for best series. His book *The Hawk* was filmed with Helen Mirren. Among his awards is the Royal Television Society's Writer's Award for the BBC play for Today *Minor Complications*, which launched the charity AvMA, promoting safety and justice for people suffering medical accidents.

His first novel in this series, *Plague Child*, was published in 2011.

From the reviews of *Plague Child*:

'A gripping coming-of-age story by the novelist Peter Ransley [and] an enthralling mystery adventure set against the backdrop of the English Civil War'
Radio Times

'Ransley writes a dramatic story of intrigue and heritage with exceptional power, in an evocation of the times seldom bettered'
Oxford Times

'Ransley has a talent for melding dramatic historical detail with a strong story that could well give C. J. Sansom a run for his money'
Spectator

'With a cast of characters that intrigues, because some of them are historically correct, and some are the product of a truly vivid imagination, this novel is one of the most exciting examples of this genre to have appeared in a long while'
Ballarat Courier

PETER RANSLEY

PLAGUE CHILD

Harper
Press

Harper*Press*
An imprint of HarperCollins*Publishers*
77–85 Fulham Palace Road
Hammersmith
London W6 8JB

This Harper*Press* paperback edition published 2012
1

First published by Harper*Press* in 2011

A catalogue record for this book is
available from the British Library

ISBN 978-0-00-731237-5

Typeset by Palimpsest Book Production Limited,
Falkirk, Stirlingshire
Printed and bound in Great Britain by
Clays Ltd, St Ives plc

MIX
Paper from
responsible sources
FSC
www.fsc.org **FSC C007454**

For Cynthia, Nicholas and Imogen,
Rebecca and Lochlinn

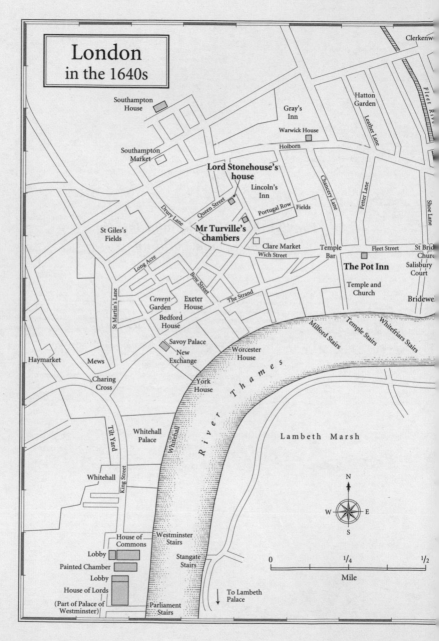

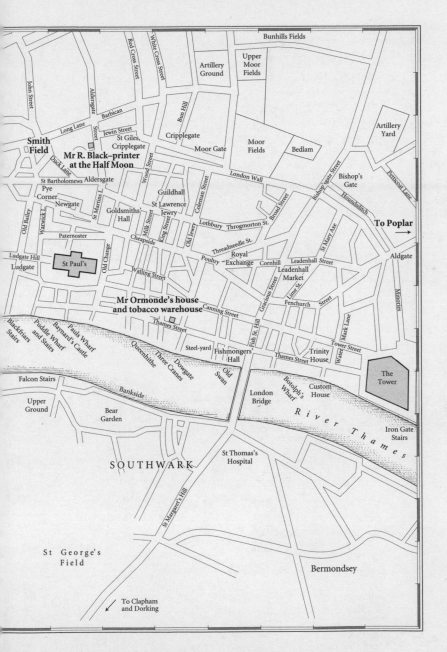

Prologue

One cloudy September evening in 1625 Matthew Neave drove the cart, loaded with the bodies he had collected, to the edge of the River Cherwell. Seven bodies: they would not pay him much for that.

While the horses drank he finished off the last of his bread and cheese. The bread was hard and dry and he softened it from his flask of beer as he waited for the light to go. He never went near the plague pit before dark.

In early summer, at the start of the plague in Oxford, relatives would lie in wait for the cart. Fear of the disease was overcome by the fear of hell that their loved ones (and they later) would suffer if they did not get a Christian burial in sanctified ground. Matthew was stabbed and nearly thrown into the pit in one fight before the watch was called.

But as people died or fled, and that remorseless hot summer reduced the remainder to a numb apathy, the disturbances petered out. Nevertheless, when he heard the sound of a galloping horse, Matthew put down his flask. Beer dribbled unnoticed down his stained fustian jacket as he stared over Christchurch Meadow.

He couldn't make out the rider at first for the trees, but the horse was a black gelding, a gentleman's horse. The horse cleared the trees. The rider was dressed in black. He was masked, although the day had not been hot. The mask might hold a nosegay of herbs to protect against the plague, but Matthew was taking no chances.

He picked up the knife with which he had cut the cheese and retreated to the cart – the stench of its rotting bodies better protection than any weapon.

The man reined in the horse well short of him.

'Matthew Neave?'

'Who wants him?'

The man took off his mask, but kept the herbs it contained to his face. Matthew dropped his knife and pulled off his hat, words drying in his throat. This was no gentleman. The horse was better bred than the man riding it, but for Matthew Mr Ralph was of much more immediate concern than any gentleman.

Mr Ralph was Lord Stonehouse's steward. A yeoman's son, he had acquired a small estate in his own right, field by field, the painful struggle to build it showing in the deep seams of his face. The deepest seam was a jagged scar running from his right cheek to his neck.

'There's a dead child at Horseborne. Bennet's farm.'

Several miles away, over Shotover Hill, on the edge of Lord Stonehouse's estate.

'A plague child, sir?'

'Yes.'

Matthew knew this was wrong, knew this was trouble. He had caught the disease when he was six. The agonising black boils under his arms burst and he had survived. They threw the rest of his family in the cart and left him locked in the house alone.

The Plague Orders, no doubt reflecting most people's conviction that the disease was God's punishment, specified that victims should be quarantined for forty days and forty nights. For over a month Matthew had been locked in alone, kept alive by the pottage and weak beer passed to him through a window by the only neighbour who would go near him.

Since the few who survived did not catch the plague again, what had nearly killed Matthew now provided him with his bread and, in a plague year like this, meat. Some people thought Matthew a cunning man because it was said he could predict who was going to die of the disease and who was going to live. Perhaps the steward kept his distance now not just because of the bodies, but because he had heard these stories.

Matthew scratched his head. He knew every case for twenty miles around. Someone might have escaped from quarantine, but that was unlikely. It was even less likely that the disease was still spreading. The cold sharpness in the air, the dwindling number of bodies, told him the outbreak was practically over.

Matthew shook his head slowly. 'Horseborne, sir? Can't be.'

As painstakingly as he had built his small estate, Mr Ralph had built his voice, away from Matthew's slow burr, mimicking the cool mockery of his betters.

'I'm afraid it can. It's still spreading.'

The clouds were now edged with black and the wind freshening. As if aware that the evening would be a short one, swifts were diving, skimming above the water catching flies. Soon they would go, swarms of them, vanishing into the sky. Just as the swifts knew when there would be no more flies, so Matthew knew there was no plague at Horseborne.

'I'll collect he tomorrow.'

In spite of the steward's fear, both of the bodies in the cart and the curse Matthew might put on him, Mr Ralph pulled his horse closer. His voice reverted to a country, flint-edged burr.

'You'll collect he tonight.'

'There's no papers,' Matthew answered stubbornly.

Not all the people ending up in the pit had been plague victims. Nobody worried overmuch about the poor, but when a farmer was murdered and dumped in the pit, the watch had dinned into Matthew the importance of papers which they flourished in front of him before unsealing a plague house. And Susannah, who lived with him, had dinned into Matthew the evil of denying anyone a Christian burial whom God had not touched with the plague.

From a pouch on his saddle Mr Ralph produced an order. He did not bother to move any closer, for he did not expect Matthew to be able to read it. The paper was enough. Afterwards, Matthew could not remember whether there was a signature, but burned in his mind was the falcon's talons clutching a shield, the seal of Lord Stonehouse, whose word was law.

The wind was bending the trees above Matthew and what was left of the sun was buried in dark clouds. It would take him an hour to get over Shotover Hill. He would set off in that direction and then turn back to Oxford, pleading the next day a broken wheel, or a lame horse. He went to his horses.

'I'd best go now,' he said.

'You'll do it – no excuses!'

Matthew stared at him. The steward had a reputation of being afraid of nothing, but something had frightened him. His words came out so violently the nosegay he was holding over his mouth dropped from his hand but still he pulled his horse closer.

'Here –'

There was a glint of silver in the air. Matthew caught the coin as deftly as the swifts catching the flies. His manner changed.

'Thank you, sir.'

'I will give you another at the pit. Say nothing – do you understand?'

Matthew understood that two half crowns were a crown. And that Mr Ralph would be waiting for him at the pit to make sure he finished the job.

The rain began shortly after Matthew left the meadow. It swept at him in great gusts as he swore and cut at the horses, struggling and sliding to climb up Shotover. At the top of the hill, to lift his spirits he took out the silver coin. A half crown. Newly minted that year for the coronation of Charles I.

It helped Matthew forget he was soaked to the skin. A half crown! More than a labourer's wages for a month. And another at the pit!

He was so intent on the coin that he was only dimly aware of the approaching coach, the driver lashing the horses to pick up speed at the start of the hill. The cart, rattling and bumping down the incline, had drifted into the centre of the road. He yanked at the reins and sparks flew as he pulled ineffectively at the brake.

The horses of the approaching coach reared. Matthew glimpsed the driver's angry face and felt the sting of a whip across his cheek. He lost the reins and the cart lurched, with a grinding of wood against stone, into the ditch.

He shouted and cursed after it, then searched for the coin, which had jumped from his hand. He shoved aside one of the bodies which had been thrown from the cart, before giving up, dropping his head in despair. Then he thought of the other silver coin, waiting for him at the pit. He flung the body back in the cart with the others and covered them with the thick bundles of hay with which he disguised his cargo.

The near-side wheel was buckled and grating against the side as, just before Horseborne, he found the track to Bennet's farm. The name meant something to him, but he couldn't remember what.

The track was a thick, gluey pottage of mud, leaves and dung, pockmarked by cattle and horses. Overlaying them were the recent, deep ruts of a coach.

It was now almost dark and the rain, which had slackened, dripped steadily through the trees. The cart rattled and jerked through a small copse, a branch wrenching at Matthew's hat before the open gate of the farmyard.

He stopped at the door of a prosperous-looking wattle-and-daub farmhouse. There was no red cross on the door. And something else was wrong.

There was no dog. Who had ever heard of a farm without dogs? Then he remembered. Bennet was a farmer who, returning from market drunk, had been murdered. The farm had been bought by Mr Ralph to add to his nearby lands, and was not yet tenanted.

Feeling increasingly uneasy, he approached the door, stopping abruptly. A pair of eyes glittered at him from the bushes. He was about to run when he realised the gaze was unblinking. They were jewelled eyes, set in the head of a falcon, the centrepiece of a magnificent pendant whose gold chain was entangled in the bushes. He knew where it came from. There would be a reward for it – a substantial one. He had lost silver, but found gold. He stuffed it inside his jacket and knocked at the door.

He expected Widow Martin, or some other fuddled midwife, but the woman who answered the door was another shock. Like Mr Ralph, she was not quite gentry. Kate Beaumann was a gentlewoman's lady, as God-fearing as her sober black indicated, and she was plainly as shocked to see him as he was to see her. They knew each other, for it is surprising how many people, from all walks of life, will seek out the services of a cunning man. She had a warm, kindly face, which reminded Matthew of the good neighbour who had kept him alive during the plague. She was in her mid-twenties, but there were already streaks of grey in her hair, and her eyes were red with weeping. Her dress, like her pattens, was splashed with mud.

He touched his dripping hat. 'Evening, Miss Beaumann.'

Without a word she beckoned him to follow her, shutting an inside door quickly, but not before he glimpsed a weakly guttering fire, a birthing stool, and a spattering of blood on the rush-covered floor. She led him into a stall where the farmer would have kept a sick animal. On the straw was a small shape wrapped in a linen apron.

'Take him.'

When he didn't move she picked up the object and thrust it into his arms. The little bundle was cold and wet. Part of the covering fell away from the baby's face, which carried none of the telltale plague spots or scars. The child looked to Matthew to be stillborn, or to have died shortly after birth.

'He don't look no plague child,' he said.

The harshness in Kate Beaumann's voice was as unexpected as her kindly face. 'He was a plague to us,' she said.

Without another word Matthew left, half-running to the cart. He took off the apron before dropping the baby on the cart and covering it with the bundles of straw. The apron was fine linen, Flemish possibly. Kate Beaumann's muddy skirt suggested she had dumped the child in the fields to die. That was as common as death itself.

The mystery was why Kate did not leave the child there. Or bury it. Or throw it in the river. One baby was much like another. But bodies could be found.

Mr Ralph's urgency and fear all but spoke out loud there must be no risk of that. Perhaps the child had some special feature, or birthmark. If that was the case, the pit was the ideal solution to the problem.

Put there to destroy the plague, lime ate quickly into bodies and faces, dissolving them in a few days into an unrecognisable slime. No one would go near the pit, let alone lift a body from it. Someone wanted to prevent anyone from recognising, or claiming he recognised, the features of the child at the bottom of his cart.

Matthew shrugged. His hand closed round the pendant, feeling the outline of the jewelled bird and the links of the chain, one by one. Then his hand stopped stroking it. Suppose he was accused of stealing it? It was risky, far too risky to return it. The horses, which were dragging the cart more and more slowly, needed shoeing and the blacksmith would melt the gold down. Broken up, the stones he could sell one by one at Witney Fair, or Oxford, with the linen apron, which Susannah would wash and press.

He was musing like this, the rocking of the cart sending him into a half-sleep, the reins slipping gradually from his fingers, when he first heard the stuttering cry.

He had been asleep. Dreaming. There was nothing but the wind, the weary stumble of the hooves and the creak of the cart. But there it was again. Unmistakable. A baby's cry.

Hadn't he feared, from the very beginning, that this was wrong? Hadn't Susannah warned him, time and again, of the evil of throwing someone who had not died of plague into the pit? The baby had been clap-cold dead – now it had come back to haunt him.

As the cry increased into a pitiful wail, he crossed himself in terror, lashing the horses in an attempt to escape from the spirit that he believed was pursuing him, he was now convinced, into hell. It was the hell he had somehow escaped as a child, but knew he had always been destined for; a pit, not of fire, but of bodies slowly eaten, burned, then re-formed, only to be eaten and burned again, forever being consumed, writhing in lime.

PART ONE

At the Half-Moon

November 1641–September 1642

I

That was the story which I eventually got out of the man I believed to be my father, Matthew Neave. There were various versions, each more colourful than the last and, of course, there was what happened next, but that has to come in its proper place.

We lived in Poplar, which some people said was a land of heathens and barbarians, because we were outside the walls of the great City of London and were not freemen. I could not understand that because in Poplar Without, as it was sniffily called, we had much more freedom. There were few laws, and I never saw a constable. I loved it there. Named after the tall, shapely trees that lined the High Street and the marsh, it was still half farming land, breeding cattle that lost little fat on the short drover's road to Smithfield. But the farmers were being pushed back by the huddling mass of small houses being knocked up every day.

These houses were unlike the tall buildings of the City, which struck awe in me when I first saw them. Rackety, timber-framed houses with narrow, gabled fronts, they were home to some of the first Huguenot refugees who had fled from France and taught me to call my hat a shappo and swear about the Pope in French. But the houses were mainly run up for shipyard workers like Matthew.

Visitors from the City called the shipwrights a canting crew because, they said, they were rogue builders, outside the Company of Shipwrights and the law of the City. But to me they were magicians who carried great ships in their heads. In the yard at Blackwell I watched these visions become hulls, then skeletons, growing prows and masts, as I ran for buckets of pitch or an adze for Matthew in his sawpit.

When snow covered the Isle of Dogs and ice gradually thickened over the Thames it was always warm here. With bare feet and wearing nothing but breeches I filled and carried baskets of wood and coal for fires to melt the pitch, mould the iron and make the steam that would bend the wood, miraculously to me, into the shape of the shipwrights' drawings.

With fires going on through the night when a ship had to be finished, no wonder it looked like hell on earth to the wealthy City people who commissioned the ships. And smelt like it. When an east wind blew, smoke from the lime pits of Limehouse combined with that given off by the coal to make a choking, noxious brew.

We lived in hovels and many were miserable, but I was happy. Unlike my fellows, I was not beaten. Matthew beat Susannah sometimes, particularly when his wages were paid and he had been to the Black Boy or the Green Dragon; but he never beat me. He would shout at me and curse me, and his hand would go to his belt or pick up a piece of wood, but at the last moment he would stop himself, give me a strange look and walk away muttering.

Once I asked him why he never beat me.

He laughed as if he was never going to stop. 'Dost thou want to be beaten?'

'No, no, Father, but everyone else is.'

He hit me on the head, knocking my hat off, but it had no more force than the slaps Susannah gave me.

'There,' he said. 'Dost like it?'

'No,' I said, 'but that was no beating.'

He stopped laughing. 'Thou art a curious child,' he said.

I did not think I was curious, but curious things happened to me.

Most of the children I knew had only a vague idea when they were born, or how old they were. There were too many of them. But I knew I was born in the year King Charles was crowned, towards the end of September. I say towards the end, because the day seemed to vary. It was always when the weather grew chill, the mist clung to the marsh and the dry seed pods of bog plants rattled in the wind. I would be up at first light, my lids gummed to my eyes, taking the snap of bread and cheese from Susannah when she would say: 'The will o' the wisps have been, Tom.'

My eyelids would fly open, I would drop my snap and rush to the front doorstep. There was a cake with icing on which TOM was written, in bold letters of yellow marchpane. It was the most delicious cake – I have to say the only cake – we ever ate. The inside was bright yellow, and full of fruit. We had no oven and the baker in the High Street sold only bread and pies. I searched on the marsh, but never could find the will o' the wisps' oven. Matthew warned me never to catch them, or even see them, or they would bake me as well, and TOM would be inside as well as outside the cake.

But I was determined to catch them and, one foggy September, real will o' the wisp weather, I begged Susannah to wake me. I must have been five or six and all that week I rose shivering and stared bleary-eyed through the holes in the oiled paper of the window.

On the fifth morning I dozed off, waking with a start. I leaned out of the window. The cake was there – I had missed them! The street was empty, except for a woman in a hooded, grey cloak and a peaked stove hat like a witch's. She must have heard me, for she stopped and began to turn. At the last moment I ducked away trembling, afraid she was a will o' the wisp in disguise, and would turn me into a cake. By the time I told myself this was stupid (I was always having such conversations with myself, as lonely children will) and looked again, she was disappearing into the swirling mist.

One Easter Sunday after the service I saw the cake in the church hall. It looked exactly the same, the marchpane glittering, but they had made a mistake with the name. Instead of my name it said GLORIA. I picked up a knife by it. Whether I was going to put my name on it, or cut a slice, I cannot remember, but the knife was twisted from my hand by the minister, Mr Ingram, who proceeded to thrash me. Susannah heard the noise and pleaded for me.

'This is Tom.'

'Ah. Tom. Yes. I remember.'

What he remembered I was not to learn for a long time but, again, I got that curious look. Through my tears I tried to tell him it was *my* cake, not Gloria's. He was startled I could read, and it happened like this:

Susannah's great treasure – practically her only possession – was her Bible. She could not read, but knew whole passages by heart from the services at the church and where to find them.

'Blessed are the poor and meek,' she would say, tracing her finger over the passage, 'for they shall see God.'

I would stare in wonder at the passage, knowing we must be blessed for I could see well enough how mean was the tiny room where the wind blew through gaps in the oiled paper at the window, even though I could not see God.

I thought if I could only understand the words, I would see Him. One day I pointed to a passage and said to Susannah: 'I . . . am . . . the . . . good . . . sh-sh—'

'Shepherd!' she cried out.

She was so steeped in parables she thought it was a miracle. I had suddenly been given the gift of reading. Shaking, tears of joy glistening in her eyes, she pulled me into the street for the neighbours to hear.

A sceptical woman opened the book at a passage Susannah had never recited. When I looked dumbly at the page, Susannah first thought I was being stubborn, then that she had done wrong by making a show of me like a travelling bear and God had taken His words back as a punishment.

She was so stricken by this and by the grins and jokes of the neighbours that I went to the passages she had so often recited to me that I knew by heart, and pretended to read them. I even put in stumbles and hesitations so that Susannah, with joy on her face again, could correct me.

The neighbours were awestruck and, not wishing to lose this reputation, I applied myself diligently to try and make the pretence real. And on that day, when I thought my cake had been stolen, Mr Ingram began to teach me himself. He explained that the cake was a simnel cake, with saffron and fruits of the East, a symbol of resurrection, of rebirth. I could not understand what this had to do with the cake on my doorstep, nor who Gloria was, unless it was one of the will o' the wisps. He laughed and said it was not a name at all – it was short for Gloria in Excelcis Deo – Glory be to God on High.

And that was my first lesson in Latin.

One day, when I was ten, a great gentleman came to inspect the *Resolution*, a five hundred-ton armed merchantman in which he had an interest. It had his flag fluttering from the mast; a falcon with an upraised claw. I saw the gentleman staring at me as I put down a bucket of boiling pitch and went off to collect another. He said something to the shipwright, who called over Matthew. Curious, I took my eye off the pitch I was tapping, which splashed over my bare leg. I had been burned before, but never as badly as this.

Yelling and screaming I ran to the pump to douse it, but the gentleman had me see the barber-surgeon who dressed the wound and gave me a cordial, London Treacle, a mixture of herbs and honey dissolved in wine, which some of the men said they would wound themselves to have. It was the first wine I ever drank, and I lay in the shipwright's office, among the drawings and the model ships they made before they built the real thing, and fell asleep.

Did I dream of the gentleman because he had been kind to me? Or was it real? I do not know, but I have a shifting memory of an old man's face bending over me, a wispy tuft of hair rather than a beard below his lips, which smiled one moment and tightened the next, just as his dark eyes looked cloudy and troubled, then stared down at me with penetrating, frightening shrewdness as though they could cut right into my heart and soul, like a surgeon's knife.

When I questioned Matthew about him as we prepared to go home, saying he looked concerned and kind, Matthew laughed bitterly.

'Kind? Aye, he's kind all right. One of those gentry-coves who would be kind enough to send you to Paddington Fair.'

He was not looking at me but staring towards the river, where the tide was on the turn and a boat was being cast off. Often in his stories he told me that one day we would leave on the tide to a distant land, and I thought they were just stories, but now there was something in his voice that told me he wanted to be on that boat, and made me clutch at his hand.

'Paddington Fair – send me to Tyburn? He wouldn't! Why? What have I done?'

He laughed. 'Nay, do you not know when I'm joking?'

Still in the manner of a joke, he took me to a fire on the edge of the yard where there were few people.

Some in the yard said Matthew was a cunning man, because he polished their thumbnails until they gleamed in the firelight, and saw their future in them. I had often begged him to tell mine, but he had always refused. Now he built up the fire, squatted by it, and stared into the flames.

I had seen him do this with the others. 'Are you going to tell me my future?' I said, polishing my nail in great excitement.

He grinned. 'Nay, Tom. I shall need more than a nail for thy future.'

His face, lit by the fire, seemed all eyes. The dock was quiet. The frantic hammering and sawing and shouting and swinging of timber was over. The gentleman was pleased with the ship, and they were taking on board canvas, ready to run up sails. Two men approached, arguing. Matthew waited until they passed, then undid his jerkin, then his shirt, which he never took off in winter. Under that was a belt, attached to which was a pouch. He started to take something from the pouch, then thrust it back.

'Say nothing about this, or I'm a dead man!'

I can now see that many of his jokes were made to ward off the fear which, at some level, was always with him. Back then I understood nothing but the sheer naked force of that fear, all the more terrible since it came so unexpectedly from someone who had always seemed, to me at any rate, a simple, jovial man.

Constantly looking about him, he took something from his pouch which seemed to have a fire of its own. It was a pendant, with a falcon staring so furiously from its enamelled nest I ducked back instinctively, for fear it would fly at me. Its eyes, Matthew said, were rubies and in one of its talons it gripped a pearl, irregularly shaped, as if it had just been torn from the earth.

I reached out my hand for it, but he cuffed it away. 'Ah ah!'

His fear seemed to recede as he gazed at it. He smiled, caressed it almost, murmuring to himself. A log settled and the gold chain glittered in the spurting flames. He addressed the pendant rather than me, seeming to enter into some kind of a trance with the red-eyed falcon. He saw a lady, he said, a real lady, with hair as bright red as mine.

'Will I marry her?'

'Nay, nay. Not her. You will make a great fortune. And lose it.'

'A crown?'

He shook with laughter. He seemed to have returned to his normal self. I loved his laughter, which made his cheeks and his belly shake, for, although he was always making fun of me, there was kindness in it.

'Rather more than a crown, boy.'

He put the pendant in the pouch, and pulled down his shirt and jerkin. The falcon seemed to flutter as it disappeared, reminding me of the bird on the flag flying on the old gentleman's ship.

'Is the pendant something to do with the old gentleman?' I said.

He seized me by the throat. For a moment I thought he was going to make up for never beating me by throttling the life out of me. 'Who told you that? Who told you? Answer me!'

'No one!' I choked. 'The bird is like the one on the ship's flag.'

He laughed, releasing me. 'Nothing like! Nothing like at all.'

I thought he was lying. He whirled round at a movement in the shadows, but it was only a dog searching for scraps.

'Tell me,' he said, 'if you ever see a man – he calls himself a gentleman these days – with a scar on his face.' He pulled his face into a smile that was not a smile, and drew his finger down the line of it, on his right cheek, down to his neck. 'He works for the old gentleman. Meet him, and you wouldn't think the old gentleman so kind.' When I said nothing, he pushed his face into mine with such a sudden ferocity I jumped in fright.

'Do you understand?'

I nodded dumbly. I understood that the old gentleman, the man with a scar and the pendant were somehow connected. And I understood that Matthew was a thief, for how else would he have got the pendant? I did not mind that, for Poplar was full of people running away from something: cutpurses, refugees, apprentices, debtors, whores. But I thought it was something more than being a thief he was running from, and I minded very much not knowing what it was.

'I don't understand what is story and what is truth,' I said.

He roared with laughter. 'If people ever knew the difference between those two,' he said, 'the world would be a very different place.'

He would say no more, except, 'You're a strange boy, a very particular boy,' as he took me home, all kindness again.

That night I woke up hearing him arguing with Susannah downstairs, where they slept. I slept upstairs with sailors they took in as lodgers.

'A boat?' she shouted. 'I've never been on a boat in my life! Where would we go?'

I heard no more because he beat her. The next day he told me we were going on a boat to Hull. I had seen so many built I was passionate to go out to sea and bombarded him with questions about what part of the Indies Hull was in and were there parrots and elephants?

But before the boat sailed, they came. A waterman brought them, and a shipwright took me to them. Matthew was nowhere to be found. Fearfully I looked up at the faces of both of them, but there was no scar that I could see.

Master Black was dressed to suit his name, in sober black, brightened only by a froth of fine linen at the cuffs and collar. He had a cane, and walked with a slight limp. The man whom I came to call Gloomy George was a thin man with narrow suspicious eyes, always looking about him as if he was afraid his pocket was about to be picked.

Susannah went into one of her trembling fits when I was took home, but instead of the words pouring out of her, she seemed scarce able to speak. The two men almost filled our tiny room. Susannah ran to a neighbour, Mother Banks, for weak beer, but Mr Black took one look at the pitcher and refused it curtly.

Gloomy George brought out a Bible from the case he carried. I thought then they were from the Church, come to test the truth of me being a miracle, because I had been given the gift of reading. He opened the book at Ecclesiasticus. My heart would have sunk into my boots if I had had any boots; for though I loved the New Testament, which is about love, I hated the Old for it is as full of revenge and hatred as it is of long words. I stared with mounting panic at the passage, which was about wisdom.

'My son, learn the lessons of youth,' I managed well enough; stumbled at 'garnering wisdom', then, at 'Only to undisciplined minds she seems an over-hard task mistress', the words fell about me like so many pieces of ship's timber when a lifting tackle breaks.

'Wisdom is an over-hard task mistress to you, is she Tom?'
Mr Black said.

'No, sir,' I mumbled, I think truthfully, for I liked wisdom, what
little I knew of it; although perhaps I also said it because I thought
it was the answer he expected.

'Then what do the words mean?'

I stared into his eyes, as black as his garments and as cold as
frost. I shook my head, sick and ashamed. I had been found out.
Not only was I not a miracle, I was a cheat and a fraud. I can still
see Susannah's wringing hands and downcast eyes. She began to
say that it was her fault, she had boasted too much to the neighbours and God had punished her by taking the words away, but
Mr Black silenced her by snapping the book shut.

From the case, Gloomy George took out a writing table, a quill,
ink and paper. He dipped the quill in the ink and handed it to me.

'Perhaps you can write better than you can read.'

I stared at the blank sheet of paper, as I now stare at the sheet
in front of me, scarce able to believe I acted as I did.

'Come now, you can write your name, child.'

I could, in a laboured scrawl I was proud of; but I could see their
sneers and hear the contempt in their voices. I would not give them
that satisfaction. The blood burned in my cheeks and I flung the
quill from me. A spray of ink peppered the fine linen of Mr Black's
cuff. I saw the horror on Gloomy George's face an instant before I
felt the blow of Mr Black's cane across my shoulders.

I reeled forward, knocking over the writing table, ink spilling from
the horn. Another blow struck me across the head and I fell to the
floor. Susannah was screaming. Above me was a blur of boots and
the metal tip of the cane rising and falling. I flung my hands about
my head and rolled away among the mess of paper and ink. As the
cane hit the floor near me I grabbed at it and held on. To avoid
falling over, Mr Black was forced to release it.

I scrambled up, gripping the cane. If he was angry when I flung the quill, he was now astonished. He backed away, almost knocking over Gloomy George in his haste. Susannah stared, her mouth open. Smeared with ink, as well as with the blood now trickling down my face, I must have looked to the two men like a wild animal. Children did not seize canes. They did not beat, they were beaten.

I was wild, but I was not an animal. The great difference between me and my fellows was that I was loved.

In families with ten or eleven children love was in short supply. Children died too often to risk love. They were wet-nursed, lost amongst the others. Susannah had had other babies, but they were dead when they came out of her, or after a cry or two at her breast. I never thought to ask why I alone was so strong and vigorous, so determined to live.

So they cared for me too much because I was all they had; and that made me selfish and bold as I gripped Mr Black's cane, feeling a strange sense of power as I looked at the expressions on their faces. I do not know what I would have done if there had not been at that moment a hammering at the door.

My boldness left me. I thought it the constable, come to take me to Paddington Fair. My mouth went dry and the cane slipped from me. Mr Black seized it as George answered the door. It was not the constable, but the waterman's boy.

The boat had to leave in half an hour to catch the evening tide. Mr Black said curtly he would take it. His rage seemed to be spent and he did not look at me as George packed the case and Susannah wiped my face and tearfully whispered to me to apologise to the gentlemen, but I would not. Apologise to him for beating me?

'I told you it would be a waste of time coming here, master,' George grumbled. 'The boy has the devil in him!'

When Mr Black, sitting broodingly, said nothing, George rounded on Susannah in bitter reproof. 'Kindness to the body, madam, is cruelty to the soul.'

'I am sorry, sir,' she replied falteringly. 'I do not know what happened – he is normally such a good child.'

He shook his head sorrowfully. 'No, madam. You are too good to him. Every coddle you give him takes him one step nearer to hell.'

Susannah pushed me away as if I was already burning. George gave me a final, dismissive shake of the head, picked up the case and opened the door, but Mr Black did not move.

'Master – the boat.'

Still he did not answer but looked at me, his eyes seeming to bore into my very soul. Then he looked at his ink-spattered cuff and jumped up as if he was going to beat me again. In spite of the danger to my soul, Susannah drew me to her.

'Sir, there is a washerwoman here who has a most rare soap –'

'Be quiet!' he shouted, so loud that soot pattered from the chimney. 'The boy has spirit,' he said.

'Aye,' George said. 'An evil spirit.'

Mr Black gave him a chilling look that silenced him. 'I will take him,' he said.

It was a long moment before George recovered from his amazement and found his voice. 'Master! His temper is as ill as his reading.'

'Both can be taught,' he said, prodding me with his cane, as if I was one of the calves at Smithfield. 'Come – the tide will not wait.'

I was later to discover that Mr Black took for ever to come to a decision, but then demanded it be carried out immediately.

'Has he any other clothes until he is fitted?' he snapped to Susannah.

'Only what he stands in, sir.'

'No boots?'

'Boots? As to boots, sir,' she stammered, 'I was always meaning to get –'

'No boots, no matter. Hurry, woman, for God's sake!' We were already in Poplar High Street, and Susannah had run back for something, which she carried wrapped in a handkerchief. 'Order boots, two pair, when you order the uniform from Mr Pepys,' he rapped out at George.

It was not until we were at the quayside that I began to realise what was happening. Susannah was delirious with joy, which confused me utterly for I thought – no, I knew – she loved me and I could not believe she was giving me, like a badly wrapped parcel, to this brute, however fine his clothes were.

'Thou art to be indentured,' she said proudly. 'An apprentice to a printer. With boots.'

The waterman's boy prepared to cast off. The light was going, the soft, magical evening light over the water which I loved, and they had lit flares in whose flickering light men moved like shadows, stitching the sails which would be run up on the *Resolution* tomorrow.

As if she knew my soul was going to be in very little danger from coddles in future, Susannah gave me one last enveloping hug and it only struck me then that I was leaving her. I clung to her, to her smells of beer, of her herb pottage in which, however bad the times, she always managed to find me a little meat. Leaving the yard. Leaving the great boats, with their promise of freedom.

Now I would never hear the creak and groan and shudder as the *Resolution* left the dock, see her stagger, then find her sea-legs as the sails snapped taut, took the wind, and she headed out to the open sea. Now I would never go the Indies, gaze in wonder at parrots, ride an elephant, and listen to Matthew's stories.

Matthew!

I cried out for him.

'Father! Father!'

I think Mr Black was not without feeling then, for he asked a shipwright to find him. No one had seen him all day. That increased my distress. He had gone to the Indies without me. But the boatman was muttering and cursing and Mr Black gave him a curt signal to leave. He prodded at the bank with an oar and the boat began to drift out into the current.

'Wait! Wait! Dear God Almighty, I almost forgot!'

Susannah flung at me what she had carried in the handkerchief. The handkerchief fluttered into the water but what was in it landed at my feet with a thump. Her Bible. It was all she had. All? It was her greatest treasure. She stood there, waving and waving, growing smaller, dimmer, as the boatman pulled at the oars.

Tears stung my eyes but then I saw the sour smile on George's face and blinked them back. No doubt he thought this was good for my soul, but what he thought good I thought a great evil.

I glared sullenly back at George. I swore then, silently to myself, on the Bible I gripped, that I would be as evil as possible. I remembered the pendant that Matthew had stolen, the future he had seen through it in the flickering firelight of the yard, and I was determined that wherever this boat was taking me, I would end the journey either with great treasure in the Indies, or at Paddington Fair.

2

They beat it out of me. That evil. Or, if you like, those childhood fancies. Mr Black thrashed me with his cane until it broke, for which offence I was thrashed all the more with the new one. Gloomy George knocked the evil out of my head with his composing stick. But worst of all was Dr Gill, the tutor hired from St Paul's, so I could learn to compose print for textbooks on nature and the physical world, which were in Latin.

As George knocked the evil out of me, Dr Gill knocked what Latin he could into me with a ferula. This was a flat piece of wood expanding at the end to a pear shape with a hole in the middle, guaranteed to raise a painful blister at one blow.

Worse than the beating was the cellar, which I thought the coldest, dampest, darkest hole on God's earth. Even now I cannot recall it without a shudder, although I was only locked in there once before – well, I will come to that. That first time I believe I had some kind of fit in there; at any rate, Mr Black said I was not to be locked in there again, and George had to make do with thrashing me.

My only comfort was Sarah, the maid of all work, with whom I shared the garret, although at first she seemed another enemy, who spoke with an accent so thick I thought she was from a foreign country like Scotland.

'Sitha – that's thy place – that side o' beam – and this be mine.

All reet?' That beam! It was so placed and so crooked that at whatever angle I got out of bed it seemed to strike my head. 'Clodpole! Some people never learn,' she invariably said, until I yelled at her, calling her a Scottish whore. She seemed more upset by the first epithet than the second, saying she would rather be dead than Scottish. She came from Hull. From the Indies? I cried, asking her if there really were parrots and elephants there.

'Oh, aye,' she said. 'And birds that fly backwards. Come here, clothhead. Mind beam.'

She rubbed some pig's fat in the bruise, which she used for her own knocks and cuts, and from that moment, however bad the beatings were, there was always the pig-fat to take the sting out of them. While she rubbed, I read to her from Susannah's Bible. I wrote to Susannah through the minister, Mr Ingram, and got messages back carried by drovers taking cattle to Smithfield.

One of them told me Matthew disappeared shortly after I left the shipyard. I never heard from him. If Susannah did, she never told me. That cut me most of all. I never forgot them, but my memory of them gradually faded as I changed from a barefoot pitch boy into a London apprentice.

For five years I was flogged regular for construing Latin, misconstruing Latin (it seemed to make little difference whether or not I got it right), for not wearing my flat cap, for losing it, for dicing, swearing, blaspheming, going into alehouses, fornicating (talking to a bawd outside the Pot Upside Down), losing my boots (I confess I put them on the throw of a dice), attempting to corrupt (a love poem to Mr Black's daughter, Anne, of which more anon) until, in 1640, Parliament was recalled and they were suddenly too busy to beat me.

Parliament? I had scarce ever heard of it. The King had got rid of it and ruled with his own personal advisers. He had also got rid of news, which his advisers called lies and rumours, and with it a great deal of his business, complained Mr Black. Robert Black, at the sign of the Half-Moon, used to publish corantos with news of the wars in Europe, shipwrecks and the like, but the King had banned them, with threats of the Star Chamber. But now Parliament was back and London so hungry for news that printers were prepared to take risks to provide it.

The only debating chamber I knew before Parliament was the Pot Upside Down. The view of my friend Will, who chaired the debates there, was simple. Good Queen Bess (as we still called her) had won all her wars against the Spanish, the French and the Dutch. Charles had lost his. He was in debt, and needed to call Parliament to get more money. But Parliament would not raise funds until the King paid heed to its grievances on religion and taxes.

I was for Parliament – most of the London apprentices were. Our hero was Mr John Pym, leader of the opposition to the King. Mr Black printed his speeches, which breathed fire on the King's advisers for drawing him into popery, even persuading him to sell forests to papists: the very wooden walls of our ships that protected us from Spain.

How we got hold of the speeches is a story in itself; very like old Matthew's story of the plague child in its muddle of right and wrong. Reporting of Parliament was strictly forbidden. Allowed in as a messenger, I heard Mr Pym himself rail bitterly against the rogue printers who stole his speeches for money. For this abuse of privilege, he thundered, they should be clapped in the Tower.

An hour later Mr Ink (as I called the scrivener, for his fingers were always black with it), whom I knew worked closely with Mr Pym, was slipping that very same speech into my hands.

Yet Mr Pym, like my master, was a very godly man. They looked similar, with their stiff pointed beards, dressed in sober black, topped with starched white linen collars, except my master's collar was plain, and Mr Pym's finely decorated lawn. One day he called me over, staring down at me, his beard as immaculate as his linen, every hair in place as though engraved there.

'You are fortunate to work for such a godly man as Mr Black,' he said.

'Yes, sir,' I stammered, although the bruising and the blisters had scarcely faded and fortunate was not the word I would have chosen.

He took a shilling from his pocket and held out an envelope. 'Do you know that address?'

'Yes, sir,' I lied.

I would have known any address for that money, even one in the foreign country of the West End, beyond the walls of the City.

'Are you discreet?'

I did not know the meaning of the word, but again was willing to be anything for a shilling and nodded my head vigorously. Not willing to risk that the nod meant understanding, he barked: 'Can you keep your mouth shut?'

'Yes, sir.'

'Do not say anything, even to your master. Is that clear?'

I was only too happy to comply. My wages were bread and cheese, my uniform and bed; the only money I ever got was from errands like this.

The letter was addressed to the Countess of Carlisle in Bedford Square, near the new Covent Garden. It was then London's first public square. After the huddle of the City I was amazed by the spacious new brick-built houses with their porches and columns. I delivered the letter to a contemptuous footman called Jenkins who left me round the back, next to the shit heap, waiting for a reply. The heap smelt sweeter than ours, I believed then, for in it was the shit of a real Countess. Now I rather think that, unlike ours, the scavengers cleared it regular.

From Will in the Pot I learned that the Countess of Carlisle had been the mistress of the Earl of Strafford, a one-time favourite of the King, who had been executed earlier that year. She was a close friend of the Queen. So what was she doing corresponding with Mr Pym? I imagined this was a love letter I was carrying, for

I was in love myself – deeply, hopelessly, with Mr Black's daughter, Anne.

Anne laughed at my bare feet when I first came to Half Moon Court. They were big and dark as the pitch that was engrained into the skin. I flexed the huge, knobbly toes like fingers. She howled with laughter when she saw me pick up a quill between my toes, and said I was like a monkey she had seen on a gentlewoman's shoulders. Ever after that she called me Monkey.

I tried to hate her. To my shame I cursed her, not a curse like smallpox, for I could not bear anything to happen to her skin, which was like milk and honey. The curse, Matthew had told me, must be related to the injustice, and so I cursed her feet, which were like tiny mice, scuttling in and out of her skirt, bidding them to grow even larger than mine. I scraped some dead skin from the soles of my feet and put it in her favourite shoes.

When she complained that they pinched, and her mother said she had grown out of them, I immediately regretted what I had done and spent a tortured, sleepless night praying to undo the curse. To my relief that must have worked, for, as the days passed, she made no complaints about the new shoes.

Her laughter and, even worse, her ignoring me, hurt me more than any blow I ever received in that place. According to Will in the Pot, who was an expert in such matters, I was suffering from the very worst type of love: unrequited love.

Yet it was not always so. There was a time, the first autumn I was there, when we became as close as two children ever could be. In September, towards the end of the third week, my simnel cake appeared on the doorstep. It seemed to everyone a most mysterious thing, but, of course, it was no surprise to me. The will o' the wisps could transport such a cake in a trice. For George, it confirmed I had a pact with the devil and he would not touch a crumb. Sarah said there were good will o' the wisps and bad, and the cake was so delicious it had been baked by good ones. I believe she began to rub pig-fat in my bruises from the moment she licked the last crumbs from her fingers. Mrs Black consulted her astrologer, who told her the cake had been stolen, and she looked at me with deep suspicion. Mr Black, whose common sense contrasted starkly with his wife's superstition, boomed irritably: 'How can it be stolen, Elizabeth, when the boy's name is on it?'

Anne was first jealous – she never had such a cake – then intrigued. We began to play together. It started as mockery, but when she found I could tell the stories Matthew had told me of foreign lands, great ships and elephants and parrots, we used to hide together behind the apple tree in the centre of the court, or in the paper store. This went on for two idyllic months until, one misty autumn day we heard the rattle and braking squeal of a Hackney hell-cart stopping in the court. We ran out of the shop to gape at it. I took Anne's hand, with a shiver of apprehension.

Out of the coach stepped a gentleman. Through the swirling fog I saw a livid scar, running from the top of his cheek and down his neck to bury itself under his collar. He stopped to glare at us. Mr Black came out and shouted to us to come in immediately. Anne ran to him but, remembering Matthew's warning, and fearing the man with the scar had come to me for the pendant my father had stolen, I fled out of the court and hid the rest of the day in Smithfield, among the poor searching for offal discarded by the butchers.

I was flogged for that and told not to play with Anne. That only increased my desire to see her, but it was then that her haughtiness and her cruel jokes really began. I still kept the memory of that autumn, but as the years passed and she became more and more beautiful, like a gradually opening flower, and more and more distant, the memory faded until I began to wonder if it had ever happened, or whether it was just a story I was making up to comfort myself.

So there I was at sixteen, hopelessly in love, knowing nothing and caring less about the speeches I was carrying, except that I must beat the other messengers at the same game. Flapping the speech to dry it, I would run from Westminster, through the narrow streets, past the grim shape of Newgate Prison until, panting for breath through the stink of Smithfield, I would at last reach Half Moon Court where we all lived and worked in the narrow Flemish wall house with its jutting gable and creaking sign: RB with a yellow half-moon. My master would seize the copy and George his composing stick and I would prepare the press. So it was and seemed it always would be, until one momentous day.

It was November, dark as pitch, the air a fine drizzle carrying the smell of the coal clouds that hung over London when people began to stoke their winter fires in earnest. The shops and stalls in Westminster Hall, where they jostled for trade next to the law courts, were long closed. I hung about with other messengers, waiting for the House to finish its day's business. Unusually, no Members had gone home. Some of the messengers did, or repaired to the Pot. I crawled into a corner, pulled a discarded sack over myself and dozed. Distant shouting woke me. A watchman was calling the hour of midnight. The shouting was coming from the House. There was no official on the door, and I crept into the lobby.

Even I, for whom the words echoing round the chamber of the House meant as much as most of the Latin my tutor tried to drum into me, knew something extraordinary was happening. Mr Lenthall, the Speaker, had to keep calling order. There was a silence so deep my boots sounded like the crack of doom. My old enemy, the Serjeant, at the door of the chamber turned, but I slipped behind a pillar.

'The Ayes have it!' Mr Lenthall called.

What the Ayes had I neither knew nor cared, except that Mr Pym's speech would soon be in my hand and I could go. There was a tremendous uproar, more shouting and banging of feet and cries for order, before Members came out, still arguing fiercely.

Mr Pym was with an MP of about forty, with a brooding, long-nosed face and an untidy beard. I knew him only from scowling me away if I scuttled too near his feet. Normally he made long-winded speeches about draining the fens, looking as if he had just ridden up from doing so. Now there was a look of almost religious exultation on his face as he came out of the chamber with Mr Pym.

'If this had not been passed, John, I would have sold up everything and gone to Massachusetts.'

Pym smiled at the younger man, but as usual there was a look of caution on his exhausted face. 'We haven't got the new world here yet, Oliver. They're already trying to wreck it.'

He looked towards another group, in the middle of which George Goring, handsome and wild-eyed, was gesticulating fiercely.

It? New world?

Goring shouted: 'You cannot make such demands of the King!'

His hand went to his waist, and if swords had been allowed in the chamber, he would have drawn his. He moved towards John Pym, but he was already disappearing with others into a meeting room. I heard Goring mutter that there had been enough words and it was now too late for meetings.

Another group round Sir Simon D'Ewes, who in any debate found one side totally convincing until he heard the arguments of the other, were finding they had urgent business in the shires and were sending out servants to prepare the horses.

Various members strode about dictating to scriveners. Some, like Mr Ink, had portable writing tables strapped to their waists.

'What's happening?' I asked.

At first he made no answer. He was writing a clear copy from notes which, I knew, came from Mr Pym, threaded through with spidery scribbles of his own. His quill dipped. The ink flew.

Then, scarcely pausing in his transcription he said: 'The Grand . . . Remonstrance!'

Even in his haste, he uttered the words with a flourish, like that of a gauntlet being flung down.

'The Grand – what? What does it mean?'

He flung his hands to his head in frustration, tried to continue, but had lost his train of thought. He turned on me. For a moment I thought he was going to throw his dripping quill at me. Then, although he had long made it plain he thought me a miserable, unintelligent wretch, his long gloomy face relented a little.

'It is a plea to the King,' he said, 'from his humble servants to leave our reformed religion alone and not listen to malignant advisers –'

'Like his Catholic Queen Henrietta?' I broke in.

He clapped an ink-stained hand over my mouth and looked nervously around. But I thought that for the first time he looked approvingly at me.

'And a plea to listen to our humble opinions, not to dismiss Parliament when he chooses and to take money from his humble servants by taxing everything in sight: bricks, salt, even the humble bar of soap we wash with.'

Since he looked as if he washed in ink and I scarcely washed at all in winter, avoiding the freezing pail in the yard, I thought soap unimportant and the whole Remonstrance thing sounded a good deal too humble for the King to care a jot about.

Perhaps that showed in my face. His face flushed. For the first time he looked as if he had blood, rather than ink in his veins.

'But the plea is really to you,' he said.

'To me?' I said, amazed.

'To the people. This will change the world.'

This? What did he mean? Not taxing soap? I thought him a magician as his writing table bounced and the words in his head, now unknotted, flew on to the paper. He spoke as he wrote, the sonorous cadences of Mr Pym entering his voice and some of his phrases, such as 'Parliament is as the soul of the Commonwealth . . .', echoing in my mind.

It was as if he had cast a magic spell over me. The spell was in the words drying in my hand. They would change the world.

I believed it utterly. I would change myself. As I ran out into the dark night, I determined to be a reformed character, and not stop at the Pot Upside Down for a beer and a game of pass-dice with the other apprentices. Alehouses and dice were near the top of the list of the thousand things apprentices were forbidden to do.

But I must admit my pace slackened as I reached the alehouse. Although it was so late, excitement and rumours about the debate spilled out of the doors. One tankard, I persuaded myself, would help me run all the faster.

There was a stranger near the bar, a gentleman in a beaver hat and a fashionable short cloak, questioning regulars. I heard him say 'red'. My ears are sharp, particularly for that word. My hair, red as fire and just as unruly, is a curse to me. My master could spot me in an alehouse however dim the light and thick the smoke. People thought I had Scottish blood, or even worse, Irish, and, since the papists were in rebellion over there, twitted me for being a spy. I had the hot temper supposed to go with the hair and got into several fights over it.

I caught the man in the beaver hat staring at me. He turned quickly away, to address a man I took to be his servant, who had the thick neck and shoulders of a bulldog, and a face pitted with smallpox.

Sometimes the Guild used the Watch to catch apprentices in alehouses. I suddenly remembered that I was a reformed character and had sworn never to go into an alehouse again. I wriggled my way through the crowd and out of the alehouse, gripping the precious words Mr Ink had given me tightly in my hand. I really believed that those words, although I did not understand them (perhaps because of that), had changed me for good.

As I ran, I imagined how being a reformed character would turn me into a good apprentice. I would become a Freeman of the City, marry Anne, in spite of my feet, have my own printing and book-seller's shop by St Paul's Churchyard and, after a few years, become Lord Mayor of London.

So I flew down the sweet street of dreams, so deep in them I was scarcely aware of the stench (ten times worse than that of the ordinary streets) of Smithfield Market. The stink hit my nostrils at the same moment as I realised someone or something was behind me.

I dived down a dark alley, my footsteps echoing. I stopped abruptly. Was that the echo, or someone's footsteps stopping shortly after mine? I stuffed the precious papers in my pouch.

'Who's there?'

There was a shuffling whisper of a sound and I kicked out at the rat scuttering past my feet. I had been a fool to come this way. I should have gone the long way up the Old Bailey. There were vagrants here, come to fight the red kites and the ravens for what offal they could find. London, I knew, because it was on one of the pamphlets I sold, had grown bigger than Paris and so was now the biggest city in the world, attracting thousands of the poor and desperate who would kill me for the flat cap on my head.

Out of breath, I hurried into the market itself, clapping my hand to my nose. The air reeked of stale blood and urine. I jumped as ravens lumbered up from a yellow mess of intestines. The moon was up, casting long black shadows in the stalls into which the cattle were driven at dawn to be sold and slaughtered.

The whole place was deserted and silent, except for the hovering, cawing ravens. A kite swooped. He was after the rats which came out at night to grow fat in the market. Behind the barn where the hay was stored there was a clatter, like a pail going over. I saw the man's shadow before I saw him. I scrambled over a stall, and, in sheer terror, vaulted over another, a thing I'd never been able to do before. I heard him curse as he slipped in some cow-clap.

He was two stalls behind. Another stall and I would reach Cloth Fair, and the twisting closes and passages which were home to me, where he would never catch me. I jeered as I prepared to jump down from the last stall. Then the sound stuck in my throat as I saw a glint of metal in front of me. Another man came out of the shadow of the wall, blocking my way to Cloth Fair. It was the man in the beaver hat from the alehouse.

I took out the dagger from my belt, the only weapon an apprentice was allowed to carry. It was next to useless against the sword he had drawn, but he hesitated – not because of the puny dagger, but because of the ditch in the centre of the street in which a dead dog floated, and into which I was retreating.

In those streets you had to sum up a man in an instant. The indigo doublet he wore was splashed from recent meals. His cloak was patched. His face, too, bearded in imitation of his King's, pouched and veined, had seen better days. But it was the look in his eyes that told me how I might escape him. The look was a mixture of arrogance and aversion that signalled he was what we apprentices called a wall man. In the narrow streets he would, come what may, stick close to the wall, rudely facing-off approaching passers-by, forcing them into the ditch.

I made to come at him, then, as his sword came up, ducked under it and ran through the ditch to the opposite wall. I was right. He would not cross the ditch but slashed from a distance. He cut at me. The blow sliced my hat askew. I staggered but ran on and would have got away but the other man, who had no such aversion for the ditch, grabbed me from behind.

He had a grip like the jaws of a bulldog. The knife fell from my hand.

'Did you see that, Crow?' said the other man.

'Went for you with a knife, sir.'

'The little wretch insulted me.'

He taunted me, demanding satisfaction, putting the point of the sword close to my eyes then, in a whirl of movement, cutting my belt and pouch away from my waist.

I kicked and struggled but then, I am ashamed to say, I broke down. It was the sight of the papers, lying in my pouch at the edge of the ditch. One sheet was floating in a filthy pool, those precious words, which were going to change the world, shivering and leaking away.

'Please, please let me go. Take my belt, my pouch, what you like, but let me have my papers!'

Grimacing, the man picked up the pouch floating in the sewer with the point of his sword. 'Item – one pouch. Pig's-arse leather. Value?'

Crow grinned. 'Half a groat.'

I felt the wind from the sword, the point of which grazed my head as he flicked off my hat, spinning it around before dropping it with distaste into his hand.

'Item – one hat, London Apprentice's thereof. Slightly damaged.'

'One farthing.'

'Half a groat and one farthing!' he cried in mock amazement, then drew his hand across his throat, which I took to be part of the same jest until he abruptly turned away and Crow grabbed me by the hair and jerked my head back.

I hung like a chicken that has had its neck wrenched, too paralysed with fear to kick or struggle. I heard the clink and slither of a knife being unsheathed. The sound drove me to struggle and kick, trying to twist my neck away as I glimpsed the glint of the knife, but he was far too strong for me and yanked my head further back. There was a sudden flutter of sound in my ears, a blur across the patch of sky.

Crow jumped as a kite rose from his dive near us, a rat squealing briefly between its talons as the life was squeezed out of it. The rat losing its senses made me find mine.

Distracted for a moment, Crow had relaxed his grip, instinctively turning the knife towards the kite. I jerked my head out of his grip and bit his hand so savagely I felt a tooth judder and loosen. He yelled, dropping the knife. The other man was bending to pick up the pouch. He grabbed at me but I head-butted him again and again in a frenzy. He slipped on some cow-clap and fell in the ditch, his shouts choked off as he took a mouthful of it.

I grabbed the pouch with the precious words and ran as I had never run in my life before, almost knocking over the Bellman and the man who should have been watching the barn.

There were cries of 'stop thief' from behind me. The Bellman tried to grab me but I pulled away – it is always the apprentice who is guilty – running into the maze of courts, alleys and twisting passageways off Cloth Fair.

3

My master's concern was so entirely bent on the dishevelled pottage of words I unpeeled from my pouch he seemed scarcely to notice the mess I was in.

The cold, God-like fury which I had expected to fall on me fell instead on the task of turning the chaos of smeared sentences into ordered Octavo newssheets. He would have failed his God and Mr Pym (and his purse) if the speech was not circulating round the inns and the taverns where the respectable gathered that week.

Who were Crow and the man in the beaver hat? They were not common cutpurses. Nor were they from the Guild. They had been told I frequented the Pot, and that I had red hair. All I could conclude was that the words I carried really were important, perhaps they *would* change the world, and they had hunted me and sought to kill me to get them.

My guilt and misery increased as Mr Black struggled to make sense of one ink-stained page after another. At that time we all thought that the end of the world was close – George was convinced the Last Judgement was due in 1666, because, in Revelation, 666 was the number of the first beast to be overthrown. For myself, I thought it had started that night. I had had the words in my hand that would save the world, and I had lost them.

My thoughts grew so crazy I even wished they would beat me

rather than ignoring me, until Mr Black came to a page which completely defeated him.

'Parliament is . . .' he began. His eyes bulged as he struggled to decipher the words. He flung the sheet from him. 'Damn the speech! Damn the boy!' he yelled.

I picked up the sheet, clutching at a word I saw in the dark grey smudge as a drowning man clutches at a spar. The word, in a mess of obliterated ones, was 'soul'. Other words, miraculously, seemed to form before me in the smear of ink, as I remembered what Mr Ink had declaimed.

'Parliament is as the soul of the Commonwealth,' I said.

They stared at me in astonishment, waiting for me to go on, but I could not. The spar was slipping from me and I was about to drown. Then Mr Black snatched the paper back and was able to decipher the next few words:

'. . . the Commonwealth that alone is able to understand the . . . the . . .'

Again we came to a dead halt. In desperation I took the sheet from him and stared at the smudged word. I may have deciphered it, but I rather think that, grabbing into my memory, I somehow retrieved it.

'Diseases!' I said triumphantly.

Mr Black seized the sheet as again I came to a full stop. The following words were indecipherable, both to his eyes and my memory; but a politician's phrases and arguments become as familiar as his face, and Mr Black knew Mr Pym's backwards.

'Diseases that strike at the heart of the body politic!' he cried.

No poetry has ever moved me as much as that bedraggled line of political rhetoric, for it was uttered with such a religious fervour, and a look at me that was a second cousin of the look I got from Susannah when she thought that I read the Bible; while, in truth, I was piecing it together from my memory of her readings and her promptings.

'God is with us!' he exclaimed exultantly.

Gloomy George, left out of this totally unexpected communion between us, scowled at me.

'Compose!' Mr Black shouted at him. 'Don't just stand there, man – compose!'

The scowl became a look of pure malevolence as George seized his composing stick. Before, I had simply been someone to chastise and, however hopeless the task, save from sin; now I was unredeemable, his sworn enemy. The devil was a very subtle creature, who had somehow slithered and slived me into Mr Black's favours, and must, at all costs, be rooted out. That was how George's mind worked.

Even George, however, got swept up in the desire to catch Mr Pym's words and have them all over town as soon as possible. There was no faster typesetter in the City of London. If Mr Ink's fingers had flown, George's were a scarcely visible blur, dipping from case to stick and back to case again, working his own magic, reproducing the words backwards as between us Mr Black and I excavated John Pym's fine phrases.

As the night wore on we ceased to care about the increasing gap between what he had actually said, and what we invented. For the first time I had a glimmer of understanding about the power of the words we were handling. They were as explosive as gunpowder. All that was wanted was a fuse. Parliament had the right to approve the King's ministers. The right? The King chose his own ministers, by Divine Right. Parliament alone had the right to make laws. Alone? Without the King?

And there, by a miracle unsmeared, unequivocal, in Mr Ink's flowing, cursive hand was the biggest keg of gunpowder of all: Parliament had the right to control the army.

Mrs Black stumbled downstairs to see what was happening, awakening her daughter. I caught a glimpse of Anne in her nightgown at the foot of the stairs, hoping she would see from the excited chatter between me and her father that he was looking at me in a different light. But she merely wished her father goodnight, turning away from me with a wrinkle of distaste. The flicker of that nose, with its tiny upturn I thought no sculptor could copy, made me miserably, hopelessly aware of the stink and grime of Smithfield on me, to which was being added the ink I was coating on the formes, now locked together for printing.

I heard her laughter on the stair, and the hated word 'monkey'. I was too fearful to curse her again. I hated her then. I hated the whole Black family. I hated being an apprentice. I wanted, above anything else in the world, to kick my boots off and be in the shipyard with Matthew again.

After we had proofed and printed, I broke the ice in the pail in the yard, washed what dirt I could from my face and hands, and began to eat the cold pottage and drink the beer Sarah had left out. Mr Black took some wine for himself, gazing with pride at the newssheets, gleaming wet in the candlelight. There was a fine portrait of the King, hair curling luxuriously to his shoulders from his hat cocked at the front, and a more modest one of Mr Pym, his pointed beard chipped because we had used the block so many times.

Mr Black's idea was to put Parliament's explosive demands in a respectful wrapping, viz:

a Grand Remonstrance
of PARLIAMENT
to his MAJESTY THE KING
Being the onlye true & faithful reporte of the
proceedings of Parliament praying His Majesty to
adresse the most humble supplications of his subjects

I had swallowed my beer in two draughts when Mr Black said to George: 'Take some wine yourself and pour Tom some.'

George's eyebrows lifted and looked as if they would never come down again. He was only offered wine on his name day, and

Mr Black had never offered me it before; rarely had he called me Tom. I had always been 'that boy', 'sinning wretch' or 'little devil'; only lately, as I had grown almost as tall as he was, kept my boots on regular, and was suddenly useful to him had he begun to call me, albeit with heavy sarcasm, 'Mr Neave'.

Mr Black took some wine, cleared his throat, and gave me a long stare. My stomach churned. Now he was going to question me about how the papers and myself had got into such a dishevelled state. His eyes, however, were drawn back by the drying newssheets, still shining with ink in the candlelight, and his face filled with the triumph of getting the speech on the streets next day.

'Well done, Tom,' he said.

The words came stiffly and awkwardly from his mouth, for he was as unused to saying them as I was to hearing them. In fact it took a moment – several moments – before I was sure there was no hidden sarcasm signalling the reproof to come. It was only when he put more wine in my tankard and raised his glass, his face coming out of the shadows with a smile on it, that I knew he meant it.

The smile was as much a stranger to me as the words. Without warning, tears pricked my eyes. I had cried myself to sleep often enough in that place, but I had never cried in their presence. The more I was beaten, the more I resolved never to cry in front of them.

'Come, Tom,' he said, 'are those tears?'

'No, sir,' I stammered, 'no, sir,' pulling away into the shadows and drawing my sleeve over my face.

'Thou art a curious child, is he not, George?'

'Aye, sir,' said George, with a vehement look at me.

'Hard as stone when chastised, and cries when praised!'

'I am not used to it, sir,' I said.

'Ah well, Tom, that's as maybe. You were very rough when we took you, was he not, George?'

George looked as if the end of the world was not merely

imminent, but had come. 'He was, sir. The roughest 'prentice in the City. And if I may venture an opinion, still is.'

'But improving, George, improving.'

George said nothing, but Mr Black was not waiting for an answer. 'There was much to do and too little time.'

He poked the dull red coals of the fire until a few flames appeared, lighting up his face. He was not yet forty, but the flickering light threw up the furrows in his face of a much older man, etched deeply into his forehead and cheeks like the lines of a finely cut woodblock. He stared into the flames as if he had forgotten we were there. I crept closer. When he had said I was a curious child I was minded of Matthew; now I was took back to the time when Matthew gazed into the fire and drew out the pendant, and I wondered how such a devious cunning man and a straight-backed religious man could stare into the fire in an exactly similar way, even though one was looking into the future, and the other into the past.

'You do not know how much evil there was in your soul, Tom,' he said.

I shuddered. At that moment I utterly believed in the evil he had found in me: Susannah only thought me good because of my trick with the Bible.

'We prayed to God we could root it out, did we not?' he said to George.

'Aye,' George replied, clasping his hands together, speaking with an irony that seemed to be lost on Mr Black. 'We are still praying.'

'More evil than you know. More than you can possibly imagine!'

He swung round as he said this, his face moving into shadow, his voice suddenly harsh. The change from a tone of reverie was so abrupt it shook not only me, but took George aback. George unclasped his hands, took his brooding attention from me and stared at his master with the avid expression I had once caught on his face when he was listening at the door to some quarrel between Mr Black and his wife.

'I would never have taken you, never, if the business had not been bad. Bad? About to go under!'

He finished his wine, poured more, drank half of that and then walked about the room.

'Even then I would not have done it, I would have gone home to Oxford with my tail between my legs if Merrick had not offered to buy me out. Merrick!'

He spat the word out. Merrick was the printer at The Star, in Little Britain. He finished his wine with a gulp, as if he wanted to wash away the taste of his rival's name. George nodded slowly, looking at me, as if he was understanding something for the first time, though I had no idea what it was.

'That was about the time, master, you . . . er, found the money to buy the new press, the new type from Amsterdam –'

'Borrowed it!' Mr Black said sharply, as though regretting these disclosures. 'Just so! Borrowed the money!'

He half moved his glass to his lips, realised it was empty, and had a little argument between himself and the bottle. He put his glass down with resolution, then looked at the drying newssheets, his eyes gleaming with pleasure, turned back to the bottle, hesitated, turned regretfully away, then saw me, with a smile on my face at this little dance and, before I could remove it, to my utmost surprise smiled back. He poured more wine and pointed at me.

'I thought I had brought the very devil into this place, the printer's devil, did I not, George?'

'A most subtle devil,' said George, looking steadily at me.

'Oh, come, George!' His gesture included not only the well-equipped workshop, but the new cedar chest in the room where we ate, with its flagons and candlesticks – not silver, but the most expensive pewter, polished to look very like. 'Is not all this a sign of God's favour?'

George turned his steady, unblinking gaze on his master. '"Prosperity will not show you who are your friends. Or good servants." Ecclesiasticus, twelve eight.'

The drink brought out a totally different side of Mr Black. He looked as solemn as ever, but I swear there was a twinkle in his eye.

'Come, George. "Whose friend is he that is his own enemy, and leaves his own cheer untasted?" Ecclesiasticus, fourteen five.'

I had never heard Mr Black trump one of George's quotations before. George looked completely put out. Mr Black clapped him on the shoulder.

'Come, gentlemen – drink up!'

George refused, and when Mr Black moved to my tankard, said: 'The boy has had enough, sir.'

Mr Black waved him away. 'He has had but little.'

'Aye, plus what he took at the alehouse,' George said.

I jumped up. 'I did not go to the alehouse!'

'You stank of it when you came in!'

'I was in a fight!'

'A tavern brawl!'

'Stop this! You will wake the house!'

For the first time, the rebuke from Mr Black was for both of us, not just me. And, for the first time, he questioned me without automatically assuming my guilt.

'Did you go into an alehouse?'

I hesitated. Going into an alehouse had led to some of my worst beatings, and was the main reason why apprentices were thrown out of their Guilds. But that was because they drank, diced and whored. I had not even had one drink, or one pass of the dice.

'No, sir,' I said.

'Mark the hesitation,' said George.

'Are you speaking the truth?' The sternness reappeared in Mr Black's speech, beginning to fight with his conviviality.

'Yes, sir.'

George's lips moved quietly, but I caught the prayer on his lips. 'Oh Lord, guide him, let him see the error –'

'Stop that, George!'

George did so, abruptly. His pale face seemed to twist and shrink, his lips still moving but no words coming out. Mr Black turned sharply, almost knocking a chair over. He sat heavily at the head of the table, in the leather seated, high-backed chair he had recently bought, looking like a judge.

George found his voice. 'Ask him how he got into the fight.'

'I was attacked. Thieves who tried to get the speech.'

'Why didn't you tell us all this before?' George's voice was acid with scepticism.

'There has been no time!'

'Apprentices from Merrick?' said Mr Black.

'No, sir. I never saw them before. One had a sword.'

George looked up at the ceiling in disbelief, but Mr Black leaned forward sharply.

'A gentleman?'

'Yes. No. I don't know.'

'Perhaps once was?'

'Yes.'

'Describe him.'

'A thin face. A beard like the King. He was wearing a beaver hat.'

'Like half London,' said George.

'The other?'

'A lowpad. Shoulders like a bull.'

George laughed. 'It's a tale from a halfpenny broadsheet! He's lying.'

Mr Black jumped up. His good mood had disappeared as quickly as it came. He seized his cane, which had become a stranger to me in recent months. 'Are you?'

'No, sir!'

I ducked as I saw the cane move and flung my hands round my head, wincing in anticipation. But the blow never came. The cane clattered as he flung it on the stone flags. His face looked tortured. I feared he had been struck by the strange ailment that affected him at times when he would stand quite still, as if struck by some vision others could not see.

George backed away, muttering. 'The boy has cursed you. I saw his lips move.'

Mr Black shook his head, as if he was shaking off the vision, like a dog shaking off water. He seized me by the shoulders and shook me. 'Are you lying?'

'No, sir!' I sobbed, more frightened by the strange contortions of his face than the violence.

He shook me again, and pushed his face into mine. 'It's as important for you as it is for me that you tell me the truth! Do you understand, you little fool?'

I pulled away from him with a rush of anger that overcame my tears. I did not consider myself a fool and I was certainly no longer little.

'It's true – I heard one of the men asking another 'prentice about a boy with red hair and then the man turned round and saw me and I ran and then –'

'Where was this?'

The words dried up in my mouth. Normally I would have lied. Told him the street, anywhere, but the look on his face was so alarmed, so urgent, I felt compelled to tell the truth.

'The Pot.'

A sad smile played round George's mouth. 'Now we have it, sir, now we have it.'

I expected to be given the beating then. I wish they had. George was clearly relishing the thought. He picked up his old composing stick with the rusty metal end from which I still bear a mark on my left temple. But Mr Black waved him away. He gave me a look of such sadness it cut me more sharply than any whip or stick.

'Oh, Tom, Tom, I was beginning to trust you.'

Now I could not stop the tears bursting out of me and with them a torrent of words. He must have beaten more of his obsession with sin into me than I realised, but it had all been concealed from me until a little kindness let it out. That, and my realisation that the words that were going to change the world could have been lost because of my desire for a drink.

I confessed drink. I confessed pass dice. I confessed lusting after Mary, the pot girl. I confessed cursing his daughter. I confessed, although I feared it would be the greatest sin of all in Mr Black's eyes, drinking and getting into debt with Henry, Merrick's apprentice.

George was hovering, testing the position of the stick in his hand. I wanted him to beat me. I needed his savagery. But as I moved like a sacrificial lamb towards him, Mr Black stopped him. He was berating himself under his breath for not having written to someone. He picked up pen and ink as if he would write a letter there and then, then set it down and paced again.

Waiting for my punishment made it ten times worse. I felt so wretched I begged him to cancel my indentures and send me home. I would return my uniform and boots, get some clothes from the rag woman at Tower Hill and go back to my father.

He came to a full halt, staring at me as if I had said something that first of all shocked, then amused him. 'Your father? No, no, that won't do, that won't do at all. It's far too late for that. As for the boots . . .' He gave me one of his rare, dry, mirthless smiles. 'I doubt anyone else would fit them.'

The touch of levity left him. 'You are not to leave this house until I give you permission. Is that clear?'

No. Nothing was clear. Not the evil that he said was in my soul, nor the man in the beaver hat who had suddenly come into my life, causing him such consternation. But I promised to obey him.

He hesitated. 'No, I can't trust you. I can't *afford* to trust you.' He turned to George. 'Lock him in the cellar.'

George gripped me by the arm, nodding his head in approval at the gravity and the justice of the punishment. My tongue and limbs were so paralysed with fear at the thought of being locked in there at night that George got me halfway to the door before I anchored myself to the table.

'Not in the dark, sir,' I pleaded. 'Please don't lock me in there in the dark!'

'Why, Tom,' Mr Black said, an amused look on his face, 'I thought you were grown up now and afraid of nothing. Are you still afraid of the dark?'

I had made my confessions with the reason of a man, but now all reason deserted me and I whimpered my plea again like a child.

'Let him have a candle,' Mr Black said curtly.

I made no further resistance. In the early days I had learned, painfully, that it was useless and only gave George more satisfaction. George lit a candle and with the composing stick in his other hand led me down the stairs, his shadow splayed out over the low ceiling. As he opened the door of the cellar the dank rotting smell brought back to me the terror of the first time they brought me here, but I stifled it, determined not to show any more fear to George. It was very late, and the candle would last me until first light filtered through the broken plaster.

It is only when you have been punished regular that you learn instinctively to recognise refinements of such punishments. As George began to close the door on me I realised he was not going to give me the candle.

I put my boot in the door and struggled to pull it further open. The composing stick fell on my fingers with agonising force. For a moment I could not move for the pain, but the rattle of the key drove me to wrench at the door. I got it half open and grabbed for the candle. He pulled back but hot wax spilled on his hand. He yelled, dropping the candle, which went out.

There was now only a dim, flickering light from the room above. I glimpsed him coming for me with the stick. I ducked and, as he crashed into the wall, grabbed him from behind and shoved him into the plaster with such force I thought the wall was coming down. He groped feebly for the stick he had dropped but I saw it on the stair and grabbed it.

I was familiar with that stick on every inch of my body, except in the palm of my hand. The feel of it there, my fingers gripping it, that hated stick, and the fear of the dark in that stinking cell drove me into such a frenzy I lashed out at George. He ducked, but I caught him a glancing blow on the temple and the thought that I had scarred him as he had scarred me let loose such a rush of savagery it felt as if the devil George always claimed was in me was released, urging me to beat him and beat him as he had beaten me.

George slipped and fell and God knows what I would have done if I had heard Mr Black coming down the stairs sooner, but by the time I turned and saw him, he was bringing his stick down on my head.

4

I thought it was a louse. *Pediculus Humanus Corporis*, my Latin tutor Dr Gill had drummed into me, as he triumphantly plucked a particularly fat specimen from my clothes. They came out to feed at night. We were used to one another, and, unless they ventured to a particularly sensitive spot like my groin, they rarely woke me. Even then, it was more my finger and thumb the creature aroused, which hovered, waiting for it settling to feed before closing round it with a satisfying snap, at which I would instantly sink back into sleep.

But this creature was on my face, normally considered too leathery for a decent meal. My finger and thumb were throbbing, stabbing with pain as I instinctively tried to crook them to catch the louse. My head thumped like the big drum in the Lord Mayor's show. Something terrible had happened but I did not want to remember, I just wanted to catch the louse and fall back to sleep. My finger and thumb crept stealthily up to my face. They touched a sticky, glutinous mass, pausing in bewilderment before closing round the object of irritation.

All in the same instant I felt a sharp, needle-like pain and sprang up yelling, Mr Black's angry face and descending stick jumping back to me as I realised that I clutched not a dead louse but a live rat which, attracted by the drying blood on my face, was squealing and biting in my hand.

I threw it from me, screaming. I could see nothing. I blundered into one wall, cold and greasy with damp, then another before I found the door, hammering and shouting until I dropped to the floor with exhaustion.

The last time they locked me in, when I first came here, I had been playing dumb, pretending I had lost my reading. I hoped in my confused way that they would believe that, just as I had been given the gift of reading, so it had been taken away. Finding me useless, they would send me home. George, however, was far subtler than me in the twisting and turning of such beliefs.

If it was a gift, he said, and I did not use it, God would punish me by taking my sight away. Still I was stubborn and when they gave me the Bible, nonsense came out of my mouth. So they locked me in and, as the light faded, so did my stubbornness. There had always been the light of stars and the moon in Poplar, however cloudy and dim.

As the dimness in the cellar faded to black, I believed I had gone blind. I screamed and yelled and threw myself about the cellar until they released me. Mr Black had forbidden George to lock me in again. Until now.

Now, exhausted, I tried to thrust what had happened then from my mind. I was a man now, I told myself. Had not Mr Black said so? I took some courage from his unexpected praise, going over and over it in my mind. The light would eventually come, filtering through the cracks in the ceiling.

I buried my face in my hands for what seemed an age. Rats whispered and scuttled. I opened my eyes, but it was still dark as pitch. We had worked long into the night. Surely the sun should have risen by now? Perhaps it had already risen! Nonsense, I told myself. God could scarcely be punishing me now for not reading – I read all the time. But then I was struck by a fresh panic. George had wished the same punishment on me for striking him. The panic mounted. Perhaps George was dead. Whatever there was of a man in me fled and I became that screaming child again, jumping up at the ceiling, tearing at the plaster with my nails.

The cellar was under the printing shop, thus isolated from the bedrooms. Even so, I thought Mr Black must hear me, however muffled. As I clenched my fists to hammer on the door, I heard a scratching sound. It came from under the door. More rats. Trying to get into the room. I stamped my foot down. There was a cry. I jumped back in terror. Not a rat – some kind of spirit, George's spirit, muttering behind the door. Then the muttering became words.

'Stupid Monkey!'

Never had that hateful word sounded so beautiful.

'Anne?'

'Be quiet, for God's sake!'

'Is George alive?'

'Of course he's alive – no thanks to you.'

'Is it light?'

'Can't you see it's not light, stupid? Why do you think I've brought you a candle?'

I thanked God as I caught the acrid smell of tallow. Bending low, I could just glimpse the faintest glimmer of yellow from a candle which she must have set down on the steps. She told me George had been bandaged and given a cordial to help him sleep as she pushed another unlit candle under the door. She followed this with a flint.

'Thank you, Anne.'

'Miss Black. And don't thank me.' Her voice was cold and brusque. 'I only did it to stop you making such a row. Crying out like a baby in the dark.'

'You would cry here.'

'Indeed I would not!' she said, with such contempt ringing in her whispered voice my cheeks burned.

The thin band of light under the door began to waver and disappear, like the will o' the wisps dancing away on the marsh. My panic rushed back.

'Wait – the flint is damp!'

'You haven't tried it.'

I scraped my boot against the wall. 'Not a spark! Please, An— Miss Black. Give me a light from your candle. Under the door.'

The light, the blessed light under the door grew stronger. Prone on the floor, I could see the flame, tallow dribbling, glimpse her thin delicate fingers. The flame wavered and almost went out. She gave a little cry and I could hear her scrambling up, waiting until the flame grew again.

'I cannot. There is a draught – it will go out.'

'Are you afraid?' I mocked, then quickly, as I heard her step away: 'I'm sorry, Miss Black. Miss Black – is there a key in the lock?'

There was a silence. I felt I could see her there in a long willow-green nightgown which I had glimpsed before, a shawl wrapped round her shoulders, those thin fingers cupped round the flickering flame.

I tried to make my voice sound as weak and humble as possible. 'Miss Black . . . it would be easier if you were to open the door a little.'

She laughed, the contempt coming back into her voice again. 'Do you think I'm such a fool, Monkey?'

Now the word had its old, hateful ring. I only just stopped myself from flinging myself at the door in anger and frustration. I clapped my hand over my mouth to stop myself from shouting.

I did not understand how I could love her one moment and hate her so much the next. My hopes for her were as much a fable as looking in a mirror and pretending I was handsome. Add to the feet and the red hair my nose, sharp and inquisitive as a bird's beak, and you have a pretty full picture. Only my eyes, large and black as ink, drew me any kind of attention – that and my use of words which, from hating when they tried to drum rhetoric and writing into me, I had grown to love.

'Open the door?' she mocked. 'You've run away before.'

'I will not!' I cried out with a sudden passion which must have taken her with as much surprise as it took me. 'I want to run away, but I cannot run away from you!'

'What rubbish! What nonsense! How can I trust you? No one can trust you! My father says you have the devil in you. I pray for you every day.'

'Do you?'

'Ssshh.'

'What is it?'

'Be quiet!'

I became as still as the stone flags under my feet. I could hear nothing but the shuffling of rats and, distantly, the wind rattling the panes and the crack and creak of wood; the house, like the ships in the docks, always seemed to talk to itself at night.

'Do you?' I whispered.

'What?'

'Pray for me.'

'It is only Christian charity to do so,' she said, quietly, earnestly. 'To pray for a lost soul. To stop you from doing such things. Writing such things.'

Writing? She must mean a poem I had once dared to write to her. Had she read it? The thought, as unexpected as Mr Black's praise, pricked my eyes with tears. The idea that she had taken any notice of me at all, except as a figure of fun and mockery, was a revelation.

'Are you crying?'

'No. Yes.'

'Perhaps you are not quite lost, Monkey.'

Was there something softer in the mockery, or was it just my hope? There was no doubt about the sweetness of the next sound: the key turning in the lock. I sprang to open the door, but before I could do so the key turned back.

'How can I open the door when you wrote such a poem to me?'

'*Did* you read it?'

'Indeed I did not. My father said it was full of such vileness –'

'Vileness?' I said hotly. 'You think it's vile to write: "The windows of thy soule –"'

'Stop it!'

'"That when they gaze, see not me –"'

'I will not listen!'

I heard her going. The yellow glow from her candle under the door wavered and went. In that moment I did not care. It was the first thing I had ever written that said truly what I felt, and the words kept coming from my lips as though they had a life of their own.

'"I know the windows of thy soule

That when they gaze see not me

but some strange Satyre. Perchance

One idle day, they may see

These stumbling lines of poetry.

And, from these clumsy words know

I have no hope of your love, only

Hope that my love for thee

May make your eyes see me."'

The words had calmed me. Now the sounds, the shuffling of the rats, the drip of water crept back. And with them another sound, but outside. The barest glimmer of yellow light had reappeared under the door.

'Anne? Miss Black?'

'They were not the words my father said.'

'I will show you them – you should have read them.'

'I cannot read, you know that!' There was anger and humiliation in her voice.

I did not know. I had often seen her with her Bible, going to church, or opening one of the books of Lovelace's poetry we printed.

'I will teach you.'

'You!' Now there was no mistaking the total contempt in

her voice. 'You copied that poem. You did not write that stupid jingle.'

'I did!'

'Liar,' she mocked.

My anger burst out uncontrollably and I hammered wildly on the door. 'I did and it's not stupid and I love you and always will – God knows why!'

During this she tried to silence me, but it was only when I stopped I heard Mr Black's grumbling distant voice followed by Mrs Black's high-pitched tones.

'There is someone!'

I heard him say, 'It's Tom. Let him hammer away,' then mutter something. Mrs Black's voice grew louder, sharper and more urgent. 'I can hear people talking.'

Whatever Mr Black said was drowned in bad-tempered thumps and creaking of boards.

I had heard nothing in Anne's voice before but lightness and mockery. Now her whisper was panic-stricken. 'Oh God! He must not find me here.'

'Go! Go now,' I urged.

Her bedroom was off a landing one floor above Mr and Mrs Black's. She might just make it. As the light of her candle vanished I heard a door open upstairs and a moment later she returned.

'It's too late. He's coming downstairs.'

'Open the door.'

She gave a little moan of fear. 'No.'

'Open it!'

I heard the key turn and pulled open the door. She was in her green nightgown, as I had pictured it. The rest I had never imagined. That wonderful hair was locked up in some loathsome nightcap. All her haughtiness and mockery had vanished and been replaced by this shivering drab, face as pale as the candle she was holding. I thought, when I wrote that poem, as youth does think, that I knew everything about love. I looked into her eyes, wild, darting like a fearful animal, and realised that I knew nothing, except that I loved her even more.

She looked more frightened than ever at the sight of me, and backed up the steps. I snatched the key out of the lock.

'Who's that?' Mr Black called out. 'Who's there?'

Anne retreated back. I pulled her to me, clapping a hand over her mouth, afraid she would cry out. I whispered into her ear. 'Stay – when you hear a noise in the shop, run back to your room.'

I snuffed her candle out, stifling her little cry of fear, and crept up the steps.

'Who's that?' Mr Black repeated.

I heard the crack of a stair that was rotten, followed by Mr Black's muttered curse, and knew he was nearly downstairs. I slipped into the kitchen as he entered the room, holding up his candle. Its light flickered towards me. I ducked behind a chair. From there I could see into the printing shop.

As Mr Black, candle in one hand, stick in the other, approached the stairs that led to the cellar, I flung the key into the shop. It hit the press and, by great good fortune, dislodged some of the drying pamphlets, the clips holding them clattering down.

'Thieves!' he yelled, setting the candle down and running into the shop. I went after him, ducking round the press, trying to get to the door, but he saw me and blocked my way. He drew back his stick. Whatever vague plan I had formed deserted me.

'It's you!' he said. 'How did you get out?'

'Run!' I shouted. 'Run!'

'Two of you are there!'

I dodged the first blow. He had his back to the kitchen and I glimpsed Anne's petrified face as she emerged from the cellar steps.

'I can handle two of you!'

Distracted by the sight of Anne, the next blow caught me and a third sent me to the floor.

'Where's the other? Who let you out?'

I flung my hands round my head, curling up into a submissive ball as I had done so many times before to receive his blows. Then the thought of him seeing Anne drove me to fight in a way I had not done since they first took me from Poplar. Through an aching, blurred mist I saw his legs, inches from me, grabbed them, and pulled. Off balance as he swung back his stick, he went down easily, a look of great astonishment on his face, hitting the floor with such a thud I thought the house must fall down.

I was at the door, fumbling with the key, before I realised he hadn't moved, and there was no sound from him. I went back to him. Mr Black was still, his eyes closed. One wild thought after another chased through my head. I was in love. I had told her I loved her. And moments afterwards I had killed her father!

As I bent over him, his eyes shot open and he grabbed my wrist. He was a powerful man and I could not wrench away. I grabbed hold of the table to stop him from pulling me down. A chair clattered down.

'Damn you!' he panted, gasping for breath. 'Would you –'

I thought his grip would break my wrist. He pressed his other hand on the floor to push himself up. Another moment and I would have fallen. I brought my boot down on the hand he was using as a lever at the same time as I saw Anne returning down the stairs into the kitchen, as if she had just awoken. A look of horror crossed her face as her father yelled in pain and released me. I tried to say something to her, but her father made another enraged grab at me and I ran for the door, pulling at the latch and was into Half Moon Court before he reached the door shouting after me.

'Stop, you little fool – you're in great danger! Come back! I must speak to you!'

I was about to run into Cloth Fair. I stopped and turned. I nearly went back. I wish I had. I hesitated, not because of what he shouted at me, for I took his warning to be yet more claptrap about the danger to my soul, and since hell could not be worse than that dark, rat-infested cellar I decided there and then I would take care of my own soul in future.

No, it was the look of horror on Anne's face when I stamped on her father's hand that cut me to the heart and made me hesitate. Mr Black walked towards me. The anger had left his face. On it was that troubled expression I had seen when, only a few hours ago, he had praised me.

I continued to hesitate as he approached. If I returned, what would I say to Anne? Explain? Explain what? Apologise? Why should I apologise? I had taken so many beatings and I was taking no more. Even so, I stood there, until he was nearly on me, for he was my master, and I respected him and thought him a good man. Unlike George, there was never malice in his beatings, which were done only to bend me to what he thought was right.

So I stood there, hypnotised by the dark eyes set among the powerful lines of his face. He was almost close enough to touch me when I saw, above the crooked jetty of the house, the first chinks of light in the night sky.

And in a rush it brought back that dark cellar, that terrified longing to see the first fissures of light in the plaster with such force I wrenched my gaze away from him and turned and ran.

He shouted something else, but I could no longer hear him. I ran down Cloth Fair and into Smithfield, where the first cattle were being driven into market. I threw away my apprentice's blue hat, which would have marked me, and it was immediately lost among the trampling hooves. There were two herdsmen. I picked up a stick and became a third, as I had sometimes done as a small boy in Poplar.

And that stick with which I prodded the cattle's swaying rumps, and the light edging into the night sky over the great open space of the market, as I had so often seen it over the docks with half-open eyes as Matthew and I stumbled down to the yard, filled me with an overwhelming, aching desire to go home.

5

I wish with all my heart I had got back sooner to Poplar, but I dared not go the direct way through Aldgate for fear it would be watched.

I was not only breaking my bond; the very clothes on my back and the boots on my feet belonged to Mr Black. The first time I had run away, a month after I had been there, I had been swiftly caught and it had been dinned into me that I was stealing the clothes I wore, for which I could be thrown into Newgate.

Instead of going east, which I am sure they expected, I struck out for the river, with the vague hope of persuading a waterman to take me. At Blackfriars Stairs they laughed or shook their heads. But further downstream a waterman was repairing his boat, which was badly holed. I helped him, boiling pitch as I used to and caulking the boat. I slept in his hut where the fog crept in like an old friend, for I was used to it at home, rising from the marsh and making the opposite river bank disappear.

He paid me in bread, dried ling and eel, and a seaman's cap and torn jacket with which he had plugged one of the holes in his boat. The cap and tattered jacket helped conceal my uniform until I eventually made my way to Poplar High Street. The fog blurred the houses into soft, indistinct shapes, and deadened footsteps so, as with increasing excitement I neared our old house, I almost walked into a woman, mumbling an apology as I skirted past her.

'Tom!'

She was so swathed in clothes, with a scarf round her face, it was her voice I identified as that of our neighbour. 'Mother Banks –'

I went to embrace her but her tone of voice stopped me. 'I prayed you would come!'

'Why? Is my mother not well?'

'Don't you know? Dear Lord help us!'

She looked down the street. Following her gaze I saw, among the blurred line of houses, one that stuck out like a broken tooth. I ran. The door hung open. The houses next to it appeared to have suffered little damage.

The roof of our house was still intact, but the windows were gaping holes, the wood round them blackened. I pushed at the partly open door, and an acrid, damp smell filled my nose. Timber from a half-burned beam crumbled under my feet as I went into Susannah's room where she lived and slept. I heard Mother Banks behind me.

'I'm sorry, Tom. She died in the fire.'

I turned and she held me close to her.

'What happened?

She told me that, in the middle of the night, she had been awakened by shouting and had smelt smoke. By the time Mother Banks got there, neighbours had managed to get water to it, for the streets were so ramshackle there had been several fires and they had butts of water in the alley. People thought it was a candle Susannah had left burning when she went to sleep. The fire must have been going for some time before the neighbours awoke, for Susannah was overcome by the smoke.

I found the iron kettle she always had on the fire, and a twisted pewter candlestick that she had been proud of, for no reason I could think of.

'If it was not for the men staying here, it would have been much worse.'

I dropped the candlestick. 'Men? What men?'

'Lodgers.'

'Sailors?'

'Susannah said they were from the docks. They said the shipwright sent them.'

'What were they like?'

'I never saw them, what with the smoke and everything. They were there just for that night. They dragged Susannah out. They went as soon as the fire was put out.'

'When was this?'

'Wednesday.'

The day after I ran from Half Moon Court. I scrambled up what remained of the stairs. The landing where I used to sleep was secure, the room Susannah rented out scorched but relatively undamaged. And the roof, which normally caught quickly in these fires, spreading them rapidly, was scarcely touched.

I returned downstairs.

'It looks as though it started down here. You were lucky.'

'Yes. I thanked the Lord.' Mother Banks clasped her hands. 'Near the church, two whole streets went up recently. We were lucky the men acted so quickly.'

I walked round the room where Susannah had slept, and where most of the damage was. King James had said he found London 'built of sticks' and wanted to leave it 'built of bricks', but had stopped at the eastern suburbs where the marsh would not support such houses. The builders rushing up the houses for new dock workers had daubed between the timbers a mess of mortar and rags that in a fire rapidly crumbled away. The debris crunched beneath our feet as the damp fog swirled round us from the street.

I picked up the candlestick again, turning the twisted stem round and round in my fingers. I remembered once trying to sneak upstairs with it so I could read after everyone had gone to sleep. It was the only time I had ever seen her angry.

I shook my head. 'Susannah wouldn't have left the candle alight.'

She pressed my hand gently. 'She must have done, Tom.'

I pulled away from her, flinging the candlestick away. 'I don't believe it!'

She was frightened by the sudden violence, exploding out of a mixture of anger, bewilderment and grief. So was I. I couldn't stop shaking. Two men. The day after I had run away. Thinking the obvious thing, that I would come straight to Poplar. Finding not me, but my mother.

'Where is she?'

'Buried. Yesterday. I'm sorry, Tom. I'm sorry. Come with me.'

I was like a child again, going from sudden violence to uncontrollable weeping. She led me to her house, murmuring that weeping would make me feel better, but I did not believe it, did not believe it would ever be so. First to lose Matthew, for I was convinced then I would never see him again, and now Susannah . . .

Mother Banks had little coal so I went back to the wreckage of our house and foraged for pieces of half-burnt timber. Outside, the clinging, yellow fog was now so thick a muffled ship's bell rang insistently, for any ship which had not sought shelter must be travelling dead slow. She built up the fire and heated up some pottage, which first I refused to eat, but once I started swallowed greedily.

The empty plate was slipping from my fingers. I felt her gently taking it from me.

'She would not . . . leave a . . . candle lit . . .' I muttered stubbornly.

'Susannah had changed. She was not as you knew her.'

'Changed?'

'Ssshh. Go to sleep.'

'How changed?' I mumbled.

'She turned preacher.'

'A woman preacher!'

I smiled. This was the sort of story I loved in pamphlets, the sort you knew could not be true but wanted to be true, the sort that people bought for a penny or two and repeated over fires like this until many people believed it. The sort of story to fall asleep over. But this one jerked me awake, staring at Mother Banks with amazement.

Susannah had stopped going to Mr Ingram at St Dunstan's, going instead to an independent minister where they prayed in silence until a person was inspired to speak. Most of the women were short on words, and looked to the minister, as a man, for guidance; but it appeared that Susannah had what he said was the gift of tongues. She rose to her feet and held the room spellbound as her words rang round it.

She said the great tumult in London stirred up by Parliament was the Second Coming. Christ had been born again, not in a stable this time, but in a plague pit. She claimed to have been a witness to it, speaking in a strange muddle of Bible stories and things that she claimed had happened to her. Oxford became Bethlehem and King Charles Herod.

People began to come from the surrounding parishes to hear her, even those who thought she was mad, for a strange voice came out of her, and some actually believed her prophecies, that Christ was being plotted against all over again.

'What did you think of what she said, Mother?' I asked.

She hesitated. 'At first I thought it was hunger.'

'Hunger?'

'She fasted. She took nothing for days but small beer. Then . . .' She hesitated again. A log settled and threw a flickering light on her face. 'She spoke in riddles, like the Bible. She said you be her child, and not her child.'

I laughed. 'What does that mean?'

The flickering flame died and her face was in darkness. 'There was one child who was his mother's, and not his mother's,' she said.

I stopped laughing and stared at her. Her hands were clasped together and her face came into the light again. 'I prayed so much

for you to come! And when you came out of the fog like that . . . I
thought . . . for a moment . . .'

I took her hands and shook my head, unable to speak for I was
so overwhelmed by the faith and the hope in her face.

'You are not . . . He that is to come?'

She stretched out a hand to touch my face, and I took it and
kissed it and now I could not help smiling and laughing.

'No, no, Mother Banks, I'm sorry, but thank you – I am much
more often mistook for the devil! But I'm neither, I hope. I am the
same old Tom, Tom Neave, hands black as ever, look – but with ink
now, not pitch!'

I hugged her and she laughed with me, for we both needed some
laughter on that gloomy day. She laughed with relief as much as
anything else, for she had a practical bent like me; yet I felt there
was a tinge of regret and I saw again the narrow line between the
stories we tell one another and believing them to be true.

When I finally fell asleep that night in front of the dying fire,
Susannah's riddle spun round and round in my head. Her child and
not her child. For the first time I began to ask questions I should
have put to myself long before.

Had I not too easily believed stories I had told myself? That Mr
Black, for instance, had apprenticed me for no other reason than
that he had heard of my miraculous gift for reading?

A bitter eastern wind sprang up during the night and cleared the
fog. Mother Banks took me to St Dunstan's and showed me the
unmarked plot where Susannah was buried. It was in a neglected
corner where the wind cut across the marsh. It bent the trees in one
direction while the church, from the settlement of the land, leaned
in the other. There were no stones and the grass was rank and uncut,
except for the new grave.

At least it had the open view of the marsh which I loved, where
the land, patches of flood water gleaming, mingled with the tumbling

grey sky. I felt tears coming again and fell on my knees and tried to pray, but kept thinking about the two men and the fire.

We marked the spot with a little cairn of stones, and I vowed to return one day and have a proper stone made.

'Did anything happen that evening before the fire?' I asked, as we walked back.

'Nothing. Well . . .' She hesitated.

'Go on.'

'When I went out to the privy, I heard Susannah shouting and screaming.'

'Did you knock on her door?'

'No.' She swallowed nervously. 'I was frightened. You don't know what she was like, Tom. She would stand up at a meeting and shout that the Lord had come to her!'

'Is that what she was shouting then?'

'No, no, no. I can't remember. Well, I heard her shout, "God knows I don't know where he is!" Then there was silence. I thought she was calling out in her sleep.'

There was the skeleton of a new ship in the dry dock, but no men working on it when I went there after leaving the graveyard. I passed some pitch, frozen in a bucket, on my way to the shipwright's office.

He exclaimed at the size of me, saying he used to look down at me and now had to look up; and would not have recognised me but for my red flare of hair and the jutting prow of my nose. He took it I had returned because of the death of Susannah and I said nothing about the breaking of my bond, but there was an edginess about his greeting, as if he suspected something. He had a bad leg, and at the sound of a footfall outside from one of the few workers in the yard, he limped quickly to the door to see who it was, as though he was afraid of some unwelcome visitor.

Most of the workers had drifted away to find other work, he told me. After the keel of the ship outside had been laid down, the money had run out. Three gentlemen had shares in the boat. When one had been imprisoned for debt, the others had refused to pay until they could replace the shareholder. Until the arguments between King and Parliament were settled, he said, all business was marooned, like the skeleton of the ship which was slowly beginning to rot.

I asked him who the sailors were who had stayed with Susannah that night.

'Sailors?' He shook his head. 'Weren't sailors. Boatman brought them from the City. They said they were friends of yours. Hoped they might find you here.'

'Did you believe them?'

He spat and went to the window again. 'Wouldn't have them aboard ship,' he said. 'One looked like a soldier.' He spat again. 'Or had been. He had a long face. Wore a beaver hat. The other I wouldn't like to argue with. Said they were helping you find your father.'

'Matthew? What did you tell them?'

'Same as I told the other man that came looking for him, soon after he vanished.'

'What other man?'

For the first time he looked at me directly. 'In trouble, are you?' I said nothing.

He hesitated, then went on. 'I told them and the other man that Matthew was looking for a berth on a boat to Hull, or maybe a coal boat back to Newcastle.'

'Is that where he went?'

He looked at me searchingly, spat again, then moved some charts from a stool and told me to sit down. He took down a flask from the same shelf on which stood the bottle of London Treacle they gave me the day I burnt myself with pitch, and I remembered the strange dream of the old gentleman bending over me that day as I slept in this very room.

'How's your scar?' he asked.

I showed him the discoloured, slightly puckered flesh. He looked at it almost approvingly as he shoved to one side of his desk drawings of ships that might be, or might never be, and poured a dark brown liquid from the flask.

'You'll have a few of those before you're done.'

I coughed as I swallowed the fiery brown liquid and tears came to my eyes. This seemed to put him in better humour.

'And a few of those.'

He swallowed what he said was the best Dutch brandy-wine, duty paid (a wink), poured himself another and stared out at the half-finished boat in the silent dock.

'Matthew stood here, the day you went. He wanted to go down and say goodbye. He heard you shout "Father" and he very nearly went down then. But he was too frightened.'

'Where did he go?'

He pointed at the river. 'He went upstream, not down, the day after you left – the very next tide. I got him a berth in a barge. I heard him say he wanted to be dropped off somewhere between Maidenhead and Reading. I've no idea where he was going from there, but he reckoned it was a day's travel, by the green road, whatever that means.'

I embraced him. 'Thank you, thank you! You said there was another man came looking for Matthew. Just after he vanished. Who was that?'

The shipwright gave me something between a shake and a shudder. 'I never seen him before, and I'm not very particular about seeing him again. Told me where to send knowledge of Matthew, but I never had no knowledge to send him, did I?'

During this he rummaged in a drawer amongst old charts and tidal tables until he unearthed a slip of paper. The hand was crabbed and uneven, with short, angry downstrokes that dug into the paper; the hand of a man who had learned to write later in life and with difficulty, and with many loops and flourishes designed to display his status. He had written: *R. E. Esq., at Mr Black, Half Moon Court, Farringdon, London.*

The shipwright did not know who R.E. Esq was, but said he had a scar on his face, drawing a line from cheek to neck, exactly as Matthew had done when he had warned me about the scarred man over the camp fire six years ago.

Before I was out of the door he was pouring himself another brandy. I was halfway down the steps when he shouted:

'Wait! All that talk and I nearly forgot . . .'

Again he rummaged in a drawer, then another, muttering to himself before finally unearthing a coin. 'Matthew said it was yours, not his.'

It touched me to the heart when I thought that my father, even in such a panic, and when he must have needed all the money he had, had left me what he could. 'Mine?'

'Belonged to thee. That's what he said.'

Puzzled, I took the coin from him, turning it over and over, as if I could read some message from the inscriptions. But it was a silver half crown, like any other, showing the King on a charger.

6

They – whoever they were – would find me if I stayed in Poplar. So I did what I judged they would not expect. Like Dick Whittington, I turned again, walking back towards the City.

I would find out who they were, the men who, I was convinced, had killed my mother. Try and find the answer to the questions that whirled endlessly in my head like so many angry bees. Why had Mr Black taken me on as an apprentice? What was his connection to the man with the scar?

The man who could answer these questions, or most of them, was Mr Black.

The wind was driving dark, scudding clouds over the marsh when I set off next morning, after spending a second night at Mother Banks's. I reached the outskirts of the City at midday. There I stopped. I would not get far in my apprentice's uniform, and the seaman's jaunty scrap of a cap barely concealed my red hair.

Just inside the City I found the kind of market I needed. From Irish Mary at a second-hand clothing stall I bought thin britches – because they had bows that tied at the knee, which I fondly imagined to be the height of fashion – and traded my give-away apprentice's boots for a pair of shoes with fancy buckles like those 'worn at court', she said. A leather jacket tempted me, and I drew out the coin Matthew had left for me. She bit it, saying it was not only a good one, but one of the first to be minted.

'How can you tell that?'

'See? On the rim there – the lys?'

Her long fingernail pointed to a tiny fleur-de-lys, above the King's head. She said the mint mark showed that it was coined in 1625, the year of the King's Coronation.

'About as old as you are,' she cackled.

An unaccountable shiver ran through me; the sort of shiver that used to make Susannah ask: 'Has someone walked over thy grave, Tom?'

Matthew had told the shipwright it was mine and I took it back, turning it round and round between my fingers, feeling that perhaps it was a magic coin and, if I spent it, I would be spending part of my past. I reluctantly took off the expensive jacket, and put the coin back in my pocket. Instead I bought what she called a Joseph, perhaps after the coat of many colours, although these colours were those of various leather patches that held it together, larded with grease and other stains I did not care to question. At another stall I exchanged my apprentice's knife for a saw-tooth dagger. The upper part of the blade was lined with teeth that would catch the tempered blade of any sword and snap it.

The City looked different. Cornhill was swept clean. In spite of drizzling rain, groups of scavengers were out in Poultry, throwing household filth, dead birds and a dead dog into their carts. They did not argue, as they usually did, that a pile of refuse was 'over the line' in the other's ward, or, when the other cart was out of sight, dump it over the boundary. Planks were being laid so that coaches would not get stuck in the muddy streets. A group of men were arguing fiercely outside St Stephen, Walbrook, where the bells were ringing. I asked one man what o'clock it was and what was the service? He told me it was four of the clock and there was no service. They were practising the bells for the King.

'The King?

I stared at him stupidly.

'Do you not know? The King has set up a government with the Scots. He arrives tomorrow from Edinburgh to talk to Parliament.'

To talk to Parliament! I stood there, stunned. The King was going to listen to Parliamentary demands! I walked away in a dream. I felt that what Mr Ink had said was coming true, and we were on the brink of a new world.

It was beginning to grow dark, but it was too early to find Will, my drinking companion, in the Pot. I hoped to beg a bed from him. Once, when it had been too late to return to Half Moon Court after a heated debate, I had slept in his father's tobacco warehouse. I made my way towards the red kites, which always dipped and soared above Smithfield in the evening, searching, like the poor, for what the butchers had thrown away. In Long Lane I stopped. When I ran from Half Moon Court, Mr Black had shouted that I was in great danger. Just words to entice me back? Or a genuine warning? I seemed to recall a note of real desperation in his voice. I still carried my apprentice's uniform, rolled in a bundle. I turned it over and over in my hands, unable to admit to myself that the bond between us was quite broken.

From Half Moon Court came the sound of horses. A voice I did not recognise was shouting brusque commands.

A woman with a boy and girl running round her skirts came out of the market clutching a bloody bundle in a scarf, full of high spirits at finding their evening meal. The girl had a battered wooden toy and the boy tried to grab it. The girl ran from him into the street just as a Hackney hell-cart came out of Cloth Fair into Long Lane.

The boy stopped short, but the girl stood frozen in front of the approaching cart. The driver, who was riding one of the two horses, pulled frantically at the reins. The horse he was on responded but the other reared, dragging the coach forward at an angle towards the child. The child stared upwards at the rearing horse, wonder rather than fear on her face. The woman was screaming.

A man in the coach shouted, his voice cut off as he was thrown against the side. The flailing hooves were descending towards the child. Only then did she turn to run.

I flung my uniformed bundle at the horse's head. The horse shied away, whinnying frantically, falling against the other horse, hooves coming down inches from the girl as I snatched her up.

I stood there holding her while the driver struggled to calm the panic-stricken horses. I was shaking, but she seemed unmoved.

'Horse,' she said, stretching her hand out to the animal the driver was preparing to remount.

'Horse,' I agreed, stroking her hair. 'Horse.'

Her mother, sobbing with relief, was moving towards us when the curtain in the coach slid back. All I could see was the scar. A livid scar running from cheek to neck. The man had twisted round in his seat, and the scar seemed to be doing the cursing, swearing at me.

Petrified, I gripped the little girl to me. My hat had come off, and it was still light enough for him to see me. But he was righting himself, cursing and rubbing his head where he struck it.

He turned towards me. I glimpsed fine linen and eyes as cold as money. Before he could see my face I lifted the little girl high in the air, dandling her up and down in front of me to conceal my red hair. She squealed in delight.

'Are you trying to get your children killed? One less mouth to feed?'

I felt all the fear and hatred that I had heard in my father's voice when he had spoken of the man. And anger that there was not a trace of concern for the child or her mother. An almost uncontrollable urge filled me to pull him from the coach. Then the woman spoke:

'I am sorry, sir. I am truly sorry. It is my fault.'

Hearing the beseeching, pleading note in her voice, taking all the blame when the coach was travelling so recklessly, I could stand it no longer. I handed her the child and walked up to the coach.

But he had turned away with a grudging satisfaction at her apology and was now shouting at the driver, who, with some difficulty, had quietened the horses. 'Come on, come on, man! I must get to Westminster before dark.'

He shut the curtain. The driver scuttled for his whip, cracked it and the carriage lurched off. I stood there, staring after it. Although there was a chill in the evening air, my body crawled with sweat at how near I had come to giving myself away. There was a timid touch at my elbow. The woman was holding out the scarf, which wrapped the bloody remains she had scavenged. I felt a double pang: that she should offer me her supper, and that I could look as if I needed it. She whispered something to the little girl.

'Thank you,' the girl said.

I smiled, moved to gallantly sweep off my hat and bow, discovered the hat was not there, affected great surprise, which drew a giggle from the girl and a smile from the woman, and could not seem to find it although it lay in front of my eyes, which drew peals of laughter from the girl.

'It's there!'

'Where?'

'There!'

This welcome little game was interrupted by a familiar voice.

'What's going on?'

George had come out of Half Moon Court. He still had a plaster on his head where I had struck him, but his darting eyes seemed as sharp as ever. I turned away, retrieving my hat. The woman told him what had happened. All that seemed to concern him was that the coach and its occupant had gone. I moved to pick up my uniform, torn and muddied by the wheels of the coach. I felt his eyes on me, but then I heard Anne's voice.

'George, are you going?'

My heart lifted. If only I could speak to her before her father!

'I must get my coat,' George said. 'It's a chill evening.'

'Please hurry!'

'All right, all right,' he muttered.

He gave me another curious look. I bent and picked up a rotting apple from the sewer, which seemed to satisfy him I was a beggar, for he went back into the court. Under the overhanging jetties it was darker and easy to follow him, keeping to the shadows of the opposite building. Although my new shoes leaked, they made less noise than the clumsy boots. Candles were lit in the house. The last of the light always came into my window in the evening, and I could see the edge of my mother's Bible on the sill.

At least, I determined, I would take that away.

Anne came to the doorway. She wore a pale-blue, high-waisted dress which I knew to be her best, presumably for the benefit of the visitor. Over that she had put on an apron. She carried George's coat. He seemed to take an interminable time putting it on, during which he shook his head gravely before finally coming to a decision to speak.

'What has happened to Mr Black is God's visitation on you, Miss Anne,' he said.

She looked at him in terror. 'What do you mean?'

'I think you know,' he said steadily.

'Indeed I do not! Please go for the doctor.'

I stared up at the window of Mr Black's bedroom. In the wavering candlelight I could just see Mrs Black passing restlessly by the bed, peering out of the window.

George stopped buttoning his coat, glanced up at the window, not speaking until Mrs Black had passed out of sight. 'You let the devil out of the cellar,' he said softly.

'I did no such thing!' Her voice was equally low, but sharp and contemptuous, as if it was the last thing in the world she would dream of doing.

'I saw you.'

'I came down when I heard the disturbance.'

'I saw you going up.'

There was a trace of uncertainty in his voice which she leapt on. 'You cannot have done. You make too much of yourself. Get the doctor!'

Perhaps he was lying and merely suspected. Or had seen something, but, groggy after my blow, could not be sure. At any rate, he began to move away reluctantly, and my heart went out to her for standing up to him.

All would have been well, but then she added bitterly: 'You should have let him have a candle.'

She knew what she had said as soon as the words were out of her mouth. He stopped and turned very slowly. As he did so I caught the smile of satisfaction on his face. It vanished as he looked at her with grave concern.

'How did you know about the candle?'

She gave a little moan. 'Please go.'

'Mr Black needs more than a doctor to cure him. We must root out the cause of the illness: your sin.'

He spoke so solemnly, so gravely, I had to struggle against the feeling that he was right, had been right all the time, and that the devil was within me. When George and Mr Black had first brought me here from Poplar, before the boat bumped against Blackfriars Stairs, had I not sworn a pact with him to be as evil as possible?

'You must confess,' George demanded.

She staggered. I thought she was going to faint.

'I cannot tell my father – it would kill him!'

'Then you must confess to God.'

'Yes, yes. You will not tell my father?'

'If you are good, child, and accept my guidance.'

She nodded perfunctorily, turning away. I could see she was on the edge of tears. 'Please go now.'

He was insistent. 'You will? Accept my guidance?'

'Yes!'

He smiled. 'God be praised! The sinner repenteth!'

He took her hands and began murmuring a prayer. At first she submitted, head bowed, but when she tried to take her hands away he only held them more tightly, murmuring away. Half a dozen times I nearly broke out of that doorway. Half a dozen times I forced myself back until suddenly I no longer cared whether he was pure good and I was pure evil. I jumped out.

'Leave her! Leave her alone!'

Nothing George had said could have made his point better. For a moment I must have looked like some foul spirit coming out of the ground. Anne screamed and backed away to the door. George ran. 'Anne!' Mrs Black shouted from upstairs. 'What is it? Has George gone for the doctor?'

There was no sign of him. 'I'll go,' I said.

Guilt drove me: I felt that Mr Black's illness was my fault. And breaking a bond is not just a matter of throwing away a uniform and selling boots. I went because I could not get out of my head it was no longer my job. Several times a year Mr Black had these strange attacks. He would stop what he was doing and stare at me like a blind man. Once, he dropped back on his chair, missed it, and fell to the floor. The first time I was very frightened, but Mrs Black drummed into me that when he had one of these attacks I must run and fetch Dr Chapman, for my master's life depended on it.

The doctor practised near St Bartholomew's in Little Britain but, luckily, was returning from a patient only two streets away. He was a bustling little man, of great good humour.

When I first met him I had told him I hated my hair; he offered to cup me for nothing, in the light of the discoveries of Mr Harvey, who declared that blood circulated and nourished everything. If enough was taken, he said, it might drain the colour from my hair. I thought he was serious and backed away hastily, at which he burst out into roars of laughter.

Now he said slyly, as we hurried back to Half Moon Court: 'I like your court dress, Tom. Are you to be presented to the King tomorrow?'

He went upstairs laughing, but that soon died. I always knew from the sound of his voice how serious the attack was. Now his greeting and his banter dwindled almost immediately into silence. There was no sign of George or Anne. It was very quiet, apart from the murmurings of the doctor, and the occasional creaks when he moved across the floor above me. There was no chance of my confronting Mr Black, but I might get my Bible.

I opened the door to the kitchen, where a kettle was heating by the side of the fire. I crept to the bottom of the stairs; from there I could see that the door to Mr Black's bedroom was closed. There was the faint clink of metal against a basin. I had watched Dr Chapman cup him once. After tightening a bandage round Mr Black's arm he would warm a lancet in the candle flame and draw it across a bulging vein. After a spurt of blood there would be a steady flow. It would take about ten minutes.

I took a step or two up the stairs. A shadow fell across the small landing above. I glimpsed the edge of Mrs Black's dress and pulled back against the wall. Never able to stand the blood-letting, she had gone into her own room. Anne was probably with her.

I stood indecisively. I could see straight through to the print shop, and beyond that to Mr Black's small office. The door, normally locked, was open. Papers littered the writing desk and the floor around it. A chair had been knocked over. I took a candle from the kitchen and went past the printing press into the office. Mr Black must have been working here when he had the attack.

As I picked up the chair I saw it: a bound black accounts book, of the type Mr Black used to keep a note of deliveries of ink and paper, and sales of pamphlets. But on the cover of this one was inked a single letter T.

Whatever I hoped to see when I opened it, it was not dull accounts. But there they were in Mr Black's neat hand, items of purchase and columns of figures.

7 October 1640. Paid for necessaries for apprentice viz:

	£	s	d
Boots, 2pr.	1	12	4
Uniform, lined	4	10	0
Stockings, worsted		6	2
Shirts, 2	1	9	10
Cap		8	3

I flicked through the pages rapidly. There was my life in Half Moon Court, from the cost of the watermen that had brought me here and the tutorials with Dr Gill, down to the very bread and cheese I had eaten, faithfully recorded right to the last halfpenny. I stopped as a word which seemed out of place with the others half-registered in the turning pages: portrait. Portrait?

I turned back, to see an entry whose amount dwarfed all the others.

8 August 1635. Paid to P. Lely. Portrait in oils & frame. £20-0-0.

I had had no portrait done. The very idea was laughable. Only people at court had their pictures painted. No. That was not quite true. Each Lord Mayor had his portrait painted and hung in the Guildhall. I went very still.

The summer of 1635 I had taken a message to the clerk in the Guildhall and been told to wait for a reply. While I was in the waiting room a young man wandered in. His smock and hands were daubed with paint. He spoke with a thick Dutch accent and said the Mayor had gone out to a meeting, and he too was waiting for him.

He pushed my face to one side so he could see the profile and grunted something in Dutch. He said he was tired of painting old men who wanted to look young and dashing, and as an exercise he would really like someone young and dashing to sketch.

I was flattered and amazed by the incredible speed with which he sketched. By the time the clerk came with the reply, and to say that the Mayor was ready again, the painter had caught me like a bird in flight. A grin. A sulk when I grew bored with him. In profile. Staring with wide eyes straight out of the paper.

As the charcoal flew across the paper he grunted, 'The eyes you have. The nose. Everything but the hair.'

'What do you mean?'

He seemed too absorbed in the next sketch to answer. 'Turn. No no – the other way!'

I begged him for a sketch but he said he needed them all.

'Perhaps the painting you may one day see, mmm?'

He smiled, patting me on the cheek, leaving traces of charcoal and paint which I left there until they disappeared.

Peter – that was his name. I stared at the account book: P. Lely. Peter Lely. Perhaps Mr Black had commissioned him to do a portrait of himself. No. No printer could afford it, and if he could he would surely hang it prominently. Somebody had paid for a picture of me. But who? Why? And where was it?

I heard sounds upstairs; the doctor's deep voice and Mrs Black's low murmuring answer. Quickly I riffled through the remaining pages. A folded piece of paper, which I supposed was used as a marker, flew out of the book. I picked it up and placed it on the table. There was nothing of interest in the rest of the accounts, but there was a whole new section at the end. Mr Black had turned the book upside down to start the section on the last page. It was a cross between a diary and a tutor's report on my progress, or lack of it.

I was 'obstinate as a mule'. 'Bright but uncontrollable.' One day there was 'a glimmer of hope', the next total despair – 'I would have him on the boat back to Poplar if I could.'

It was soon clear that these were notes for more carefully worded reports, for there was the draft of one of them, pulling together various amended notes. Written two months ago, it declared: 'Mr Tom hath the Latin of a scholar, I have taught him a good Italian hand, he can use a fork at table, but his morality must still be called seriously into question.'

Mr Black got reports from Dr Gill. Why did he need to write these? They must be for the same person who commissioned the portrait. The accounts book answered at least some of the questions that had been plaguing me. Someone had paid Mr Black to have me educated and apprenticed; either the man with the scar, or, more likely, the kindly old gentleman Matthew had told me he represented.

Remembering the piece of paper I had picked up, I unfolded it. It was part of a letter, written on a different paper, a thick quality paper, and the hand was very different. Mr Black was proud of his hand, the simple sloping penmanship of a businessman, without flourishes, essential for something that might have to be read quickly in a dim light or a swaying carriage.

This was written in an erratic, angular hand, liberally sprinkled with capitals and with thick upstrokes and downstrokes that cut into the surrounding lines and made the words so difficult to read I had to move the paper closer to the candle. The paper was that of a gentleman, possibly one who had a scrivener to write his letters for him. I could see why he had not dictated this one.

It was a page from a longer letter:

. . . means that he now looks at the boy in a different way. He sees him as a great Folie who must be got rid of. Perhaps a Taverne brawl or some similar kind of ACCIDENT.

He has men for the purpose, who have been given a likeness and of course the boy's hair stands out like a beacon.

This matter will bring me to London sooner than I intended, but meanwhile re the accounts you sent me . . .

The page ended with some minute dissections of the cost of paper and ink. I searched frantically among the papers for the preceding page, but could find nothing. In spite of what had happened to me, I could not believe I had read the words right, and, hands trembling so much I almost singed the paper with the candle, began to decipher every word of that page again.

'What are you doing?'

It was Anne, holding the kettle. I was so still, so intent on those scrawled words, she must have taken the kettle from the fire and been on her way back to the stairs before she saw me.

'Somebody is trying to kill me.'

The words came out of my mouth lame and halting, marked with disbelief in spite of the evidence in front of me. But I must have looked so rigid with shock that she came up to me, concern on her face.

'What are you talking about?' she whispered.

'Look –'

I showed her the letter. I had forgotten she could not read. In a panic I gabbled that somebody had paid to make something of me, and now that I had failed had decided to get rid of me. It must have sounded a great nonsense, for she pulled away with alarm.

'You're mad!'

'Look –'

Even though she could not read them, I tried to show her the patterns the words made, in the vain hope that she would see the madness, the evil, in the blotches, the sword-like downstrokes.

'Anne!' Mrs Black called. 'The water must have boiled by now.'

There was the creak of a door opening upstairs. 'Get out,' Anne hissed.

'I'm not mad,' I whispered. 'You must believe me!'

We heard her on the stairs. 'What's going on? Is that George?'

'No, Mother,' Anne shouted back. 'The water's just boiled. I'm coming.' To me she whispered: 'George has gone for the constable. Stay – if you want to be arrested.'

It was only when she went that I thought of my Bible. I hurried to call her back, but she was already halfway up the stairs. I folded the letter and put it into my pocket. I went to the door and listened. It was silent in the yard, but towards the river there was the sound of rioting, in the direction of Westminster. I hoped that would make it difficult for George to find his constable.

After a minute or so Anne returned to refill the kettle. The pail in the kitchen was empty. Ignoring me, she went to the pail in the yard we normally washed in. I followed her, taking the pail from her, doing what I had done so many times, drawing my fingers over the water, breaking the thin film of ice already forming on it. I ached for normality, and the everyday action calmed us both. I dipped a jug in the water and poured it into the kettle.

'How is Mr Black?'

'He cannot speak.'

I was stunned. Water flowed over the top of the kettle as she pulled it away. I stared up at the window, where I could see the elongated shadow of the doctor move across the wall.

'I am sorry.'

'You struck him,' she said, accusingly.

'He struck me!'

'It is his right.'

'When it is just. George taking the candle was not just.'

We had instinctively drawn away from the house, into the shadows of the tree where, for that brief period, we used to play as children. 'I should never have let you out! George knows.'

'Don't trust him.'

'I must.'

She began to move back to the house.

'If he meant well by you, he would tell your father.'

She stopped. She was now in the light, and I could see that her hands, which she twisted together constantly, were white with cold. I longed to touch them, to take them in my hands, but dare not. There was a trace of the old mockery in her voice.

'And I can trust you?'

'Yes!'

I spoke with a ferocity that made her jump with fear, but then she gave me back a look of such intensity I wanted to lower my eyes but could not, or dare not. It seemed to go into my very soul in a way no preacher, nor my mother and father had ever done.

'Did you write that poem?'

'Yes – and meant every word of it.'

Everything at that moment was as sharp and clear as the moonlight on the splinters of ice I had broken in the pail. She stared back at me, trembling, but before she could speak there was the sound of someone turning into the court from Cloth Fair. At the same time I saw her mother coming to the window. I jumped into the shadows.

It was the pewterer who lived opposite. His clothes were usually dusty with the chalk shed by the plates and mugs when he took them from the mould, but now they were clean. For him, like the shipwright, business had dried up.

His gait was unsteady. He scarcely gave Anne a glance.

'Goodnight, Mr Reynolds.'

'Goodnight, Anne.'

Mrs Black had withdrawn from the window. The intensity of the moment had gone. Neither of us spoke. She picked at her apron. Suddenly she put a hand to her mouth to smother laughter.

'What do you look like!'

'Well, I think,' I said stiffly, with a stab of indignation, yet with a feeling of relief that we were back on the familiar ground of mocking banter.

I displayed my shoe. In the dim light the gap where the upper was parting from what was left of the sole could scarcely be seen, and I thought it had a particularly fine buckle.

'This shoe has been presented at court.'

'Which court?' She struggled to stop giggling. 'James or Elizabeth?'

She could not contain her laughter and I was frightened they would hear her. 'I had to change my clothes!'

'As people do in your pamphlets?' she mocked. 'Because someone is trying to kill you?'

A movement in the window drew our eyes upwards. The candles in the room threw a wavering silhouette on the wall of Dr Chapman fastening his bag. Time and again, I find, ideas come out of desperation.

'You know your numbers?' I whispered urgently.

'Of course,' she said indignantly.

Without another word I grabbed her hand and ran her into the house. Water splashed from the kettle and she almost dropped it. I took it from her and put it down. Now she looked convinced I was mad, was ready to scream. I went into the office, picked up the accounts book and pointed out the letter T, which I think she understood.

And, as I whispered the names of the purchases, she with increasing bewilderment in her face scanned the numbers. She knew some of her letters by stitching them and her numbers by shopping. We heard the bedroom door opening upstairs. I almost dropped the book, then could not find what I was looking for. She was begging me silently to go, her hands locked beseechingly.

I found the entry.

8 August 1635. Paid to P. Lely. Portrait in oils & frame. £20-0-0.

She did not understand the words, but stared in such wonderment at the number, she did not react to Dr Chapman's voice.

'I will call in tomorrow morning.'

There was no reply from Mr Black, but his wife said: 'Look – he is writing something!' I could hear the doctor go back into the room.

'Twenty *pounds!*' Anne exclaimed.

It was as much as a skilled clerk earned in a year. I told her what it was for.

'A picture! Of you? It must be something to do with the man with the scar.'

'So I imagine.'

'I hate him!' she said vehemently. 'Shouting at my father when he's ill; ordering him about. Who is he?'

I shook my head. She kept looking at the entry in the book and then at me. I do not know what she was seeing, but it was no longer a clown, a tumbler, or even an apprentice. She bit her lower lip as she often did when she was vexed or puzzled.

'Twenty pounds,' she kept saying with awe. 'For a picture. Of you.'

'A monkey.'

'Don't joke. Where is it?'

'How do I know?'

'I knew it.' The words came out in a tiny explosion. 'One day my father –' She stopped herself.

'Your father what?'

She shook her head and refused to say more. We heard Dr Chapman saying goodbye and hurried through the darkened print shop to the door. I desperately tried to think of a way of seeing her again.

'Can you bring me my Bible?'

'Where?'

'I'll write to you. Through Sarah.' I groaned inwardly again at the frustration of her being unable to read.

'I will learn,' she said, matter-of-factly, as though it was something she could do in a day or two. 'If my father cannot speak, I shall have to read. My mother is no good at business.'

'Bring the Bible to church. Sunday.'

She stood there, slight, determined, letting me out through the back door, while her mother let the doctor out of the front. There was something about her I had never even guessed at before, behind all the mockery, the trivial games, something that I can only call, even at that age, calculation.

Whatever it was, I leaned forward, before she could close the door, and kissed her.

7

I was in a daze, a dream after that kiss. I suppose you could scarce call it a kiss, more a bump of noses, a collision of my lips on her cheek, as cold and splintered as the ice in the bucket, a brief holding of her trembling slightness, as slight as the bird fallen from its nest I had once picked up in Poplar and tried vainly to warm back to life. But it opened up the whole world to me.

I was careless of my safety, oblivious of what was going on around me. All I wanted to think about was that trembling, that cold cheek, that slightness against me. For, however clumsy and brief it had been, her arms had held me.

I could well have walked into George and the constable he sought, but he must have been unsuccessful, for I learned from people streaming away down the streets that there had been a big riot outside Westminster. Mingling with the crowd, I was much more difficult to find.

One man had a pike wound oozing blood. He almost staggered into me. I ducked as he raised his stave at me, but he was only demonstrating exultantly how he had broken the head of the guard who gave him his wound. He said his radical Puritan master had equipped him with the stave and urged him to fight for the Bill.

'The Bill?'

'The Grand Remonstrance – the Freedom Bill! The King's side

are trying to stop Mr Pym from publishing it officially because it will give him control of people like me. The army!'

'Are you a soldier?'

'No, a weaver.' He held up his stave proudly. 'And a member of the All Hallows Trained Band!'

'You must know Will,' I said, for Will was an enthusiastic recruiter for the All Hallows.

'And his father!' The weaver held up his stave again and yelled: 'Ormonde! Ormonde!'

'Ormonde! Ormonde!' the crowd chanted.

Will's father was a radical supporter of Mr Pym, standing against an East India merchant, Benyon, in the City elections. Whoever controlled the City, the weaver told me, controlled citizen militias like the All Hallows, which together totalled ten thousand men.

Intoxicated as I was with Anne, I now became drunk at the thought of all this as I approached the Pot, to which many of the demonstrators were repairing. This was what Mr Ink had predicted. The appeal had been made to the people – and the people had responded!

The words he had copied and I had rescued from the dirt had done this. Or so I thought. Now the struggle was to have them officially published. Our pirated copies were in the alehouse, ringed with beer, passed from hand to hand, read out to people who could not read, people who nodded silently.

They were not talking then about rebellion. People talked of Magna Carta. Of old rights to disappearing common land, which had driven them to leave their families and come to London. Of rights to religion. And of the biggest right of all – the right to afford a loaf of bread.

I could not see Will. I was clutching a beer a complete stranger had given me when I glimpsed in the throng something that drove all this from my mind. At the bar was the man in the beaver hat. Anger fought a desire to run. I believed he had killed my mother. I had eaten little and the beer had gone to my head. Anger won and I fought my way through the laughing, shouting crowd. Now I saw the bulky shape of

Crow, and felt again the sensation of him wrenching my head back to cut my throat. Crow turned and stared round. I put my hand on my knife, sure he had seen me, but he was the sort of man who habitually glanced about him, watching his back.

'– last place he'll come,' I heard him say.

'A dog always returns to smell his own shit,' the man in the beaver hat said.

There were a couple of candles on a table as I got closer to the bar. I snuffed them out with my sleeve. Someone shouted. My approach to the bar was plunged in shadow.

The feel of the knife was quite different from my apprentice's knife, which was a toy by comparison. This knife was heavier, balanced. I loosened it from my belt. I stopped, inches from their backs. They had caught the landlord's attention.

'. . . red hair – Tom Neave,' the man in the beaver hat was saying. He drew a crumpled sheet of paper from his pocket. As he unfolded it I glimpsed one of the sketches the artist had done of me that summer. In a few lines he had caught my grin, the sharpness of my nose between the dark gleam of my eyes.

I moved closer. I tried to swallow but my mouth was too dry. There was a rent in the back of Crow's tough leather jerkin like an open mouth, gaping wider as he moved. I became drawn to it, fascinated by it.

The landlord was saying: 'Haven't seen him for a week.'

'We're working for the Stationers' Company and Mr Black,' the man said. His voice was grave and concerned. 'He's wanted for breaking his bond, theft . . . You can reach me at the Cock and Hen in Holborn . . . There's a reward of five crowns.'

The landlord's eyebrows lifted. I could see that he regarded that as a much more substantial profit than he would ever get from selling beer. But it was not this that made me lose control. It was hearing that Mr Black, whom I thought such a godly man, and who had hypocritically claimed to warn me of danger, was part of this plan to kill me.

The knife seemed to have a life of its own as I drew it from my belt. I could see nothing but the rent in Crow's jerkin, opening and closing, a perfect target.

'Tom!'

As God is my witness, I thought it was the Lord's stern voice stopping me. Crow and the man in the beaver hat whirled round, bumping into a man trying to get to the bar, who knocked into me. My knife spun to the floor.

'Tom!'

Will was waving near one of the doors. The man in the beaver hat pushed through a group of drinkers towards him. Crow immediately went to cover the other door. I could see his eyes moving meticulously from head to head. Even with my hat firmly wedged on and the dim light I could feel the red hairs crawling on my neck as if they were burning like a beacon.

Will was staring at me. All I could do was shake my head numbly at him. When the man in the beaver hat spoke to him, Will shook his head and pointed to the door where Crow was standing.

'He's run for it!' the man in the beaver hat shouted to Crow, who dived out into the street, the other man following.

I picked up the knife, staring at its blade as Will pushed his way through to me with another, older man, who wore a jump jacket, Dutch style, with a square linen collar.

'I was going to kill him,' I said stupidly.

The older man shook his head. 'You were wrongly positioned,' he said, in an educated drawl. 'You would only have wounded him. He would have turned and killed you.' He drew his finger across his throat.

Will cut across him sharply, seeing the landlord say something to the pot girl. 'Get him out of here, Luke!'

He grabbed me by one elbow and the man called Luke took me by the other and they hustled me into the night.

8

That night I slept curled up in my Joseph coat on bales of the best Virginia tobacco, in the warehouse of Will's father. Ever since then the smell of Virginia curling up from a clay pipe has meant the smell of rebellion to me. It rose from the pipes of Will and Luke when they woke me next morning. They took me through to the counting house, where there was a third man, Ben. What followed was a counting, not of money, but of me – an interrogation.

All three were members of the All Hallows Trained Band. Will and Ben were typical of many of the City's part-time soldiers: middling men fighting against the City's richest merchants, who generally supported the King. Will's father, like many tobacco merchants, was struggling to break the monopolies of fabulously wealthy spice merchants such as Benyon, his opponent in the City elections the following month.

Ben was an apothecary. Prevented from working in the City by another monopoly, the doctors, he practised medicine in Spitalfields outside the walls, dispensing herbal cures to the London poor. Ben was as quiet and diffident as his grey jacket and hose, but there was a stubbornness in his silences, a refusal to take anything for granted, that I liked.

Luke was totally different. He seemed to have only one aim in joining the militia, and that was to fight. He had just come from fencing practice, and propped his sword against a rickety table in the counting house. A pupil to a lawyer in Gray's Inn, he was the second son of a gentleman, and looked it. The achingly soft leather of his funnel boots ridiculed my shoes 'as worn at court'. I hid them under the table, my cheeks burning with embarrassment, but could not hide the shabbiness of my breeches, the stink and stains of my Joseph coat, at which he wrinkled his nose. He stared at me quizzically, as if I was one of those curiosities exhibited at a travelling fair.

'You're on the run,' he drawled.

'Yes,' I said defiantly. 'Are you going to take me to Newgate?'

'Bridewell,' he corrected, 'for petty offenders like you – unless you've actually murdered someone?'

He was looking meaningly at the knife in my belt. I jumped up, rocking the table. A week on the run had already changed me. Acting first had become a way of life. Another moment and I would have been on my way to the door, prepared to shove Luke from his stool if he tried to stop me. 'What happened, Tom?'

Ben's voice was soft, his concern calming. Ashamed now at my over-reaction, I dropped back on my stool. I told them everything, from Mr Black first taking me to Poplar, to the attempt on my life and the receipts and notes on me I had discovered in Mr Black's office.

When I had finished there was a silence, except for the clang of bells from barges on the river. Will puffed at a clay pipe of his father's best Virginia, which had gone from the 'foul stinking novelty' derided by King James to a soothing cure for all illnesses, from cholic to bladder stones.

'Is this a pamphlet you're writing?' Luke said sceptically.

'It's true!' I banged my fist down on the table, but then over the ships' bells came the much deeper sound of a church bell.

'St Mary-le-Bow,' Will said. 'It means –'

The end of his sentence was drowned by a great tumult of bells, spreading through the City from the east. Like a fire leaping from roof to roof the noise swelled, the deep-throated boom of St Katharine by the Tower, the clangour of St Dunstan-in-the-East, sparking into life the carillons of St Lawrence Jewry and St Giles' Cripplegate, St Paul's, St Martin's, St Dunstan-in-the-West and St Clement Danes until the whole warehouse shook in one huge caul-dron of sound.

Luke was inaudible, but no one needed to hear him.

'The King,' were the words he formed.

The King had arrived to talk to Parliament! All our arguments were forgotten as we joined the great crowds pouring along Thames Street, past Fishmongers' Hall and up Fish Street Hill. Shouting questions and holding our ears close to people's mouths, we gradually made out that the King had met the Lord Mayor and aldermen at Hoxton, in fields just beyond the sprawl of new building, which (if it was anything like Poplar) had come to an abrupt halt in the present crisis with half-built houses and littered wood left in muddy pools.

'The King knighted the Lord Mayor on the spot,' someone told Will.

Will groaned. 'Knighthoods for gold – the King wants the City to buy him an army!'

A burst of cheering silenced him. I wondered why the crowd, after the demonstrations last night, could be so happy about it until we reached the corner of Gracious Street. We could not move for the press of people round the fountain. Men and women staggered from it with what looked like blood on their hands and clothes.

Even Luke had lost his coolness and was shoving his way through the crowd. He yelled at me, but I could not hear a word. The bells near us stopped, others petering away, and Luke's voice boomed into my ear.

'Drink to the King! And damn his bad advisers!'

He vanished among the heaving mass, reappearing with his fine lace collar stained with crimson, his hands running red.

'The best Bordeaux!' he yelled. 'When the King favours you – you're all for him!'

I could not believe it. The fountain was running with wine. A woman carried away a pot of it. Most held out their hands and slurped it into their mouths before it dribbled away then, having lost their places, fought to get back for more before the casks that were supplying it ran out. I wriggled on my hands and knees under a drayman's apron, catching the wine that ran through his fingers, sucking it up then turning my head to the sky to catch the red rain until I lost my balance and was in danger of being trampled into the crimson mud. Whether it was the best Bordeaux or vinegar I did not know, and I did not manage to swallow very much of it, but I was certainly drunk. Drunk on the press around me, then, turning like one towards Cornhill, on the thunderous roar of the crowd coming from there. He had arrived! We were missing him! The thought was on everyone's faces as they pushed and elbowed past Leadenhall Market.

People must have been in their places for hours. The route for royal entries to the City had been the same for over a hundred years. The King had entered at Moorgate, the procession doubling back on the route of the old Roman wall, turned again at Bishopsgate and was now approaching Merchant Taylors' Hall, rising in front of us. Spectators were pressed together as solidly as a brick wall and no matter how I dodged and jumped I could see little but fluttering banners brightening the grey November day and people leaning perilously from windows shouting with one voice:

'Long live the King! Long live the King!'

Tall as he was, Will had to stretch on his toes to see. He was flinging his hands in the air, shouting with the rest of the crowd. I was pressed against a half-timbered house. Above me was a cross-beam beneath the upper-storey windows where people were leaning out. Later I heard they had paid an angel for the privilege.

'Will, for the Lord's sake – give me a step.'

He linked his hands together. I slotted my foot into them, swung my other foot on to a stud, scrabbling for a hold in the loose herringbone brickwork. Plaster dribbled on me as a hand above grabbed me and pulled me up. I clung on to a cross-beam to cheers from the people round me. When I took in the sight below me, I nearly fell back again. The streets were lined with City liverymen. A great rainbow of colour made it as bright as midsummer as another entourage passed down Cornhill, followed by the City Artillery Company, pennants flying from their pikes, pistols at their saddles. I had thought them radical, but it seemed that they had joined the crowds in succumbing to the King.

Two by two on magnificent horses, which trod so exactly to the beat of the drums it looked as though they too were awestruck by the occasion, came the great peers. Constantly in danger of falling, I kept calling out like a small child: 'Who's that, who's that with the sword?' and someone from the window, or more often Luke, who had managed to worm his way to the front, shouted the answer.

'That's the Marquess of Hertford with the Sword of State . . .'

He seemed to know who everybody was, and the significance of who had been chosen and of his position in relation to the King.

'That's Manchester . . . Lord Privy Seal . . . and that's the Marquess of Hamilton . . . fancy choosing him to be Master of the Horse . . . they're all moderate reformers . . . You see? You see?' he yelled at Will. 'The King is sending a message – he's got rid of his evil counsellors!'

I thought that wonderful news. Then I had to cling to the cross-beam as the crowd below me flung up hats and the people in the room above drummed with their feet on the floor so that the whole house shook. There he was!

'The King! The King!' the crowd roared.

I never again in my life used a woodblock of that oval face, long curling hair and pointed beard without thinking how totally inadequate it was, and without remembering that moment. He seemed to float rather than ride on his magnificent black horse, saddle embroidered in silver and gold, his gossamer-light riding cloak fluttering like wings behind him, embroidered with the insignia of the Garter, a star emitting silver rays.

Every time he raised his hand or smiled, the crowd erupted. Already from mouth to mouth the word had spread that at Hoxton he had vowed not to be swayed by popery but to protect the Protestant religion of Elizabeth and James. He looked up as he passed. He seemed to smile and lift his hand directly at me. I was near to fainting, my fingernails scrabbling as I hung on, the crowd a continuous roar in my ears. I loved him. There is no other word. The Divine Right of Kings? Of course he was divine! Were not people all along the route struggling to get close to him, held back by the liverymen – the halt, the lame, beggars trying to get relief from their sores? A woman pressed forward, holding up her blind child in the hope that for a moment he would breathe the same air.

I twisted round to follow the King as long as possible as he disappeared towards Cheapside. When I reluctantly turned back I was immediately transfixed by the woman in the carriage below. Anne was beautiful, but in a fresh and simple way. This woman was beautiful by art. Pearls glittered in her hair. Her skin was like thin porcelain, marred cunningly with a beauty spot on her cheek. Her dress was cut low and, because of my elevated position, I glimpsed more of a woman than I had ever seen before. I had no doubt in my mind who she was.

'The Queen!' I shouted. 'Long live the Queen!'

The woman looked up and smiled. The eyes were not artifice. You could not paint them. They were such deep blue they were almost black, and full of humour. The porcelain round them cracked with tiny laughter lines before she was whisked away and it was a moment before I realised that people round me were howling with laughter.

'The Queen has been and gone, you idiot!'

'That's Lucy Hay!'

'Countess of Carlisle.'

'Strafford's whore!'

The Earl of Strafford had been one of the royal advisers hated not only by Parliament but by many on the King's side for his ruthless, near lawless, drive for power. There was so much feeling against him the King had been unable to prevent his impeachment. With great reluctance, he had signed the death warrant for his execution in May that year.

'Now Strafford's gone, she's John Pym's whore!'

'Changes beds as she changes sides!'

There was more laughter and a fight broke out below. I took no notice of the vile accusations made about such a beautiful woman, who, because she was at court, must I thought have attracted to her some of the spirituality of the King. I was overwhelmed by the thought that I had been to her house, even if it was little nearer than her shit heap, and that, if I ever delivered letters again for Mr Pym, I might catch a glimpse of Lucy Hay.

'Look at him!'

'He's in love.'

'Come and join us!'

Drunken hands stretched out for me. I realised how much my arms were aching and gladly let go of the cross-beam, whipping up my hand to be caught by someone above me. Another hand grabbed me by the collar. It was as I thrust upwards from the stud I was standing on and grabbed for the sill above me that I saw the pennant. It fluttered from the guard of one of the out-of-favour peers, judging by the distance he was behind his King. Inscribed on the pennant was some kind of bird, I knew not what, but I felt I had seen it before. It appeared and reappeared as the wind caught it, as if the bird was really flying. A falcon. I *had* seen it before! As though it were yesterday, I was back in the dockyard with Matthew, carrying pitch to the *Resolution*, which was flying the same flag, the falcon, in honour of the great gentleman who commissioned it.

There he was! Stiff on a horse, as if he rode little these days. He winced as he stared round at the crowd and I saw that face. That beard. That kindly look. No, not so kindly now, screwed up like crumpled paper, greying eyebrows knotted together in a frown but there was no doubt in my mind he was the gentleman who had bent over me while I slept after I burned myself with pitch. The gentleman Matthew had been frightened of, and after whose visit Mr Black had apprenticed me.

'That's him! That's the man!'

I must have been out of my wits. I pointed. Saw the gentleman crick his face upwards, staring at me as I hung for a moment by one hand. They tried to grab me but the man holding me lost his grip and I fell on to the people below. A man went sprawling, cursing. Others cheered. Luke shouted something. Will and Ben were coming towards me but I pushed and shoved and wriggled and fought my way through the crowd to get to the man before he passed. I reached the liverymen, barring the way with staves. I seized the stave of one of them and threw him off balance. What drove me forward were the words in that scrap of a letter I had found in Mr Black's office: 'he now looks at the boy in a different way'.

It must have been written by the man with a scar, on the old gentleman's instructions. I had one object and that was to reach the gentleman who had, for some reason, decided to make something of me then, like a potter discarding a faulty vessel, determined I was 'a great Folie' who must be got rid of.

Why? That was the question I wanted to hurl in his face: Why?

Perhaps I even shouted the word. In the blur of what happened I cannot remember. The procession had come to a stop. I ducked round one reined-in horse and was a few feet from the gentleman staring down at me. I appeared so suddenly his horse reared. I tried to catch its reins as the gentleman slipped in his saddle. All around me people were shouting. Riders were fighting to control their bucking horses. I felt the stinging cut of a whip.

'Make way! See to my father!'

The voice was that of a rider who had his horse under perfect control. I caught a glimpse of the falcon emblazoned on his cloak as he urged his horse towards me. His face was like the old man's but smoothed out, with a neat, spade-like beard. His sharp grey eyes were those of a man of action who is brought to life by other people's panic and disorder. He broke through the press of people and bore down on me, his head low over his horse, his eyes narrowed along the sight of his down-pointed sword. To him I must have looked like the game he hunted on his estate. Or vermin, more like. Someone was shouting in my ear but I was like one of the rats in the dockyard, hypnotised by a stray dog which had trapped it. The point was inches from me when a stave knocked it away. The sword ripped through the shoulder of my coat, spinning me round. The rider's horse bucked, but he controlled it, and turned the horse towards me again.

'Run!' the voice yelled.

It was Luke. He dragged me through the confused mêlée and shoved me towards Will. 'Run, you little fool! Run!'

9

They took me back to the warehouse, where Mrs Ormonde insisted on giving me a bed in Will's room. Ben rubbed a cool salve into my shoulder. He reminded me of Matthew, except there was a sense of order in the herbal cures he carried in a battered leather satchel. Luke watched, sitting on the end of the bed. 'What on earth were you doing?'

I did not answer, determined to say nothing more, since he had ridiculed my story. I had thanked him for saving my life, but being so indebted to him made it all the harder to stand his patronising manner.

The throbbing in my shoulder was already going down as Ben put the salve back in his satchel. 'You shouted "That's him." Who did you think the old gentleman was?'

'Were you trying to prove your story?' Luke persisted. 'The pitch boy and the peer?' I tried not to listen to him, turning my face into the pillow, but then his tone changed. 'Risky way of proving it, but effective. I saw him looking at you, and I'm sure he knew who you were.'

I sat up, staring at him, but in that irritating way of his he went off at a bewildering tangent. 'It looked as if the younger one just took you for a madman. But he wasn't properly dressed. He should have been wearing a ceremonial sword, not a rapier.'

He wrinkled his nose, in that fastidious way he had, as if he had smelt something bad. He had taken off the lace collar, stained with wine. He brushed some speck from his breeches. Alone amongst us, he looked almost as pristine as when we had set out for the procession, and, unlike Ben, totally out of place in such a Puritan household.

He sighted down an imaginary rapier and lunged towards me. He smiled, but a shiver went down me. Perversely, part of me didn't want to hear what he was going to say. The salve was working and the bed, which had the first feather mattress I ever slept on, made me realise how achingly tired I was. Now all I wanted was for it to be a story and to doze off into sleep; but he brought me fully awake. His matter-of-fact tone became more chilling.

'It was an Italian rapier. Bologna, at a guess. He should have been wearing a good old English broadsword and cut his man down. But that's clumsy and much less effective. It's the thrust, the *stoccata lunga*, not the cut . . . the point, not the blade – if you really want to kill a man.'

There was a relish, a ghoulish intensity in Luke's voice that brought back with sickening clarity the smell of the horse and the young man's eyes, one almost closed, the other focused along the rapier, as if his eye were part of the blade.

'You mean he was prepared?' Will put in.

'Yes. Apart from the rapier, he was dressed perfectly. I should know whose coat of arms that is . . . The falcon . . . it's on the tip of my tongue . . .'

'Was he one of the people in the Pot?' Ben asked.

'No. They were low-pads,' Will said.

'The man in a beaver hat looked like a soldier down on his luck,' Luke put in. 'Did you hear what they said at the bar?'

'They said they were from the Stationery Office. The soldier asked the landlord to contact him . . .'

'Where?'

'The Hen . . . No, the Cock and Hen in Holborn . . .'

'Mercenary inn,' Will said. 'Where they're recruiting for the war.'

'There isn't going to be a war,' Ben said.

Unlike the others, he refused to believe that people here would destroy their own country as they had done in Europe. The English were not that stupid. King and Parliament had patched up their quarrels for fifteen years, so Ben said, and would continue to do so. He had joined the Trained Band because of an interest in treating wounds, which he was convinced were much more likely to happen in exercises in Artillery Fields than in some mythical war.

Will's sister Charity, who was about Anne's age, brought me a posset. Her black dress had a starched cotton collar and she had the simplicity of those Dutch portraits which their artists did before they came to London and burst into colour when they painted for the court.

Astonishingly, Luke took on some of that simplicity as soon as she entered the room. His wit deserted him as she talked to him with a directness that cut through his diversions and flippancy. He was modest where he had been arrogant, listened where he had interrupted, bending with a sober face as Charity expressed her concern.

'I put your lace collar into water, Mr Ansell. There was blood on it.'

'Blood?' he said, startled.

I remembered the fountain of wine and could scarce check a smile. There was no drink in that Puritan house except a bottle of Dutch schnapps for use as a physic.

'Oh yes . . . blood,' Luke said, attempting a dismissive wave.

She came close to him, staring anxiously at the stain on the top of his doublet. 'Are you hurt?'

'Hurt? No no no . . .' he stammered. 'It was n-nothing . . .'

He caught my smile, gave me a savage look, half warning, half pleading, tried to recover his composure, stumbled against the foot of the bed, and hurried to open the door for Charity as she left to go to prayers. He returned almost immediately, his face flooded with excitement, snapping his fingers in triumph.

'Falcon! Lord Stonehouse, third Earl. Seat Highpoint House, in extensive lands near Oxford. King Charles's Master of the Court of Wards until about five years ago, when he fell from favour for dragging his feet paying Ship Money. That's who the old gentleman is!'

10

I slept late next day, and would have slept later, if it was not for Luke and Will dangling a bag with the stench of a neglected stable before my nose.

'What on earth is that?'

'Raven's wing,' said Luke solemnly.

'Approved by the Queen to remove the curse of red hair and turn it into fashionable black.' Will spoke like the hawker in Cheapside from whom they'd clearly bought it.

'Suitable for court.' Luke gave me a small bow.

I was suddenly very fond of the red hair I had hated all my life. 'You're not putting that on me!' I grabbed the canvas bag from Luke, peering at the evil-smelling black slime which had the consistency of loose turds, before jerking my head away. Luke tried to seize the bag. I dodged, drawing back my hand to hurl the bag at him.

'Do you want to be killed?' Will snapped.

He had an authority which Luke, with all his clowning, lacked. Slowly I lowered the bag. They told me they had been to the Cock and Hen in search of the man with a beaver hat. It was, as Will had told me, a recruiting centre for mercenaries. The religious wars which had devastated Europe for thirty years were petering out, and every other ship coming into London brought soldiers of fortune, looking for the highest bidder. One of them was the man in the beaver hat.

'His name is Captain Gardiner,' Luke said. 'He's a distant cousin, a poor relation of Lord Stonehouse.'

I took one last feel of my red hair and silently handed the revolting mess to Will. In the yard I dipped my head in a freezing pail of water, shook myself like a dog, and shut my eyes.

'Good for lice, too,' said Will.

'Turns them black instead of red,' spluttered Luke.

I shuddered and gagged as they rubbed the evil-smelling slime into my hair. 'It's foul! How long do I have to stay like this?'

'All night.'

'What?'

The worst moment was when Ben came next morning to find me propped up in bed, the mixture set into a hard clay on my head. He demanded to know what was in it, for if there was ceruse, a form of white lead, I might not only lose my colour but my hair.

I stared fearfully at myself in a pewter mirror as Luke, like a sculptor, chipped away at the clay. My hair was still there, not quite black, but a dusty dark brown. The effect was startling. Even Luke was silenced. Then he began laughing again as I touched my face to make sure I was the stranger who faced me in the mirror.

The bells were ringing as I approached St Mark's, Mr Black's local church, the following Sunday. Their sound was recognisable all over the ward and beyond, because one of the bells was slightly cracked and seemed to limp along after the others. I looked like a devout Puritan, with a square white collar and a black jump jacket and breeches of Will's, cut down by Charity. My darkened hair framed my face under a wide-brimmed felt hat. I looked towards Mr Black's pew. He was not there, George taking his place with Mrs Black. My heart leapt when I caught sight of Anne – and leapt again when I saw she carried my mother's Bible, which she had promised to bring me.

After the service I stayed seated, apparently still in deep prayer. Anne passed me so close her skirts almost touched me, a whiff of damask roses in the pomander she wore reaching me. Behind my hands, raised in prayer, I winked at her. She gave me a startled look, almost dropping the Bible, then slipped it on the bench beside me.

Outside, Anne dropped back while her mother and George talked to Benyon, the East India merchant standing as a King's man against Will's father in the City elections. I was surprised to see him there, for Mr Black despised his politics and his religion – St Mark's was a 'halfly reformed' church and Benyon was always urging a return to sacraments and ceremony – but it gave us the opportunity we needed.

The same thought in our heads, we went behind a mausoleum dedicated to Samuel Potter & Relic. She kept darting guilty, nervous glances towards her mother and George like a cornered animal. I was afraid to touch her in case she would flee.

'Thank you for the Bible, Miss Black,' I said.

She swallowed a smile at the formality. 'Tom, Tom, I must not see you again.'

'Then you must not call me Tom, surely.'

'Mr Neave.' Now she could not keep the smile back, although she was near to tears. 'You fool – what do you look like?'

'I have become a Puritan.'

I mimicked the stiff dignity of George, who from round the edge of the mausoleum I could see, hands clasped behind his back, nodding gravely to Benyon and the minister, Mr Tooley, who had joined them. She dipped her face into her hands to contain her laughter. As soon as she stopped I doffed my hat, starting her off again when she saw my hair.

'Stop it, you fool, stop it! What on earth have you done with your hair?'

'It's called Raven's wing.'

'Raven's –'

She clapped her hand over her mouth to curb the laughter.

Slipping in her heavy, wood-soled pattens, she clutched at me. I caught her and almost immediately released her, for I was still frightened she would fly off like a bird, but in a sudden movement she held me so tightly I gave a little gasp. She buried her head on my chest. Still apprehensive, I brought my hand tentatively down to smooth the hairs blown from under her hat across her forehead. Her eyes were shut, as if she was asleep. Sunshine briefly lit us and warmed us and she murmured something as if dreaming, and my hand stroked her gently, but otherwise neither of us moved or wanted to move.

'Anne,' her mother called. We stood motionless, except for my stroking hand.

'Anne?' Louder and querulous.

Anne's eyes shot open. She stared up at me with a fierce, wild, hard, desperate look that softened briefly into one of deep, penetrating tenderness such as I never thought I would see in her grey-flecked eyes.

'Anne?' Mrs Black's pattens clacked on the path.

'God forgive me,' she whispered. 'I must not see you again. Don't try and see me, Tom. Please. Please go.'

She pulled away, waved to her mother and began walking slowly back to her. I followed her, in my devout pose, clasping my Bible. Mrs Black stared at me, then returned to the conversation. I caught a snatch of George saying: 'The King is right. Pym has gone too far!' before Anne, fearful I would go right up to them, darted behind an urn, beckoning me frantically.

'Go the back way,' she hissed.

'Not until you tell me what you feel for me.'

She picked up a stick and struck at some weeds. 'I feel nothing – nothing!'

'That's not true! I saw the look in your eyes.'

'The look in my eyes!' she mocked, and now the grey eyes held all the cruelty they showed when she used to make fun of my monkey feet as a child. But I met their gaze steadily until finally she turned away with a shrug, giving the weeds another savage blow.

'Tell me you do not love me,' I said. 'And I will go. I'll never try and see you again.'

She did not seem to hear me. She began to clear the weeds she had cut. I asked her again to say she did not love me, and I would walk away.

'I cannot,' she muttered. Among the weeds were nettles which must have stung her, but she seemed unaware of them.

'Cannot? What do you mean?'

She gave a little moan and I thought for a moment she was going to bury her face in the nettles. 'It is a sin to love you.'

At first all I heard was that she loved me. I moved to hold her, but her pleading agonised look stopped me and I retreated at once, for I would do anything for her, now that I knew she loved me. I had something that I had to ask her.

'When I found that book in your father's office, about the money spent on me, and the portrait, you said "I knew it!" What did you mean?'

'I had seen that book before.'

She was silent for a moment and looked towards the group. It was an unusually mild winter's day, the sun breaking strongly through the clouds. George was still in full flow, Mrs Benyon was showing Mrs Black the gilded panelling and plump leather uphol-stery of their coach, while the coachman lit a pipe and turned his face towards the sun.

It was the autumn day, she told me, when we were playing together as children, and the man with a scar arrived and Mr Black called us in. When I ran away, her father took her into his office, where he was going over the accounts book with the man. She had never seen her father so stern, and yet so frightened.

'Frightened? Mr Black?' I said.

'So was I.' She trembled at the memory of the gentleman striking the table and shouting: 'It won't do, Black, it won't do! Keep the boy close!'

The man had bent down to her so the scar almost touched her upturned face and she could smell the wine on his breath. 'You know what Tom Neave is, don't you? A plague child!'

Only then did she drop the weeds she was gathering and realise her hands were blotched red from the nettles.

'What did he mean?'

She scratched her hands wildly. 'I don't know! I don't know!' Turning to look back towards her mother, she said, 'They told me not to come near you. They believe you're evil.'

'That's George,' I said contemptuously. 'He's a liar and a hypocrite.'

'He's not!' she said vehemently. 'He's kept the business going! Without him, I don't know what we'd have done! He does much work for Mr Benyon.'

'Benyon?' I could not believe my ears. 'He's a Royalist! Does your father know?'

'George shows him what he prints.'

'Are you sure?'

'He gives him proofs, but I cannot read them. George knows someone paid my father to take you. He says he warned him you were evil, and now his illness is God's punishment.'

'What nonsense!'

'He told Father I let you out of the cellar. I thought he would go mad! It's worse because he can scarcely speak. He writes – tries to write . . .'

She buried her head in her hands, stumbling about blindly. Blood ran down the backs of her hands where she had scratched them.

'Anne – where are you?' Mrs Black called.

'Coming!' she shouted. 'I've stung my hand. I'm just getting some dock leaves.'

She wrenched up a fistful of dock leaves. I seized her by the hand.

'Anne – when he said I was a plague child, did you think I would get black boils?'

Unexpectedly she began to laugh. 'Yes. I looked for them every day.'

'Did you see them?'

'No.'

'Do you think I'm evil?'

'The devil is clever,' she said, with a penetrating directness.

'George says.'

'He says nobody knows who you really are. Where you've come from.'

It was true. Everything pointed to me not being Matthew and Susannah's child. Matthew had fled to Poplar not only because of the stolen pendant, but because of me. A plague child. What did the man mean? So far as I knew, I had never had the plague. A chill ran through me. There was a law that made it a hanging offence to 'talk, feed, entertain or employ any wicked or evil spirit'. This, the Church believed, was the greatest offence against God: *maleficium* – making a pact with the devil.

'Anne, you can't believe I'm an evil spirit!'

My face must have looked so desolate, so woebegone that she laughed and held me. 'No, no, no, Tom – not when I'm with you, not when you look like that.'

She kissed me impulsively. I had never seen her more beautiful, although her face was reddened with half-shed tears and her hat was awry, allowing her fair hair to blow in unruly tangles in and out of her eyes.

The crack of the coachman's whip made her jump as if she had felt the lash. 'But when I see my father lying there . . . You said if I told you I did not love you, you would go.'

'But you *do*.'

'I *cannot* love you.' She was crying now, the tears blurring the words. 'I promised my father . . . I swore on the Bible I would never see you again. And here I am, God forgive me. Promise me on your mother's Bible you will not try and see me again, Tom.'

Her eyes were so blinded with tears, her voice so desperate, and I loved her so much, so much that I would do anything for her that the words were out of my mouth before I could stop them: 'I promise.'

11

That December, that Christmas is a total blank to me. I cared about nothing: life, politics, words – everything had the taste of dry bread. I joined the All Hallows Trained Band and went with Will, Luke and Ben to Moorfields for what I thought senseless drilling practice. But I needed something senseless: 'Trail your pike . . . Palm . . . Charge your pike!' Or, with a musket: 'Put in bullet and ram home! Remove scouring stick!'

The pikemaster, Big Jed, was a coal heaver, a huge man whose gentle manner belied his words. His mood fitted mine. He was a veteran of the London riots who declared the pike manual had been written by gentlemen who liked pretty pictures. He took the smiles from our faces and the jokes from our mouths with two short, chilling sentences: 'This is a pike,' he said. 'It kills people.'

I thought my love for Anne would fade eventually. I prayed for this to happen, but it only seemed to grow stronger. Evenings were worst, when I saw the red kites floating above Smithfield and longed to walk down Cloth Fair, just for a sight of her.

Just before Christmas the City's Common Council elections were held. The King's supporters lost their majority, George's friend Benyon losing his seat to Will's father, John Ormonde, but even that did little to lift my spirits.

I earned my keep at the Ormondes by running messages for

Mr Pym. The riots grew worse. Apprentices – now being called Roundheads, because of their close-cropped hair – responded by taunting the Royalists as 'Caballeros', after the despised Spanish troops, a word which became on Londoners' tongues 'Cavaliers'. Throwing myself into politics was one way of trying to forget Anne. I helped organise demonstrations preventing bishops from entering the House of Lords, removing the King's majority that had becalmed the Commons' reformist legislation. The Lords were now approving legislation, reported a gleeful Mr Ink, at an unprecedented, most unparliamentary speed.

Even a move by the King to prosecute him for treason did not seem to concern Mr Pym, for that would take time, and time was now on Mr Pym's side. Splashed with ink, shaking his cramped fingers, Mr Ink told me there was a Bill to deprive the bishops of their seats permanently. Second reading. A Bill to remove the King's power to raise an army without Parliament's consent. Third reading. A Bill . . . He pressed a letter in my hand to be urgently delivered to the Countess of Carlisle and rushed back to transcribe yet more Bills. As I was crossing Bedford Square, a coach approached at such speed I was forced to dive to the pavement, falling and losing the letter in a pile of swept-up snow. By the time I had picked myself up and retrieved it the coach had jerked to a stop outside her house and the Countess was coming down the steps. I was as transfixed as when I had mistaken her for the Queen in the royal procession. She had no need for a queen's jewels. Her eyes glittered and her cheeks glowed in the sharp air. She wore a fur cloak over an embroidered dress of green silk. Her tight ringlets of hair quivered as she berated a footman who was ordering a boy to clear scraps of snow from the steps.

'For the Lord's sake, Jenkins, let me pass! If I don't hurry it'll be more than my leg that's broken!' She slipped at the bottom of the steps, righted herself and turned to him. 'Can you do it?'

'I'll try, ma'am.'

'I'm not interested in trying! You must!'

He gave a little bow. As his head dipped I saw him shut his eyes briefly and clench his teeth as he kept his feelings under control. She took a letter from her cloak to give to him, and in the same moment saw me, letter in hand, gaping. So did Jenkins. He vented his pent-up feelings on me, snatching my letter and shoving me away.

'Off!'

I slid, found my balance, and as he went back to her, gave him the apprentice's finger and slouched away.

'Wait!'

Thinking she could not possibly be addressing me, I trudged on, until Jenkins grabbed me by the arm.

'You – boy! Come here.' She beckoned me impatiently. 'Yes – you!'

I went reluctantly, so reluctantly that Jenkins gave me a couple of shoves to propel my progress. I skated towards her, only just stopping in front of her, gazing at the ground, convinced she recognised me as the boy who, clinging on to the window ledge at the royal procession, had looked down her low-cut dress.

'Look at me.'

It was like being asked to look at the sun. She had that kind of brightness, that kind of perfection that belonged in imagination, hinted at inadequately in battered woodcuts of goddesses, but was now before me in full glory. She was supposed to have had smallpox but I could not believe it. There was not a pit, not a blemish in the perfect white skin of her neck, in her cheeks pinked by the cold. She was supposed to be old, all of thirty, but I could not believe her to be much over twenty. She was supposed to be in love with Mr Pym, but much as I revered his words and his courage, I refused to believe such a divine woman could love old bones.

She was staring at me inquiringly. I realised in a panic she had said something to me, and I had not heard a word.

'Has he a voice?' she said to Jenkins, who gave me a sharp prod.

'Yes,' I said, finding it, but barely.

'Can you take this letter to Mr Pym?' As I opened my mouth she anticipated my reply, waving it away impatiently. 'I mean now, during the debate, interrupting him?'

It was impossible for strangers to enter the House during debates, but it seemed equally impossible to say that to her.

'Yes.'

Another savage prod from Jenkins. 'Yes, ma'am!' he said. 'Don't you know how to speak to your betters?' He turned, unctuously apologetic to the Countess. 'I'm sorry, ma'am, it's the times, the rabble –'

'Oh, do be quiet, Jenkins!' She gave the footman the letter. 'Give it to him,' she said, as if it was not quite safe to move close enough to hand it to me direct.

Jenkins gave me the letter with a look of pure hate, and I added him to my lengthening list of my enemies in this world. I took the letter, but still stood there, unable to stop gazing at her.

'Go on,' she shouted. 'Mr Pym's life depends on it! Run!'

I ran. For her I would do anything. Fly like Mercury, who should be the messenger of such a goddess.

'Stop! Wait.'

I jerked to a halt, almost falling in the snow again. She was running to the coach. She was a woman who expected everyone to keep up with her rapidly changing thoughts.

'Come on! Don't just stand there!'

I had no idea then that she had the reputation for doing the unbelievable, the unthinkable. I ran back, watching her as she got in the coach, her dress lifting, petticoats momentarily frothing round her galoshes.

'Get in.'

I stood there dumbly, frozen as the snow. She lifted her eyes to heaven, as if asking God why she had to deal with nothing but imbeciles. 'You'll never get there in time! Jenkins –'

An appalled Jenkins sprang forward, slipped, saved himself by clutching at the open coach door, gave me another look of hatred, this one shot with disbelief, shoved me in and slammed the door. She rapped on the panel and the coach jerked away, throwing me against her. Her face flickered with disgust at the contact. I grabbed for a swaying strap like a man drowning, heaving myself into the opposite corner. I hung on to the strap as the coach rattled out of the square into Bow Street, dizzy with her scent, which clung heavily round me. In the great stink of London I had grown so used to taking short, exploratory breaths that it was a novel sensation to breath in so deeply, to abandon myself to breathing. I was amazed to find there was not one scent but many; jasmine and lavender that intoxicated the senses, only to be stimulated again by a sharp whiff of cinnamon.

There was a screech of brakes and I lost my strap, banging my head against the front of the coach and losing my hat. Carts and coaches going into the Strand were jammed in front of us as tight as mutton pies in a cook's oven. A carter and the driver of a Hackney hell-cart were yelling at one another.

'London is getting impossible – you'd be better running,' she commanded.

As I fumbled for the door latch, she saw a gap open up between two carts. Snatching up a stick with a silver knob, she hammered on the partition, shouting: 'Go through the Piazza, Alfred!'

The door flew open as the horses veered sharply left and I was thrown out, half-hanging from the coach. I hung on to the door desperately, the cobbles a speeding blur below me, before the horses jerked sharply right into the Piazza, flinging me back inside. Dazed by her scent and the blow to my head, I managed to shut the door again and dropped back in my seat. She was so intent on the driver getting through she was either unaware or unconcerned about this, but as we made good progress along the Piazza I felt her eyes on me.

'You have red hair.'

Convinced she had recognised me as the youth hanging from the window, gazing down at her breasts, I felt blood rushing up my neck, burning my cheeks, tingling in my cursed hair.

'Black . . . black, ma'am,' I stammered.

'Do not correct me,' she said sharply. 'It is red at the roots. You have dyed it. Extremely badly. Why?'

'It is the fashion, ma'am,' I tried, as the coach careered down St Martin's Lane, pedestrians diving for the safety of the posts that lined the narrow sidewalk.

'Fashion? Nonsense. Look at me.'

A new note had crept into the sharp command, one of curiosity, perhaps even of interest. Reluctantly I turned my head. I have no idea what she was going to say because I was so transfixed by what I saw I moved impulsively towards her, a movement that silenced her. I had last seen it in the docks in Poplar, glinting in the evening firelight when my father had told me my fortune. The jolting of the coach had parted her cloak, exposing the pendant between her breasts which in the dark of the coach seemed to carry some of the glitter of that firelight in the jewels that formed the bird's eyes as it stared at me, grasping a pearl in its talons.

Unable to stop myself, I parted her cloak to see the jewel more clearly. With the flat of her hand she gave me a stunning blow on the ear.

I fell back in the seat, reeling from the blow. In that brief, closer look, I had seen it was not the same pendant at all, although it was very like. The bird in my father's pendant was a falcon, with rubies for eyes. This bird was a magpie, with diamonds for eyes.

'I'm sorry,' I mumbled, 'ma'am. I – I forgot myself. My father –'

I huddled into the corner, feeling sick from nearly giving him away, and from the swaying coach, which was fighting its way past Charing Cross.

'You were looking at the pendant. There's only one other like it. Have you seen it?'

'No. No.'

'You're *his* boy, aren't you?' She was leaning closer, eyes bright with curiosity, like the magpie in her pendant.

I stared up at her. I had suddenly changed from being the meaner sort of person, or not even that, merely a pair of legs that ran messages, to becoming a real person. *His* boy? Did she know who my father was? Older and wiser, I might have pretended I *did* know, in the hope of drawing the information from her. But raw as I was, my reactions so close to my skin, I responded with such ferocity she pulled back.

'Whose? Whose boy? Tell me!'

'Whose? Why . . . Mr Pym's, of course!' She smiled, but only after I caught the vexed bite of her teeth on her full lip, and something I did not expect to see in her eyes: apprehension. It was nothing as naked as Matthew's fear when he showed me the near relation of this pendant, more a cautious, civilised version of it, but it gave me courage.

'You didn't mean Mr Pym's boy. What did you mean?'

'Don't be impertinent!'

She picked up the stick with the silver knob. Whether she would have struck me or had me thrown out of the coach, letter or no letter, I did not discover; for outside Whitehall a guard in livery stepped out into the street, holding up a pike, bellowing for the coach to stop. Alfred jerked back the reins. Through the Palace Gate I glimpsed a large group of armed men. Some were in court dress – bright slashed doublets and wide-brimmed feathered hats – some in the sober Dutch jerkins mercenaries wore; all had swords and some wore pistols. Before I could see more, the Countess was hammering with her stick on the partition.

'Drive on, drive on!'

The coach lurched forward, the guard jumping to one side with an outraged yell: 'Stop! In the King's name!'

'Drive! Drive!' the Countess hammered. 'Drive, you fool!'

The confused and terrified horses reared, then leapt forward. Fleetingly I saw the guard behind us commandeering another coach, with better results. Alfred hung grimly on to the reins rather than guiding them. At any moment I thought he must be flung from his seat. In the coach it was impossible to hold on. My strap broke.

We cannoned into one another, then were immediately thrown against the sides of the coach. Shouts from pedestrians, from a carter pulling out of the way were lost in the drumming of the wheels, in the creaks and groans of the coach, which seemed about to part from its harness.

Another coach approached and would not give way. Alfred pulled at the reins. Half lost them. It seemed we must collide. He cracked his whip at the oncoming horses. As they reared, he yanked his horses away from them. The Countess shut her eyes. The collision flung her against me. She clutched my arm. There was a drawn-out and horrible grating sound which made me wince and shut my eyes. The coachmen were yelling at one another but our coach was still moving. Alfred had steered it into the narrow gap between the other coach and the posts that bordered the sidewalk. They ripped into the side of our carriage, slowing it sufficiently for him to get the horses back under control.

She opened her eyes. There was a look on her face not of fear, or even anger at the damage to the coach, but exhilaration. We collapsed back in our seats, saying nothing as, a broken wheel clacking at intervals, the coach limped into Westminster. I had already snatched up the letter from the floor and was struggling to open the jammed door when she seized my hand impulsively. 'Run, Tom, run! Get this letter to him before those men come for him!'

Tom! She knew my name! This thought hammered in my head as Alfred yanked open the door. She called me Tom. Perhaps she really did know who I was. The idea thrilled through me as I tumbled out, running into Mr Ink in the lobby. I gabbled to him that I must take the letter to Mr Pym and without a word he hurried me towards the chamber. In the shadowy approach there were two guards, and beyond them the Serjeant at Arms, in hose and full ceremonial uniform. Mr Ink's eyes gleamed with excitement. It was as though he had been waiting all his life for this moment.

'I'll deal with the guards,' he said. 'You get past old Pompous Breeches.'

I slipped into the darkness cast by a column. I could hear Mr Pym's sonorous voice. 'The army for Ireland is being assembled and my Lord Warwick has a four-hundred-ton vessel victualled and armed . . .'

Mr Ink was arguing and gesticulating that he must get through to Mr Pym. I crept along the wall. The Serjeant at Arms had his broad back towards me.

'The vessel could carry six hundred men and is ready to sail from the Port of London –'

I could see Royalists howling protests. The Speaker took a point of information from Sir Edward Hyde.

'Are not the normal ports of embarkation for Ireland Chester and Bristol? Is this not an attempt by the honourable member, under the guise of fighting the papists, to bring an army into London against the King?'

I was ten, fifteen steps away from Mr Pym. It was my intention to dart past the Serjeant and run to Mr Pym, but as I prepared to launch myself he turned and blocked my way with his vast bulk. I held out the letter.

'For Mr Pym.'

He gave me a scandalised look. 'What by Satan are you doing here?'

'He must have it now!'

In the Serjeant's jowled face was all the outrage of procedure being violated. Mr Ink was taken away by one guard and the Serjeant called on the other to take me. The Serjeant would not even touch the letter. He said a similar letter had been delivered to Mr Pym containing a plague-sore dressing. I knew this to be true. It was supposed to have been delivered by a papist out to murder Mr Pym. Convinced he had foiled a similar plot, he seized me with the grip of a bear. I kicked and yelled, tears of frustration stinging my eyes.

'The letter is to save his life, not kill him! The King has soldiers on his way here!'

'Serjeant.'

It was the Speaker, William Lenthall, a mild-mannered lawyer of about fifty, with a carefully pointed beard and moustache and hooded eyes that made him look half-asleep. He had a quiet, almost timorous voice that was effective in an uproar only because MPs were forced to stop shouting in order to hear him.

'You have a letter for Mr Pym, Serjeant?'

'I believe it to contain another plague-sore dressing, sir.'

It was a measure of the jumpiness of the House in those days around Christmas, when every day brought rumours of plots and counter-plots – there had even been a move for Parliament to move to Guildhall for its greater protection – that Speaker Lenthall had left his seat. I could see Mr Pym rising. MPs on both sides were craning to see.

'Ask the messenger if he would be good enough to open it,' Mr Lenthall said courteously.

I broke the seal, showing there was nothing inside, and without any comment, question or fuss, Mr Lenthall gave it to the Serjeant to take to Mr Pym. Neither seemed in any particular hurry. I remembered the swaggering courtiers buckling on their swords at Whitehall, the weathered, sabre-cut faces of the mercenaries, and in an agony of impatience watched as the Serjeant ritually bowed to the Speaker's chair before crossing the floor to Mr Pym. He seemed to take an eternity to unfold it, then read it, then refold it carefully before clearing his throat to speak.

'Mr Speaker, it appears His Majesty will shortly appear in this place to arrest me' – roars of dismay drowned his words – 'to arrest me and four other honourable members: Mr Hampden, Mr Haselrig, Mr Holles and Mr Strode. I request your permission to withdraw.'

Speaker Lenthall showed the first signs of tension, drumming his fingers on the arm of his throne-like chair.

'You have my permission, Mr Pym,' the Speaker said. 'Which I suggest you take with all possible speed.'

While all eyes were on Mr Pym, I crept into a niche at the back of the room and crouched low to the floor.

The Serjeant, robbed of his arrest of a poisoner, glanced at the spot where I had been. I squeezed further into my hiding place, holding my breath. Mr Pym and three other members hurried towards the lobby, but the fifth man, William Strode, rose to make a speech. Never one to compromise, he declared now was the time to confront the King.

'Come on, Bill,' a member said. 'You don't want to spend another ten years in the Tower.'

But it seemed that was exactly what he did want. Only when there was the rattle of an approaching coach outside did Mr Pym lose some of his dignity and coolness and shout: 'It won't be ten years – it'll be the block! Get him out of here!'

Two of the burliest members grabbed Strode and manhandled him past the Speaker's chair, spittle flying from his mouth as he protested vehemently about the rights and privileges of Parliament. The five members disappeared as there was a chatter of voices and laughter, and the clatter of boots on the stairs from Westminster Hall into the lobby. The rest of the House talked with nervous anger in small groups.

The Speaker settled back in his chair and said: 'Order! Order! Sir Edward Hyde made a point about embarking troops for Ireland from the Port of London. Does anyone wish to answer that?'

The members took his cue and returned to their places. Edward Hyde rose and said perhaps he could amplify his point and members listened attentively, as if there had been no interruption. The drumming of boots and the clank of swords outside the lobby ceased. The door opened.

Edward Hyde took off his hat. All the members rose as one, removing their hats. I could see only the effect, not the cause, but as all eyes were on the opening door I poked my head out to see the King, taking off his hat, entering the chamber alone. He nodded and smiled at Edward Hyde and some other members whom he counted on his side. He seemed so at ease, and so courteous, it could have been taken for a friendly visit – had it not been for the gnarled face of the Earl of Roxburgh, glowering as he stood in the doorway, exposing a troop of soldiers loosening the swords in their scabbards. Some of the younger courtiers grinned and cocked their pistols. It was the mercenaries who chilled me. They stood silent and still, eyes staring coldly into the chamber, hands hanging loosely near angled swords.

'May I trouble you for your chair, Mr Speaker?' the King asked.

Mr Lenthall got up and sat on the benches. The King looked quickly near the bar of the House where Mr Pym usually sat, then referred to a paper about the impeachment of the five members for treason which had been tabled, and which, he said, members must consider urgently. Treason was such a serious charge, he continued, that the accused must be taken into custody while Parliament deliberated. He stared round the silent chamber.

'Is Mr Pym here?'

The shuffling and clink of swords from the soldiers in the lobby died into a complete, prolonged silence.

I could see the King's white-gloved hand tighten on the arm of the chair, which he had made his throne. I gazed at his magisterial profile in awe. It was the same face which had glowed from the uproarious welcome of the people on his return to London barely six weeks ago. I expected that face, with its immaculate triangle of beard, framed by the brilliant white stiffness of his collar, to glow again, to say some magic words which would lift everyone to their feet, cheering and shouting. Then, as the silence continued, I expected him to thunder wrath and retribution. So did many of the other members, whose hands instinctively crept to empty sword belts, weapons not being allowed in the chamber. What I least expected to hear from the King's mouth was a note of petulance.

'Mr Speaker, are the five members present?'

Lenthall fell to his knees. 'Your Majesty, I can only see and speak as this House directs.'

The abject man on the floor suddenly grew in stature as the King, rising from his chair, diminished.

'Very well. My eyes, I believe, are as good as yours.' The King stared round the benches on one side, and then the other. I could see one hand gripping his hat, the other clenching and unclenching, but he kept the composure in his voice, even managing a lightness in his words. 'I see the birds have flown.' He put his hat on his head and walked away.

Roxburgh came to life. 'Make way! Make way!' The army in the lobby abruptly became a rabble, those at the front now pushing and shoving against those packed at the back, who had no idea what was happening. As the last set of boots left the lobby and clattered down the stairs, the chamber erupted.

'Privilege! Privilege! Privilege!'

Sir Edward Hyde and the King's party looked desolated, shaking their heads despairingly at what one muttered was a naked invasion of rights. Others were talking loudly, violently across one another, convinced that if the five members had been there they would not just have been arrested, but butchered on the spot. Many crowded round Lenthall, slapping him on the back, amazed that this gentle, self-effacing man had shown such courage, some declaring that only God could have put such words in his mouth. No one took any notice of me as I got up and walked out of the chamber. I could not understand why I did not feel triumphant that Parliament had won such a stunning victory. Instead I felt empty, as if I had lost something and would never find it again. All I could see was that lonely figure of the King, putting his hat on his head and walking out of the chamber.

12

The next day London erupted. 'Privilege! Privilege! Privilege!' the mob roared – and I roared with them. The story of the King invading Parliament spread from mouth to mouth, the Cavaliers and mercenaries who had accompanied him multiplying by rumour into a small army.

Will shook me awake that morning, almost unable to speak from excitement. 'Get up! The Trained Bands have been called out.'

He told me the City had formed a Committee of Public Safety. The King had lost control of the City militia. People believed his Catholic Queen had persuaded the King to join the papists. In pamphlet after pamphlet I read horrific stories of atrocities committed by Catholics on Protestants in an uprising in Ireland. Women in the City of London feared that, like the Protestants in Ireland, they would be raped and their children massacred. In Milk Street that night I saw two women with a cauldron of boiling water poised on the sill of a first-floor window, from which yesterday they might have flung the contents of a chamber pot.

In vain the King asked Lord Mayor Gurney to give up Pym and the other members sheltering in the City. All the Mayor could give him was a sumptuous meal at the Guildhall, while the rioters congregated outside.

Normally I kept clear of the big riots. I feared seeing Crow and

Captain Gardiner, the man in the beaver hat, who knew my radical leanings; but there had been a call for our Trained Band to muster in Coleman Street, near the Guildhall. Once, I was sure I saw Crow's bulky shape in the crowd, and kept my hand on my knife. Torches lit the faces of the King's dragoons guarding the Guildhall as they tried to calm their restive horses before the swelling, angry crowd. Only a short distance away, in Coleman Street, Mr Pym and the other members were dining, the sauce for their meal beating drums calling the Trained Bands to muster. I fought my way through the crowd towards our standard – *For God and Parliament* – being held aloft by Big Jed, and joined Will and Luke outside the radical church of St Stephen's to help build a makeshift barricade across Coleman Street.

To my astonishment, Luke said he had married Charity that afternoon. It was one of many such marriages in the militia, provoked by the feeling that we would soon be on the march. I helped him lift a bench from the church and pile it on the barricade.

'You are not marrying Anne?'

'No, no. That's over.'

He looked at me slyly. 'You prefer the Countess?'

'And her carriage,' I managed, but the banter rang hollow. For hours at a time I managed to stop thinking about Anne, but then I would see someone in the street I thought was her, or smell the damask roses she used in her pomade. Then, as now, I would hurl myself into activity, struggling to forget. We picked up another bench and manoeuvred it through the church doorway.

'I heard Anne was with someone else.'

I dropped my end of the bench so rapidly he lost his grip, howling with pain as it fell on his toe.

'Who?'

'I don't know – it was just alehouse gossip.'

There was still a gap in the barricade and I wriggled through it. I forgot my vow not to see her. I pushed and elbowed my way, but outside the Guildhall I found myself wedged in a solid mass. There was a great roar as the gates opened. A spurting flare of torches lit up the glittering gold and red of the King's livery as his carriage pulled up outside the Guildhall. The crowd fell silent as the King emerged and brushed something from his cloak before getting calmly into his carriage. The muttering began as a group of the King's dragoons cleared a way slowly through the crowd with the flat of their swords, and built until the crowd found its voice again, thundering 'Privilege! Privilege!' Pamphlets were flung at the coach, and I glimpsed the King's white, frightened face. It was hard to believe that, less than two months earlier, the same crowd had given him such a rapturous welcome and I had thought him divine.

Seizing my chance, I darted into the passage beaten by the dragoons before it closed up again. I burst into a run, but I was now in full view. A voice bellowed, almost in my ear:

'There he is!'

It stood out in the crowd, that scar, a living presence. The cold metallic eyes held me hypnotised. I might not be Matthew's son, but I had inherited from him the fear of that scar. The man pushed his way towards me. In front of him was a man I had not seen before. Thin and wiry as a greyhound, he stood a foot taller than most of the crowd, slipping through it towards me as if he was oiled. He was near to grabbing me when a stave thrown from the crowd caused a dragoon's horse to rear. Another dragoon slashed at the rioter. The man with the scar was shouting at me but I forced my way through the crowd until I reached an alley. I ran blindly. It was part of the City I did not know. When I reached a narrow street I tore down one alley after another, until the shouts of the riots dwindled, and all I could hear was the sound of my running feet and my panting breath.

I had no idea where I was. There was only a scrap of moon, but it was reflected from the ice in an unearthly glow. I leaned against a slimy wall, slowly recovering my breath. I did not even hear them, they must have approached so carefully. Looking up, I saw, silhou-etted at one end of the street, the bulky shape of Crow. At the other was the man in a beaver hat, his hand on his sword. They were so sure of me they did not even move. Neither did I. It seems strange, but for a moment I almost welcomed them. It was not just that I was tired of running, it was what Luke had said:

I heard Anne was with someone else.

Even if it was just alehouse gossip, what hope was there for me? It came back to me, with redoubled force, that I had sworn on the Bible never to see her again. In that moment, with the three of us standing as frozen as the ice, I felt for a moment it would be better to die if I could not see her again. But my instincts, my legs, propelled me into a narrow alley. Crow and Gardiner were in no hurry to follow me, and I soon found out why. It led to a church huddled between two narrow passageways. The gate to the other passageway was locked.

'Convenient,' Gardiner said to Crow, drawing his sword, flour-ishing it towards the graveyard, which was above the small flight of steps. Like all the churches crammed into the City, where people fought for space, in death as in life, to be buried in their own piece of holy ground, the graveyard was crowded. There was a pile of unburied coffins at one side of the steps. Crow indicated them with a grin.

'Perhaps we can borrow one of those.'

I ran up the steps, holding my knife, ducking behind the coffins, which rocked unevenly. On top of them was a body in a shroud.

'Making it easier for us, Tom?' Gardiner mocked. He drew his sword.

Gravediggers, like the scavengers, had either not been paid in the crisis, or taken to rioting, or joined the militia. Rubbish piled up; bodies were left unburied. The stench of rotting flesh brought bile into my mouth. As Gardiner began to ascend the steps I pulled the shroud from the body. 'This one has the plague!'

Gardiner laughed and drew back his sword, preparing to lunge. 'You're lying! You wouldn't go near it if it had.'

'I'm a plague child!' I yelled, pushing the body to the top of the steps. Gardiner backed away slowly, sheathing his sword. He drew his tongue over his lips. 'Shoot him,' he said, matter-of-factly.

For the first time I saw that Crow had a pistol. I stared down the long barrel, seeing every rifled groove and Crow's eyes above the backsight, and prayed to live then, for God to forgive me for ever wishing to die, but there was a blinding flash and a searing pain before everything slid from me, as if I was falling into a dark, bottomless pit.

13

Hell is not knowing. Not knowing where voices are coming from, what they are saying. Hell is burning fire and soaking sweat, pain you eventually do not want to end, because if it does, you know it will start again, and waiting is the worst thing. No, that is not true. The scar is the worst, just as Matthew told me. That was why I shut my eyes, feigning sleep when people came into the room.

There was the scar, and another man. There was a doctor who put a splint on my arm and bandaged it. He would have bled me, but the scar said I had bled enough, for God's sake. There was a girl in black they called Jane, who drew the curtains with quiet hands, lit the fire and left food, which I began to eat when the fever slackened a little, but only when I was left alone.

One day I was sipping the pottage she left me when a short, fat man walked, or rather rolled, into the room. From his well-turned calves to his plump cheeks, everything about him was warm and genial, except his eyes, which sat upon a second pair of cheeks and were shrewd and watchful.

'Caught!' he said, rubbing his hands gleefully. 'I told my learned friend you are like the little mouse who only comes out to eat when the trap has been laid.'

There was something in the way he said 'trap' I did not like. My hunger banished, I dropped the spoon back on the plate. 'Am I in Newgate?'

'Newgate?' He broke into fits of laughter. 'Much worse than that. You are in my house near Lincoln's Inn. I am a lawyer. People can escape from prison, but they can never escape from the law. Is that not right, Mr Eaton?'

I turned to the wall as the man with the scar entered. 'Awake, is he, Mr Turville? I was hoping he'd never come round, and that would be the end of our problem.'

Needles of pain shot through my shoulder as he gripped me to pull me up. I screamed, sweat breaking out over my whole body. The scar was a livid flickering wound which seemed about to eat my face before I twisted away.

'That's enough!'

There was a new note in the other man's voice. He sat on the bed, which sagged under his weight. He had a heavy smell of musk. 'Come – you are not in prison, nor going there.'

'More's the pity,' the man he called Eaton said.

Turville ignored him and spoke gently, soothingly: 'Come, Mr Tom, sit up. We must all have a good talk together, mmm? Sit up, there's a good boy.'

He touched my shoulder. It was nothing to the pain of Eaton gripping it, but I was as much afraid of his gentle manner as I was of Eaton's violence. I was exhausted, worn away by not knowing, while people made knowing remarks such as 'my dear Tom' or 'Mr Tom'. I sprang up, almost knocking him from the bed, screaming at him, pointing to Eaton.

'He's tried to kill me! He wants to now – look at him! I can't bear him near me, I can't bear to look at him!'

The outburst took what little energy I had and I fell back on the bed. The smell of musk nearly overwhelmed me as Turville pulled the blankets back over me. 'That's nonsense, Tom. Mr Eaton brought you here – he saved your life! His man shot Crow as he was about to shoot you!'

If my body was exhausted, that took away my sanity. I raved at them. Saved my life? The man with the scar? Who had driven Matthew away and whose men, I believed, had killed Susannah? The fat man got up and had a whispered conversation with Eaton.

'Wear a scarf, man! He's had nightmares about your scar. We'll never get anywhere like this.'

My fever became worse. The next time I saw Eaton he had a high scarf knotted round his neck, covering the worst of the scar, but still I saw it: in the coals that warmed the room, in the branches of a tree outside the window. I even imagined a man with a scar was measuring me for the drop from the gallows.

When Eaton stopped coming I gradually recovered. Turville would not explain why he was keeping me there. He insisted I was not imprisoned, although I was locked in. It was for my own safety, he protested, because I was so disturbed. When I asked for my clothes, he said they were ruined and he had ordered others; but they never appeared. I discovered from Jane that Turville was Lord Stonehouse's lawyer, and Eaton his steward.

Now I was totally bewildered. Was I, suddenly, in Lord Stonehouse's favour? Or was there a more sinister motive? Politely, unctuously, Turville evaded all my questions.

Jane nursed me back to health slowly, although I remained so weak and lethargic I could scarce get out of bed. I knew from the familiar way Turville touched her they slept together. I saw her flinch from him and when I remarked on it she broke down and told me her story.

She was a maid at Highpoint, Lord Stonehouse's country seat, until a gentleman – she refused to say who – had ruined her. Her mother, Mrs Morland, who was the housekeeper, had disowned her. Jane had lost her position. Eaton, who dealt with such problems, had placed her in Turville's household.

A strange bond grew between us. She had had a child who had died. She knew from what she had overheard that I came from a similar liaison in the past, but could give me no details. In a curious way, I believe she took me for the child she had lost. She told me that the sweet posset I enjoyed contained opium and other herbs to keep me drowsy until they had completed their plans for me. I stopped taking it, throwing the posset into the chamber pot. She heard Turville telling Eaton I was love-sick, but would be cured by the end of the week.

'Cured? What did he mean?'

'I don't know. But Mr Turville said it when Mr Eaton was drawing extra money for Mr Black.'

'Extra money? For what?'

She shook her head, her hand trembling as she fumbled in the pocket of her apron, brought out a key for my room, and pressed it into my hand.

'His bedroom is the first room you come to on the next floor. Your clothes are in a chest near the dressing table. Leave the key in the lock. They will think I've been careless.'

'They won't believe that!'

She shrugged. 'Turville is meeting Mr Eaton tomorrow at nine o'clock. His study is on the first floor. As soon as you hear them go in, dress. There is a passage in the hall leading to the back stairs. Before you reach the kitchen, turn right down another passage. The door there will be open.'

I pleaded with her to come with me, but she refused, saying she would never find another place. But I could write a letter for her to her mother, who was very ill. She wanted her mother to forgive her for what she had done.

For what she had done! But I wrote it and promised to send it to Mrs Morland. Or perhaps, I thought, as I fell asleep that night, I could deliver it. Mrs Morland had been involved with the consequences of one liaison with a gentleman. I wondered if she had been involved with another . . .

Next morning I waited by the door until I heard Eaton's harsh voice, Turville greeting him and the closing of what was presumably his study door, before opening mine. I could see right down the well of the stairs, to a small portion of the black-and-white floor tiles of the hall. I took another couple of steps and caught my breath. On the stairway was a magnificent picture. It was of a great house, with a sweep of turrets and Dutch gables, and, above the columns of a stone porch, a three-tiered clock tower and belfry. There were tiny figures in parklands and fields running down to a river: labourers working, a lady taking the air. In one corner of the picture was a signature, *P. Lely*; in the other, *Highpoint, Oxon. 1635.*

I crept down another flight. From below I could hear a murmur of voices, coming from what must be Turville's study. A heavy smell of musk drew me to Turville's bedroom. The door was open. His four-poster bed took up most of the room. He was fond of red; crimson silk curtains hung from the tester and scarlet cushions were piled on white rugs. I skirted the bed to reach a chest of drawers, opening the first. Linen. In the next I found my jacket, looking at it in dismay. It was crusted with dark, matted blood, and the sleeve had been ripped off, presumably by the doctor in order to extract the ball from my arm. I searched frantically, but could find neither britches nor shirt. Turville's breeches would go round me two or three times.

It was in the bottom drawer that I found them. The breeches and doublet were an austere dark blue, but the material was a rich velvet even Luke could not afford. The linen shirt with its fine lace cuffs was something I could only dream of. I tried on the shirt. It fitted perfectly. So did the doublet and breeches. By the dressing table there was a new pair of boots. When I slipped on the soft leather an eerie shiver passed down my spine. Never had my large, clumsy feet found such an elegant, comfortable home.

I stared into the dark, lumpy Venetian glass and started back. The dour Puritan had gone. My fiery red hair had returned. Had I been ill for so long, or had the dye been washed out? I did not know. My beard had grown. The clothes might have been tailored for me, yet I remembered no tailor. I sat down abruptly on the bed. Another shiver ran through me as I recalled, when thrashing about in delirium, believing I was being measured for the gallows. I clearly had been measured for something else. These were not the clothes of an apprentice, nor even a businessman like Mr Black. They were the clothes of a gentleman.

Even my hands had changed. The ink had disappeared from my palms and fingertips. Perhaps they had been scrubbed. Only traces of ink remained in the cuticles and the fleshy part of the palm. These were not my hands, any more than the reflection was that of Tom Neave. I felt a pang, a sense of loss, as I stared at them. Since I had graduated only from the pitch of Poplar to the ink of Farringdon, I had never seen these strange pink palms before.

I jumped as the clock in the hall struck the half hour. As I slipped down the stairs, keeping to the edge where they were less likely to creak, I could hear someone pacing restlessly in the study. There was a strong smell of tobacco. Another flight and I would be in the hall. A board cracked. I froze. In the silence it sounded like a pistol shot. I thought I heard someone in the hall. I ducked behind the banisters then crept down a few more steps and peered into the hallway. I could see no one.

'I should have let them shoot him!'

Eaton's voice exploded so suddenly I fell down a step, clutching at the banister rail.

'And lose everything?' Turville said sharply. 'Patience, Mr Eaton, patience! Wait until today's over . . .'

Wait until today's over? His voice dropped into a soothing murmur and I could hear no more as I crept downstairs. There were no other sounds now but the tick of the clock in the hall and the distant clatter of pots in the kitchen. I passed the clock and turned into the passageway. Leaning against the wall, pipe in hand, was the tall man, rangy as a greyhound, who had chased me through the crowd the night I was shot. There was a pistol in his belt. He took a puff at his pipe and smiled at me. I ran for the front door. It was locked. The man came up behind me and grabbed me. I kicked and struggled but, still weakened by my illness, could do nothing more than break his pipe. Still with a smile on his face he picked me up as if I was no more than a baby, carried me back upstairs and dumped me outside Turville's study before knocking on the door.

14

Eaton flew into a rage. He knew nothing of the clothes, and thought that Turville and I had planned this together. Only when I assured him I had stolen the key from Jane and found the clothes for myself, and Turville in his oily manner said that they were 'a contingency' I was not meant to see, was Eaton reduced to a glowering silence.

On the wall behind Turville's desk was a map, which from the picture outside I could see was of the Highpoint estate, with the house dominating forests, water meadows, villages and churches. Turville prowled round me as if I was a thoroughbred horse for sale at a fair. Far from being angry at my deceit he seemed so pleased I felt increasingly uneasy. What would have led to a beating from Mr Black, here seemed to meet with approval. Even Eaton could not stop staring at me. And the most remarkable thing of all was that he – the man with a scar, the source of all my nightmares – was frightened. Perhaps that is too strong a word. But he was certainly agitated, pacing, cracking his raw knuckles, gazing out over a large garden, before swinging back to gaze at me.

'The clothes are a stroke!' Turville rubbed his plump hands. 'They make him, Mr Eaton!'

'He is like,' Eaton muttered.

'Like? He is very like!'

They were looking at a picture in the centre of another wall, which I now know was a Van Dyck. At first I did not recognise Lord Stonehouse. It was only partly that he was so much younger. Mainly it was because he looked so happy. This was painted long before his hair had greyed and the lines on his face deepened into the penetrating frown I had seen in the royal procession. The picture was a family group with Highpoint House in the background. Next to Lord Stonehouse was a modest-looking woman with features that bordered on the plain, but whose face was touched into beauty by happiness. What might have been too idealistic was made real by the restlessness of the older boy trying to pull a stick from a spaniel's mouth, and the younger boy clutching fretfully at his mother's skirt.

'He has the Stonehouse nose,' Turville said. 'Aquiline.'

Aquiline? Suddenly the nose I had always despised had the bleak arrogance of an eagle. Or a falcon. Perhaps it had given rise to the family symbol. I could see it – or fancied I could – repeated in the faces in the painting.

Turville put his hand on my shoulder. 'If he continues to be in the dark, how can he see the dangers?'

'Are you saying I should tell him?' Eaton said.

'An edited version, Mr Eaton, an edited version. And I am not *saying* – I can only advise. He is your responsibility.'

His responsibility? Eaton was not wearing a scarf and as he came towards me, preparing to speak, the scar quivered like a second mouth. I flinched involuntarily. Turville lost patience.

'You,' Turville said to me, with a severity he tried to make playful by wagging his finger, 'owe Mr Eaton a very great debt.'

'Like a Tyburn prisoner owes his hangman,' I said bitterly.

Eaton jumped up. 'I'm taking no more of this, Turville!'

'Please, Eaton – let the boy speak! It has been difficult enough for us, God knows – think what it must have been like for him. Start at the beginning. Why did you run from Mr Black, when he was only trying to protect you?'

Protect me! I thought the answer to his question obvious enough, but as I gave it Turville shook his head, pulling a handkerchief from his cuff and wiping his brow and his hands. When I came to the letter from Lord Stonehouse saying I was a 'great Folie' who must be got rid of, Turville groaned out loud.

'You see, Eaton, you see?' He turned to me. 'Lord Stonehouse is not trying to kill you – that letter was not from him! It was from Eaton, warning Mr Black you were in danger from Richard. It is *Richard*, not Lord Stonehouse, who sees you as a great Folie who must be –'

'Have a care, Turville, have a care!'

Now Eaton certainly was frightened. He jumped up with such speed he sent his chair careering backwards. My eyes were not drawn to his scar now but to his hands, which gripped the back of another chair. He could pass for a gentleman but for those hands. They were the deeply weathered hands of a countryman who worked the land, not just rode over it. His knuckles were like knots of wood and his nails bitten. I suddenly saw my hands, in years to come, if I stayed a printer. He pointed a finger with a yellowed misshapen nail at me.

'He is an act of charity, Turville! Nothing else. That is what my lord told me. And that is what he is until my lord tells me otherwise. I know when to keep my mouth shut. I have done it for thirty years and I am not going to throw everything away now for this little brat!'

'The war changes everything, Eaton!'

'War, what war?'

'The King is in Oxford, raising an army.'

'An army! Both sides have sent letters to the lord lieutenants of all counties. Parliament orders you to send your soldiers. The King commands you to send your troops to his army.' Eaton snapped his fingers in contempt. 'Some have been stupid enough to take sides. Most are shitting themselves. Nobody has declared war. Nobody will.'

Turville kept trying to interrupt, snatching his handkerchief from his cuff, filling the air with musk, wiping his forehead. 'Suppose they do? And the wrong side wins? You would lose everything then. As would I.'

'Which is the wrong side?' I asked.

They stared at me as if they had completely forgotten about me. From being almost at each other's throats, they were thrown off balance. Turville recovered first. 'Ah, Tom, there you have it. Which is wrong and which is right? Mmm? The boy has a head on his shoulders. Come, Eaton, it is time we got off the stool. Otherwise we will by caught with our breeches down.'

In the hall the clock chimed eleven. Both of them looked towards the sound, and then at each other. I remembered overhearing Turville telling Eaton to wait until the day is over. And the puzzling words Jane had picked up about me being cured of love when the week was out came back to me.

'What is happening today?' I asked.

Again they glanced at one another before Turville spoke. 'Why, Tom, this is happening – this auspicious meeting. A little earlier than we, er, planned – but that's of no consequence, is it, Eaton?'

Eaton looked from me to Turville and back again. Then, as the last chime of the clock echoed into silence, he seemed to reach a decision. He came over to me, lowering his face into mine, speaking with a frightening intensity. 'I wrote the letter, part of which you saw. It was a warning to Mr Black that you were in great danger. It is Lord Stonehouse's son, Richard, who sees you as a "great Folie", not his father.' He pointed to the boy in the picture, trying to wrest the branch from the dog's jaws. He gave me a bitter smile. 'It is that delightful boy, whom I have rescued from whores and gambling debts, who has been trying to kill you, while I have been entrusted by his father to see that not a hair of your precious head is harmed.'

The scar quivered. There was a rank animal smell about him which brought acid to my throat. I fought a desire to back away. 'Not harmed? Is that why you have a prig downstairs, ready to shoot me if I leave?'

This amused Turville, who flung up his hands in delight. 'You see, Eaton – he's as suspicious as you are. Understandable, under-standable! The poor boy was frightened.'

'Gibson shouted at you to warn you,' Eaton said. 'We knew you would be at the Guildhall. So did Gardiner. Gibson lost you, but saw Gardiner and followed him. He shot Crow. Unfortunately, Gardiner got away.'

'Then Eaton carried you here, at some danger to himself . . .' Turville put in.

'More to my coat,' Eaton said resentfully. 'Ruined it. You were bleeding like a pig.'

'A charge to the estate. I'll warrant you've not missed charging that one, Mr Eaton,' Turville said, with a wink at me.

I stared stubbornly at them. 'When I ran into the royal procession I saw Lord Stonehouse ordering Richard to kill me.'

'Saw! Saw!' Eaton clenched his fists in rage at me.

Much more composed, Turville sat at his desk and linked his fingers together. 'Did you hear Lord Stonehouse say that?'

I said nothing.

'He told Richard not to harm you. I have it from his lordship.'

'He came at me with his rapier!'

'Of course he did!' Eaton turned away from me as if could not bear the sight of me any longer. He looked at the boy in the picture wrestling with the dog, mimicking a gentleman's voice surprisingly well. 'I'm sorry, Father, I didn't hear you. My one thought was to protect you!' He turned back to me. 'I had to apologise to Lord Stonehouse for that. He blamed me, of course. I have nearly lost my position because of you!'

I trusted neither of them, for with every truth they told me, I felt they kept another one back. If anything, I preferred Eaton's testimony, for it was drawn from him with such bitter reluctance I felt it must be true. And, as he went on, it seemed incontrovertible that Eaton had indeed saved me from Gardiner and Crow.

'I am very grateful to you, sir,' I said, as if a tooth was being drawn from me.

'Well done, Tom!' cried Turville. 'Now, shake hands with your guardian.'

My guardian! The twisted world that I had fallen into got worse and worse! This raw, brutal creature who had driven the man I believed to be my father away in terror, and who inhabited my nightmares – my guardian! The thought of shaking hands with him made me sick to the stomach, but I felt I owed my life to him and forced myself to hold out my hand. He took it with a hand as hard and rough as rusted iron and with a smile – I took it to be a smile – that held much more of distrust and caution than friendship.

Turville rang for Jane, who came in trembling, and looked at the scene in amazement. He told her to bring drink to celebrate what he called this happy reconciliation, smiling at her as she put the glasses in front of us.

'Does Mr Tom not look a perfect gentleman, Jane?'

'He is a gentleman,' she said, the blood rising in her cheeks.

'Oh, mark the roses in her cheeks, Eaton! If only I were young again and I could grow such flowers there, like our young poet Mr Tom.'

She stared away from me, growing rigid as he patted her flaming cheeks. I jumped up, unable to stop myself. 'Leave her! She does not like it!'

There was a silence. Turville lost all his joviality and his eyes blazed with anger at me. Eaton grinned. Jane completely lost her usual composure, twisting her hands in agony. 'I – I am sorry, Mr Turville.'

Turville regained his joviality as quickly as he had lost it. He told her he understood perfectly, with a wink at Eaton which made me want to strike him, but I knew I was only making things worse for her. She left without looking at me and I cursed myself for opening my mouth.

The wine was a sweet sack. Trusting nothing in that house I scarcely touched mine, even when Eaton swallowed a second glass. I told them it made little sense to me that Lord Stonehouse did not want a hair of my head harmed, while his eldest son was trying to kill me.

'D'you hear the logic in that, Eaton!' Turville cried. 'The money on that education was well spent.'

'Logic?' Eaton stared at the painting gloomily. 'You need more than logic to deal with that family. His lordship has no idea his eldest son is trying to have you killed.'

'Why don't you tell him?' I asked in amazement.

Eaton looked at me not with anger now but contempt. His outburst seemed to have exhausted him. He dropped on to a chair back to front, as if he was riding it, lowered his chin on to his clenched hands and stared broodingly at me. Turville smiled benignly.

'Innocence, Mr Eaton,' he said, 'is a quality to be treasured not despised.' He coughed, drew his handkerchief and wiped his brow and hands. His voice became suddenly sharp. 'You are not to repeat any of this until and unless we give you permission to do so. Is that clear?'

It was perfectly clear, but I said nothing. Turville wiped his brow again, although there was no sweat on it. Eaton smiled. They seemed to enjoy each other's discomfort.

'I will deny this conversation. So will Eaton. Do you understand?'

I said nothing. He clenched his hands, thrust his handkerchief in his cuff, pulled it out again and continued to speak in sharp, clipped tones. 'Lord Stonehouse would not believe us. We have no firm evidence it is Richard who is trying to have you killed. Even with evidence it would be a risk. Lord Stonehouse is . . . unpredictable. Richard is his eldest son. Lord Stonehouse knows his faults, but I would not want to be the person telling him that Richard is attempting the cold-blooded murder of –'

Eaton sprang up. 'I hope you know what you're doing, Turville!'

'– of someone to whom his father has extended such a great, indeed an unprecedented act of, er, charity.'

Reluctantly accepting this legal description of me, which was as clear as London fog, Eaton slowly sank back into his chair while Turville told me that, at the age of sixty, and in indifferent health, Lord Stonehouse had one urgent, overwhelming concern in life – the succession of his great estates. Richard should inherit them. He expected to do so. But at the age of thirty-six his main achievement in life had been to lose a small fortune on a non-existent sugar plantation. And another on whores and gambling, muttered Eaton. Even more unfortunate from Lord Stonehouse's point of view, Turville continued, Richard's wife had died leaving him two daughters and no sons.

Slowly, the fog began to part in places. I began to form a picture of the family. Lord Stonehouse's wife, Frances, had had a rare combination of sweet benevolence and shrewdness that held together not only the family but the whole estate. Turville and Eaton both concurred on that. She knew everyone in every farm and village, knew and cared about every birth and death. She would listen, advise and, if she felt help was merited, give it. Her way of saying no made even the most disappointed feel they had been given something. Five years before I was born, Frances had died. The happiness that filled the painting disappeared. Richard became arrogant and headstrong. In spite of a generous allowance, and constant promises to reform, he was so heavily in debt his father feared that, under him, the estate would rapidly disintegrate.

Richard was confident his father would not, and indeed could not, take action. The estate was entailed – legally bound to the eldest son. That bond was hard to break. But someone of Lord Stonehouse's power and influence with a clever lawyer – Turville smiled modestly – might circumvent parts of it. And there was a substantial amount of money and London property outside the entail. Lord Stonehouse took steps to change his will and leave as much as possible to Edward, the younger son. I gazed at the boy in the picture, clinging anxiously to his mother's hand.

'There's another one,' muttered Eaton.

Edward, a clergyman, was less concerned with the estate than his church, and less concerned with that than his laboratory, where he searched for the philosopher's stone. But his son, James, was the apple of Lord Stonehouse's eye. Then the plague struck Edward's parish. Edward survived, but James and the rest of the family died. Edward eventually married again, but Lord Stonehouse's grief was slow to heal.

Turville leaned closer to me, his voice dropping. He was older than he looked, the vanity of powder hiding the veins in his cheeks and pits in his skin. 'It was six years ago, in the depths of this grief, that he saw you.'

'In the shipyard.'

'Just so.'

'Just so! Just so!' Eaton mocked Turville's equable tone. He said nothing was 'just so' at Highpoint. Turville tried to stop him taking more wine, but he might as well have tried to stop a hunting dog in full cry. The words came out like the spittle that flew with them, an extraordinary mixture of pride and venom, power and frustration. 'I am Lord Stonehouse's scavenger. I clear up the messes he and his sons make.' He stabbed his bitten fingernail at Turville. 'He makes them legal. You –' he stabbed the fingernail at me '– you are the worst mess I have ever had to deal with and you go *on* and *on*, *year* after *year* after *year*!'

Turville shook his head apologetically at me, bouncing about on his chair as if it was hot. 'Come, Eaton, come –'

'Come, my arse!' He smashed his fist on the desk. 'I have taken the brunt of this bloody business!'

'Mr Tom might be –'

'Might be! Mr Tom! Oh, he's Mr Tom, is he? Mr Tom Might Be!' He stopped, Turville's agitation cooling him a little. 'Mr Tom.' He gave me an ironic little bow and looked at the painting. 'Mr Richard, Mr Edward, Mr Tom.'

'The situation has changed, Tom,' Turville said. He smiled, a smile I trusted less than Eaton's surly bluntness. 'We need your help. We need to find out who you really are. And quickly.'

I looked from one to the other. 'Changed? What situation?'

A shaft of winter sun played over the desk, lighting up dust motes still settling where Eaton had struck it. It was so quiet I could hear the ticking of the clock in the hall. Then Turville spoke, forming his words as carefully as if he were writing a legal document.

'In spite of everything Richard did, in spite of Lord Stonehouse's threats to change his will, or steps to do so, we were resigned to Richard inheriting. Though we indicated to his lordship, as near as we dare, the disastrous consequences, it made no difference. Richard is the eldest son. He drives his father nearly out of his mind, but he loves him and in the end he always forgives him.' Turville cleared his throat. 'You, Tom, were an old man's whim. We were convinced you would never be more than that. But, during your illness here, something happened we never foresaw. While Lord Stonehouse has been organising an army for Parliament, Richard has told his father he is joining the King.'

15

Did I change in that instant? Yes. Did they? Certainly. I felt I was no longer in borrowed clothes, while, in some indefinable manner, their attitude shifted. In no way did they become servile. They were still very much in control. Yet when they called me Mr Tom the mockery was less certain, the irony diluted. I was still in a kind of limbo, not to be acknowledged or spoken of in polite society. One false move could be very dangerous for the three of us, Turville said, as though we were already plotters together.

Now, with me bursting in, looking like half a lord at least, and the drink in him, Eaton overcame his reluctance to break his master's ban. Once he began to talk, he was like a dam breaking and he held me as spellbound as Matthew ever did over an evening fire as he told me about that dark September evening, sixteen years before.

Eaton talked jerkily, as if he was back on his bay gelding, riding towards Highpoint that night. Just beyond the lodge, he told me, Lord Stonehouse's coach swerved past him out of the driveway. Henry, the coachman, did not acknowledge him – a sign that this was business that must not be talked about. In the back of the coach he glimpsed a woman with hair as red as fire. Another woman pulled down the blind as the jolting, rocking coach flashed past.

In the reception hall he heard a violent argument between Lord

Stonehouse and his two sons, Richard and Edward. Edward's shrill voice cried that the child was John Lloyd's bastard. Eaton winced as Richard savagely broke in: 'You surely know what she feels for her cousin Lloyd, Father? Did she not tell you whose bastard it is? You were with her!' A door slammed and there was silence. Mrs Morland, the housekeeper, was cleaning a dark pool of liquid from the floor of the gallery room – a task with which she would not normally demean herself.

Eaton was summoned to Lord Stonehouse's study. His lordship was now alone, very calm, ominously so, carefully pressing his signet ring into the still molten wax of a plague order. In the tone of voice that he might use about uncollected rents or diseased cattle, he told him a baby had died of plague at Horseborne. It must be removed before the contagion spread.

Relating this, Eaton never looked at me once. Now he did so, fingering his face as if he were adjusting a plague mask. 'I found Matthew Neave, the driver of the plague cart, and told him to collect the dead child.'

'My father never drove a plague cart!' I shouted.

Eaton ignored my outburst. 'I waited for him near the plague pit. He showed me the dead baby, then flung it in the pit. I paid him –'

I brought the birth-coin out of my pocket and slid it across the desk. That silenced him. Turville craned across to see it. His eyes became suddenly sharp. 'You've seen Matthew Neave recently? You know where he is?'

I shook my head and told them how I had come by it. Eaton scoffed and said it could be any coin. I turned it over so they could see the fleur-de-lys on the rim, above the King's head, showing it was minted in 1625, the year the King was crowned.

'It was a half crown?' Turville asked Eaton.

'One to collect the body. Another to throw it in the pit.'

I shuddered and slipped it back in my pocket before Eaton could reach it. He was close-fisted enough to want to take it, saying that

Matthew had cheated him by showing him a dead child from a plague family already on his cart.

A month or two later, he said, rumours began to circulate among the villages on the Highpoint estate that Matthew Neave's common-law wife, Susannah, had given birth to a healthy male child. As she was nearly forty, childless, and had shown no sign of pregnancy, it was thought a miracle – or a spell cast by her husband, who was known to be a cunning man.

'When I rode up to their cottage,' Eaton said, 'they were gone. Pots, pans, plague cart, child, everything. Gone.'

Eaton had spent himself. It was as if he had ridden through that rain-soaked night again, telling the story. He sat like a wind that has blown itself out, chin resting on his linked hands, knotted together like a tree root, staring pensively at me. Turville poured more wine. This time I swallowed mine at a draught. The ray of winter sun had moved slightly, lighting up something in the painting I had missed before. I jumped up, Turville grabbing at his wine as I brushed against it. The woman's russet-coloured dress was modestly cut, much more so than Lucy Hay's, but there was no mistaking it. Suspended by a gold chain, half in and half out of her dress, was the pendant Matthew had shown me over the fire that dark Poplar evening. The head of the falcon peered at me over the edge of her dress, ruby eyes seeming to glint accusingly at me.

'What is it? What is it, Tom?'

Eaton's voice was urgent, hoarse, catching in his throat from talking. He used my name for the first time. He wanted something, and I was sure from the way he looked at the picture it was to do with the pendant Matthew had stolen. They were both like dogs hunting, bellies down, breath held, ready to spring.

'What is it?' Eaton repeated.

'Is she my mother?'

They both laughed. 'Lady Frances? She had been dead five years when this happened,' Turville said.

'Who is my mother?'

'A whore and a thief,' Eaton said.

I flew at him, taking him unawares. My fist struck him on his scar. He cried out, his head jerking back, his drink spilling on his jacket. He grabbed me in a grip as tight as prison chains.

'Go to your head, do they, those fancy clothes? You are nothing without us – *nothing!* I could just as easily throw you in a pit! And this time I'd make sure you were dead.'

'Then why didn't you let Gardiner and Crow kill me?' I shouted.

Turville laughed. 'He has you there, Eaton.'

Eaton pulled me to him until I feared he was going to throttle me. Turville scrambled up. 'Leave him, leave him, for God's sake. Eaton, you fool – he has his mother's temper. And you are as mad as you were then!'

The clock struck twelve. Eaton suddenly smiled at me as it chimed, then at Turville, and pushed me away. I was too desperate to hear about my real mother to worry about these strange exchanges between them. They told me she had captivated all the Stonehouses, father and sons. She lived on an adjoining estate and was, said Turville, of gentle birth.

'Gentle? Margaret Pearce!' Eaton slapped his thighs in derision.

Turville said she died shortly after my birth. Her companion in the coach, Kate Beaumann, had left the district and they had been unable to find out what had happened to her.

'Have you seen her?' Turville asked. 'Short woman. Always wore a grey cloak, winter or summer.'

I had a memory of myself in Poplar, gazing through holes in oiled paper to catch a sight of the will o' the wisp delivering my cake and seeing a cloaked figure, but dismissed it as fanciful. I had been too frightened to see much, for fear of being turned into a cake.

They were gazing at me intently. 'A plain woman –' Turville continued.

'Not plain!' cried Eaton, then almost immediately: 'Yes, plain. Plain as bread is plain. About this high.' He put his hand to his chest. 'Quiet,

West-country voice. Ye had to dip to hear the lady. Dark hair. Well, it was dark. I suppose it now be as grey as her cloak. Have you seen her?'

This time it was more of a plea, but I shook my head. What little I knew, however fanciful, I was determined to keep to myself, while finding out as much as I could from them.

'It doesn't make sense!' I cried. 'Why would Lord Stonehouse have me thrown in the pit – then change his mind and have me educated?'

Eaton jumped up. 'Because he was tricked, humiliated by your mother – I only know the half of it, the gossip, the rumours. When you were born he was convinced you were *not* a Stonehouse.'

'Until he saw you in Poplar, ten years later,' Turville said quietly. He steered me over to the portrait, his hand almost a caress. 'Saw the flaming red hair and the Stonehouse nose – Roman, wide-bridge – and the set of the deep black eyes . . .'

'Unless he was seeing what he wanted to see,' Eaton put in sourly. 'He was in one of his rages – about to disinherit Richard. Again! He paid Mr Black, through me, to apprentice and educate you.'

I stared at the portrait, felt the curve of my nose. 'But . . . but surely Lord Stonehouse can find out who my father is?'

Eaton gave me an incredulous look. 'Ask his sons, you mean? They denied it that night. Anyone seeing his lordship would have denied it. Now? Worse. Edward married again after the plague death of his first wife and child and has a young family. He don't want no bastard turning up! Nor does Richard – he fears for his inheritance.'

'At least Lord Stonehouse must know if I am *his* child!' I blurted out.

Eaton laughed. He laughed outright. It was one of the few times I ever saw him do so. He laughed until his body shook and he broke out into a fit of coughing. 'If a bitch on heat runs loose a dog may cover it, but he don't know how many other dogs have been there, do he?'

I could feel my cheeks burning, but bit back my feelings, digging my nails into the palms of my hands.

Turville's hands flew into the air with pretended outrage. 'Mr Eaton – show some delicacy, please!'

Eaton stopped laughing. His voice was bitter. 'If he don't know love ain't poetry, he won't get very far, will he? Neither will we.'

He turned away again to stare out of the window. I could not help feeling that Eaton was not seeing the garden but the fields and woods of Highpoint on that dark rainy night. I wondered what had caused such bitterness, and how it was connected with the night when I was born, as Turville continued, choosing his words with care.

There were signs, he said, that Lord Stonehouse was beginning to think of me as more than an act of charity. Now that Richard had joined the King, he had ordered Turville and Eaton to find out as a matter of urgency who my father was. Again he stressed they had strict instructions to tell me nothing – but had come to realise that, without my help, they would get nowhere. Turville linked his hands together and stared intently at me.

'Shortly before your mother's companion, Kate Beaumann, disappeared she told the housekeeper that the locket part of the pendant contains proof of who your father is.'

I was very still. Eaton swung round from the window but did not approach me. For a moment the only sound was the wind rustling the trees outside.

'We know Matthew has it, because word reached me he once tried to sell it. Do you know where he is?'

I shook my head.

'Come, Tom,' said Turville gently. 'We are on the same side, are we not?' When I said nothing, he tapped a file on his desk. 'We have been gathering information about where Matthew might be. Will you help us find him?'

I felt a sudden surge of excitement and hope, which I could not conceal. I had no illusions about them, but, if they needed me, I needed them. I had lost Anne because I did not know who I was.

At best I was a bastard, at worst George's evil spirit. But if I was the bastard of a lord, even Mr Black might forgive me.

'What will happen to Matthew if I do help?'

'Nothing. In fact – no promises – but he might get a small reward for, er, helping us to find the pendant.'

Eaton bit his lip but said nothing.

Turville smiled at me. 'I told you Eaton! I knew from your file, Mr Tom, that beneath – shall I call it your poetic wildness? – there is a native shrewdness that would tell you where your best interests lay.'

My file! From shelves of land litigation and law books he took a file with a falcon crest and THOMAS NEAVE on the cover.

Thomas! I had been Tom all my life and now I was to be Thomas. Thomas Neave Esq. Dizzily, as he opened the file, I saw letters for me to be indentured, educated, my portrait commissioned. Turville, beaming at my excitement, painted a glowing picture of what might be in prospect, if I played my cards right. A house in Drury Lane was far from a remote possibility . . .

'A house!'

'Ssshhh –' Turville put his finger to his lips and looked nervously around, as if there were ears in the very panelling. Once again he stressed that if Lord Stonehouse knew they were telling me this it would ruin everything. I must not expect more than three servants, he went on.

'Three –' I dug my nails into the back of my hand to make sure I was not dreaming.

He said he was sorry there could not be more, but it would be politic to display a Puritan frugality in contrast to Richard's excesses. Faintly I said I would struggle to manage on three, as across the garden square came the distant sound of church bells. One of the bells had a dull, cracked peal.

'That sounds like my old local church, St Mark's,' I said.

'It is in that direction, certainly,' replied Turville.

Again there was that complicit exchange of glances. 'Be done with it,' Eaton said. 'Tell the boy. Now he knows where his real interests lie.'

Even when Turville, speaking now in his measured lawyer's phrases, told me that Anne Black had married, or – as the clock in the hall struck the half-hour – to be precise, would be married at one o'clock to George Samuel Sawyer, I did not believe it. If she could not marry me, I was arrogant, blinkered enough to think she would never marry. Least of all to Gloomy George! It was absurd. Laughable. She would never, in this world or another, marry someone so *old!* Gloomy George?

It was Eaton who brought me to my senses. His eyes, normally dull as old coins, flared into life at some painful memory. 'Love!' he snarled. 'Forget it. There's only one thing that matters –' he flung out a finger towards the estate map '– soil! Land! The *seat!'*

Eaton's bitter outburst wrenched me out of the cosy, self-satisfied belief that Anne would never marry anyone but me. I remembered the reports George gave Mr Black when he found me with Anne and saw them as the jealousies they were. When Mr Black was struck down and George took Anne's hand, telling her to confess to God it was her fault for letting me out, I saw it as the love-making it was. I was so lacerated by my own stupidity, I did not move. They took my silence not as shock, but acquiescence. Turville now laughed openly.

'I was concerned you might be foolish, Mr Tom, but now you know what is at stake you see the world a little differently, eh?'

The brief fire in Eaton's eyes flickered out. He grinned. 'His lordship saw what might happen. He gave strict instructions to Black you two were to be kept apart. You can thank me for that.'

'I can just see his lordship's face,' Turville said.

'Aye!'

'The daughter of a *printer!'*

They laughed and Eaton clapped me on my back. I sprang up. I shoved my chair at Turville, catching him in his fat stomach. He gasped and staggered backwards into the shelves. He bounced from them to grab me, but a heavy ledger slid from the top shelf on to his head. As he reeled groggily I ran past him, but Eaton's outstretched arms were waiting to clutch me. I vaulted on to the desk, kicking at him as he tried to pull me down. He gave a grunt of pain as, with another leap, I made it to the door, slamming it shut after me.

'Gibson!' he yelled.

Lean-muscled, relaxed, Gibson kept his eyes focused steadily on me. I hesitated. Perhaps a window. There was one across the landing, but I would never get it open in time. Gibson read my hesitation and grinned up at me. Behind me, Eaton was cursing as he pulled open the study door. I ran down halfway down the stairs then jumped, curling my arms round my face, hitting Gibson like a ball from a cannon. Both of us sprawled there dazed, Eaton and Turville gazing down on us. At the end of the passage to the back, Jane, who was carrying a pitcher, stared in amazement.

In a better state than Gibson, for his head had struck the tiled floor, I scrambled up, but he grabbed my leg. Another moment and I would have been down, but there was a thud. A grunt. The tiles around me were shattered with broken pottery. A shower of water splashed over me. My leg was released and I pulled myself up just in time to avoid Gibson, who gave me a bewildered stare, eyes glazing. Beyond him, a look of sheer amazement on her face at what she had done, was Jane, holding the handle of the broken pitcher in her hand. I stood there watching Gibson, as he slowly keeled over, falling into a pool of water and shards of pottery. Jane reacted first, beckoning me to follow her down the passage. Another passage bent off to the right. The door at the end of it was open to the yard, from which she had collected the water.

I turned to plead with her to go with me, but hearing the others running down the passageway she gave me a push and gestured violently for me to flee.

16

Blind rage drove my feet. Rage at my stupidity turned into rage against Anne. That she could even think about marrying anyone else was bad enough, but my old enemy George . . .

When I had struck George with his composing stick I wished I had killed him. There must have been murder in my face as I ran past Smithfield, for people pressed against the wall to avoid me.

Passing Half Moon Court I remembered something Anne had told me and turned towards the house. There was one chance. The door was locked but I knew the stone under which the key was hidden. I stopped. The table was laid with the wedding feast: game pie, a whole carp, a goose on a spit, fat dripping from it, conserves of fruit and pitchers of beer and wine. I ran into the print shop.

'Sa-rah?' Mr Black called from upstairs. 'That . . . you?'

So he was still too ill to go to the service. Mixed with guilt for being a cause of his illness was a surge of hope that my plan might work.

I ran into the print shop. Machinery gleamed; frame, quoins and hammer were neatly placed by the polished stone, ready for the next imposition. Whatever else I might say about George, his work was of the highest standard. The title of a pile of tracts brought back to me George's sour, doom-laden voice: *The Sinner's Seven Steps to Hell.* The sinner in me knew he would not make much money from that. It would scarcely pay for the paper. Yet there was an air of prosperity about the whole shop, to say nothing of the wedding feast.

I went into the paper store. There I found the source of that prosperity: a pile of Royalist tracts, baled up and ready to deliver. I ripped open a bale and took one: *Fighte for the King's Peace*. The imprint claimed it had been printed at the White Horse, Oxford, the King's headquarters. I could not believe, as Anne had told me, that Mr Black knew about this.

But it was easy to believe, when I ran upstairs, that he scarcely knew about anything. He still thought I was Sarah, for he was half sprawled out of bed, groping for a quill he had dropped. Papers were scattered round the bed. He had been struggling to sign his name again, but had lost his fine Italian hand and his signature was reduced to a spidery scrawl.

'S-arah, lift . . .'

I put my hands under his arms and tried to lift him. My bad arm cried out and he slipped even further out of the bed. I gave him another heave. If he had been his old weight, I would never have managed it, but the crackly skin seemed to slip over his bones as I pulled him against the pillows. He stared at me, or at least half of him did. Half, the right half, seemed the same Mr Black. The same dark eye fixed at me sternly, half of the lips quivering as if to issue an order. His left cheek was a frozen whirlpool of flesh, the eye half shut, immobile.

I covered my face. I could not bear to see what I had done. If I had not fought with him that day and run away this would not have happened. I could see now why Anne had sworn to him not to see me again.

'C-closer.'

The words, or half words, were so mangled and slurred it was a moment before I deciphered them. I was afraid to go closer. He was the embodiment of my sin, a monster whom I could only barely look at through the chinks between my fingers.

''oser!'

An angry, bitter snarl. It must have contained some remnants of the old Mr Black for, still sitting, I shuffled reluctantly, obediently along the bed towards him, still with my hands before my face.

'Let . . . see you.'

I flinched as I glimpsed his right hand curving towards me, but did not pull my head away, fully expecting a blow, indeed suddenly desiring my old punishment. Instead, his hand touched my hand, prising my fingers from my face. His touch was so gentle, so unexpected, and in such contrast to the scowl permanently locked in his face, that I burst into tears.

'Oh, sir, forgive me, forgive me for what I have done!'

To my astonishment the man I had always known as unyieldingly hard and obdurate put his arms round me, or, to be more accurate, his good arm.

'Should . . . told . . . you.' There was a long, agonising gap between the words, during which both parts of his face seemed to be fighting with one another. But the stern, judgemental side was frozen, while the side which had smiled at me after we had put the Grand Remonstrance together, and which I had really only discovered just before I had run away, seemed to have been set free. His right eye glowed with the animation of both while he fought to move his lips into what I realised was a smile. 'Should . . . told . . . you . . . many . . . things . . . many . . .' He stopped, exhausted.

'She must not marry George, sir!' I said.

'She . . . not . . . for . . . you,' he managed.

'I – I – love her, sir.'

'George . . . good . . . man,' he said.

Nothing had changed after all. I felt anger boiling up inside me, just as it had when they had tried to beat me into the shape they wanted me to be. 'I never thought George would convert you to the King's cause,' I said bitterly.

'King's . . .?'

I held up the pamphlet. He slowly began to read it, then dropped it, his face reddening. I feared he was going to have another fit.

'She must not marry George, sir,' I pleaded. 'If you refuse your permission, it can be stopped, even now!'

The church bells ceased ringing. In the penetrating silence his mouth quivered open, then closed.

'Do you refuse your permission? Mr Black?'

He stared at me, his mouth quivering, closing. I picked up a sheet of paper from the floor and a quill, and dipped it in the ink.

17

I ran past the memorial where she had stung herself on nettles that day. Stumbled on the church steps. Sprawled on the porch. Caught the words of the minister resonating: '. . . in sickness and in health, forsaking all other . . .' I scrambled up, panic stricken that she was about to say 'I will', and ran into the church.

'I will.'

It was George speaking, a George with his face scrubbed till it gleamed, George who even on this joyous occasion was encased in a black doublet and breeches and sent the words rolling round the church with a sense of doom. Anne's simple, unadorned white dress made the contrast between them even starker.

The minister, Mr Tooley, turned to her. 'Anne, wilt thou have this man to be thy wedded husband, to live together, after God's ordinance –'

'She won't!' I shouted. 'I mean, she can't – her father forbids it!'

For the second time, the first being when I appeared in Turville's study, I saw the power of being a gentleman, or, at least, looking like one. Even a rich merchant like Benyon hesitated to interfere, particularly when he heard me tell Mr Tooley about Mr Black's anger at George printing seditious material. Parliament now ruled the City, and these were serious charges. Benyon sent one of his servants scuttling from the church. The congregation was in uproar. Mr Tooley shouted: 'This is a house of God, not a playhouse!' as he took me into the vestry, with George, Anne and Mrs Black.

Anne refused to listen to me. Every time I opened my mouth she cut in with: 'You broke your promise.'

'I had to! You cannot marry him – he has been cheating your father!'

'You broke your promise never to see me again.' Tears filled her eyes. 'You promised, you promised!'

'I've seen your father.'

'My father! You've seen my father? You'll kill him!'

She covered her face with her hands.

'He's forbidden the wedding!' I cried.

'Forbidden?' She took her hands from her face and looked wildly at me.

In the drab confines of that vestry, with its hanging black robes and notes of parish meetings, George recovered himself. 'How can it be true?' His voice throbbed with indignation. 'Did we not talk to him before we left? Did he not bless us?'

'Is this true, my child?' said Mr Tooley sternly.

Anne twisted her thin fingers together until I thought they would break. 'Yes. Yes. As much as he could speak.' Her mother came over to put her arm round her, but she thrust her away and rounded on me. 'Why do I keep believing you? I can't believe a word you say. You promised not to see me again and now – now – today of all days –!'

She broke down in tears and her mother took her to a bench in the corner. I could not help trying to go to her, but Mr Tooley grabbed me on one side and George on the other. 'Worse than a thief is a liar, Mr Tooley, for he steals the truth from your mouth,' George said.

His quoting from his favourite Ecclesiasticus brought back all the sanctimonious homilies he had beaten into me over the years, which bruised and enraged me far more than his composing stick. I struggled to control my anger as I drew a piece of paper from my pocket. 'I have proof.'

George tried to take it, but Mr Tooley held out his hand and I gave it to him. He read it out. '"I withdraw consent for the marriage of my daughter, Anne Black, to George Sawyer." It is signed Robert Black.' He frowned. 'Why would he do that? At this late hour?'

I explained again about the pamphlets supporting the King that I had found. George hotly denied any such printing.

'What has been going on, Mother?' Anne said, with a sudden show of spirit.

'Nothing!' Mrs Black cried, but looked increasingly uncomfortable. 'I have thought of nothing but you, of seeing you safe.'

George took the piece of paper. 'The apprentice has written this! For that is what he is, in spite of his stolen clothes. Thanks to him, poor Mr Black is unable to write.'

'He can!' Anne broke in. 'Let me see –'

'There is no point in you looking at it, child,' her mother said. 'No more than me.'

'Aye,' George echoed. 'Praise the Lord you cannot read such a foul deceit.'

'I can read!' Anne cried, then her voice faltered. 'A little. And I have been learning to write.'

'After I forbade it?' George said, in a freezing tone.

She stared at the floor. Mr Tooley looked away. It was as though they were married already, and whatever the minister thought, he would not come between husband and wife. He used to talk in his sermons of the virtues of an obedient wife, who knew enough reading and writing to perform her household tasks, but not enough to read the Bible, which was dangerous, for it needed a man to interpret it. I began to sense what had been happening at Half Moon Court since I had left; George taking control of business and Mrs Black, fearful of the future, only too compliant in letting him do so. Anne, left with much of the nursing of her sick father, seemed to have developed a deeper relationship with him than they were aware of.

'N-not learning to write as such,' she stammered. 'But my father has been learning again like a child and I, I have picked up things. That is all.'

'Leave us,' George said, scarcely less dismissive of her than of me when I had been an apprentice. Anger boiled up in me when she quietly returned to her mother. Her steps were slow and controlled. I could not believe this was the same person who had laughed at Gloomy George with me only two months ago.

'Wait –' Mr Tooley showed her the piece of paper '– is this Mr Black's hand?'

'I wrote what he wished to say and he signed it,' I said. 'After I showed him the proof of the pamphlet George is secretly printing for the King's party.'

'There is no such pamphlet!' George said. He looked at Mrs Black. 'Is there?'

'I have not seen one,' she replied.

'Is this Mr Black's signature, Anne? In his present state?' Mr Tooley asked.

'It is like . . .' She hesitated, then whispered: 'I do not know.'

'Tom!' Mr Tooley fired the question at me like a ball from a musket, so abruptly I jumped. 'Did Mr Black sign this?'

'It is what he said to me.'

'Answer the question! You are in church, God's court, which is higher than any court of law.'

It was suddenly silent outside the vestry room, except for whispering and shuffling, which sounded like the rats creeping towards me in the cellar, in my recurrent nightmare. It was the culmination of my childhood, that question. A blur of questioning faces passed in front of me. The old gentleman when I burned myself with pitch, his face asking who I was. Susannah opening the Bible. What does this say? Mr Black, stern, uprighteous. Have you your letters? I wanted to cry back a question to all of them. Which one of you has told me the truth? Not Susannah. Not Mr Black. Not Lord Stonehouse, although each knew a piece of it. In that tawdry vestry room, with its creaking table and tattered piles of greasily fingered prayer books, I felt one lie had piled on another, like one brick on another, and I feared to add to them, lest the chinks of light I had revealed would vanish, and I would be walled up in a cellar of deceit for ever.

The truth was that I was sure Mr Black did not want Anne to marry George. Anne would be condemned to a kind of death, not life, if she married him. That was the real truth. The unimportant legal truth was that Mr Black's hand could not hold the quill, and I signed it.

'Tom?' The faces all dissolved into that of Mr Tooley. He had thick, bushy eyebrows which gradually knitted into one as I remained silent. 'God waits for your answer.'

George, who had been straining forward like a dog on a leash, relaxed visibly. He smiled at Anne and took her hand. 'There must be some hope for his soul that he cannot lie in God's house.'

Anne pulled away from him, staring at me with a look that was like acid in my face. She kept silent but the words were in that look as plainly as if she had said them: Why do you come here to ruin all this? To tell another lie?

Mr Tooley expelled a sigh, which sounded as if it had been pent-up ever since he asked the original question. His voice and demeanour became more than ever that of a judge. 'Tom Neave, I am bound to take your silence as evidence of guilt. As a court will tell you, the laws of the realm hold forgery to be a most serious crime, much more serious than running from your master. Mr Henderson –'

He called for the churchwarden, who evidently had his ear to the door, for he opened it immediately. Much of the congregation had crept forward as closely and showed no signs of moving.

'The wisdom of Solomon, Mr Tooley!' cried George. 'You condemned him by his own silence!'

18

Useless running, even if I had any life left in my legs. They had called a constable, and there was another in the congregation. Gripping me by the arms, they led me down the aisle, where I had once dreamed of walking with Anne. Mr Tooley was urging everyone back in their places so that the ceremony could continue. There was another couple waiting outside – everyone was getting married because of the approaching war.

'Forgery,' said George to Benyon.

'Forgery!' Benyon gave a low whistle and shook his head. 'A felony.'

'The very day I brought him upriver with poor Mr Black I predicted it.'

'A hanging job!'

The words spread through the congregation like a spark falling on dry tinder. Snatches of conversation came to me as I stumbled down the aisle. Forgery. A felony. A hanging job. Always knew he would mount the ladder. Take the morning drop. Mr Black, dead? Murdered in his bed! Then he forged his signature to try and stop the wedding. The devil is in him! It was as though, with no fancy preliminaries like a trial and Newgate, I was already on my way to Tyburn. From bearing composed, set, wedding smiles when I had entered the church, the faces of the congregation now bore a hanging-day flush. Necks craned, eyes protruded, as they elbowed and pushed to see me.

'Hanged?'

I heard Anne's voice rising above the rest. I jerked to a stop, pulling away from one of the constables. Mr Tooley was bending over her, making soothing, placatory gestures. George came to join him in a little huddle. Mrs Black got up from the front pew, clutching at her hat, and joined them in a mounting argument. Out of it came a whirlwind. Every part of Anne seemed to be in furious motion. Her hair flew, her large liquid eyes and her quivering mouth seemed to fill her face. Her words rang round the church.

'Why? Why? Why cannot we go and ask my father if he did sign it?'

Mrs Black began to speak, but a freezing glance from Mr Tooley stopped her. He struggled to keep his voice low, but in the awestruck silence it reverberated round the stone walls. 'Anne, do not listen to other people. There will be a trial. I do not know what will happen. No one does.' As she opened her mouth to reply, his voice struck the exasperated tone no one in the church had ever dared to disobey. 'Anne – do you wish to be married or not?'

She bowed her head. There was a huge collective sigh from the congregation. Mr Tooley waved the bride and groom peremptorily back into position to take their vows. Mrs Black scuttled back to the front pew. The constables gripped me by my arms again and led me into the porch.

'Five minutes!' Anne's voice echoed round the church.

I turned at the door to see Anne bringing her clenched fists down on her hips with such force I thought she would break into pieces.

'It is five minutes to my father, Mr Tooley – *five minutes!* Marriage is *my whole life!*'

The arrivals for the next wedding stared at us as we wound through the graveyard, past the mausoleum to Samuel Potter & Relic. We must have looked a curious procession; Mr Tooley led the way with Benyon and Mrs Black, who struggled to keep her hat on in the wind, then came the bride and groom, Anne staring straight ahead, George murmuring into her ear, casting glances back at me, who stumbled between the two constables, both of them gripping me so close we must have looked like a creature with six legs.

It was the longest five minutes of my life. It now seemed the height of stupidity to have forged Mr Black's signature. But there was the secret printing George had been carrying out, the proof of which Mr Black had read – although how much he had really taken in I did not know. George clearly believed this would be outweighed by the forgery, which I had all but admitted by my silence. His face as he glanced back bore the expression I knew only too well from childhood: anticipation of my punishment to come.

As we turned into Half Moon Court, Mrs Black let out a cry. The curtains of Mr Black's window were drawn. Sarah was standing on the doorstep and Mrs Black and Anne ran towards her. All my previous fears were dwarfed by the thought that I had killed him.

'All but,' Sarah scathingly said. 'You nearly managed it this time, with the upset you gave him.'

She said she had left the house to buy fresh bread and had returned to find him in a terrible state. She had made him a draught and he was now asleep. While Mrs Black hurried upstairs to him, the rest of us filed through the parlour, where the smell of new bread had joined that of the game pie and the goose, which was still sizzling on the spit, and then into the printing shop. Mr Tooley demanded proof of the seditious material.

Under the eyes of the constables I went straight into the paper shop. There was no sign of *Fighte for the King's Peace*, or any other Royalist pamphlets. Nor was there any sign in the shop of the formes from which it had been printed.

I struggled to keep calm. I could not meet Anne's eyes. George stood watching me, head slightly bowed, arms folded.

'It was there – I swear it was there!'

Anne turned away. George's arms encircled her. I felt Mr Tooley's eyes follow me as I searched every shelf and bench. I remembered

Benyon sending his men out of the church. 'Sarah – did Mr Benyon's men come?'

'Aye. In a coach. To tell me the feast would be delayed.'

'Did they take anything?'

'I don't know. I was upstairs, with Master.'

'It *was* there!' I said to Anne. 'You *must* believe me!'

I could not bear the look on her face. She turned away from me. She looked as if she had just been told that a loved one had died. Although Sarah had no love for Miss Hoity-Toity, she recognised grief when she saw it.

'Come on, tha's getting married. Remember?'

Anne did not seem to know where she was, or what had happened. 'I'm sorry,' she whispered. The words were barely audible. Whether she was sorry for me, or saying it to me or in general I had no means of knowing, but George took it as a personal apology to him. He was magnanimous, forgiving and sorrowful at the same time. 'It is one of her best qualities, Mr Tooley, to try and see the good in people. Mr Black and I struggled to find it in him for years. But you have just demonstrated, my dear – more eloquently than I have ever been able to – that there is nothing there.' He reflected. 'Nay, there is worse than nothing.' He had combed his thinning hair over the mark on his forehead where I had struck him, but the wind had disturbed it and it flushed red as he levelled a finger at me. 'He is possessed – possessed by the devil!'

It was not the words, for I had heard them many times before, albeit never so extreme and violent. It was not even their effect on Anne, who had a look of terror on her face. It was George opening his arms to her that made me fly at him. It took everyone by surprise, including me. My momentum knocked Mr Tooley aside and slammed George against the press. As he fell to the floor my hands, which seemed to have a life of their own, went round his throat. I fully intended to kill him. I had no thought of what would happen to me – in my own mind I was hanged anyway. Whatever happened, he must not marry

Anne. He must not touch her, poison her mind – the words hammered in my head as I fought to keep my grip on George while the constables tried to drag me off. I really think I was possessed. When they finally managed to pull me away, George was not dead, far from it, but at least he could not speak. That was something.

The print shop looked as though a storm had struck it. Blocks, type and paper were scattered about the floor. They bound my arms tight behind my back. Even then, they moved round me cautiously, as though I was a rabid dog who might suddenly bite. One constable's lip was thickening, and a dribble of blood leaked from the corner of his mouth. I saw this in flashes as I came round, gradually aware of the blows I had received. How long Mrs Black had been there I do not know, but she was telling Mr Tooley that Mr Black wished to see me upstairs. See me upstairs! I could scarce climb one of them. Mr Tooley dismissed this. He would not put Mr Black under any more distress.

A violent hammering came from the room above. Plaster pattered down on us. Before Mr Tooley could stop her, Anne was halfway up the stairs to her father. The minister linked his hands and shut his eyes as his lips moved in what, I imagine, was a prayer that God should bring to an end, one way or another, the longest wedding he had ever witnessed. Mrs Black shook plaster from her hat.

'Mis . . . cre . . . ant!' bellowed Mr Black above us, in a howl of distorted syllables that brought Mr Tooley from his prayer and me to my feet. His voice might be slurred, but it still held all the vengeful power that both he and George derived from the Old Testament. It reawoke old shivers in me, and brought George's voice back, albeit a thin reediness rattling in his throat, round which he was tenderly wrapping a silk scarf. 'It is only right for Mr Black to see the miscreant, Mr Tooley. I told the poor gentleman, when we took the boy from without, that we were bringing the devil into this city.'

Mr Tooley, who now looked as vengeful as Mr Black and George, took the letter on which I had forged Mr Black's signature, and led the way upstairs. At that moment, I believe, I would rather have climbed the ladder at Paddington Fair than those stairs to Mr Black's room. He was a fearful sight. Exhausted by thumping with his cane on the floor, his eyes were almost closed, his head nodding on his chest. His hair, still luxuriously thick but largely grey, fell down in mottled streaks, except for one clump, plastered by sweat to his forehead. He was supported partly by pillows, and partly by his hand gripping the cane. It was the successor to many such canes, but to me it looked very like the cane he had beaten me with on the first day I saw him in the shipyard.

Mr Tooley approached him, stopped awkwardly, then coughed. Mr Black's eyes jerked open, travelled up to the minister's face and then stared directly at me. I would have fallen on my knees if I had not been held up by the two constables. How could I have reduced this upright man to this? Tried to destroy his daughter's wedding? Truly the devil was in me! George stepped forward, taking off his hat and indicating me.

'Here he is, Master,' he said.

'Aye.' Mr Black struggled up on his pillows, his voice for a moment almost normal. 'Here he is.' Anne rushed to the bed and arranged the pillows. He sank back on them with a sigh, keeping his eyes on her all the time. 'You thought to . . . disobey me . . .'

She did fall on her knees. 'No, Father, no! I thought – I thought –' As his speech became clearer as he looked at her, hers was blurred by sobs, so she could scarcely form the words. 'I – wanted to be – sure what your wishes were. Tom – he – brought a letter.'

'This!' said Mr Tooley, producing the letter.

I shut my eyes as Mr Black stared at the scribble I had written, but I could not shut my ears when Mr Tooley began to read the lines about withdrawing consent. I opened my eyes when Mr Tooley abruptly stopped reading. Mr Black was holding out his good hand. He took the letter and read it. I began shaking and could not stop. I was not only a rogue and a fraud, I was that most foolish of rogues: one who did something so inanely stupid he was bound to be found out.

Mr Black gave me a look of such searing gravity I opened my mouth to blurt out what I had done and beg his forgiveness. Only the gleam of triumph in George's eyes stopped me. I would not give him that satisfaction. I glared sullenly back at him, just as I had done in the boat all those years ago, although it was now carrying me remorselessly not to treasure but to Paddington Fair.

'Is that your signature, sir?' said Mr Tooley.

'That?' Mr Black peered at the sheet of paper. 'That miserable . . . spidery . . . scrawl . . . my signature?' He spat out the words with scorn, then muttered. 'Miscrean—'

Mr Tooley expelled a deep, resigned sigh and signalled to the constables to take me away.

'Aye,' Mr Black muttered, nodding his head, still staring at the sheet of paper as I passed the foot of his bed. 'That is . . . what . . . I am reduced to.'

'Wait!' cried Mr Tooley, stopping us so abruptly at the door we all collided with one another. 'Are you saying, sir, it *is* your signature?'

'What?'

Mr Black clutched the piece of paper, staring up at him. Anne, who was being helped up by George, repeated the question. There followed a period of confusion such as I had endured before writing the fatal letter, until Mr Black thrust out the letter, almost striking Mr Tooley, and cried: 'Of course . . . it's my . . . damned sig . . . nature, sir!' A stunned silence was broken by Mr Black exploding into a fit of coughing and Sarah and Anne rushing to his aid. Everyone began speaking at once, George shaking his head and telling Mr Tooley his poor master did not know what he was saying, until Mr Black made his meaning clear by dropping the letter and taking from under his blanket the pamphlet I had shown him of George's secret printing.

'Miscreant!' he yelled, thrusting his stick with such force at George it sent him staggering backwards.

'I knew it! I knew it! I knew you were telling the truth!' Anne's arms were round me, her face streaming with tears.

'Anne – in front of the minister!' cried a scandalised Mrs Black. 'You are getting married!'

'Aye,' said Sarah. 'But to which one?'

The small bedroom was like Bedlam. Mr Tooley wanted to know whether there was to be a wedding or not. The constables did not know whether they were arresting me. Or George. Or neither. Sarah kept asking what she was supposed to do with all the food. Mrs Black collapsed in a chair, crying she did not care what Sarah did with it. Give it to the poor! She could never show her face in church again! I stood there in the middle of it all, dazed.

I was consumed by the fear that the success of my falsehood had been bought only at the cost of Mr Black's sanity. Surely he had become too confused to have any idea what he was doing. Amidst the babble, he was staring directly at me. He beckoned me closer. The good side of his face was strangely contorted, as though he was on the verge of having a fit. His right eye twitched. Fearing I had brought on his final spasm, I moved towards him, then stopped. There was no doubt about it. His right eye was closed in an outrageous wink. He pointed to the cane, which I gave him, silencing everyone with thumps on the spot where he signalled so regularly that little chips of wood had broken away. There was no sign of George, but in the silence I heard the door close downstairs.

'Food,' said Mr Black.

'You mean – what to do with all the food?' said Anne.

Mr Black smiled and nodded. He pointed with his cane to the Bible that always lay at his bedside, and Mr Tooley picked it up. I think he expected the Old Testament, but Mr Black chose the New.

'Luke,' he managed, 'fifteen –' He fell back exhausted, but Mr Tooley seemed to know, or divine which verse and pointed at it. Again

Mr Black smiled and nodded, and Mr Tooley read it. His voice shook a little as he did so:

'Then bring out the calf that has been fattened, and kill it; let us eat and make merry; for my son here was dead, and has come to life again, was lost, and is found.'

19

They were some of the happiest days of my life, that spring and summer. While the country was slowly tearing itself apart, I seemed to have come together as a person. War threatened, but never came.

Every day I expected to see Eaton ride into the yard at Half Moon Court. I wrapped up the clothes I had escaped in, ready to give them to him. I wanted to have no obligation to him; but would not take the risk of returning them. When Eaton never came I supposed he and Turville had given up on the idea of me ever being a gentleman. The money Mr Black had received regularly from Eaton stopped. With it, it seemed, went the risk to my life. Crow was dead. For a time I saw Captain Gardiner on every street corner, but as I kept up the military training and grew tougher and stronger my fear diminished.

I heard nothing of Matthew and no longer cared about finding my real father. That wink Mr Black gave me, and that reading from Luke, was as good as – nay, a thousand times better than – any blood a father has given to his son. Anne continued her dual mission of helping Mr Black to write again and, through the process, learning to write herself. Sometimes I joined in, but I felt I spoilt the atmosphere between them, for it was impossible to conceal our feelings for one another. One day I snatched a kiss. I saw Mr Black staring rigidly at me with his good eye and pulled sharply away, fearing his wrath – until, once again, he gave me that outrageous wink.

But as I grew closer to Mr Black, and he depended on me, Mrs Black scarcely spoke to me. She knew nothing about George printing for the King, she said – and if she did, I think she was secretly proud of it. She dismissed politics as an alehouse argument dressed up in fine words which never brought food to the table. For her, everything had been settled. Her daughter had been about to marry a man who was a pillar of the community and did business with one of the richest men in the city. Now all that had been snatched away. And for what? A grubby apprentice with big feet who had gone through endless pairs of boots and who had bewitched her poor sick husband, which had been proved beyond doubt by her astrologer! Prodigal? That was certainly the word! Didn't it mean wasteful? Spendthrift? Most certainly. Except he had nothing to spend.

Mrs Black was right about that. There was no money. Mr Black, who gave me long and painful instructions on how to run a business that no longer existed, insisted there were ample funds. The cash box in which he kept money to run the business was empty. I suspected George of taking it, but Mr Black was so confused, I had no means of knowing how much, if anything, had been there. All there was to live on were the lead and tin tokens shopkeepers issued because there was such a shortage of small coins. Worth a halfpenny or a farthing, Sarah kept them in small leather bags for the butcher, baker and dairy. There was a cry of triumph when anyone discovered odd ones in a drawer, and a celebration when a small hoard was discovered in a pitcher.

When the last of the tokens bought us only rye bread and no cheese, I remembered the tumultuous day I had witnessed when the King had attempted to invade Parliament. I wrote my first pamphlet, borrowing money from Will for the ink and paper to print it. I gazed at the proof I pulled with the fond pride of a father for his first child:

PRIVILEGE!
How MR PYM & Parliament
Were Saved
The Mysteriouse Messenger Revealed
& the Kinges Evil Advisers Foiled

It went through so many runs I had to reset the battered type. Its success brought in other business and I was courted, not as a gentleman, but a pamphleteer; courted and reviled, for the pamphleteer was seen as the lowest form of writer, seditious, licentious, even worse than a playwright, a whore in print, bought one day and thrown away the next. Occasionally I grew tired and disgusted with myself and wrote some poetry, but as these sold even less than moral tracts I went back to my stories, preferring to be reviled and read than not read at all.

Mrs Black, however, began to look more kindly on me. With more money coming in she was able to afford a better class of astrologer, Mr Lilly. He found an error in the cheaper one's calculations. Mercury was in conjunction, not opposition to the sun and I was therefore a messenger, not a devil.

I could now afford a doctor for Mr Black, but he seemed to have benefited more from having no doctor at all. His speech had returned, slowly, albeit hesitant and slurred, and he was able to host the celebration of the fulfilment of my indentures. Seven years I had been there. Seven years – and at last I could throw away my uniform, my boots and my cursed hat!

On a hot, humid, August day, Big Jed carried out tables and set them up under the apple tree. To mark the great occasion, he said, I was 'excused pike' for a week – but in truth drilling with a pike or shouldering a musket at Moorfields had fallen off. Fear of all-out war had dwindled as there seemed to be only isolated skirmishes far from London.

Will, Ben, Luke and Charity came. She was with child, and as a treat (and perhaps practice) brought her small sister Prudence and brother Tenacious. Pamphleteers were there, like Crop-Eared Jack, who had had an ear cropped for his radical views. I most wanted Mr Ink to be there, but to my disappointment he had not arrived when Mr Black rose to make his speech. There was a rumble of thunder from the coppery blue sky, but Mrs Black said it was passing. She had bought the day from Mr Lilly, who had told her there would be no rain.

Mr Black declared that the mysteries of the Guild had been satisfied, albeit after some debate about conduct (much laughter and thumping of the table).

'Tom . . .' His voice shook. 'You are now free. You m-may now . . . go into an alehouse.'

There was a great shout of laughter and another rumble of thunder, which Mrs Black dismissed with a wave of her hand.

'You may even play . . . p-pass-dice.'

There were more cheers and someone said he felt a spot of rain but Mrs Black said he was imagining it.

'And . . . and . . .' He stopped, leaning on his stick. Mrs Black got up anxiously, but he waved her testily away. He was unable to get the words out and I thought it was illness, but then, when he did speak, realised it was emotion. 'You are . . . now . . . f-f-free to . . . m-marry.'

Anne's hand crept into mine. Mrs Black smiled. The rain sluiced down. Laughing, half-drenched, we were toasted in the house until the rain cleared and the sun came out again and we saw a lonely figure, dripping wet, under the apple tree.

'Mr Ink!' I cried. 'Dear friend – you got here just in time!'

'I was delayed by the news.' He looked dazed, twisting his hat between his fingers, from which an inky rain dripped.

'News?'

'The King has raised his standard in Nottingham.'

It had been expected for so long, but was still a shock when it came. What we did not expect was Eaton. He rode into the courtyard that evening, on his black gelding. He was almost civil, for him. He gave me a small bow, almost mocking, and called me Mr Tom. Just as he had done for seven years, he saw Mr Black in his office, the difference being that this time I was there. He said the King raising his standard had drawn Lord Stonehouse's attention to unfinished business.

'I . . . I have no business with Lord Stonehouse,' said Mr Black steadily.

'You have a contract, sir.'

The contract concerned me. In effect, Eaton said, I was indentured not to Mr Black but to Lord Stonehouse. We put up a very spirited defence, telling him I was now free. The Guild had approved it. Furthermore, no payments had been made by Lord Stonehouse that year, and that had broken the contract. Eaton clenched his fist, controlled himself with an effort, and tossed a letter on the desk to Mr Black, telling me if I wished to discuss the contents I should appear promptly at Mr Turville's chambers at nine next morning.

'I have no wish to discuss anything, sir,' I said.

'Very well. I bid you good evening, gentlemen.'

I saw him off. When I returned to the office I thought Mr Black had had another fit. He could not speak. I seized the letter that lay open on his desk. Lord Stonehouse had bought the freehold of Half Moon Court and given Mr Black one month to quit. I knew that any move Mr Black made from the house he loved would kill him.

20

I took out the parcel containing the austere dark blue doublet and breeches, not to return but to put on. Once more, I was a gentleman. But I did the last thing Eaton expected. I went not to Turville but to Queen Street, to Lord Stonehouse's town house, determined to face the puppet-master, not his puppets.

I went there, my words all prepared, like the speech of a player, but as I approached my courage began to drain away. I knew that, in spite of Mr Pym and Parliament, and the rioting crowds, without the moves behind the scenes of some of the richest and most powerful peers in England, peers who had fallen from favour with the King, there would have been no revolt. Pamphleteers called them the Great Twelve – peers like Warwick, Bedford, Essex and Stonehouse. No wonder I slowed, my legs shaking as if I had the ague, as I approached Queen Street.

The street was wider and more imposing than the streets of the City. The classical façades of the four-storey terraced houses were uniform straight lines of stone and brick, with none of the comfort, the crookedness, the narrowness of wood. There was no place to hide. No comforting alleys. A constable eyed me from his sentry box at the end, but was distracted by a coach demanding entry, and I slipped by on the other side of it, past a scavenger who was sweeping up shit as the horses lifted their tails. The air was different. Not country air but air you could breathe without grabbing for a nosegay every turning or so. I did not need to ask for Lord Stonehouse. There in the centre of the terrace, the size of two or three of the other houses, was Falcon Lodge. Giant pilasters flanked windows crowned with triangular pediments. Above the main entrance, carved in a stone shield, was a falcon with a threatening, upraised claw.

It was a cloudy but warm day, and the double doors to the entrance hall were open. From the street I could see into the black-and-white checkerboard tiled hall, lined with pictures and Greek busts. Servants scurried about in green silk livery embroidered at the chest in silver wire with the forbidding falcon. Lord Stonehouse's role in the Great Twelve was to head the Committee of Requisition and Intelligence. This, I discovered later, was the official name for plunder. Most prominent Royalists had left London. Their houses were being seized and searched for arms or letters as well as silver plate, which was to be melted down for coinage to pay the militia. The raider usually took a percentage of the choicer pieces for his trouble. In the City, old scores were being settled under the guise of legitimacy. Benyon had fled with what he could cram in a coach before his fine house in Thames Street was stripped by rival merchants. All this meant a constant flow of visitors to the house in Queen Street.

A corpulent man descended from a coach handing a card to a servant, who dropped it into a silver salver where there was a nest of similar cards, calling out to someone I could not see: 'Sir Samuel Pope on the Marquess of Hamilton's business.' My foot was in the air, almost on the first marble step. The servant's eye rested on me. It had the beady, penetrating look of the falcon. It was then I lost heart. What could I say? 'Thomas Neave, on the business of bastardy'?

I walked on, with a pretence of casually idling by. It was as I returned that I heard him. The whole street heard his rich, savage tones through an open first-floor window. There were interruptions in a quieter voice, but they were swept away. 'Is that all you have come to tell me? That you have *not* changed your mind! I don't know how you dare come here when your friends have fled! Do you think I'll protect you? . . . Do not interrupt me! . . . Sincere? If I could believe that!'

The other voice broke through, higher-pitched but just as virulent, a voice at the end of its tether. 'I am, Father, I am! I believe in this more than anything else in my life!'

'You believe in nothing but the throw of the dice! You're gambling Parliament will lose and you'll get the estates!'

'That's a foul thing to say! You're wrong! You're going against your God, your King –'

At that point Lord Stonehouse must have remembered the casement window was open. He strode over and shut it. His face was distorted with anger. He was breathing so heavily he rested for a moment, closing his eyes, before swivelling round and disappearing from view. The servants all had their backs to me, straining to hear. It was an impulse, done as the thought was entering my head. I sprang up the steps and picked up a card from the bottom of the salver, holding it out as the servant turned. I had noticed that a number of servants ferried guests through, and I was gambling that this servant had not dealt with the gentleman whose card I proffered. He stared at the card then coldly at me. My stomach lurched to the bottom of my expensive leather boots but then 'Sir Andrew Marham!' he called, tossing the card back into the salver. What I had not seen from the street was that the next barrier was a scrivener, half-hidden behind a pillar.

He had his head turned towards the elaborately carved balustrade of the staircase – another falcon, with coneys and hares caught in his talons – catching another tirade from Lord Stonehouse on the first-floor gallery, before a door slammed, followed by a shattering of glass. The scrivener, a small wizened man with spectacles, winced. 'Not the best day to see his lordship, Sir Andrew,' he said, before frowning. 'Sir Andrew?' He consulted a list in front of him. His voice rose. 'Sir Andrew is already waiting.'

Behind me I could hear the approaching rap of the servant's shoes on the marble floor. I felt everyone's attention was on me. In desperation I did the only thing I could think of – I produced the truth, even if I had to gild it a little. I smiled. 'Thank goodness he has not gone in to his lordship.' I took a handkerchief from my cuff, with a flourish I had learned from Turville, and wiped my forehead. 'I am Sir Andrew's secretary. He forgot some papers. And I must give him a message.' I drew from my pocket the letter Turville had sent evicting Mr Black, which bore the magic seal of the falcon.

The rap of the servant's shoes approaching me stopped. The scrivener picked up his quill. 'Your name, sir?'

'Thomas Neave,' I said stupidly, but automatically. He stopped in the act of dipping his quill. I feared he knew the name from my pamphlets. He peered up at me sharply, but evidently deciding that my rich blue velvet and lace could not possibly clothe a gutter object like a pamphleteer, wrote in his book *Thomas Neave Esq.* which, I must admit, gave me a thrill of pleasure. He directed me between statues of Mars and Minerva to a reception room with an oval ceiling painted with nymphs being chased by satyrs.

Three gentlemen, deep in conversation, one of whom was presumably Sir Andrew, looked up and then ignored me. I was full of myself with the success of my deception. I would seize the right moment, see Lord Stonehouse, and be gracious but firm. I would appeal to his better nature in telling him I wanted nothing from him but my own life. It never occurred to me that he might not have a better nature, that it might have been lost a long time ago.

Sir Samuel, the corpulent man from the coach, who occupied most of a silk upholstered couch, shook his head as the distant argument above ebbed and flowed. He gave it as his opinion that if Richard Stonehouse did join the King he would be finally disinherited. A lean, clever-looking man, squeezed into a corner, who turned out to be Sir Andrew, disagreed. Whatever happened, Lord Stonehouse always forgave his eldest son. What mattered to Lord Stonehouse was blood. The third man, whom they called Jacob, was much younger than the others. Perched uncomfortably on a squab, hungry to join in, he said there was a second son.

'Edward!' Sir Andrew smiled. 'He has milk, not blood in his veins.'

'Mother's milk, at that,' murmured Sir Samuel, and the two men laughed.

Stung, the young man declared that he had heard, on good authority, if Richard was cut off, a bastard stood to inherit. The other two laughed uproariously at this. Sir Samuel clapped the young man on the back, dislodging the papers he was carrying, and almost squeezed Sir Andrew from the couch with the shaking of his stomach.

'You have swallowed that one!' Sir Samuel glanced towards me as I stared studiously at a satyr chasing a nymph across the blue sky. He wiped his eyes. 'You are good value for a dull wait, Jacob. Depend upon it, sir, there is no such person. He is a figment of Lord Stonehouse's imagination, put about to bring his errant son to heel. Unfortunately, it has had the opposite effect.'

I was beginning to enjoy my entry into good society when I heard Eaton in the hall, cutting across the well-fed tones of Sir Samuel with a voice as sharp as vinegar, demanding to know who was waiting. I cursed myself for giving my own name and shot to the door to see Eaton picking up the scrivener's book. I slipped across the hall towards a door, but as I reached it the handle began to turn and I glimpsed the livery of a servant emerging. Beside me was the statue of Minerva. There was just enough space to squeeze behind it as Eaton exploded.

'Thomas Neave!'

'Sir Andrew's secretary, Mr Eaton.'

'Sir Andrew's –'

I pressed myself as tightly as possible behind the statue but the stone curve of her skirt bulged into me so part of my doublet protruded. Eaton strode towards me. If he looked down he was bound to see me, but his eyes were on the waiting room. He marched in, the abject scrivener and the servant on duty in the hall trailing after him. There was a confused babble of voices. I did not stop to hear the outcome. The hall was empty. I ran up the grand stairway and on to the gallery. The walls had alcoves at intervals containing looking glasses and richly wrought cabinets. Passing a pair of double doors I heard the murmur of voices close to the door. Lord Stonehouse's was so different from the violent hectoring tone that at first I did not recognise it.

'This is for you and you alone . . . I can trust you in this?'

'Yes, Father.'

'The doctors say I have one year. Perhaps a little more.'

There was a commotion downstairs. From the gallery I could see Eaton haranguing the servants. Doors were opening and closing. Eaton hurried across the hall towards the stairs. I darted down a corridor. Tried a door but it was locked. I heard the double doors opening and slipped to one of the alcoves behind a cabinet as Lord Stonehouse and his son came out. In the alcove looking glass near the top of the stairs I saw Eaton hurrying up, stop and hesitate. Lord Stonehouse had his arm round his son. He gave Eaton a single, angry look and the steward slowly retreated.

It was the first time I had seen Richard at such close quarters. Ringlets framed a face that was so handsome it made me catch my breath. His eyes were dark and piercing and shone with tears that he was struggling to hold back. 'I cannot change my mind. I cannot!'

'I know, I know! I did not tell you for that reason, but – we may not see each other again.'

'Don't say that!'

Lord Stonehouse smiled. I had seen that smile before, but always believed it was a dream. It was not the smile of a ruthless man who had ordered Eaton to have me thrown into the pit, or to evict Mr Black from his house, but that of the man who had bent over me years ago when I had fainted from the pitch burn. 'Well, well . . . I believe you are sorry!' he said to his son.

Richard could not speak then, but flung his arms round his father.

I looked away. Richard had hired two men to kill me. It was difficult, almost impossible to believe. I wished I had not come. Not seen this. I had come thinking them to be purely evil men whom, if I could not fight, I might at least outwit. Lord Stonehouse laughed. He had a rich, deep laugh which transformed his face – there was a memory in it of those happier times I had seen in the portrait with his wife Frances. 'It is strange . . .' he said.

'What?'

Choked with emotion, his father's voice was an almost inaudible murmur. 'I am proud of you.'

'Proud?' Richard grinned in astonishment. 'I can't remember you ever saying that to me before.'

'I can't remember you ever doing anything you really believed in.'

He stared across at a portrait of Charles I. Richard followed his gaze. If they had looked to one side they would have seen me as I pressed back into the alcove, but they only had eyes for their King. Richard stood up, straight and proud, his voice now welling with emotion. 'I do believe in him.'

'I know. I can see that now. I wish, I wish I could, but . . . God go with you, Son.'

'God bless you, Father.'

Again they embraced, then Lord Stonehouse strode back into his room. Richard walked across the gallery towards the stairs. Every muscle in me tensed. As soon as Richard Stonehouse went downstairs, and before Eaton had a chance to come up, I planned to be in Lord Stonehouse's room. What I had just witnessed gave me hope. Underneath his ruthlessness was a man of deep feeling, who would, I was convinced, listen to my appeal.

I darted from the alcove as Lord Stonehouse went into his room. I had a glimpse of rich hanging tapestries before I caught sight of Richard Stonehouse returning up the stairs. I froze. Any movement would betray me. I sucked in air, too scared to let it out in case he heard me. Richard entered the room and I heard him say: 'My hat.' He came out almost immediately, putting an elaborately feathered contraption on his head as he walked away. I slowly let out air and took in more to still my pounding heart.

He was almost out of sight but, not quite satisfied with the set of the hat, stopped at one of the looking-glass alcoves to adjust it. His fingers stilled. It was a split second before I realised he could see me in the glass. I do not think he quite believed what the glass told him. Perhaps he thought I was a ghost, for I could not move or say a word. I wished I was a ghost, that I could vanish as abruptly as he thought I had appeared. The venom in his eyes held me mute like a rabbit trapped by a snake.

'You,' he said softly. 'You.'

He came close enough to touch the velvet of my doublet. My clothes seemed to act on him like a match to gunpowder. When he had nearly run me down at the royal procession I looked like a laughable freak in my second-hand clothes. Now, while I was no match for Richard in his fastidious dress of a courtier, from the large, florid rosettes on his shoes to the plumes in his hat, I unmistakably had the look of a gentleman. He had half unsheathed his sword when he saw his father standing at the door. Lord Stonehouse's mouth hung open. He blinked and blinked again. If Richard thought he saw a ghost, his father was convinced of it. I opened my mouth:

'I —'

It was the only word I uttered. The personal pronoun was enough. I existed. I was alive. Richard ignored me. He would not speak to me. I was unspeakable. The words he said to his father were acid with anguished bitterness. 'Couldn't you wait until I was gone?'

'I had no idea he was here!'

'He let himself in, I suppose?' His sword came out in a blur of movement which brought the point to my throat. He expected me to skip back but I would not. Moments before I had been so moved I'd had the impulse to embrace him and his father. Now I stared back with a hatred that matched his own. 'Bought this fine lace with his wretched, seditious pamphlets, I suppose?' With a flick of the blade he ripped away my lace collar. I instinctively jerked back. From that moment they ignored me. I had torn open an old wound and with every word they lacerated it further.

'I have not seen this boy for years and that is the truth!'

'You old hypocrite!'

His father's face reddened so, I thought a blood vessel had burst. 'Do not dare talk to me like that!'

'Proud? You were proud to be rid of me, weren't you?'

'That is not true! I meant every word I said.'

There was such agony in Lord Stonehouse's voice I struggled to interrupt, to clear up the misunderstanding, but I might as well have tried to walk through a hurricane. They pushed me to one side against the balustrade. Down in the hall I could see the servants, the waiting visitors and Eaton staring up. He gave me a vicious look, but even he dared not interrupt. Eventually, when they had torn their voices hoarse, Richard walked away down the stairs, only then seeming aware of the spellbound people in the hall.

Lord Stonehouse stood at the top of the stairs. Broken veins throbbed in his cheek, and spittle soiled the linen at his neck, but he was an impressive, forbidding figure nonetheless. He was tall and had not run to too much fat. Muscles stood out in his arms which could still control a horse or wield a sword. His hair was shorter than his son's and had more dark than grey in it. He was carelessly dressed in black, his status shown only by the small gold-and-enamel medal of St George at his throat, the insignia of the Garter, worn, perhaps, to remind his son that he had once been a close confidant of the King. He was so used to an audience and too powerful to care what they thought, that he addressed his son as if there was no one there.

'Richard! Come back . . .' The first word was a command, the last ended in a plea. Richard caught the tone and hesitated. He turned, his face, which was as haughty and as proud as his father's, was also awash with the same uncertainty, with a longing to return to the way they had originally parted before he saw me. If one had moved down a step, or the other up, they might have done so. But each was too proud to do so, and as if regretting his conciliatory tone Lord Stonehouse jerked his head towards his room and said gruffly, 'Come.' But when Richard turned away the old man's rage burst out: 'I'll have you arrested!'

Richard unsheathed his sword, the blade almost catching the scrivener as he fell back against his desk. 'I'll see you in hell, Father,' he yelled. 'You and that impostor!'

21

I was locked in a closet. All that long day, after the violence of Richard's departure, there had been a brooding silence, broken only by whispers and the sound of carriages arriving and departing. The closet was an annex to the library, now used as a storeroom for correspondence seized from Royalist families. A passage marked by Parliamentary intelligence on one blotted page pleaded with a relative to '. . . take the Children & the Family Plate to the Countrie before the Harveste is inne and this Dismal Businesse begins'.

It was evening and the candles were lit when two servants took me upstairs. They would not answer my questions, or even look at me. They knew, as servants always know, that I was the plague child, and treated me as if I was still contagious.

I was taken into Lord Stonehouse's study and motioned to a spot some distance from his desk. Lord Stonehouse sat in a pool of light from the candelabra burning over his head. With him was a man I took to be his secretary, who gave him papers to sign. Lord Stonehouse drank some wine, belched, moved to sign a paper, then stopped.

'Eight horses?'

'Eight, my lord.'

'I know the Duke of Richmond's stable. He has twelve fine Barbary horses. Find what has happened to them, will you, Mr Cole?'

'Yes, my lord.'

He pushed the paper away unsigned. His voice remained equable, unemotional. 'Horses and plate. Any soldier, officer or no, convicted of stealing them must not only be hanged but kept hanging as a warning to the others. Anything else?'

The secretary indicated me, bowing as he withdrew. Lord Stonehouse stared at me as if he had forgotten all about me. I am sure this was not an affectation. He had the administrator's ability to dismiss one problem entirely from his head while he dealt with others. He looked at me as if I was a piece of paper on his desk. 'You thought you would plot against me, did you?'

'P-plot, sir?' I stammered, in bewilderment.

A bony finger jabbed me in the back. 'My lord,' Eaton corrected me. He had been so still in a corner he had merged with the dark tapestry behind him.

Lord Stonehouse's voice was as cold as his look. 'Step forward. Look at me.'

I forced myself to look at the man who might be my real father. At that moment I cared little. I had lost any desire for a real father, particularly one who condemned you to a pit at birth.

His linen was crumpled and there were wine stains on his collar. Yet this very carelessness of dress spoke more eloquently of power than the finest clothes. His face was long and gaunt and his nose slightly hooked, like the falcon that was his symbol, and his jet black eyes had the bird's unyielding, penetrating stare. It was hard to believe this was the man whose emotional parting with his son that morning I had interrupted. His voice had the rasping harshness of another bird, a rook.

'You chose your moment well.'

I had spent the day regretting bitterly the misunderstanding, the rupture I had caused between father and son. 'I am sorry, sir,' I mumbled wretchedly, jumping as I got another prod in the back: '– my lord.'

My very abjectness goaded him to a sudden fury. I learned later that, like many strong, obdurate men, he could not abide weakness. I saw Eaton flinch, his scar curling into his cheek, for he knew what was coming. Lord Stonehouse leapt up. 'Sorry? Sorry! You will be sorry! Did you think you could come in here and pick up your inheritance like that?' He snapped his fingers in my face. 'Did you? Did you?'

Spittle struck my face. I tried to answer, but it was impossible against this violent torrent of words. He raged at me, saying he had atoned for what he did. He had clothed me. He had educated me. God knew, he could do no more! And how did I repay him? By destroying his relationship with his eldest son. Despite all their endless arguments they had always been reconciled, but now it was over, and I was the reason for the final rift. He was only stopped by a fit of coughing. He leaned against his desk, breathing heavily, taking a swallow of wine. Red veins flared on his cheeks.

'No news of Richard?'

Eaton re-emerged from the gloom of the tapestry. 'No, my lord. You were considering whether he should be arrested. Shall I –'

Lord Stonehouse flung the glass at Eaton, who only just ducked in time. 'Arrested? Arrest my son? For the only noble thing he has ever done?' Eaton wiped the dregs of wine from his face. The look of hatred he gave Lord Stonehouse's back was so savage that the ones he had given me seemed mild in comparison. Lord Stonehouse came back to me. His anger was spent, replaced by the cold remorseless look he had displayed at his desk. I preferred the violent, uncontrolled fury. I remembered the reports on me which, year after year, must have passed over that desk, pages read by these cold eyes, which I felt knew every blemish, every sin. Uncannily, he seemed to read my mind.

'When I first brought you from that slum, the first reports suggested you would be hanged. You are but a step from it now.'

'Why?'

'Why? He thinks I have to have a reason to hang him, Eaton.'

Eaton laughed. It was short-lived, for Lord Stonehouse gave him a long, cold stare before coming so close to me I could smell the wine on his breath. 'I could have you hanged as an impostor. There is no proof who you are.' His black eyes that never left my face told me he would do it, as easily as he had signed the plague order to consign me to the pit. 'Who put you up to this?' he said softly. He darted a look towards Eaton and the look of fear on the steward's face sent a shiver through me. 'Put – put me up to what?'

'You think you can walk in here and claim your inheritance, do you?'

'No, my lord! That that is not what –'

'It was deliberately planned, wasn't it?

'I don't know what –'

'Who told you my son was going to be here?'

'No one!'

'Liar!' He felt my doublet. 'The finest velvet. Who bought you this?'

Again he shot a look at Eaton. Guilt was written all over the steward's face. I saw it all then. I remembered Eaton's panic when he first saw me in the clothes. His saying to Turville they were going too far. Desperate that Richard should not inherit and ruin their rich livings, they had painted an optimistic picture of my prospects. The town house they talked about now seemed like a dream; perhaps there never were any such prospects of inheritance, apart from a fantasy in Lord Stonehouse's mind, or simply as a threat to use against his son. Eaton and Turville had plotted to sell me at the right time – and I had turned up at a spectacularly wrong one.

He fingered the doublet again. 'Who gave you this? What have they been telling you?'

The words were almost out of my mouth, but I bit them back. If I told him the truth he would be convinced I was part of a plot with Eaton and Turville. 'Nothing! I bought these clothes myself.'

I glimpsed the look of relief crossing Eaton's face. Lord Stone-house picked it up too; he read things into every nuance. 'You?' The word was loaded with disbelief and contempt. He would have got the truth out of me but for that contempt – contempt at the very idea that a miserable wretch like me could possibly earn money to afford such clothes. That riled me, for my pride was as great as his, but it was a different sort of pride; the pride of seven years of honest work and toil. The sale of my pamphlets had begun to make me more money than I had dreamed possible and I could – just – have bought the clothes.

'Yes – I earned it!' I spread out my hands. Every crevice of my hands down to the whorls of my fingers were once again engrained with ink. The work I was so proud of was beneath his contempt. And no argument would convince him once he had decided he was right. He shook me so my head rattled. I lost my temper, grabbed him by the shoulders and pushed him from me.

I felt I was at the end of a journey which had begun with my rescuing from the mud those words that were going to change the world. The words had started the process, and the army would finish it. But if this was one of the men who was leading the army, one of the Great Twelve whom Mr Pym himself deferred to, what hope was there? His words were twisted and devious. They were not the words of hope, of change, but of double meanings and despair.

He was so shocked I had dared to lay a finger on him, he gaped at me open-mouthed while words poured out of me. I told him about rescuing the words from the mud, about how I thought he was a great leader like Mr Pym, but all he was interested in was hanging a man for stealing Barbary horses and turning an honest printer out of house and home. Eaton turned away, wincing, expecting Lord Stonehouse to explode as I said all that and more. Oh, I said all kinds of twaddle, things I had picked up from Crop-Eared Jack and barely understood, but I made up for my lack of understanding with passion and belief while he stared at me as if I was a creature just dropped from the moon.

When he had got some kind of breath back he picked up a bell from his desk. Still I kept on talking, starting from the very beginning when he had picked me up in the dockyard when I had burned myself. It was him, I knew it was him, I said, when he looked about to deny it. I said everything I might have said to him if I had been brought up by him instead of his money. When two burly servants came in and seized me, the story had to be cut pamphlet size. In short, I told him, I had not come for treasure.

'Treasure?' he said, with a puzzled frown.

'I mean inheritance. I have come for this –' And I pulled out the letter he had sent Mr Black.

'Wait!' He motioned the servants to release me and took the letter. He stared at the falcon seal. I thought for a moment that it was a trick of Eaton's and he had never seen it before, but it was so unimportant to him he had forgotten it. He read it through to remind himself of it before looking up. 'You came here for this?'

'Yes, my lord.'

'Is that all?'

There was that sharpness of disbelief in his voice that set me off again, sounding like Crop-Eared Jack in his pot, saying I was the very last person to want an estate. Landowners seemed to forget that there was a Charter of the Forest as well as Magna –

'Be quiet!' he roared. He gestured towards a painting of Highpoint House. It was much larger than the one in Turville's house and, I realised, done at a much later date, for the village that straddled the river was not there; perhaps it had been removed because it spoiled the view. 'You would not have that?'

'I would not, my lord.'

'Then you are a fool.'

Riled again, and having nothing to lose I said: 'I see what problems it brings you, my lord.'

His black eyes bored into me. I felt the servants, one at either side of me, staring stiffly ahead, hands twitching at my elbows, ready to lift me away like a course at dinner. Then he grunted and smiled. It was a smile bitter as vinegar, but still a smile. 'Not, perhaps, such a fool,' he muttered. The hands of the two servants stopped twitching and returned in unison to fold behind their backs.

He looked at the letter again. 'You came here for Mr Black?'

'Yes, my lord. He has been like a father to me.'

He winced, and walked up to me, giving me a piercing look. 'Like a father?'

'Yes, my lord.'

He turned abruptly away so I could not see his face. He crumpled the letter as he walked towards the window, pieces of wax from the seal crumbling from it and pattering on the floor, leaving a little trail behind him. It was quite dark now, candles glowing in the houses opposite. A window was open but the air was thick and warm and as still as the servants guarding me. It was so quiet I could hear their breathing and the creak of their shoes as they shifted slightly. Eventually he tossed the letter on his desk and swivelled curtly to Eaton. 'You did not tell me any of this.'

Eaton came to life. 'It was all in the reports, my lord. The devil in him, the temper, the –'

'No, no, not that, Eaton, not that.' The old man walked restlessly away. Then, like a lawyer suddenly finding a flaw in a case, he pounced on me. 'But the wonderful Mr Black, like a father to you – you ran away from him!'

Triumph shone in his eyes. I was a fraud, making up a story to show what a wonderful son I was – and would be, in contrast to his own. It was a plot to get his estate from him. Plots were wrecking my life every time I tried to build it up. I was done with plots. He would see the worst in me anyway, whatever I said, so I flung the words bitterly at him: 'I ran away because your son's men tried to kill me.'

Eaton winced. He looked as if his scar had been freshly reopened. I remembered Turville saying he would not want to be the man who, without the most incontrovertible evidence, told Lord Stonehouse his son was a cold-blooded murderer. He stood quite still for a moment, then dismissed the servants, ordering them to stand outside his room. His face had the bleakness of those winter days that are never far from night. Eaton retreated into the shadows. Lord Stonehouse sat in the pool of light looking for the first time what he was, one of the most powerful men in England – or at least in that part of England opposed to the King. All my bravado left me. I began to shake and could not stop. His silence was the most awful thing, much more so than his violent, unpredictable temper, which was at least human; the measured way in which, with a key from a bunch at his waist, he unlocked and opened a drawer, had me convinced he was going to draw out a black cap.

Instead, he took out a file of papers. When he went through them, my shaking increased, although it was from a different cause. I recognised immediately Mr Black's flowing, Italianate script, of which he used to be so proud. With my printer's eye I could read upside down as well as in reverse. As Lord Stonehouse turned the pages I caught 'devil beat out of him' . . . 'Latin good, but morally' . . . 'outstanding' . . . 'if not in hell first'. They were the carefully written versions of the drafts I had seen in Mr Black's office, submitted once a quarter for the last seven years of my life. It was to this office, this desk they had come. Lord Stonehouse had made notes in the margin in a cramped, hurried scrawl. What moved me was not the notes – I could not read them – but that he had made them at all. Whatever the truth about my parentage, I realised I meant something to him and I saw him then, for the first time, as my benefactor.

Unlike the harshness with which most children were raised, the love and warmth with which Susannah brought me up made me look upon those arid pages of moral progress, or lack of it, with gratitude. They had given me an education. Without them I would never have met Anne. I could not stop my eyes filming over. He looked up as I dashed my hand quickly over my eyes and stared at me sternly, tight-lipped, expecting perhaps repentance, a confession for my part in the plot he imagined – anything but the two words that came awkwardly out of my mouth.

'Thank you,' I said.

He stared blankly at me for a moment, then gave me a glare of suspicion. 'For educating me,' I stammered. 'For giving me a chance to use words to –'

'Enough!' he said curtly. For the first time he looked uneasy, unsure of himself. Then he returned to the pages in front of him, checking dates, rapping out a series of questions about the time when the first alleged attack on me – as he put it – took place. Exactly as Eaton and Turville had warned me, he demanded proof. 'Why did you think it was my son who hired these men?'

'I didn't. I thought it was you.'

'Me?' He laughed. 'After spending all this money on you?'

It poured out then, in a strange mixture of gratitude and bitterness. I told him of the letter Eaton had sent Mr Black, warning him of the danger Richard posed to me, and that I mistakenly thought it was him, Lord Stonehouse, who had grown tired of me; that the experiment or whatever it was had failed and he was discarding me as a potter would throw away a piece flawed in the firing. When I came to the royal procession and said I thought he had ordered his son to run me down, he hammered on the desk for me to stop. 'You thought I was ordering him to kill you?'

'Yes, my lord.'

His sharp eyes darted from me to Eaton. 'I shouted to Richard to stop,' he said curtly. 'He said he did not hear me. That he feared my life was in danger.' He suddenly rounded on the steward. 'Do you believe that, Eaton?'

'It is possible Mr Richard did not hear you, my lord.'

'Possible, aye, possible! But what do you *think*, man?' Eaton was silent. I began to see how the two men fed each other's suspicions. 'Why did you not tell me any of this, Eaton?'

The question was put very softly. Again Eaton did not answer. Thin beads of sweat had collected along the line of his hair, and one trickled slowly from his forehead and down his cheek. I never thought I would feel a shred of sympathy for that crude, violent man, but it ran through me then. He was like an animal fearing a trap.

'Mr Eaton saved my life,' I said.

The effect of this on Lord Stonehouse was remarkable. I cannot explain it, except by saying that the two of them were like a man and his dog. The dog, having been brought up brutally with scarcely any acts of kindness, responds blindly to orders, always fearing that brutality might reappear at any moment, for no apparent reason. But even the most primitive relationship has a long history, and in that history there are shared experiences which force them more closely together. This seemed to be one of those moments.

'Why did you not tell me all this, man?' Stonehouse said. Now some of the pent-up tension and bitterness I always felt simmering in Eaton charged his reply. The dog was showing his teeth. 'It was one of Mr Richard's periods of reform, my lord. I feared you would not believe me.'

Lord Stonehouse met his eyes, then gave a long sigh. 'Nor would I. Nor would I. You are quite right, Eaton. I told him he had nothing to fear from this boy, but on the gallery I could see . . . he almost had his sword in him!' He gave a deep sigh, finished his wine, went to the open window again and stared out. It was so quiet I could hear a candle guttering as its wick ran out. 'Get Turville,' he said. He pointed to me. 'And get him something to eat.'

22

On the way down the stairs Eaton murmured: 'Well done! I did not know you had it in you, Tom.' He spoke as if he was already half-convinced we had plotted my entry into Queen Street together. Perhaps that would be how he described it to Turville. I pulled away from him angrily, in a state of utter confusion. I had come to this place to be open and honest, rid myself of the plot that was destroying our lives at Half Moon Court, free myself to marry Anne, only to become mired deeper. Eaton seemed to enjoy the look of hatred I gave him, treating it as a bond between us. 'That's the spirit, Tom! Turville don't trust me and I don't trust him. That's the way we get on.'

In high good humour he bullied the servants, ordered his horse and 'vittles for Mr Tom' before leaving. The two servants who had picked me up like a course at dinner looked now about to serve me it. They guided me deferentially down an oak-panelled corridor, approaching a large dining hall which contained a gleaming mahogany dining table as long as a ship. Lord Stonehouse was sitting alone at one end of it. I was almost through the doorway when the servants coughed (they did everything in unison) and steered me adroitly away. Lord Stonehouse did not notice. Besides his setting there was one more cover. He was ordering a servant to remove the silver cutlery, plate and glasses. I suppose they had been laid for Richard, in what might have been their last meal together.

After a meal of game pie with the secretary, Mr Cole, I was taken up to Lord Stonehouse's study again. His voice had resumed its curt tone.

'You are not to wear those clothes again. Is that clear?'

'Yes, my lord.'

'I will decide what station in life you occupy. Meanwhile you will dress like Mr Cole.'

I said nothing. It seemed I was right. Turville had exaggerated Lord Stonehouse's plans for me, partly to draw me away from Mr Black and Anne, partly so he could promote me at the right time as a puppet in line for the inheritance, whom he and Eaton could manipulate.

Abruptly he barked out: 'Eaton has told you about the pendant?'

It was useless to deny it. 'Yes, my lord.'

He stood up, and picked up a seal from his desk. I flinched; for a moment I thought he was going to throw it at me. Instead, he kept rapping it on his desk, punctuating his words as he spoke. He told me that, when Matthew and Susannah and – he coughed sceptically – a miracle baby had vanished from the estate, he sent Eaton to find them, but the trail was cold.

Lord Stonehouse went to the window and stared out at the dark street. Six years later, he said, after he had picked me up in the dockyard, Eaton set out again on Matthew's trail. He almost caught him when Matthew tried to sell the pendant.

Taking a candle from a sconce, he held it up to illuminate a picture hanging behind his desk. It was of his wife, Frances, painted later than the one in Turville's chambers. I learned later it had been painted shortly before she died. In one hand she held a white rose, the symbol of love. The other pointed to the falcon pendant at her breast.

'I believe it contains the secret of your birth. I will not rest until it is found. You are to find it, with Eaton's help, then I will decide what to do with you. Is that clear?'

He put back the candle and picked up the bell to dismiss me.

'I will find the pendant, but I want nothing from you,' I said. 'Apart from one thing.'

For a moment I thought he was going to throw the bell at me. 'Go on.'

'The house at Half Moon Court. And my freedom.'

'To do what? Marry old Black's daughter?' He put down the bell and roared with laughter. I thought he had no sense of humour, but there were tears of laughter in his eyes now. 'Come, come, if you are not careful I will end up liking you! You are my – whatever you are. I have made you what you are and you will do as I say. Marry a printer's daughter, indeed!'

I dug my nails into my palms as I felt my temper slipping. I preferred his anger to his laughter, which mocked everything I believed in. 'I am a printer!'

'Of course, of course.' He picked up Turville's letter to Mr Black. 'I know this was a ruse to get you in here –'

'It was no ruse!'

He gave me an incredulous look. His smile was condescending. 'You think you love this girl, do you?'

'As I believe you loved your wife, my lord.'

'Don't be impertinent!' he cried angrily.

I was about to retort that commoners could have the same passions as lords, but he had been moved in some way that stopped me. He walked up to me, round me, then seemed to forget all about me, going to the picture of his wife, muttering something I could not hear, before finally swinging round.

'Very well then. Very well. Sit.'

He pointed to a desk Mr Cole used, which had paper and ink, and instructed me to write that in exchange for the pendant Mr

Black would receive the freehold of Half Moon Court in perpetuity. He put in various legal phrases and conditions, but that was the essence of it. I was unable to determine whether he was serious, or treating the whole business as a joke, but it certainly put him in much better humour. He said my hand was far too educated to be that of a gentleman, and perhaps I was a printer after all. Mr Cole and a servant were witnessing my signature when I heard the familiar urgent drum of hooves and Eaton's shout to the stable boy.

Lord Stonehouse was in absolute control of himself again. He told the servant to send Eaton up immediately. He instructed Mr Cole to make the necessary legal arrangements to imprison Richard, where he could stay until he had reflected on his condition. He smiled at me as he said this, taking the piece of paper I had signed. I could see him using it when Richard had reflected, as the prelude to yet another reconciliation. It did not matter to him that Richard had tried to murder me. That must be a misunderstanding, exactly as my unfortunate blundering into their meeting had been. I did not care at that time. All I cared about was Anne.

'Well, well,' Lord Stonehouse said, his good humour bubbling over. 'You took your time Eaton! I have discovered this young gentleman is determined to be a printer! What is it, man? Are you hurt?'

Eaton looked as if his scar had been slashed open anew. He brushed at the blood which smeared his collar and coat. 'Not mine,' he said. 'Turville's. He's dead. The file on the pendant has gone.'

23

It seemed never to have occurred to Lord Stonehouse that the ransacking and pillaging of Royalist houses, which he had organised with such ruthless efficiency, could ever happen to him, or those he dealt with. He never thought that Richard, who time and again had come to heel, would really rebel. And it certainly never occurred to him that while all his life the law had been his exclusive property, during war there might be two laws. Or none.

As we went down to the stables, Eaton told me there was no sign of Jane or the other servants at Turville's house. It was believed they had fled. He chose a grey mare for me which, he said, with a sly look at me, was docile, for I had done only a little riding at Moorgate Fields. She almost threw me as soon as I was on her, and I told Eaton I was glad he had not chosen me a lively one. He grinned as he controlled both horses and said the best way to learn how to stay on was to be thrown a couple of times. He seemed to have recovered from the shock of Turville's death remarkably quickly, saying more than once that if this did not blacken Richard in his father's eyes, nothing would.

'We don't know it was Richard,' I said.

'Of course it was Richard!'

'Did anyone see him?'

'He knew what he was looking for,' he said shortly. 'Keep close! Keep close, damn you!'

He kept getting ahead of me and then reining his horse back impatiently. His eyes darted nervously from side to side at every alley. There was no curfew, but it felt like one, for the streets were almost empty. He told me that bands of militia had already marched north to join the Earl of Essex to form a Parliamentary army.

I told him about the agreement I had made with Lord Stonehouse. He slapped his sides with laughter and said he had never heard such a good story.

'Why, Mr Tom, I do believe you're an honest man!'

'I like to think so,' I retorted.

He touched his hat, half mocking, half deferential, and put on his country burr. 'When we gets the pendant, my lord, you shall have Half Moon Court and I shall make do with Highpoint. How's that for a game of soldiers?'

He laughed and fell into a deep, musing silence until we reached Gray's Inn, where he led me over the grass. There was the cock of a pistol, sharp as the crack of a whip in the quiet night. Eaton called out softly to the guard he had left. A constable had been sent for, but not found. It seemed the constables had gone to war as well.

The door was open and the clock in the hall was ticking, slowly, quietly. It was the only sign of normality in the chambers. Papers were strewn down the stairs. He stopped me sharply, clapping a hand over my mouth. He had not washed and his hand had the rank smell of stale blood. Although the guard had been round, Eaton was still suspicious of a trap. I thought he was being absurdly cautious, but then I heard it. There was the creak of a board, a little animal-like grunt then silence.

Eaton slipped back to the guard and took his pistol. I crept up the stairs. A thin moonlight came through the landing window, lighting up a bloody boot-print on some crumpled papers. Eaton pulled me back, and kicked open the study door.

He was swinging the pistol round at body height and did not at first see the crouching figure on the floor. As he aimed, I picked out in the darkness the shape of the cap she habitually wore and shouted a warning.

Eaton lowered his pistol. 'Damn you, Jane – I nearly shot you!'

She did not move. She was cradling something or someone, moaning softly. As I went towards her, paper clung to my boots. I touched her gently but still she did not move.

'Jane. It's me – Tom.'

Eaton lit a candle. Jane was cradling Turville's head and murmuring gently to him. Turville's right hand was half hacked off. Near it was a pistol he must have been holding. There was a great wound in his side and I realised the papers were sticking to my feet with blood. I turned away as the rich game pie I had eaten came up, burning in my throat.

'Throw it up,' said Eaton. 'You can't make more of a mess.'

He was staring down indifferently, as if he was looking at a slaughtered animal on a farm. I forced myself to swallow back the bile, kneeling down with her, putting my arm round her. Still she did not respond but kept on stroking the dead man's cheek, murmuring that she would get a doctor, he would be all right. Only when I said he needed a minister, not a doctor, did she turn to me with a sharp animal cry. I held her shaking body, but she pushed me away, lifting his head again as if she was trying to make him more comfortable, stroking and kissing him. I watched helplessly, feeling I knew nothing about life or love. With the look of surprise in his open, staring eyes and his pock-marked skin devoid of powder, he was even uglier in death than in life. He had taken her in when she had been ruined, but he had used her, and I was sure she had been severely beaten when I escaped, but from the way she held him, and continued to kiss him, you would have thought he was the kindest, most wonderful man on earth to her.

'A fine son! A credit to his father!' Eaton swung the candle round the dishevelled mounds of paper, the empty shelves, to catch sight of the picture behind Turville's desk. It had been slashed diagonally, decapitating Lord Stonehouse's figure. The cut had been made with such force that half the canvas, with Frances smiling happily, curled outwards. 'Van Dyck. In the inventory at thirty pound,' Eaton muttered.

A pile of old legal parchments cracked under his boots. He gave a sudden cry. The cut in the picture exposed the panelling behind, part of which had been pulled open. It was a cunningly concealed cupboard, which would probably have escaped notice. But the vehemence of the sword blow had cut into the woodwork behind, splintering the edge of the door, normally hidden by the panelling.

'He has got my papers!'

'What papers?'

Eaton cried he was done for now. He was like a man demented, searching among the litter of papers on the desk and floor. He kept returning to the aperture and feeling inside, although he must have known there was nothing there.

'He has me now!'

'What do you mean?'

He swivelled round, towering over me and I realised that, such was his distress over his loss, he had forgotten I was there. He forced a smile on his face as much as the scar would allow him. He pointed to the torn map on the wall.

'Listen, Tom. I have cared for that estate. Not Lord Stonehouse. Not his sons. I know every copse, every blade of grass, the people who pay and the people who don't. As a reward, Lord Stonehouse bought me some pieces near it: mean thankless pieces of land. Without those papers, I may lose them. That's all I mean. Do you understand?'

He spoke so soft, and his voice was so chilling, that all my old fear of him flooded back. He had been so indifferent about the fate of poor Turville he would think nothing of seeing me dead on the floor with him. 'Yes, yes I think so.'

'So long as you have it clear.'

'I have it clear.'

'Good. We must get after Matthew.'

'You know where Matthew is!' I cried.

'Might be. The details were on the papers Richard has taken.' He pushed me to one side, seized Jane and demanded to know what had happened, what she knew. Terrified, she would not let go of Turville, and he continued to grip her until I yelled at him.

'Leave her! You won't get anything out of her like that!'

Only then, when he saw a practical reason for a vestige of kindness, did he send his man for a minister, while I took her downstairs. The larder had been looted, but the fire was still burning and I sat her there, found a half-drunk flask of wine, mixed it with honey and warmed it over the fire. The honey came from the garden and as she smelt its familiar elderflower scent some of the vacancy left her face.

Gradually she told us what had happened. The cook saw Richard across the gardens with a small group of men demanding entry at the gate. Alarmed, she ran to tell Turville. Turville laughed at her fears – he had spent a lifetime calming that boy's rages and deflecting his demands. Nevertheless he loaded the pistol in his drawer, and sent Jane for the constable. She could not find one and, returning, saw Richard through the upstairs window shouting: 'In the King's name!' and wielding his sword. There was a violent crash and a cheer – perhaps the moment when he slashed the picture.

Terrified, she hid in the coal shed. Through the chinks in the walls she saw Richard stuff some letters into the pouch of his saddle. Like the others, he was cloaked dark. His high black riding boots bore no Cavalier tassels or lace and his wide black hat no feathers. She heard their raised voices arguing. One, whom Richard called Colonel Royce, said they must ride north immediately and join the King. Richard swore at him and said if they wanted to use Highpoint, they must ride east.

'Highpoint – east?' Eaton gripped her by the shoulders. 'Highpoint is west! East? Are you sure?'

She was sure. Like the devil, Richard turned his back on the setting sun and went east, the others following him.

Eaton tried to pull me out of the kitchen. He wanted to leave there and then and ride after Richard.

'But where?'

'Poplar! The sewer where you came from!'

'Poplar? Why?'

He was too frantic to leave to say more. He ran outside to his horse, shouting for me to follow him. When I refused to leave Jane, he threatened to go alone. I argued that they were hours ahead of us and we would make better progress in the morning. Slowly, unwillingly, he returned. He had the same look on his face as I had seen in his exchanges with Lord Stonehouse: a mixture of reluctant obedience and hate. The estates, as he had just told me, were his whole life. Some part of him still believed, or hoped, or hoped to persuade his lordship that I was a Stonehouse. I might be the key to the estates. He would not, could not, go without me.

From that moment, I must confess, I began to take some secret pleasure in this, scarcely admitted to myself. That this man, who had once carelessly ordered my death for a couple of half crowns, of whom I had lived in mortal terror since Matthew had warned me about him, should, however savagely, come to heel! It was impossible not to feel satisfaction, impossible not to act as if I was a Stonehouse. He expected it. He expected that arrogant tone, that tilt of the chin, and I found myself very gradually, over the days that followed, assuming it. At first I did it as a joke, strutting, miming my part, but as it tempered his attitude and made him easier to deal with, I almost forgot I was doing it.

I was as desperate as he was to get hold of the pendant – but to gain my freedom from the Stonehouses, not become one of them. To be free to marry Anne. I soon stopped trying to convince Eaton of this, however, because it was clear he thought it the greatest of all jokes.

Eventually a minister was found, and only then would Jane leave Turville's body. While I was comforting Jane, a message came from Lord Stonehouse instructing Eaton to meet the solicitor who would replace Turville. Muttering that he was always expected to be in two places at once, Eaton arranged to meet the solicitor the next day at a tavern near Lincoln's Inn, where we would stay after returning from Poplar.

I lifted Jane on to the back of Eaton's horse and we took her to Half Moon Court. Eaton stuck to me as close as a barnacle to a ship. I led Jane upstairs so Sarah could take care of her.

When I returned downstairs I was startled to find Eaton sitting like a ghost in Mr Black's high-backed chair. He would not leave, and when I told him I was sleeping on the floor, proposed to join me, saying the boards were damned comfortable compared to some places he had slept. When he saw the expression on my face he clapped me on the back and laughed. 'Don't worry, Mr Tom, I won't murder you in your sleep – you're far too valuable!'

He folded his coat up as a pillow and did indeed look as comfortable as if he was on a feather bed, seemed in fact to greet the floor as an old friend. Falling asleep is a strange time. People tell you things they would never say in the daylight. He told me he was a foundling brought up by the parish. A mouth nobody wanted. He ran away, sleeping in hedges, barns and stables. He poached and stole in every corner of Lord Stonehouse's estate. He was whipped by Lord Stonehouse and sent back to the parish. He ran away again and was caught tearing a hare from the jaws of the hounds before the hunters reached the pack. This time he was whipped so severely his cheek was cut open. It festered and left a permanent scar. Lord Stonehouse loathed poachers, but he was intrigued by this wild animal who could swoop on a partridge with the silence of a hawk, who seemed to know the courses of every hare, and, more importantly, every poacher. He was at first tolerated, then used for the information he gave, then employed as stable boy.

Eaton's eyes closed and he curled up like an animal, instantly asleep. It was a long time before I followed him as, in the semi-darkness, I watched his scar rise and fall.

24

In the shock and confusion at Half Moon Court early next morning at Eaton's presence – not to mention Jane, who upset Sarah by rising first and lighting the fire – Eaton said there had been a great misunderstanding and we had come to an agreement. Though the nature of that agreement was not made clear, Mr Black was beside himself with joy, and seized Eaton's hand.

I had kept my word to Lord Stonehouse and taken off the gentleman's clothes, with a strange mixture of regret and relief. I could see that, in Eaton's eyes, by removing the clothes I had removed some of the veneer of a Stonehouse. There was a sarcastic twitch to Eaton's smile when he saw me in my army buff jerkin and breeches. It was as if I had been demoted to the ranks. He had a ribald, if repetitive sense of humour I had never suspected, and kept ordering me to 'make ready . . . present . . . fire!'

He saddled my horse on one side of the apple tree, while Anne came to say goodbye on the other. The weather was changing, and the first leaves were beginning to drop. She kicked at a small pile of them, and wanted to know why I had changed my clothes.

'Because I'm in the army.'

'Then why aren't you with Will and the rest of the unit?'

I felt there was too much to tell her in too little time. Well, that is not quite true. For some reason I felt uneasy about telling her of the strange meeting with Lord Stonehouse. To be back in Half Moon Court was to breathe a different atmosphere. Washing in the pail in the yard as I had always done. Changing in the print shop where the very smell of the ink was pure fresh air to me. And above all there was Anne's expression of sheer delight when she saw me.

'Why are you going off with *him*?' she whispered, with a sidelong glance at Eaton. 'Are you going to look for the pendant?'

I laughed. That summer I had told her everything I had learned at Turville's. But then I had dismissed it as a fantasy, a piece of trickery dreamed up by Turville and Eaton, which in part it was. The pendant, and the Stonehouses themselves, seemed like a story in a pamphlet. Now it was real, I felt strangely uneasy about telling her. And I felt Eaton's mocking eyes on me while he tightened the girths on the horse. I knew what he was thinking – what a great joke it was that I would ever give up the possibility of a great position, and one of the largest estates in England for her.

'It's an army mission,' I said. 'I'm not allowed to tell you.'

'You're a terrible liar, Tom! My lord.' She gave me a mocking little bow. The smell of damask roses intoxicated me as she came right up to me, whispering in my ear. 'Tell me. Tell me the truth.'

Branches rustled as Eaton picked a couple of apples from the tree. I broke away from her. 'I've told you!'

'Touch the tree!' she demanded.

It was a game we used to play in our brief childhood together, before Eaton had warned Mr Black to keep us apart. Once you touched the tree, you were solemnly swearing you told the truth. Irritated, I moved to put my foot in the stirrup.

She gave a cry, 'Don't leave like this, Tom!' and grabbed at my arm. I fell backwards, almost knocking her over, and we were in each other's arms. 'I'll always love you, whatever happens,' she said.

I kissed her. 'I'll always love you, whatever happens,' I said.

I touched the tree, and she put her hand on mine. Eaton whistled softly as he held my horse for me to mount.

Rain in the night had washed away some of the stink, and there were bursts of patchy sunshine as we cantered down Aldersgate. I felt a sudden surge of happiness. I had no idea what was going to happen on the road ahead and I did not care, for I felt I had the answer to everything. I did not even care about words changing the world at that moment. There was one thing that did not need changing. Would never change. I saw love everywhere: in a mother comforting a crying child, in a man bantering a girl selling apples, even in an old man and woman bickering as they might have done for years. The grey mare seemed to pick up my mood, her restlessness going as I patted her.

'Have you fucked the girl?'

I pretended not to hear Eaton, urging the mare forward, but Eaton overtook me with accomplished smoothness. His scar did its twisting smile, disappearing momentarily in his cheek. 'I thought not. I knew a woman like that.'

I stared at him in astonishment. He had never before displayed feelings for any creature, least of all women. 'Proud,' he went on, his lips tightening, staring ahead of him. 'Wants you and no one else. Wants you, aye, and that's very good, but that type wants you like a man wants a woman and that's bad, very bad. Unnatural.' He dropped to a walking pace as a troop of militia crossed Lothbury, flying a standard: *God is with us – who can be Againste us?*

'You're right not to tell her what's going on. But don't make the mistake of not having her, Mr Tom. She's as ripe as the apples on that tree. Don't leave it too late. Pluck her now – before she knows she can't marry you.' He gave me a lascivious grin.

He disgusted me. I was no Puritan. If Luke or Will had said such a thing it would have been different. But it was as if he had taken my mood of hope and love and trampled it in the filth that the horses were throwing up round our boots. I kicked the mare viciously, unleashing an unexpected burst of power in the startled horse that had been as placid as I was a second ago.

A couple of straggling soldiers dived for the wall as the horse abruptly careered towards them. I bounced in the saddle, slipped, half lost the reins, just managing to retrieve them as she went at terrifying speed round the corner into Broad Street, straight towards some market stalls. I shut my eyes. She seemed determined to vault them but veered at the last moment. A woman screamed. Children cheered, shouted 'Runaway!' and threw vegetables.

Round the next corner I was flung one way, then the other. I lost one stirrup then the reins again. Approaching me was a Hackney hell-cart. Its brakes screeched, on and on. The driver was one obscene yelling mouth. I grabbed at the saddle. I was slipping off. The cobbles were rushing up to meet me. A hand gripped me and thrust me back into my saddle. Then it grabbed at my horse's reins and yanked her to one side of the hell-cart. There was not enough room to pass, and Eaton pulled down the rearing horse and quietened it. The hell-cart driver got off his horse shouting. Eaton gave him one look, and he went away muttering. He turned to me, his voice shaking.

'Don't you ever do that again!' he said.

I had not a breath to respond with, and scarcely the energy to hang my head. I hope I was never as hard and cruel with a horse as Eaton was, but it was Eaton who taught me how to control a horse on that ride to Poplar. I lost count of the number of times he shouted to me to keep my toes out and my knees in, until I was doing that unaccountable thing, rising and falling with her, becoming at moments one creature, as if I had her legs, her power. She had a white blaze on her forehead and I began calling her Patch – an obvious name which perhaps the stable boy used, for she immediately responded to it. After our escape from the hell-cart, I felt we were not just horse and rider but companions.

There is a bleak, lonely stretch of marsh just before Poplar. We were going at what I thought was a gallop when Eaton suddenly, with no warning, took his whip to his horse and streaked away. Patch jerked after him, almost leaving me behind. I lost everything Eaton had taught me and clung on. Then somehow the horses seemed to draw closer. My hat went. My hair streamed. I saw his glance of surprise over his shoulder as I began to gain on him. I took my whip to Patch. Eaton had released the childhood wildness I had in Poplar. Yelling and whooping, I was as savage as he was. We were neck and neck before he slowly pulled away again, finishing a length in front.

He grinned. 'That's it. Give her the whip. Show her who's master.' He took an apple he had picked at Half Moon Court and bit into it. 'Just ripe.' He held it out to me. I shook my head and would not look at him. He ate the apple as he ate all food, as if he never knew where the next meal was coming from, laughing from time to time, but I finished the journey in stubborn silence.

Eaton had so little trust in anyone that he disclosed only the bare minimum, and only when he had to. It was not until we were nearly in Poplar that he told me what was in the file on Matthew that Richard had stolen. Matthew had been traced to the Oxford area where he eked out a living as a cunning man. Lord Stonehouse's intelligence network had intercepted two letters addressed to K. B. J. Ingram, minister at St Dunstan's Without, because they were sent from Oxford, a Royalist stronghold. They were thought to concern jewellery smuggled from London for the Royalist cause until Lord Stonehouse saw them and realised they referred to the pendant.

One letter, as Eaton remembered it, said the pendant could not be destroyed, for there were 'forces against it'. It was signed with a red cross.

'Matthew's signature,' I said, remembering his grisly humour of signing his name with a plague cross. 'But why is he writing to Mr Ingram about the pendant?'

'He's not. He's writing to KB, who is at Mr Ingram's.'

'KB?'

'Kate Beaumann.'

'Kate – the woman who was my mother's companion?'

'Just so,' he said. 'Just so.'

And now he, in his turn, rode on in silence.

25

I took him the marsh way, round the back of St Dunstan's. On Susannah's grave there was a pot of fresh wildflowers, primula and bog iris. I was about to dismount but Eaton gripped my arm and pointed towards the row of almshouses. He had the keenest sight of anyone I ever knew. I could see nothing untoward. The almshouses looked calm and peaceful. But it was unusual that no one was about. Our horses picked their way between the graves. Descending towards the almshouses, I saw what Eaton had picked up in the distance: churned-up earth under some trees where a group of horses had been tethered overnight.

The door to the main almshouse, where Mr Ingram lived, was ajar. Eaton shoved the door fully open with the toe of his boot. The hallway was a mess of muddy footprints. He gestured me to stay still, ducking his ear to listen. I could hear nothing but the constant sough of the wind over the marsh. There was a small office where Mr Ingram saw parishioners. Papers were scattered about, and coats were in a tumbled pile in a small cloakroom.

As we approached his living room, I caught a sour smell which brought back the burning of my mother's house. Before Eaton could stop me, I pulled away from him and ran into the living room. Some books were scattered on the floor but otherwise everything was in order. Then I looked through into the bedroom. Sprawled out, arm hanging over the side of a simple box bed, was John Ingram. Eaton pushed me to one side and put his ear to Ingram's mouth.

'At least they left him alive,' he said. He pulled down the coverlets. I turned away. If getting the pendant meant this, I wanted none of it. 'Come on – lift him! If you've not seen worse than this, you're a lucky man!'

Ingram was clad in the coarse linen shirt he habitually wore. Beneath it he was naked. There were burn marks on the soles of his feet, his ankles and up the inside of his legs. He had wet himself and the sour tang of it mingled with the smell of the burned flesh that clung to him. Eaton seemed unmoved by this horror. But his desperate need for information was of much more use to poor Mr Ingram than my pity. We stripped the bed and turned the mattress. As we did so my foot kicked against a poker. It had been dropped while hot, for the floor where I picked it up was charred. While I looked for fresh coverlets, my boots crunched over dead coals and ash. The sound opened Mr Ingram's eyes. He gazed at us in terror, and Eaton pulled me in front of him. 'Talk to him – he don't want to see an ugly brute like me!'

I tried, but he did not seem to recognise me, twisting away, muttering that he had told us everything he knew, until his eyes closed and he drifted off again. Maybe, in my buff jerkin, I looked too similar to the men who had tortured him. I went into the kitchen to find something to give him. It was a large one, with a baker's oven, since it served all the almshouses. I opened a cupboard. From it came a powerful smell of spice, but there was little in there apart from a yellow powder. I wished I could remember what herbs Matthew would have used for those dreadful burns. I opened the pantry and started back as I saw a ghost-like figure. The figure gave a cry as I pulled out my knife and I realised, just in time, who it was.

'Mother Banks!'

Flour was stored in the pantry, and she had knocked over a sack of it in her hurry to hide, terrified the men had returned. I went to hug her but she backed away, her terror unabated. 'It's me – Tom!'

'I know who you are.'

'I thought you were a ghost!'

'I thought you would make me one,' she retorted bitterly.

She was cold and distant, quite unlike the last time I had seen her, when she had comforted me after Susannah's death. She kept looking at me as if I was a stranger and when she saw Eaton I had to beg her to stay. I thought at first it was my uniform which she associated with the men who had come, but then, with a sinking heart, realised what it was. She was avoiding me just as Anne had avoided me, years ago, when Eaton had told her I was a plague child. She would not touch me, or even come near me. When I did, her lips moved in silent prayer. I was a creature of ill-omen. First I brought death to Susannah. Now this.

I persuaded Eaton to leave her while she treated John Ingram, making a salve of herbs, soap and oil of roses, mixed with egg white. Eaton went through some papers in the office, but found nothing.

I put some order into the little cloakroom, picking up a hat, crushed by the imprint of a muddy boot. It was a stove hat, most unlike anything Mr Ingram ever wore. Near it was a woman's grey cloak. It was short, very short. Kate Beaumann must have left in a hurry to leave this here. Perhaps she saw the men arrive and fled. Idly, I dropped the hat on my head, looked at myself in a mirror, and was still. Then I put the cloak round my shoulders. It was exactly what I had believed a will o' the wisp or a witch would wear. Exactly the shape I had seen as a child, disappearing into the swirling mist, when I had tried to see who was delivering my cake.

I went back into the kitchen and sniffed at the spice and the saffron-coloured flour. It was not September yet, but it was all there – all the ingredients to bake a simnel cake.

'Maybe Mr Ingram told them nothing,' I said, when I returned to Eaton.

'Oh, he did, he did.'

'How do you know?'

'Because they stopped. We shall have to give him some of the same medicine.' He rattled the fire irons in the grate. John Ingram started up, syrup dribbling down his chin.

'No!' I cried.

'I was joking!'

I was not so sure he was. He claimed he had a conscience as much as the next man, and only meant to show the irons to him. Where was the harm in that? It would make him cough, and save us a deal of trouble. I warned him that if he so much as touched him I would go and he would get no further help from me. He was like a boiling pot being taken from the heat to be reduced to a slow, bubbling simmer.

He touched his hat. 'Very good, very good, my lord. We are to do this the straight and honest way?'

'Yes.'

'Very good. What, er, precisely is that way?'

'I will think of something.'

'How long will that take?'

'I don't know.'

He tipped his hat, scratched his head and smiled. 'Very good. Meanwhile Richard might be torturing Matthew, who brought you up like a loving father. Then finding and destroying the pendant.'

I turned away, but with his long stride he overtook me as I reached the door. 'Such are the consequences of the honest, straightforward way, my lord. Just so we understand one another.'

His scar beat like a pulse, hypnotising me. I feared him much more when his temper was controlled and his eyes held that curious smile, for it was as if he was looking into my very soul, and he saw things there I did not know, things I did not want to know. He glanced at Ingram, who was dozing, Mother Banks gently wiping syrup from his lips. He brought his lips to my ear. 'If you want the pendant, we are going to have to do worse things than this.'

I ran outside. Wind rippled the marsh grass, like waves in the sea. It carried the first drops of rain and in it what I had always imagined to be the will o' the wisps' voices. The rain was falling faster, streaming down the windows through which I could see piles of prayer books on the sill. I went into the office, and there it was. The cover was coming away from the spine. It was smaller and lighter than I remembered, when I had first learned to read from it. Eaton's sardonic smile deepened when he saw it.

Ingram was asleep, or pretending to be. Mother Banks looked at me warily, but the prayer stopped on her lips when she saw the Bible. Perhaps she still believed the words had come to a child who could not read. Eaton, I am sure, knew the story. I struggled to ignore him as I opened the book and found the familiar page.

'I am the good shepherd . . .'

'The miracle child returns.' There was no mistaking the sarcasm in John Ingram's voice. His eyes were still closed. A speck of syrup gleamed on his lips.

I remembered the joy on Susannah's face. She believed. She made it a miracle. Miracles were what you believed. 'The good shepherd lays down his life for his sheep –'

'Whereas the hireling abandons the sheep.' Ingram opened his eyes, giving me a steady, accusing stare, licking the globule of syrup from his lips.

'Only if you do not help us,' I said.

'Help you! When you have brought the wolf with you?'

'He is not in the fold. I will keep him out! I swear it.' He turned his face away. 'Kate Beaumann baked a simnel cake here, didn't she?' I said.

There was a long pause, with only the sound of the drumming rain. A slow smile flickered across Mr Ingram's face. Eaton crept away, and hunched over the dead fire.

'Every Michaelmas,' Mr Ingram said. 'She made me swear not to tell you, but as you now know . . .' He stared out of the rain-streaked window. 'Every Michaelmas. I told her it was the wrong time of year, it was a resurrection cake for Easter, but she used to smile and say, "That's right, Mr Ingram. A resurrection."'

The wind blew in gusts now, throwing rain against the window, as Ingram told us how a plague cart arrived in Poplar seventeen years ago. A plague cart.

Three people and a baby. In a plague cart! Crouched in the grate, Eaton stared at the streaming window, as if he could see the cart arriving. It was weather like this, Ingram told us. Winter early. Their cart would have been turned away, but one of the occupants, although she was dressed like Matthew and Susannah, had the voice of a lady. And she had a letter from Mr Stevens, minister at Upper Vale, near Highpoint, where he, Ingram, had once been curate.

Eaton swore softly. 'I thought I'd seen you before.'

Ingram's fear of him seemed to have gone. Rather, it was Eaton who appeared to grow fearful of what he might say, yet increasingly eager to hear it. Shadwell had no love for Lord Stonehouse, Ingram went on. There had been some scandal at Highpoint House, after which Shadwell was evicted from his living. The lady, Kate Beaumann – she gave her name then as Mrs Turner – said in the turmoil that followed the scandal she also lost her place. Lord Stonehouse had called in loans and forced the sale of the small estate where she held a position. It was given to his steward, for his services during the scandal.

Eaton shook his head violently. He sprang up. 'That's not true! I –' He clenched his fists but seemed more liable to do damage to himself than Ingram, flailing his hand against his side.

The first years she was here, Ingram said, she was a tortured woman. She said her connection with the child, and who she said were his parents, must never be revealed, for it would be a danger to him and to her. In the church she made long prayers of penitence for some unmentionable sin about which she said she could only unburden herself to God.

'After you went to London, Tom,' he said, 'she used to take the cake to London and stay with a lady there. When the men came yesterday she was on her way to tend Susannah's grave. She must have seen them and fled.'

'Why did she write to tell Matthew to destroy the pendant?' Eaton asked.

Ingram looked at him steadily. 'She said it was evil.'

Eaton swore under his breath. 'You said nothing to Richard Stonehouse about Kate Beaumann?'

'Nothing.'

'Thank God. What *did* you tell him?'

'Where letters to Matthew were sent: for collection at the Blue Boar, Oxford.'

While Eaton ran out to see to the horses I said goodbye to Mr Ingram. He pulled me close. 'Do not tell him, but once I saw the seal on a letter from the woman she stays with in London. She is the Countess of Carlisle in Bedford Square. Kate may have fled there first.'

Eaton rode hard. For the first few miles he did not seem to care whether I kept up with him or not. Then, as the horses tired, with the thick mud splashed up to their manes, he preserved a sullen silence.

'That's the first time I've heard God on your lips,' I said. He looked at me, startled. 'You said thank God Richard did not know about Kate Beaumann.'

'Did I?'

He dug his spurs viciously into his horse's flanks, driving it into a gallop, which only ended as we approached Aldgate. There had been talk of fortifying and trenching the main entrances to London. Nothing had been done, partly because the City feared that trade, disrupted already, would be stopped altogether. But there was an increased guard that held us up while they checked our business, to Eaton's increasing irritation. When we were through he looked as if he would resort to silence, but he twisted in his saddle, his eyes like fresh wounds as he looked at me. His words, the self-derisive ring in his voice, remain with me, livid as his scar.

'Before you were born that night, I had asked her to marry me.'

26

Eaton had arranged to meet Turville's replacement at the Seven Stars in Carey Street, an inn patronised by lawyers who dealt with litigation and debt. We reached it by early evening, Eaton sending a dispatch to Lord Stonehouse, saying we would leave at dawn next morning for Oxford. He said no more after his confession – for that is what it sounded like. I do not know if I was more astonished by what he told me, or by his manner of telling it. For a moment he was full of remorse and regret. I never before saw him regret anything, unless it was measured in acres and rents.

I closed my hand round my lucky half crown, which I kept in my jerkin pocket. Whether I was right to regard it as lucky, I still did not know. Whatever had happened on the evening when I was born had spread ill-luck and remorse in an ever-widening circle of people, like a stone thrown into a pool.

While Eaton met the lawyer, I went across Covent Garden to the Countess of Carlisle's house in Bedford Square, where Mr Ingram had told me Kate Beaumann might have fled.

As I walked up the steps, I felt like a small boy again, sent round the back to wait by the shit heap for replies to messages. It was my old persecutor, Jenkins, who answered the door. Determined to burst my way in, I had my foot ready to jam the door, but he opened it with a flourish. Not a muscle of his face moved as I stumbled forward in astonishment. He bowed to me.

'They are expecting you, sir.'

They? Expecting me? He took me upstairs under a ceiling elaborately moulded with floral and leafy scrolls, before leading me into a panelled salon. Perhaps it was Lucy Hay's sense of humour, but on one side were portraits of King Charles and his party, by Van Dyck, and on the other somewhat cheaper pictures by Lely of Bedford, Stonehouse and other lords who supported Parliament. Jenkins announced me, with a good deal of relish and even more ambiguity as the 'gentleman you are expecting, my lady'. The Countess was seated in what looked to me like a throne at first glance, but was merely an upholstered chair with elaborate gilt arms. The magpie pendant she had worn in the coach sparkled at her breast. She indicated a chair, but I thought she was giving me her hand to kiss and bent forward.

'Oh, don't be a fool,' she said, irritably. She talked as she had done in the coach, as if there was no time to waste. 'Sit down. You got my letter?'

'No.'

She had sent it to Half Moon Court. A letter with the Countess's seal must have caused a sensation there. I could imagine Mrs Black snatching it from Sarah's greasy hands, holding it up to the light, and putting it prominently on the chimney piece where any visitor might see it. I was so hypnotised by this thought I did not at first realise there was someone else in the room. With his trim beard he looked so like a life-size version of the battered woodblock we had printed with the Grand Remonstrance, I was not sure until he spoke that he was real.

'Now we shall be in his scandal sheets, Lucy!' he said, then when I stood there tongue-tied: 'You look as if you've seen a ghost.'

'I – I was expecting someone else, Mr Pym.'

'The King, perhaps?' He roared with laughter, and pointed to Lucy Hay. 'I wouldn't put anything past her.'

'A – a lady called Kate Beaumann,' I stammered. 'I thought she might be here.'

'I wish she was,' Lucy said, then to Mr Pym: 'This is –'

'Oh, I know who he is.' Unlike his thunderous speeches in the House, his voice had the soft burr of Somerset, where he came from. He took my hand. 'The man who mangles my prose, smuggles me out of the House . . . Thomas Neave – or should I say Stonehouse?'

'Neave, sir.'

'Well, well, we shall see.'

He looked at Lucy. She unclasped the pendant, holding it before a candle. It dazzled me as much as the other, but in a mischievously wicked rather than a menacing way. The magpie had a little cluster of tiny pearls in its enamelled nest, perhaps symbolic of the gossip she picked up in one place and flew with to another, the gossip that had saved Mr Pym.

She pressed a garnet on one side of the nest, held it down, then pressed its fellow on the other side. I sprang back instinctively as the magpie flew towards me. Inside, I glimpsed the portrait of a man, but she was too swift to close it before I could see who it was.

'Ah,' said Mr Pym. 'Now we shall never know where her heart lies.'

Lucy told me she had been presented at court the same day as Frances Stonehouse. They had become friends and ordered the same style of pendant from an Italian jeweller. Through Frances, Lucy came to know Kate Beaumann, who lived on the neighbouring estate. She knew my story through Kate, who believed Frances's pendant was lost. Matthew had told her, when they first came to Poplar, he had never seen it.

'Kate only found out recently that Matthew was lying,' Lucy Hay said.

'Because I told you –' I burst out. 'In the coach! I didn't mean to but –'

'The boy's sharp,' Mr Pym said. 'You're right, as usual, Lucy. He may do.'

'Do?' I said.

He waved my question away. 'Lord Stonehouse has told you to find the pendant?'

'Yes. He –'

'We know he's considering you for the inheritance. We have our intelligence too. But Lord Stonehouse is . . . changeable. And he is not well. We cannot afford the inheritance to go to either of the two brothers – the enormous power and influence of the Stonehouse name going to the King!'

He was standing, making a speech now, his voice sonorous. I was even more dazzled than I was by the pendants. Enormous power and influence . . . Stupidly, I had never considered this. I was a person who ran with speeches, or copied them, or set them in type. Not a person who made them. He paused, standing directly in front of me. His voice rapped out.

'Suppose you do inherit? Will you support us?'

My throat was so dry with excitement it was a moment before I could speak. 'Yes, Mr Pym,' I said. 'I would do anything for you.'

'Good! Good!' He squeezed my arm with a politician's certainty, as if everything was settled, the pendant found and the inheritance secured.

'Suppose,' said Lucy Hay drily, 'he is not a Stonehouse?'

She had a remarkable capacity for bringing him down to earth, but he had an equally remarkable capacity for leaving it. Politics, for him, was just as much a question of belief as religion.

'Look at him,' he said. They both walked round me, gazing at me from different angles, as if I was a marble statue. 'Look at the nose. The chin.'

Lucy Hay tilted it. Her hand was warm, and she left a heavy smell of musk and sweet marjoram clinging round me as she moved away. 'I admit everything looks Stonehouse, except for the dreadful hair, which is that of his mongrel mother but –'

'He's not only a Stonehouse, he's the old man's child,' Pym said decisively.

'You just want him to be! How can you possibly know that?'

'Because when I was at Highpoint I got lost and found myself in the wing he kept unchanged since his wife Frances died. I went into her old bedroom. Hanging there was a portrait of, er . . . this fellow, youth –'

He had forgotten my name. 'Tom,' she said.

'Tom, I know he's Tom,' Pym said irritably. 'Tom, painted when he was about –'

'Twelve,' I said. 'By Peter Lely.'

He jumped a little, as if a statue had spoken. 'You know Sir Peter?'

'Only as a model.' I told them about the trick, my errand to the Guildhall, by which he had sketched me.

'How were you dressed?'

'As an apprentice.'

'You see!' Pym turned triumphantly to Lucy. 'Lely painted him in the height of fashion. Highpoint in the background. Dog at his feet. Lace dripping from his collar, from his funnelled boots. Plumed hat hiding completely his red hair. Gloved hands holding a little cane. Did you ever have such clothes?'

'Only in my dreams,' I said.

Only in my dreams! It was not until I left, dazed, still in a trance, that I remembered the contract I had signed with Lord Stonehouse. I did not want to be Lord Stonehouse. I wanted Anne. And, at that moment I wanted her so badly I almost went to Half Moon Court. Almost.

It was dark when I got back to the Seven Stars. Eaton was beside himself, thinking I, like Kate had disappeared. He assumed I had been to see Anne, and I did not disabuse him. He was very drunk and I was about to go to the room that he had booked upstairs when two late travellers, a man and a woman passed. Eaton's eyes followed the woman. So did mine. She was wearing a cloak, and was about the same height as my will o' the wisp, and moved with the same quick grace. But when she turned to address her companion I saw she was far too young to be Kate Beaumann. That shape, that gliding grace had compelled me to strain to try and catch a glimpse of her face. Eaton had exactly the same, hungry compulsion, and at the same moment that each of us felt a small, irrational tug of disappointment, our eyes met. We turned sharply away from one another, like two men discovering they have the same secret vice. And it was that discovery, as much, or more than the drink, that started him to talk.

He sat so close to the fire, his boots began to singe. He never looked at me. It was as if he was talking to himself, unpicking a long-crusted-over scab. As Lord Stonehouse's scavenger he told me – or told the fire – he was hated throughout the vast estate, from Edgehill in the east to Grey Horse in the west. He relished it. It made his job easier. Fear was a great inducement for people to pay their rents. Labourers and even some of the richer yeomen threatened unruly children that the black horseman would get them. He enjoyed hearing them scream and run to hide as he approached a farm. He had no use for company, living alone in the steward's lodge.

One day he was at Earl Staynton, on the fringe of the Stonehouse lands and the Pearce estate, where Margaret Pearce lived with her sick father and her companion, Kate Beaumann. The Pearces were an old family that had once had a greater estate than Lord Stonehouse, but had fallen into decline. Poachers went unchecked in Rowan Wood, whose ownership was disputed between the two estates. Eaton set traps for them. He nearly caught a poacher running away, but in his eagerness to get him ran into his own trap.

The iron teeth bit through the leather of his boot. At first he was more enraged by missing the poacher than the pain, until he realised he could not reach the teeth and was losing blood. It was Kate Beaumann, walking on the edge of the Pearce estate, who heard what were more his savage oaths than cries for help.

The pain was excruciating when Kate found him and he was near to fainting, which he had never done in his life before. He thought it was misfortune upon misfortune when he saw it was a woman, but she took the pinion out as he directed her, then, with a stout piece of wood, managed to prise the jaws apart.

He was over a month recovering, during which she visited him with Margaret Pearce. He was surly and ungrateful – he had no language with which to express gratitude. But when he returned to work he suggested to Lord Stonehouse that Rowan Wood should be divided between the two estates. Margaret Pearce's father died. For the first time there was a period of peace between the two families, Margaret's friendship developing with Lord Stonehouse and his two sons.

Water had always been a problem on the neglected Pearce estate. It was Kate who came to Eaton for advice about a spring that had stopped flowing. Limping away from her – for a bone had been broken and was proving slow to heal – he sneered that he had always known she expected payment for freeing him from the trap. Her reply was to bring him a salve for his foot from Matthew Neave, the driver of the plague cart, known to be a cunning man with a gift for herbal cures. When his foot was strong enough, Eaton went up to the hills above Earl Staynton, found the fall of rocks that had blocked the spring, and freed it.

When Kate came to thank him, he denied all knowledge of it. From that moment their relationship, although he did not call it that, grew. One day, during the summer of 1625, that terrible summer when the sun beat down from a copper sky and the plague spread through Oxford, she asked him if he knew a minister who would perform a marriage outside the parish. Eaton was the holder of many secrets, which was precisely why she asked him, but they were all ones he had prised out of people. Never before had anyone, certainly not anyone like Kate, entrusted him with anything like this.

His first thought was that it concerned Margaret, but Kate denied this. In any case, now Margaret's father was dead no one had any hold over her. Kate said the information was for a friend. Suspicious of everything, Eaton investigated that. He could discover no such friend. Then it dawned on him that the friend might be himself. He laughed at the idea. She would as soon marry his dog! And he had never felt the slightest desire to marry anyone. But, usually a heavy sleeper, he found he could not sleep. He kept seeing her plain, almost placid face, usually with a smile on it, whatever insults or grunts he threw at her.

He had no illusions about himself. He was rough and uncouth, but he had acquired money, property. He began to wash and dress more like the prosperous man he was. He told her that the Reverend Mark Stevens in Upper Vale was in debt and would carry out the service she required, no questions asked. She was grateful but nothing more was said. Their dealings were like this. A request was made in the guise of a remark, which the other picked up without further discussion.

Now he was convinced Kate was going to marry someone else, and was desperate to keep it from Margaret Pearce, who relied on her so much she would put every obstacle in her way. Yes, that must be it! He had been a fool to think she would even look at him! But he was tortured by his feelings for her. He had to know the truth. But though he struggled dozens of times to talk to her about it, the words would not come. He could talk about dogs. Hawks. Scheming, lying tenants. But love . . .

It was the first, and I think the only time I heard the word on his lips. I do not know whether I was more surprised by that or by the eye nearest to me gleaming wet in the guttering candlelight. The fire was low, ash softly clinking in the hearth. From the distant stables a horse whinnied as the doors were closed for the night.

It was Margaret Pearce who brought it out into the open. Seeing the change in Eaton, she said that he must have a secret love. Nobody but Margaret Pearce could talk to him – or Lord Stonehouse – like that. She was so beautiful, said it with such grave concern, without a glance to Kate, that he fled. Kate followed him and in an agony of confusion his feelings came out. He nearly fled again, but she stopped him. She said she was complimented, and he had many qualities that he was denying to himself. She needed time to think about what he had said. He did not know what she meant by qualities, or how he could deny something to himself if he really wanted it. But he was overwhelmed that she had not dismissed him out of hand.

He was silent for a long time, staring into the dying, softly settling fire. The candle had gone out and I was in a pool of darkness. I felt like an intruder, hunched on a stool, legs stiff from riding all day, until the cramp cried out in them and I was forced to move. He looked round startled, as if he had completely forgotten I was there. Frightened he would not finish the story, I said: 'What happened?'

He glared at me. 'You happened! All hell broke loose in the big house. Your bitch of a mother had you! Where the hell you came from, I don't know. What happened? I don't *know* what happened! That's the worst thing. All these years . . . I never spoke to Kate again. I never saw her. I never held her. I never even touched her. That's the worst thing!'

He lashed out with his boot at the fire, scattering the glowing embers into the hearth and went blindly away, knocking over a chair.

I slept little. His torment started a similar turmoil in my head as I tossed and turned. I was leaving Anne and I might never see her again. I could not believe I had so lightly agreed to Pym's plan. Oh yes, I would be Lord Stonehouse. The great peer! The peer of the people. Solving the nation's problems. Previously, if I ever thought about it, it was a fancy. But Pym was at the centre of power. It was no longer an idea, a fantasy, but a real possibility.

I buried my head in my pillow. What had I said? If I became a peer, I could never marry Anne. I scratched at a particularly virulent bed bug that they probably reserved for the lawyers who frequented this place, which seemed to be burying its way inside me like these poisonous thoughts. I felt her last kiss, saw her standing by the tree.

Promise me you'll come back. Touch the tree. I had such a burning, overwhelming desire for her I sprang out of bed. I felt someone watching me. For a moment I thought in my half-sleep it was Kate, who, although I had largely been unaware of it, had been watching me all my life.

But in a room that was eerie with moonlight, it was not Kate but Eaton, still on a window seat. I had no idea how long he had been there. Perhaps I had been talking in my sleep, and he had been listening to me as I had been listening to him by the fireside. Whatever else we were to one another, we were linked by a common bond. We knew that we would never rest until we found that pendant, and discover what had led up to that night, seventeen years ago.

All he said was: 'There's light enough.'

He had packed our saddle bags. He kicked the stable boy awake and we rode through the moonlit streets, empty and silent but for the occasional night watchman calling the time, and found our way on to the road west.

PART TWO

Highpoint

September–October 1642

27

We were out of London and beyond Chiswick village before dawn. As the sun rose over green fields my spirits lifted with every breath of good air. Lord Stonehouse had replied to Eaton's dispatch, instructing him to use Highpoint House as a base for the search for Matthew. The house was at a strategic point north of Oxford and Lord Stonehouse wrote that he had ordered Will's militia unit to meet us at Chipping Norton, thirty miles from Highpoint. This, Lord Stonehouse wrote 'woulde meete both the purpose of Parliament, and my owne desired purpose to find the pendante'.

The King was thought to be 'cominge down confidently from Shrewsbury,' Lord Stonehouse wrote, to march on London. The Earl of Essex, the Parliamentary commander, had left London on 9 September to an enormous citizens' send off, with earnest prayers and great applause, and orders to capture the King. Once he was out of the hands of his evil advisers, he would see the wisdom of Parliament's measures and there would be peace and prosperity in the kingdom.

And what a kingdom! I had never before been in the country. Poplar, I now realised, with its High Street of timber-framed houses and narrow, gabled fronts and bleak marsh was without, not country. I gazed with awe at field after rolling field where stubble was being burnt, and soil turned before the winter frosts, at a deer – Eaton had to tell me what it was – which broke cover from the edge of a forest.

My heart swelled at the sight of all this and on that first day, at our first stop, before we broke our bread and cheese, I sent up a fervent prayer to God to thank Him for giving me this small place in Parliament's great enterprise. Eaton, who said he was not a great one for prayers, chewed his bread in silence and looked at the weather. I could have stayed there for ever, breathing in that sweet air – it was the first time I realised I had been breathing sea coal and stink all my life. I turned my face to the sun, but Eaton was already on his horse saying we had better make progress before the rain.

'God has given us good weather!' I protested.

'He ain't told the birds that,' Eaton said.

We were on the edge of a forest and the birds were silent. The birds were right. The first drops had that remorseless persistence which told Eaton it would last all day. By late afternoon we rode into a sullen blanket of dark cloud approaching from the west. The roads were riddled with potholes and thick with a pottage of mud and stones churned up by the marching armies and their baggage and artillery trains. Herds of cows and sheep driven in their wake to feed them added to the shit and chaos.

Between overhanging trees we passed a column of Parliamentary soldiers chanting a psalm: 'Let the saints be joyful, Let the high praises of God be in their mouth . . .'

It was a psalm we often sang at Moorfields when drilling was over. Lifted in spirits, I joined in: '. . . and the two-edged sword in their hand . . .'

There was a crack, and splinters of wood showered amidst the men. A pile of wood lay on the verge, and I thought someone was chopping it. Everyone continued chanting with gusto: '. . . to bind their kings with chains, and their nobles with –'

Another crack, and a soldier in front of me fell against his colleagues. I stared at him in wonder. What I believed to be chips of wood was splintered bone. Half his shoulder was missing and his arm was a muddle of mangled flesh and leather jerkin. The ball had spun him round in front of my rearing horse and he stared for a moment stupidly at his arm hanging from the remains of his shoulder. There was the most dreadful animal scream I had ever heard. I thought it was from the horse, but then saw it came from the man's mouth, which seemed to swallow up his whole face.

Like me, I am sure the troops had never seen action before. The front of the column was still chanting and marching, while the back was shouting for help. The officer, who was an ironmonger I recognised from Artillery Fields, yelled: 'Deploy! Deploy!' He pointed to where the shots had come from. But this was what the Cavaliers had been waiting for. As the troops ran to take up positions on the outskirts of the wood, a group of dragoons rode down on them from the rear, swords drawn, shouting, 'For God and the King!'

I drew my sword and was struggling to turn Patch round in the churning mud when Eaton cut at her with his whip. She lurched forward, almost throwing me. It was all I could do to keep on the saddle as she careered away. When I started to get her under control, Eaton lashed her again until we were out in open country and the cries and screams had faded away.

'Coward!' I yelled at him. 'You made me desert them – leave them to die!'

'We have our own business to do,' he said.

Tears of anger burned my eyes. 'We have Parliament's business! They are our colleagues, in the name of God!'

'You may be a Roundhead,' he said shortly. 'I only bother about my own head. And if you must sing psalms, keep your voice down. God may hear them, but so can the Cavaliers.'

I was so bitter and angry at him the words were out of my mouth before I could stop them. 'You are a sad, lonely Godless creature and I cannot believe any woman could ever love you!'

He bit his lip, and jerked his horse forward, saying nothing more.

It was as if I had broken a confidence in even referring to it. I felt the urge to ride after him and apologise, but then burned with shame and anger at deserting my colleagues. I began to ride back to them, but stopped, fearing to run into the Cavaliers. By the time I turned to follow Eaton, he was almost out of sight. I kept on thinking he would look back, but he never did. Eventually my spirits lifted. It felt good to be free, without his morose, watching presence.

It began to grow dark and chill. I came to a small farm and asked for lodging, but the farmer drove me away with a pitchfork and a snarling dog, saying that he wanted no more tickets. Tickets could not buy bread!

I discovered that, whatever their sympathies, people were already at breaking point, being forced to billet soldiers for tickets which – in many cases – were no more than worthless IOUs, and though I had money no one would trust me. Soaked to the skin, I was tempted by the warmth of a charcoal-burner's kiln, but seeing the way the burner and his son eyed my horse and baggage, forced myself to move on. My new-found love of the country rapidly turned to fear. It was as dark as Mr Black's cellar, only the scuffles and cries were not rats, but those of wolves or spirits. My horse was stumbling. I was hopelessly lost. It was my town nose, more than anything else, that saved me, the smell of smoke taking me to a straggle of buildings that turned out to be the outskirts of Beaconsfield.

He was waiting outside an inn, smoking a clay. The rain did not seem to bother him. It dripped from every corner of his hat and cloak as he gazed up at me sardonically. This expectation that I would come to him, depended on him, filled me with fresh rage. I kicked savagely at Patch, but she refused to budge from the water she was sucking. I lurched forward, grabbing ineffectually at the harness and began to slip from the horse. The stable boy caught me as I fell in an exhausted heap.

Eaton stared down at me, puffing at his pipe. 'Try elsewhere, if you like. You won't get in.'

I snarled at him I was not hungry, but the smell of pottage deflated my pride. I never slept so soundly, before or since. He woke me at dawn, to the remorseless patter of rain. My clothes were warm, but still damp.

We did not make more than a dozen miles a day, sometimes less. We were shot at by both sides. It is difficult to believe, but in those early days, and even later, you never knew whether you were meeting friend or foe. If there were uniforms, they were regimental ones – little help at shot distance if you did not know whether the regiment's commander had declared for the King or Parliament or (as happened not infrequently) had switched sides. After a musket ball took away my hat we adopted the general custom, which travelled by mysterious word of mouth, to wear the orange scarves of roundheads, in the hope that at least we would be shot by the enemy. Cavaliers wore red ones.

Eaton, through the Stonehouse intelligence network, picked up news at inns along the way. Essex had successfully joined Midland forces in Northampton, but many of his troops were untrained volunteers, ill-fed, unpaid and on the point of mutiny, until fresh funds arrived from London. The King was first reported to be in Shropshire, then Worcester.

I refused to listen to Eaton when he said nobody knew what they were doing, and said hotly that Essex was a veteran of the Dutch wars. It might be that Prince Rupert, the King's cousin and feared cavalry commander, had won a skirmish or two, such as we had seen. But when the Parliamentary forces came together they would impale the Royalists on their pikes.

'If they ever find one another,' Eaton said.

It was true there were practically no maps. Signposts, if they existed, were removed or twisted round to confuse the enemy. With the weather and the sporadic fighting, it took us near a week to get to Oxford, rather than the two days Eaton had expected. The city was still supposedly uneasily neutral; the University was wholeheartedly for the King, but the citizens were mainly for Parliament. It had stopped raining, but pools of water lay on Christ Church Meadow. I stared in awe at what I took to be the spires of churches and cathedrals and said it must be a very Godly place.

Eaton laughed. 'There are more sinners than saints in those places. They are the colleges – seats of learning,' he said, with a sarcastic edge. 'That's Magdalen, where Richard Stonehouse learned to gamble.' He pulled down his hat and raised his collar.

I thought that made him even more conspicuous, except it hid his scar, but I wedged my hat more firmly over my red hair. 'Is he here?'

'The Stonehouses are everywhere. Lord Stonehouse bought parts of the city the colleges don't own.'

It was beyond the meadow, outside the broken wall of the city that I saw it. The crude red crosses on the wattle fencing had faded so as to be scarcely visible. I realised what it was more from the clay thrown up, marked with white streaks, and most of all by the way people shunned the place. I stood quite still, staring.

'Do they own that?' I said.

'The plague pit? The dead own that,' he said, almost cheerfully for him. 'If you'd have been thrown down there, we wouldn't be having all this trouble.'

We stabled the horses at the Green Man, not far from the plague pit, as he said the city was not safe. We removed our orange scarves and walked to an inn near the centre, the Dog and Pheasant, too mean and small to have stabling. He would not risk me going near the Blue Boar, to which Matthew's letters were directed, although I argued I was more likely to get information than he was. He returned surly and out of sorts, saying he had got a groat's worth of information for a crown. Matthew had gone. He had taken the road to Woodstock and Chipping, in the direction of Highpoint.

We went to bed early to make, he said, an early start in the morning. But I was asleep less than an hour when I heard the outside door close. His bed was empty. From the window I saw him emerge on to the street. I had been cooped up all afternoon and, still angry he had not taken me to the Blue Boar, I scrambled downstairs to follow him. It was quite dark and there were few people about as he strode into a market square.

I stopped in terror as I saw the falcon glaring down at me. It was as big as a red kite and would have dropped on me like a stone if it had not been made of that material. It was the emblem, in place of the common wood sign, of an opulent inn, the Stonehouse Arms.

My fright caused me to duck back into a dark doorway, and it was as well I did, for at that moment Eaton turned, staring. He had the stillness of someone who hunts, eyes and ears focused for every movement, every sound. I began to breathe again only when he turned and went down a dark alleyway at the side of the inn. I hesitated to follow him, for I feared he would be waiting for me at the end of it. The sound of laughter drew me cautiously towards a lighted window. At a table, roaring with laughter, was Captain Gardiner. With him was Richard Stonehouse. They were having a mock sword fight with lighted candles. Wax splashed over food and glasses as they sparred. Sipping wine and watching them with a mixture of indulgence and distaste was a man who, from the sharp curve of his nose and his eyes, even though they were partly hidden by thick spectacles, could only be Edward Stonehouse.

I ran. I could not believe I had been stupid enough to trust Eaton, who was no doubt on his way to join them. No doubt also he had told me his stories to persuade me that he had – what had Kate said? – qualities he was denying to himself. I ran faster than I have ever run in my life, determined to grab my pack and get out of that place.

The sight of that trio and my anger at my own naivety threw me into such a panic that it was minutes before I realised I was lost. I came to the river, doubled back, saw an alley I was convinced I knew and found myself back in the market square again. Everything

I had was in my pack at the Dog and Pheasant – my money, even my knife. The inn was so mean, few knew it. People I asked shook their heads. A drunk was convinced he knew it, but then kept contradicting himself – keep going left from the main square, no, right and when you come to, what's the name of the inn? – that I left him in despair. He followed me, shouting abusively that he knew exactly where it was. Finally in desperation I decided that, pack or no pack, I would leave the town. At that precise moment I recognised the crumbling jetty of a house. The inn was in a street next to it.

Back inside I snatched up my pack and retrieved my purse from the crack in a beam where I had hidden it. I was ramming it into my pack when I heard the outside door slam and Eaton greeting the landlord.

I took out my knife, pulled the bed-cover over me and pretended to be asleep. He stopped whistling when he came into the room, and I forced my breathing to be regular. I smelt beer on his breath as he bent over me and I gripped my knife. Something, bug or lice, began crawling up my leg but I dare not move. At least, I thought, he would not kill me. He needed me too much to get the pendant from Matthew.

His boots fell one by one and, as usual, he was instantly asleep. But every time I shifted the old timber creaked and groaned and I sensed his eyes on me. I felt I had no sleep that night, but awoke to find a meagre dawn light stealing through the window, and Eaton, booted, pack slung over his shoulder, standing over me.

The cover had slipped from me. He looked at the knife, still near my hand. 'Taking no chances?'

Still half-asleep, I did not know whether he was real or nightmare and snatched up the knife. It caught in his coat and with a cry of annoyance he grabbed at my wrist and took the knife from me. 'Look at my coat!'

I should have had it out with him there and then, but he had my knife, which he was putting in his belt. I stared up at him sullenly.

'What is it, Tom?'

I pretended to be too sleepy to answer. I could be as cunning as he was. If I could get to my horse, I had a chance to escape. On our way to the horses he proposed to get breakfast at a baker's he knew. I picked up my pack, dashed water in my face in the yard, and followed him through the quiet streets. Before I had always been the one full to the brim with chatter and questions, trying to break through his grim silences; now, perversely, he bombarded me with questions. Was I ill? Had he upset me in some way? I preserved a silence as dour and taciturn as his ever was. This was not so difficult at first, for sleep still clung to me, as it seemed to do to the day. It was dank and dark in the alleys and there was a sallow greyness in the streets as if some of the clouds building overhead had drifted down amongst us. The few people about huddled into their collars without looking at us.

The one person who was unmistakably and thoroughly cheerfully awake was the baker. I wanted to hurry past, wrapped in my silence, but Eaton stopped to buy a loaf and a small beer. I sullenly refused both. Eaton raised his eyebrows, for I normally had a fearsome appetite. He shrugged and sat on a bench outside the baker's, smacking his lips as he swallowed the beer, declaring he could taste the nutty, Oxfordshire barley which made real beer, not your London piss.

There is nothing like the smell of newly baked bread in the morning, particularly when you have had little to eat the night before. The loaf was so hot Eaton jiggled it from hand to hand as he divided it with scrupulous fairness. The delicious, eddying steam made my mouth water and my stomach contract, but it was the mocking way he broke it, as if, God-forsaken as he was, he was aware of doing a parody of the Last Supper.

'I will not break bread with you,' I said.

He shrugged, put the rejected portion carefully in his pack and munched the other, with great sounds of enjoyment as we walked along.

It was as if I had woken in the middle of a nightmare, and was now walking through a parable. The rising sun seemed to pale and weaken, the houses become hovels and the hovels waste ground on which nothing grew as we approached the plague pit. Seeing a cart nearby Eaton struck off the path, up the track towards the pit. When I did not follow him, he called back. The bread and beer had put him in great good humour.

'Do you not want to see what you were saved from, my lord?'

I hung back. I felt the urge to run but my legs had turned to water. Eaton reached the rough fence, smeared with crude red crosses. The smell of lime, sharp as a knife, was carried to me by the thin wind, but it was not sufficient to obliterate the undercurrent of rot and decay, or keep away the flies, which hovered round the head of the carter who was laying down more lime. The man doffed his cap.

'Mr Eaton! Got anything for me?'

Eaton looked back slyly at me. 'Not today, Bryson. Bit late in the season.'

Bryson agreed, and declared it had been a bad year, but things were picking up. Fever was spreading through the troops, and there was good business in burying them. He was heading north, beyond Highpoint, where the two armies were circling.

'They had better begin, while they have some men left,' he joked. Their conversation sickened me, but at the same time I felt a great thrill of excitement that this noble conflict that would settle the fate of England was about to begin. I determined to be there, to distinguish myself or die. If I lived, I would write the greatest pamphlet on the war ever printed.

Fired with these thoughts, I turned from them and hurried away. Where the greenery began to grown again, beyond this charnel ground, I saw the inn where we had stabled our horses. I had no idea where Chipping Norton was, where I was due to meet Will, but God would put me on the right road.

I heard Eaton hurrying behind me, and quickened my pace. 'Tom . . . what is it?'

There was something I had never heard in his voice before: concern. But I knew it to be as counterfeit as a faker's coin. I stopped so abruptly he almost bumped into me, and I rounded on him. 'I saw you leaving the Stonehouse Arms last night.'

To my amazement he laughed and readily admitted it. There was almost a kind of relief in his laughter. 'I thought I heard someone following me. Is that all?'

'All? When you go into an inn where the Stonehouse brothers and Captain Gardiner are staying?'

'I see. I see.' He walked for a few steps in a deep, penetrating silence. 'And you think I am laying a trap for you, do you?'

'What else am I to think?'

'Yes, what else are you to think? You're as little trusting as I am, Tom, and I like you none the less for it.' We were now at the inn and he pointed to a bench, but I would not sit down. 'Did you see me go into the inn?'

I had to admit I did not.

'Talk to Richard Stonehouse or Gardiner?'

'No.'

He told me he went to the stables to talk to Lord Stonehouse's spy about Richard's movements, so we would not cross them.

'Why didn't you tell me you were going there?'

'You were asleep. And I knew you would have this reaction.' He spoke suddenly with all his old violence, his harsh voice charged with contempt, but whether it was aimed at me, or perhaps himself or life in general I never knew. 'After I killed Crow, and all I've said about Richard destroying the estate, do you really think I would work for him?'

'Yes. If you thought he was going to win.'

His scar throbbed as if it was going to leap out at me. Then he turned away, struggling to control himself. He picked up a stick from the hedgerow and slapped his side continually with it. 'I thought I was the strangest of God's creatures because He left me to the devil and I was happy with that, for it was very simple. People were afraid of me and I knew where I was.' He turned and levelled the stick at me. 'But He made you stranger. He made you honest Tom Neave, or whoever you are. Honest, but not stupid, a combination I have not seen before.'

He tossed the stick away. 'Going off, were you? You'll need this.'

He gave me my knife and strode back to the stables, where our horses were saddled. If I could not make him out, I could scarce make myself out either. While he went into the inn to pay the bill, I could easily have escaped, but I was now loath to part from him.

When he came out of the inn, I said: 'I went to where Kate Beaumann stayed in London.'

He mounted his horse, listening intently while I reported what the Countess had told me. He stared over the browning landscape at the twisting road. 'Ah. She is ahead of us. Thank you.'

He said not another word, staring at the road ahead, and might well have been riding alone, for all he said or acknowledged me. We crossed meadows and forded a river until we struck what I believe was an old green way, a drover's road over the downs. I remembered what the shipwright had told me about Matthew taking the green road, and felt a surge of excitement. This must have been the way he came when he escaped with the pendant, years before, high over the downs, a way marked with mysterious cairns and crosses. In the far distance, a white horse cut into the chalk seemed to move with us in the swirling mist. Eaton pointed his whip towards it, and said that was where the Highpoint estate began.

We dropped into an area disputed by both parties. There were sounds of gunfire and the boom of cannon. In the valley below us a castle was under siege. As we descended, coming near the main way, Eaton rode into a copse, gesturing me to keep silent. In the distance rode a party of about twenty, wearing the red favours of Cavaliers. Eaton, whose eyes were keener than mine, said one of them was Richard, and urged me along faster.

In that God-forsaken valley we rode through a village where Parliamentary soldiers were stripping the lead from a church to make bullets. They wanted us to join in their 'pilgrimage' to liberate the church from papism. But it was one thing to hate bishops, another to watch books – which to me were living things – and crucifixes being thrown into a fire round which drunken soldiers danced. We hurried away through the churchyard. Eaton stopped by a gravestone, inscribed with the name Sir Henry Pearce and bearing a coat of arms on which was a wildcat with a raised paw.

'The Pearce arms,' he said. He pointed to the wildcat. 'An apt symbol for your mother.'

He went into one of his silences, refusing to say more, except that the Pearces were old nobility who, a century ago, owned most of the valley we rode through.

Back on the green road, I was shocked to find that, while the soldiers were celebrating, Eaton had stolen a couple of pistols with balls and powder. He shrugged and said we were too ill-equipped to have scruples; we were only plundering the plunderers. That at least was true. In the pack of one soldier I had seen stolen plate, while a cottager pleaded in vain with an officer for the return of the hams she had cured for winter, for she and her children could not eat the ticket she had been given, which I read out to her when I tried to help her: *To be Redeemed by Parliament Three Hammes. Sgnd J—— (Cpt).* I was told by the captain that everyone must make sacrifices for the good of all. I had no answer to that, for I had said exactly the same thing in pamphlets, but with a great deal more fervour when I wrote it than I felt now.

There was no news of Will and the unit, but the captain told us that Chipping Norton, where we were to have met them, was held by the Royalists, so we pressed on towards Highpoint.

What little breaks we had were more to rest the horses, for we could doze on their backs. It rained steadily, but Eaton found dry hollows that smelt rankly of foxes. Though we had a leather under-sheet and a scrap of blanket, we depended on each other for warmth. The main torment was lack of food. There were troop movements all round us and Eaton would not shoot a rabbit or light a fire; instead we ate berries, which he said he had lived on one winter as a child, before he learned to hunt, and they gave him the strength he needed, but all they gave me was the flux.

I awoke one morning, the sides of my stomach cleaving together, to hear a sound in the undergrowth. I felt for the pistol under my pack as I peered through the leaves. The horses, tethered nearby, reacted to the sound and I followed their gaze to see a stag alertly sniffing the air. With a full stomach I would have admired its magnifi-cent antlers and praised God for the beauty of its creation but, famished, I could only see meat, a gift from God. Eaton was asleep. His warnings held me in check, but we had seen no soldiers the previous evening. My mouth filled with water and I could almost smell the venison steaks sizzling over a fire. I cocked the pistol under the pack to kill the sound, but it still alerted the stag. His head was taut, his ears shivering. In a moment he would run. I fired, but as I did so the pistol was knocked up from my hand. The stag fled, twigs and leaves raining down and a host of roosting birds rising up squawking.

Eaton snatched the pistol from me. 'Damn you, sir! Would you shoot your own deer?'

'My my own . . .' I stuttered.

'Lord Stonehouse's. Stonehouse or no, he would have had you strung on a gibbet if you'd shot that stag.'

'Are we at Highpoint?'

'We crossed the boundary yesterday forenoon when we left Barrow Down and entered the Great Forest – hist!'

He clapped his hand over my mouth. At first I heard nothing, but as the birds swooped and settled, in the still morning air picked out several voices. Wordlessly Eaton made a stirrup with his hands and got me to climb a tree while he swept everything into our packs and untethered the horses. It was the birds fluttering up again that led me to their movements. I glimpsed a bloodstained bandage on a head, a red favour.

'Cavaliers. About five of them. One of them wounded.'

'Mounted?'

'No. They have seen our tracks.'

He swore softly. 'They want our horses.'

I was mortified at my stupidity in bringing this on us after Eaton's warning but he said not a word in recrimination. We were among tightly bunched trees and bushes where it was impossible to ride. Eaton led us along a narrow track. With the difficulty of managing the horses, we could hear them gaining on us.

'Stop! In the King's name!'

'Half a mile and we're in the clear!' yelled Eaton. 'Mount up!'

Throwing myself on to Patch's back I ducked as low as I could, following Eaton weaving between the trees, branches whipping at us, the bigger ones almost knocking us from our saddles several times. It was a fallen tree that did for us. My horse, with its lighter weight leapt it, but Eaton's stumbled and threw him. He was up almost immediately, but the delay cost us vital time for a clear run across open ground, which I could see temptingly through the trees. They were not far from us, yelling and whooping like hunters closing in for the kill.

I would still have gone for it, but Eaton had a cooler head for calculation than me.

'Reload your pistol.'

He tethered the horses, flung himself down before the fallen tree and brought out his own pistol. Whether he left the horses in full view as an irresistible temptation, I do not know. Certainly the fact that their blood was up and the prospect of two horses between five men made them reckless. A man with a sabre was ahead of the rest, shouting he would have the black gelding. Eaton left it so late to fire he was almost on us, swinging his sword. The ball caught the man in the chest, but his momentum was so great he ran on for another couple of steps, the blade of his sword clanging down close to Eaton. I stared in horror as he coughed blood, his eyes fixed on me with a glazed stare, but Eaton rolled him over, taking the flintlock from his belt. He aimed it at one of the retreating Cavaliers, but it clicked uselessly against the charge. He flung it down and began reloading his own.

'That will make them rather more cautious,' Eaton said. His eyes gleamed. His habitual moroseness had gone and he seemed almost looking forward to them coming on again. There was silence among the trees, but I caught a movement on one side, then the other.

'They're surrounding us,' I whispered.

'Aye. If they're sensible, we're done for. We have two shots against four. If the bastards go off. Untether the horses. Keep down as I showed you.'

'What are you going to do?'

'Cover you.'

'But –'

'Go!'

I wriggled away from the fallen tree as he had taught me, using what cover I could, skirting the bush to which the horses were tethered and untied them. I grabbed the reins but the movement of the horses raised a cry from one of the Cavaliers.

'They're running for it!'

As the Cavaliers broke cover, Eaton stood up with his pistol. 'I have one shot and my friend has another. Which of you fine gentlemen wants the balls in their hearts, to give your good friends the pleasure of the horses?'

Eaton's putting the matter like this so divided the Cavaliers they stopped, glancing nervously from one to another, staying just out of range of the pistol. The scar which had once so terrified me must have been, to them, every much a weapon as the pistol. The nearer we got to Highpoint, the more he had picked and rubbed at it, until it was a weeping sore. Now he looked a fearsome sight, a man with a contempt for death, standing in the open, holding them with his gaze while backing imperceptibly towards me. He spoke out of the corner of his mouth.

'Is my stirrup free, Tom?'

'Yes.'

'Put your foot in yours.'

One of the men made a move for his flintlock. Eaton fired, missed and ran for his horse, leaping on with the agility of a far younger man.

'Stay low on the horse – they will not shoot at that!'

We careered forward, weaving between the last of the trees. Across a valley, like a mirage, I saw statues that seemed to dance round a fountain as I was bounced this way and that, and beyond them a great white building whose endless pilasters and chimneys flickered through the trees. It was my first view of Highpoint and almost my last. I felt the wind of a shot and Eaton fell right in front of my horse. I tried to swerve round him but the hooves caught him.

I dismounted. He was quite still. His forehead was bleeding. His jacket was torn at the back and blood was soaking through. There were a number of shots, one striking a nearby tree. I bent over him, feeling his breath on my cheek and struggled to drag him into the shelter of a tree. Eaton's black gelding had bolted, to be seized by two of the Cavaliers, who were arguing over him. I could not see the other two, but there were more shots as I managed to get Eaton behind the tree, next to my horse.

His eyes opened. 'Leave me! Let them have your horse and run for it!'

I crawled to get his pack and there was the crack of another shot. Either they were reloading incredibly quickly or more had joined them. The pack had been split open in the fall and I pulled out his spare shirt. He tried to get up to protest again, but gasped in pain and fell back. I turned him over and ripped the back of his jacket open with my knife, wincing at his wound, which was steadily ebbing blood. I stuffed the shirt over it as tightly as I could and turned him back so his weight would help stop the flow. His eyes began to glaze over like those of the other dead man and I could not check the sobs as I knelt there, remembering that once I would have given anything for him to be dead, but now I would give anything for him to live. I prayed Our Father – what I could say of it, for the words choked in my mouth.

The prayer brought some life back to his eyes, but not I fear to his soul, for it was an angry spark of life. 'None of that! Leave me to die – it's better for you! Go!'

He pushed me away. I overbalanced and as I scrambled up saw a movement in the trees. One of the cavaliers darted to a tree not far from me. Eaton's hand was quivering above his body as if he was still feebly trying to push me away. Through the last of the trees I could see the fountain, which seemed to make the pilasters of the house shimmer in the air. He was right. I could leave the horse and slip away through the trees. But instead it was as if he had infected me with some of his detached, bitter anger at life. I picked up my flintlock and wriggled behind Eaton, who was now quite still. I lay as if dead, using Eaton as a convenient rest for the pistol. When the Cavalier ran forward I waited as Eaton had done and shot him with some of his cold anger.

As I watched him fall I heard a sound behind me and turned too late to avoid the pistol butt coming down on my head.

28

The sky had miraculously changed to an aching blue, across which perfectly formed white clouds floated. Nine muses rode on clouds blown by Cupids with pink, fat cheeks. They, in turn, were being chased by goats. Goats in heaven? One of them appeared to be eating a cloud, wispy fronds of it clinging to his beard. I could hear it munching, its hooves rapping on the sky as it gripped another piece of cloud. Surprisingly, there was pain in heaven. The light was so bright it forced me to shut my eyes and I struggled to turn my body, indeed discover whether I still had a body, then wished I hadn't as a wave of nausea swept over me. I had a body, but it consisted principally of bruises.

This was more like purgatory, with a tantalising glimpse of heaven. Yes, I was suspended between the two places, for I heard the hooves and smelt the stink of the goat as it bent over me.

'Tom . . . Tom . . .'

I opened my eyes a fraction, gripping the goat's beard.

'It's real.'

The goat had turned into Will. The sky tilted – clouds, Cupids and goats falling towards me, then righting themselves as I was mercifully carried away from the blinding sunlight of the windows and my senses slowly returned. I was being carried under an ornate, swaying ceiling on a makeshift stretcher, composed of a soldier's coat slung on two pikes.

Big Jed grinned down at me. 'Peaceful use of the pike,' he said. 'Not in the manual.'

He and another soldier deposited me on a truckle bed in a withdrawing room where Luke was sitting, alongside a statue of Mars with a musket hanging on his sword arm, and another of Minerva, hung with coats and packs. The marble tiles were grey with mud.

'Welcome home,' Luke said. I struggled up on one elbow, gazing at the incongruent muddle of classical figures and drying clothes, at Will leaning against a pillar, and Luke who even in that place managed to have a clean shirt with carefully turned lace cuffs. 'It is your seat, isn't it? Not bad, as estates go.'

I sat up further, very gingerly. From the room I could see into the great hall from where they had taken me, through shattered windows that looked out on to an avenue wide enough for three carriages. There was no wind, and the water of the fountain seemed to hang motionless in the air. Beyond lay gardens that dropped imperceptibly to the river below, the land on the other side rising from the tumbling, fast-running water, up to the wilderness of the Great Forest. I understood what Pym meant about power. Kings had stayed here and to give them an acceptable setting, Lord Stonehouse's ancestors had almost bankrupted themselves.

While I stared at the scene in awe, Will told me they had fought with a strong unit of cavaliers at the Battle of Highpoint. His voice had become more clipped, casual, like a dispatch to his colonel.

'They were horse and we were foot, of course, so we had no chance on open ground. Held them with pike at the ford for a while, although we lost some good fellows there, didn't we Luke?'

Luke said nothing. He took some tobacco and a clay from his pack.

'Retreated to the house in good order –'

'We were scared shitless.' Luke tore off a plug from Mr Ormonde's best Sweet Virginia. His hands were shaking.

Will went on as if he had not heard him. Later, I realised they were both shocked by what they had seen, but reacted in different ways.

Will talked constantly, issuing orders to passing soldiers. Luke was as flippant as ever, but his jokes had a bitter edge.

'Their army charged up the approach there –' Will took his sword, propped up against Mars, and pointed through the shattered windows.

'All twelve of them,' muttered Luke.

'We drew them inside with a feint, ambushed them from the landing up there. They fled in disorder, but we had secured their horses –'

The clay slipped from Luke's fingers as he tamped in the tobacco and broke on the tiles. He swore. 'Oh, come on, Will. They came in to plunder. We had run up there to hide. I had a lucky shot on one of the bastards and you knocked a bust of Caesar on another. When they tried to run away, their horses had been taken by some of our good fellows, who deserted and buggered off back to London. I wish I'd joined them.'

He grinned, but I thought he was only half joking. In the absence of his clay, he twisted at his wedding ring, on which was engraved: *Noe heart more true than mine to you.*

'I am to be a father,' he said. 'I had a letter from Charity.' I stared at the ring enviously as he kissed it. He had held her properly, discovered the mysteries of love. Their hearts and souls were mingled in another mystery, a child; whatever happened, they would be together, whereas if I had died in the forest, my soul would mingle only with the rotting leaves, without discovering my father or becoming one. Such melancholy, and a feeling of the old bond with Luke over matters of the heart, made me put out my arms to embrace him, but he shoved me away.

'You stink, Neave!'

It was as much comfort to hear that name as a hug. It felt as real as bread, while Stonehouse and this magic palace had the substance of a philosopher's stone, which the alchemists are always discovering one day, only for it to vanish the next.

I asked if Richard Stonehouse had been one of the band that attacked them. None of the men matched his description. Will had heard he was riding to join Prince Rupert near Banbury. This, if true, was both a comfort and a puzzle; for I could not understand why Richard had not come to take Highpoint. Perhaps, I thought, the glory of riding with Prince Rupert had been even greater than the desire for his inheritance.

The men who tried to steal our horses were the rump of the band who attacked Highpoint. Luke said they had heard the firing, and he had only just stopped his man from killing me when he saw my red hair.

'What happened to the man I was with?' I asked.

'We brought him back here,' Will said. 'Since he was with you.'

'He was cursing us. Telling us to leave him where he was. Fine fellow,' Luke said.

I sprang up. 'He's alive?'

Luke shrugged. 'Probably dead by now.'

The wounded got little treatment. A surgeon might treat you if you were a gentleman, or high enough in rank, but then you were billeted on some unwilling family to nurse. Will's unit was exceptional. Ben insisted that if the wounded were not picked up regardless of rank he would go, denying the troops even the limited form of treatment he could offer.

He stood at the end of the long table where the servants normally ate. There were a few truckle beds, but most of the wounded soldiers were laid on straw spread over the table.

'Wait!' Ben snapped. He was tying a crudely fashioned splint to the arm of a man who was groaning in pain. He turned to me. 'Take that filthy shirt off. Go away, Luke.'

'Ben, it's –'

'I know who it is.'

Luke went away. I took off the shirt and watched, while Ben warned his patient not to try and loosen the splint, for the tighter it was, the quicker the bone would heal. The mild-mannered man I knew in

London had gone. His lower lip stuck out stubbornly. His skin had a grey, tired pallor and he worked with a dogged bitterness. In one of the truckle beds I saw Eaton, or at least his scar. It was rising and falling steadily. Where once I had run from it in fear, I ran to it now and I fell down on my knees and thanked God.

'None of that,' Eaton mumbled restlessly. 'None of that.' He was so hot it was like kneeling in front of a furnace. His forehead seemed to crackle and bubble with sweat, and there was a sweet smell about him from some herbs Ben had used to try and cool him. He gave a sudden cry. 'I did it for the estate! D'you see that? Keep it together! Keep it together!' He seized my hand with a grip which was a mere ghost of his old violence.

'It's Tom.'

'Tom?' His eyes opened, but I did not know how much he took in. 'Tom? Tell him to go away. Now. Before it's too late.' He pushed at me feebly. I overbalanced and another hand grabbed me.

'Leave him!' Ben cried angrily. He called an orderly over to Eaton and led me away. 'I'm trying to bring the man's fever down and you send it sky high!'

I apologised. 'Will he live?'

Ben shrugged. 'The ball didn't lodge, and only chipped the bone. His mind seems more diseased than his body – he doesn't seem to want to live. What have you done to him?'

'Me? Nothing.'

'He keeps going on about you. Who stuffed that shirt on his wound?'

'I did. Sorry. Was it wrong?'

'The devil to get off, but you probably saved his life.' He scratched his head. 'Then I don't understand why he's so angry at you.'

29

Highpoint had become two worlds. During the fight most of the servants had fled. The soldiers occupied the ground floor, while the first, which was almost untouched, was run by the assistant housekeeper. She was a quiet woman, Will told me, but her look was full of the Bible and the soldiers did not dare to venture upstairs to cross her. She spent most of her time looking after the real house-keeper, Mrs Morland – Jane's mother – who was seriously ill. She had remained upstairs, nursing her patient, while the soldiers fired from the nearby gallery. Soldiers' stories grow in the telling like pamphlets, and there was already a legend that during the firing she went out to the gallery to reprimand them for swearing, and stayed to read them the Bible.

Eaton grew worse, his fever deepening. Ben refused to let me see him and I determined I must get back on to the trail of Matthew and the pendant alone. I found the pack I had lost in the forest. Most of its contents were gone, but the letter I had written for Jane to her mother was still there. I determined to brave Mother Preacher – as the soldiers called the woman in charge – both to fulfil my promise to Jane and in the hope of finding out what had happened in this house when I was born.

I went upstairs through a maze of empty, echoing corridors, seeing no one, stopping transfixed when I came to an enormous room. I had never seen such a library before. Amongst shelf after shelf of priceless books was a portrait of Lord Stonehouse, staring dreamily, his finger keeping his place in a book which, I saw on closer inspection, was Machiavelli's *The Prince*. On a scroll above the shelves was painted: *Homo doctus in se semper divitias habet* – a learned man always has wealth.

And power, I thought, symbolised by the book in the painting. How else did you get the wealth to buy the learning? Each one of the hundreds of books cost a labourer's wages for several years.

Somewhere a door opened and closed. I ran out into the corridor, but saw no one. I went down another corridor, hung with Flemish tapestries of the seasons. At the end of it stood a pair of double doors which drew me to them. I did not need to see the portrait of Frances Stonehouse to know it was her bedroom. Opposite it was a portrait of James I. The room was spotlessly clean, but the oak furniture had a dark, brooding heaviness that belonged to a previous era. A faded, fringed carpet covered a table. Half-burnt candles, petrified in their holders, had been left just as they were snuffed out when Frances died. In this room, Charles, whose divided people were about to fight one another, had not yet ascended the throne. Everything had stopped here, more than twenty years ago.

Not everything.

My heart thudded painfully as I stared at myself. It was a portrait of a boy I had never seen before, yet it was me. There I was, when I had run to the Guildhall that morning with a message from Mr Black, and an apparently bored painter, Peter Lely, had stopped me to improvise some casual sketches. But I was no dirty, unkempt apprentice, grinning and excited about being sketched. Just as Mr Pym had described, I was elegantly dressed, with a dog at my feet and Highpoint in the background.

Lely had kept my grin, but he had turned it into something else, something halfway between a cheeky smile and one of superiority. It was partly a lie – or so I felt – and partly the truth. It was a boy on his way to manhood, a picture of what might be, rather than what was.

I wanted to stick my tongue out at him, but could not quite do so. The truth was, I rather liked him. No, it was more than that. I was captivated by him. I took off an imaginary hat and swept it with a flourish in a deep bow. Then I stood quite still as a thought struck me. How did I know he was me? I had only ever seen myself in distorted glasses, or in dark, still pools.

'Are you sure?'

The voice was so quiet and the question so apposite I thought for a moment it had arisen in my own head. But I turned and there she was, standing by the door. I did not believe she was real at that moment. She had appeared, out of air. She was the will o' the wisp, the good spirit who had looked after me throughout childhood.

'S-sure?' I stuttered.

'You want to be Lord Stonehouse?'

I could not answer. Ridiculously, I wondered why she was carrying a garden trug of herbs and not a simnel cake, which I had not had that year. Afraid she would vanish, I went towards her and touched her face. She sprang back, startled, herbs spilling from her trug. I picked them up, mumbling an apology. 'I was not sure you were real.'

She laughed. Eaton had been rather flattering to say she was as plain as bread; she was quite ugly, with a snub nose and pocked cheeks, rather like those weathered gargoyles that spew rainwater from churches. But her laughter and her voice, as perfectly pitched as plainsong, transformed her. Then she became grave. 'I did not want to be real, but I have to warn you to forget the pendant, forget the Stonehouses.'

It is strange how awkward and obdurate and downright unhelpful a spirit becomes when it turns into flesh and blood. Kate Beaumann would not deny she knew where Matthew was. She had been on her way to him when she learned Mrs Morland was very ill. Then she had been trapped by the siege. But she refused point-blank to tell me where Matthew was. That would lead me to the pendant, which was the source of all the evil that had happened. Her sole purpose was to find it and destroy it, and nothing would shake her from that. She refused even to tell me what had happened at my birth. I was so desperate I told her Eaton was with me, thinking it might advance my cause.

She stood there looking every bit as fixed as a stone gargoyle, then hurried away. She was gone so quickly I was afraid she had turned into a spirit again. I had to run to catch up with her, pleading with her to see Eaton, telling her that he seemed to have lost the will to live.

'Then leave him to die,' she said, without changing her pace.

'What has he done?'

Now she stopped. 'You, of all people, to ask that!'

'I mean to you.'

'Ask him.'

I was shocked by her tone, which had some of Eaton's own savagery in it, but she refused to say any more. All equanimity left her. Herbs dropped from her trug again and I picked them up, following her trail, to find her outside the housekeeper's bedroom, her lips moving in an almost inaudible prayer which I dare not interrupt. Gradually her breast stopped heaving beneath her plain brown dress, which was only relieved by a snow-white collar. I put the herbs in the trug and asked if I could see Mrs Morland.

'You want to ask her about the night you were born?'

I avoided the question. 'I have a message from her daughter.'

Mrs Morland's bedroom was the hottest place in that huge, draughty building. Sprigs of lavender crackled on the fire, but its sweet scent could not hide the pervasive smell of sweat and the stink of the piss-pot a young maid was removing. In the flickering light of the fire, under a nightcap, I could just make out the still, wasted outline of a woman's face. Kate dismissed the maid, but when she saw me she stopped so abruptly to do an elaborate curtsey, she forgot she held the piss-pot, spilling some of the contents.

'Sorry, sir . . .' she stuttered. 'But you are so like your picture.'

Either the noise, or the sound of a male voice, broke through Mrs Morland's fragile sleep. Her voice was disjointed. 'Rose . . . Who is it?'

'The young master has come, Mrs Morland,' Rose said.

'Nonsense!' Kate said sharply. 'It is one of the soldiers.'

But Mrs Morland attempted to struggle up, peering one way, then another, with eyes that were so pale, so milky blue they could have seen little. 'Mr Richard – is it Mr Richard come back?'

Kate tried to intervene but Mrs Morland pushed her away and seized my hands. I struggled to tell her I was a soldier, but she felt my face, the curve of my nose and was in such a confused state she was convinced it was her Mr Richard who, it rapidly became clear, had been her favourite.

I began to read the letter I had brought from Jane. I thought Mrs Morland would not only forgive Jane but express joy in Jane forgiving her. Nothing could have been further from that fond imagining.

'Forgive her? When she brought shame on the family!' She made my flesh crawl with disgust. I tried to pull away, but she gripped my hands more tightly. 'You're too good, Mr Richard. You always had a warm heart, like you had with that other harlot, whose son has come back to plague you. But I'll keep an eye out for him!'

'Will you?' I murmured.

'I saw the bastard being born . . .'

Kate gripped my arm. There was a look of outrage on her face that – as she put it later – I should be preying on a dying, confused woman. I shook her away, feeling no qualms after what Mrs Morland had said about Jane. 'The old goat!' Mrs Morland chuckled.

'The old goat?'

'Your father! Planning to marry Margaret Pearce.'

'Lord Stonehouse?' I said, stunned.

'You were all in love with her . . . You for her looks. Edward for her good works. My lord for both. I knew what was in his mind!' Her hands shook with something that continued, after all those years, to outrage her so much she spat the words out. 'He told me to change Lady Frances's room!'

Her face suddenly creased in pain and she clutched at my hands. Kate gave her some cordial, which she swallowed with little grunts, never letting go of my hands. A small drop of sweat coursed down her forehead, which Kate wiped away. Again Kate motioned me to go as Mrs Morland's eyes closed and she sank back against the pillow, but when the old housekeeper began to murmur drowsily in disjointed, jerky phrases, she listened as intently as I did.

'That day . . . last day of summer. Cold coming. Rain in the air. My lord due from London. Every fire laid, every surface polished. I took some things from my lady's room, leaving the door open. When I returned, Margaret Pearce was in that corridor. Said she got lost. Lost! That was when the thief took the pendant!'

She struggled for breath and it was some time before she continued. 'My lord late . . . black as the clouds coming over the forest. Horse lost a shoe . . . groom his job.'

She chuckled and a quivering sliver of pale blue eye appeared, struggling to focus on me. 'You made yourself scarce. So did Edward. But not *her*! He melts like sugar in water with her. In the library they were . . . "You know how long I've loved you," my lord says.'

I felt she was raving, slipping into nonsense, and tried to loosen her grip on me, but it immediately tightened.

'Were you there?'

'Of course I was there! What do you think keyholes are for – keys?'

She choked with laughter at this, fought for breath, then continued with more urgency. 'She just stood there. So did I, I can tell you!'

'What did she say?'

'She laughed.'

'Laughed?'

The memory seemed to give her fresh energy and she sat up. 'The bitch laughed! "You don't understand," he said. "I'm asking you to marry me." "That's what I came to talk to you about, my lord," she said. Brazen! Just like that! I thought the end of the world had come. It had. For her.'

Her head darted about, as if she was trying to see through a keyhole.

'Couldn't see her. Bell rang three times. That's me. Three for Mrs Morland for trouble inside, two for Mr Eaton for trouble out. "The lady's fainted," he said. Fainted! I could feel the crown when I put my hand up there – excuse my language, Mr Richard, but I know you're a man of the world. "The lady is with child, my lord," I said. He went as white as this sheet! I took charge. He'd made enough of a fool of himself, fathering the bastard. And this was woman's work.'

'How do you know I – it was his child?'

'Of course the bastard was his! He'd been after her all summer, hadn't he? If Eaton had done his job properly you wouldn't be in this mess now – but you'll see to him, Mr Richard, won't you . . . you've come back, as you said you would, to see to him . . .' Her voice flickered like a dying candle. She lay back on the pillow, the taut lines of her face relaxing, as if she had confessed all her sins and was now at peace with the world. 'Keep evil and shame from this house. That's all I've ever . . . tried . . . to do.'

30

The cold, raw brutality of Mrs Morland's story struck me numb. I could picture the others, but in spite of being drawn in such lurid colours, my mother, Margaret Pearce, remained a shadowy person. In spite of what Mrs Morland said, it was hard to believe Lord Stonehouse was my father. My impending birth seemed to have come as a shock to him. Eaton had told me Kate had asked him for the name of a minister who would perform a marriage outside the parish. My mother's visit to Lord Stonehouse was linked to that, surely? What a fool I had been. All this time I had been searching for my father, but the key to everything surely lay in my mother. I determined immediately to try and talk again to Kate, but that night Mrs Morland died.

It was as if, having unburdened her soul to Richard, as she thought, she had no more to do in this life. And it seemed that Eaton would shortly join her. Ben, for once, was no comfort, quite the reverse. He was usually equally interested in the patient and the disease; here he was repulsed by Eaton, but had what I thought was a ghoulish fascination with the disease, which he described as a sickness of the soul.

'Mark the wound,' he said to me, as if teaching a student. 'It is almost healed. But the humours are so out of balance it has broken out in another place.' He pointed to the scar, oozing a yellow pus, and made a note in his commonplace book, which he wrote up every day. He had a drawing of the scar which, he said, most interestingly, had increased in size over the last two days. He closed the book. 'He will not eat or drink. He has a day, perhaps two. I shall be sorry not to see him out.'

'Why is that?'

'Have you not heard? We are leaving.'

It was true. I had been so caught up with Mrs Morland and my own affairs I had not noticed men loading up the baggage train to leave at dawn the next day. I pleaded with Will to leave a small body of men to defend Highpoint, for Mrs Morland had been expecting Richard to return. Will refused. He had lost too many already. The King had succeeded in reaching Shrewsbury, and it was feared at any moment he would break out and march south to London. Essex was at Worcester and Will had received an urgent dispatch to join him.

If it was not raining that autumn, it had merely paused and was threatening to return. I found Kate in the kitchen garden where she was picking herbs. The edges of her cloak were dark with recent rain and drops clung to the backs of her hands as she snipped marjoram.

'I am sorry I upset you over Mrs Morland,' I said.

Her voice was equable, but condemning: 'I thought you wanted to reconcile her with her daughter, Tom.'

'I did! I did! But she was so bitter and unforgiving!'

'You did not correct her when she thought you were Richard.'

She moved to a row of lavender, snipping spikes of it, a weak cautious sun colouring raindrops on each spray as she threw them in the trug. I was suddenly so exasperated by her calmness, condemning everything and answering nothing, I burst out: 'Would you have married Eaton if I hadn't been born?'

She staggered as though she had been struck, dropping the trug and spilling some of the contents. All the colour drained from her face and, afraid she was going to faint, I led her to a bench in an arbour. I kept on saying how sorry I was, but she cut short my apologies with a curt gesture. She was breathing heavily. I went to the trug, rubbed lemon balm with lavender and the rainwater clinging to it, and gave it to her in a lime leaf as a small pomade.

She smiled faintly. 'Matthew's son.'

'Amongst others.'

She began to breathe more easily. 'Eaton told you . . . What did he tell you?'

I now felt guiltier than ever about betraying the secrets Eaton had told the dying fire at the Seven Stars rather than me, but once I had started I had to continue. Perhaps I gave a poetic gloss to his coarse, abrupt story, put into it feelings of his I assumed from the bare facts he related. She said as much but, as if my own heart was in her hands, I pleaded his case, saying that if you just took what happened, what he did, however clumsily and bluntly he carried out his actions, did they not show that he was genuine, that he was – well, I had to say it, I had to – in love with her?

She was shaking and I thought she was crying, then I saw she was laughing. 'Oh, Tom, Tom, it is as if you are making love to me!'

'He would use these words if he could, I swear it!' I cried passionately.

'You can see into that man's heart, can you?'

'Yes, yes, I do believe I can, yes.'

She laughed until tears welled into her eyes. She picked at the lavender spikes, dropping them into the lap of her dress as if she was a little girl playing lovers' fortune, then abruptly the tears came in earnest and I realised her calmness was not calmness at all, but a door tight shut on feelings that had been locked away since the day I was born.

I put my arm round her and anyone coming into that garden would have thought us lovers, in spite of the disparity of our ages.

For a moment she clung to me, then rose to go, but a squall of rain swept over the garden. We pressed back against the accumulation of dusty, snapping twigs and dead leaves in the arbour, staring at the curtain of rain in front of us.

'Why did he tell you all this?'

'Because he heard you were alive. He thought he might see you again. From that moment he changed.'

'Changed? That man?'

'Yes!'

'Tom, he is fooling you, as he fooled me.'

'It was as if he was dragging the words out of a deep well.'

'That, at least, is like,' she muttered.

The squall died away as quickly as it had arisen, and the sun crept out again. In my vehement movements I had edged into the rain and became aware that one sleeve of my shirt was clinging to my arm. Part of her cloak and hair were dark with rain. 'You think he told you the truth?' she murmured.

'Yes, yes, I do. No man could invent such feelings.'

She sighed and shivered. I realised how wet we were and urged her to go in before she caught a chill, but she refused, saying she had to talk now, or she never would. She had thought it all best buried, that my happiness depended on it. Now I had been drawn to this cursed place, it was the lesser of two evils to tell me what part of the truth she knew.

Over the years, she had given me more than simnel cake on my birthday. It was she who persuaded Mr Ingram to begin teaching me my words with the Bible. What began as an atonement for her sin – well, she would come to that – ended as, why not say it, a labour of love.

'You asked me if I would have married Eaton if all this had not happened? Did he not tell you, I *did* answer him?'

I shook my head. She shivered again, and again I pleaded with her to go in, but she said it was not the cold that made her shiver but the memory of that day, that summer creeping back to her. It had begun, as Eaton had told me, when she released him from the trap. Before then she knew him only as a person hated by the Pearce family, whose once vast estates had long been in decline. Margaret Pearce was an only child. Her mother was dead, her father a stubborn man who had lost most of his money fighting Lord Stonehouse's encroachments on his land. When he died, the estate was close to ruin. The only thing he left her that was not mortgaged was his hatred of Lord Stonehouse.

I listened spellbound. People had talked about my mother, if they had talked at all, as if she was a whore in a penny pamphlet, but no one had brought her to life as a real person.

'She was beautiful?' I asked.

'And witty. And intelligent. And charming. Like you.'

'I am charming?'

'Oh, Tom! Listen to yourself!'

'My feet are too large for me ever to be charming.'

I splayed them out sulkily and she laughed. 'And she was ruthless.'

'I am not ruthless! Far from it!'

'No. Not yet.' Although the sun grew stronger, and it was now quite warm in the arbour, she shivered again. 'I see so much of you in her. That is what I am afraid of. I did not see her as ruthless then. I thought I knew everything about her – until that day.'

She was silent for a while before telling me that she was used by Margaret Pearce. Well, that is what companions were paid, fed and sheltered for – mostly sheltered, in that house. But most companions are also confided in. She thought she was, but she was not. Margaret Pearce had a way of saying things, in violence or exaggeration or in their opposite, lightness and mockery, both of which Kate could not take seriously, until it was too late.

Margaret Pearce believed Lord Stonehouse was as responsible for her father's death as if he had murdered him. And she believed his soul would not rest in peace until she had taken her revenge. How did she plan to do this? By no less than taking over all his estates as he had almost swallowed up her father's. To Kate Beaumann this was an excess of grief and loss which, with patience and needlework, would disappear. But they did not.

'I shall have one of them, Kate. Who do you think it should be? The father is an old goat, but he is my lord and must take pride of place. But when he dies, where should I be? The estate is entailed to Richard. So Richard it must be, it seems. He is devilish handsome, but a complete boor! I cannot *imagine* spending my life with him! Edward, at least, has pleasant conversation and a head on his shoulders, but is as weak as water. And he is a second son.'

To Kate, listening as she stitched a sampler, this was like one of the chapbook legends of villains and heroes Margaret used to read with her childhood sweetheart and cousin, John Lloyd. She was deeply in love with John, who wrote passionate letters to her from Ireland, where he was fighting the rebels. Kate could not see her jeopardising that love for any Stonehouse. If she was alarmed when Margaret ordered the most sumptuous mourning clothes in damask and brocade for her father's funeral, it was only because she was already deeply in debt.

The service was in Highpoint church, deemed a great expression of forgiveness by Lord Stonehouse to his old enemy. The living had once been in the gift of the Pearces, and there were still more Pearce effigies and coats of arms than there were Stonehouses in the Norman church. It did briefly cross Kate's mind that Margaret's plans might not be complete nonsense. The Pearces were an older, nobler family than the Stonehouses.

In black, Margaret Pearce looked even more beautiful, startlingly so. Yet her grief was genuine. When the minister said: 'Death unites us all,' her 'Amen' echoed fervently round the old stone walls. The sound drew all eyes to her grief-stricken face, her white perfect skin and her large, liquid eyes, hollowed by sleeplessness, framed in black, except for her flaring red hair. Even Lord Stonehouse, normally as unmoved as one of the effigies of his ancestors, turned his face away abruptly, and was heard to remark that it reminded him of his long grief over his wife Frances.

Margaret Pearce became a constant visitor to Highpoint, keeping her black thoughts away, she said, by devoting herself to charitable work for the deserving poor on the Stonehouse estate, which had been neglected since Frances's death. Perhaps she expected a better relationship with the Stonehouses over her land. Perhaps that would have happened but for Eaton, who blocked all progress. Then came the time when Kate released Eaton from the trap, and later, he freed the stream to water the Pearces' remaining land at Earl Staynton. Margaret was ecstatic. 'He is in love with you,' she said. 'This will save the estate. You *must* give him some encouragement!'

Well, of course, she talked like that, as she talked, in her wild, private moments, of taking over the Stonehouses' fortune. Kate gave Eaton no encouragement. She was, in fact, repulsed by him. But Eaton's goodwill was their lifeline. That was why Kate got the salve from Matthew for his injured leg. That was why she continued, fighting her repulsion, to see him. He gave advice for the Earl Staynton land, even sent some of his men there. The land improved beyond recognition. Astonishingly, she discovered, within that surly, brutal man, feelings which shied away like a nervous horse when she tried to approach them.

She fell silent again. She was breathing heavily, and now she did not look at me for a while; like Eaton telling his story, she seemed scarcely aware I was there. Margaret got rid of the maid who dressed her – for economy's sake, she said. She was sick every morning for a while, would not call the doctor but told Kate to collect a remedy from Matthew. It contained ergot, for getting rid of an unwanted child, although Kate had no idea of that at the time.

Margaret told Kate to ask Eaton for the name of a minister who would perform a secret marriage, saying it was for a friend. Did Kate believe that? It was rather that she did not question it. Of course she was naive, blind to what was going on, but she was living in her own enclosed world. Eaton proposed. She found she did have feelings for this strange, uncouth man. And she certainly had feelings about not wanting to be a companion for the rest of her life. She told him she would give her answer the following day.

The final strange action that brought everything to a climax was when Margaret declared she would sell Earl Staynton. After all her promises that she would rebuild her father's estate, let alone take over the Stonehouses', this was astonishing. But she needed the money. Why, she would not say, but Kate believed she intended to flee to London. It was the early afternoon of 20 September 1625. Eaton rode over on his black gelding to give Margaret a price on Earl Staynton, and to hear Kate's answer to his offer of marriage.

Kate half thought, half hoped that he would recommend Margaret not to sell. Where would they live? Whatever his feelings for Kate, Eaton could not escape from a lifetime's habit of hard, grasping dealing. The price he gave was reduced by the money owed to the Stonehouse estate, and by the work he claimed to have done on the Pearce land; it was a fraction of what Margaret expected. She accused Eaton of cheating her and ordered the cart – their carriage having been sold long since – to drive her to Highpoint. Kate felt cheated also, and refused to talk about marriage. Eaton would not go, but followed her around like a dog, saying he would not leave until she answered him. She retired to her needlework, but when, an hour or so later, she heard the sound of a carriage and came out, he was still there, pacing, his hat in one hand, his whip in another.

Henry, the Highpoint coachman, touched his hat. 'You are to get in, ma'am.'

'Why? What has happened?'

'Don't know, ma'am, but you are to get in and come to Highpoint.'

As Henry lowered the steps, Eaton struck the crop of his whip against his boots. 'I need an answer!'

'No,' she shouted, as the coach lurched off down the pot-holed driveway. 'No, no, no!'

Kate shouted the words in the kitchen garden so loudly that startled birds flew up and two soldiers crossing the top of the garden turned to stare, but she seemed totally unaware of them and me. It was as if she was back in that rocking coach, trembling with fear.

The servants at Highpoint were in a state of confused upheaval. She heard the raised voice of Lord Stonehouse and ran up the stairs and along the landing, where she saw him and his two sons. Richard had an amused look on his face which he was careful to hide from his father. Edward, who had only just taken to wearing spectacles, kept pushing them back as they slipped down his nose.

'She has cheated me, she has cheated all of us, sir!' Lord Stonehouse cried.

'She – she is a married lady, Father,' Edward said.

Kate had never seen Edward like this. Usually meek and deferring, he met his father's gaze defiantly, hands clenched. Margaret married? At that moment, to Kate, it seemed impossible. She was even more bewildered by Richard's remark, as he squeezed his brother's arm protectively.

'Married. Aye. But to whom?'

His father glared back at him, then saw Kate. 'Library!' he barked. She scuttled away. This was women's business. The men seemed to have automatically congregated in one half of the house, and the women in the other. When she lost her bearings in her panic a maid took her to the library. Her chopines made a muddy pattern in some water on the floor, and she remembered thinking how curious that was, because Mrs Morland was such a fastidious housekeeper. Margaret Pearce was stretched out on the floor, a cushion under her head, with Mrs Morland next to her. She stared up at Kate and smiled. It was a weak smile, part greeting, part relief, for she had been in severe pain, but still a smile, and it enraged Mrs Morland as if Margaret Pearce, of all people, had no right to it.

'This is a foul business, Miss Beaumann,' Mrs Morland said.

'Foul?' Kate said, bewildered at her manner, for she thought Margaret had merely fallen ill.

'Foul!'

She pulled up Margaret's dress violently, tearing one of the underskirts as she did so. They were wet, and Kate realised where the water had come from. She stared at the distended belly, the straining, partly torn sex, the dark, reddened shape of something, something which had been struggling to get through. It had stopped, but was beginning another attempt to thrust its way out, the lips of Margaret's sex peeling back. Kate stared in horror, for she knew what that something was. Samuel Pearce had been a strict Puritan, allowing few books in the house, apart from the Bible. One of those was Stephen Batman's *The Doome Warning All Men to the Judgemente*, a chronicle of every prodigy and monstrous birth ever recorded. As Mrs Morland pulled the dress down, Kate remembered that the list proved beyond doubt that indecent, adulterous sex led to the birth of monsters. There were children born with two heads, limbs or fingers missing, twisted or malformed bodies. She was convinced such a monster was about to appear.

'Get her up!' Mrs Morland snapped at her. 'Get her up while she is between times!' She gave Kate an accusing look, as good as saying she must have known, and was a party to this outrage.

How they lifted her, Kate never knew. She was small, and Mrs Morland lean and tall, and Margaret tilted over between them. The maid who had taken her to the library helped get her down the stairs, but as soon as Margaret began talking Mrs Morland dismissed the maid. Margaret reeled between them into the hall. She sounded drunk, but there was no smell of wine about her.

'I am to be married to Lord Stonehouse! What do you think of *that*, Kate? I am to be Lady Stonehouse! You see – it's all come true! It's all come true!' She half-slipped on the tiled floor. Kate lost her grip momentarily, but Mrs Morland kept hers and with savage momentum half dragged Margaret across the slippery floor before Kate caught up. 'Thank you, Mrs Morland,' Margaret said. 'Is my carriage ready?'

Then the pains caught her again. Mrs Morland watched with a smile of grim satisfaction as the coachman Henry helped her into the carriage. Margaret fell across Kate, digging her nails into her hands and biting one of the leather straps, but could not stop a scream tearing from her.

'Wait! Wait!' Mrs Morland hammered at the coach door. 'You know what you have to do?'

'Do?' Kate stared at her, bewildered.

'God's wounds!' Mrs Morland twisted her hands together in frustration, then clapped one hand over her nose and mouth in a smothering gesture.

'I can't do that!'

'You'll be all right. The cart will come for it.'

Having left Highpoint land in accordance with his instructions, Henry breathed more easily, and he, at least, showed some pity on them. Before leaving the cold damp farmhouse, he gathered wood and struck a flint to light a fire. Kate had no idea what to do. She felt she was in the presence of evil. Several times she nearly left, but every time she opened the door, Margaret muttered or screamed and flung out a clutching hand, groping for hers. Kate found water, and heated it, and some dirty cloths. The head came out and it was sticky and wrinkled but, to her surprise, looked normal. For a while, whatever was coming out of Margaret seemed stuck, as exhausted as the mother. During these moments Kate prayed. She heard a clicking and fumbling sound from the mattress where Margaret lay. Margaret kept mumbling something, but Kate shut out the words by praying harder to ward off the devil which was slowly but surely slithering into the world.

The wind blew in swirls, clattering a pail outside. Finding chinks in the crumbling chimney, it whirled spatters of rain hissing into the fire. As if it was part of that sound, part of the violence outside, the thing came out suddenly in one violent eruption. Kate thought with relief the sticky mass was dead. Steeling herself, she picked it up. It slipped from her fingers. Instinctively she grabbed it. The thing shuddered, warm against her, quivered, its mouth trembling and to her astonishment gave a high-pitched, stuttering, but increasingly strong and certain and very human cry. He was normal, flawless. She held him to her and he seemed to fit perfectly in her arms, something that she had never known was missing until now and all her fears and imaginings were swept away. For a moment.

Margaret's eyes opened, her hands moving towards the child. Kate felt a strange reluctance to let the child go. Nevertheless she was passing him to the mother when she started back from what looked like the hypnotic eyes of a snake, the darting glitter of its forked tongue. Another imagining! But the reality was worse.

In her hand Margaret had a jewel which Kate knew well. She also knew that Lord Stonehouse prized Frances's pendant above any other of his possessions. Firelight glinted in the falcon's eyes, as it seemed to stare accusingly at her. Panic filled her as she thought of Lord Stonehouse's man arriving and seeing it. She put down the crying child and tried to take the pendant from Margaret, saying she was mad to steal it.

'It is what I am owed,' Margaret said. 'It is what I've been cheated of! I was going away with the child's father.'

'His father?'

'One of his fathers. That evening. That afternoon. All we needed was the money.'

One of his fathers? What was she raving about? There was a cunning, crazy look in her face and the words came out of her mouth in jerks, like the child had come out of her belly, but there was a terrible kind of sense in what she said. If Eaton had brought the promissory note for the land, they would have gone. The child, probably, would have been born later, in secret, not brought into the world suddenly, by the crisis. The words tumbled out of her, a vehement savage retribution. She clung on to the pendant more than she held on to the child, saying it was her hold on the child's father, for the secret compartment contained proof of who he was. But gradually, spent and exhausted, her grip on the pendant and, Kate thought, her grip on life began to weaken. Muttering that if anything happened to her, Kate was to keep it for the child, saying again and again that her hold on the child's father was in the portrait compartment, she fell into a deep but troubled sleep.

Kate took the pendant from Margaret's slackening grip. The wind snatched the farmhouse door from her hands as soon as she unlatched it. She flung the pendant away as far as she could throw it.

The child was asleep in his mother's warmth. The snake that attached him to her had stopped its strange beating. Kate bit it off near to the child's belly, as she had once seen a midwife do and, although there was no sense in it, in view of what she intended to do, tied the remains carefully and tightly. Then she tried to smother him. He kicked, struggled and cried. His mother stirred. Kate began to weep and tried again. She could not do it. She realised she was still wearing the linen apron she always wore for her embroidery work. She wrapped it round the child and took him to the most exposed place she could find where the east wind cut across an open field, and there was no shelter from the rain. Then she fell asleep in front of the fire, as exhausted as if she had given birth herself.

The distant sound of a cart awoke her. She ran to the field. The child was cold, wet and quite still. She ran back to the farmhouse with him. It seemed to take forever for the muttering, cursing driver to draw up and knock at the door. It was a shock when she opened it to see it was Matthew Neave with the plague cart.

'Evening, Miss Beaumann.'

As if it was a normal evening, normal business!

'He don't look no plague child, Miss Beaumann.'

The shifty manner, scarcely looking at her, but accusing her never-theless, as if she was complicit, responsible! It brought out all the outrage in her, the God-fearing side of her, and she was as bitter as Mrs Morland when she shoved the child, cold as stone, at him. 'He was a plague to us, Matthew!'

Matthew shrugged, took him and went away whistling. Whistling! As if he'd made a fortune! As soon as she slammed the door shut, the recriminations began. She had pushed the sin out of the door: why did it remain with her? In her? She cleaned away all traces of the childbirth, threw the snake on the fire where it seemed to hiss and spit at her. But she could not clean away the feeling that she had committed a mortal sin. What was worse was she could not understand why. It was not her child, not her sin, she had done her duty, but there it was, she could still feel his slippery warmth in her arms, hear his first cry . . .

The good-hearted coachman Henry arranged for a friendly carter to take them home the next day. Margaret was struck by a fever. The craziness that had been in her when Kate and Mrs Morland took her out to the coach at Highpoint took root in her mind. Sometimes she knew about the child, sometimes not. Sometimes she was on her way to Highpoint to see her lover, but which lover was never clear. Always she raved about the pendant. She had to take the pendant. Kate must see that! Taking the pendant was taking his wife, becoming his wife. She spoke about a marriage, sometimes it was as if she was going through the ceremony with Kate, but whether the marriage was a fantasy or a real one was impossible to say. Always her rambling ended with the pendant. 'Keep it close,' she used to say. 'It is the secret of everything. Keep the pendant close.' She lingered two months before she died.

Lord Stonehouse refused to allow her to be buried at Highpoint, so the funeral took place at Shadwell, where the servants were buried. Eaton was at the service, but Kate was barely civil to him. He was as coarse and blunt as usual, seeming unaffected by the whole business. She could not believe that she had once had feelings for him, that inside that brutality she had seen – well, never mind that. She shut her ears to him, except when he asked her if she had heard the stories about Matthew Neave's miracle child. Then she flew at him. She had done what Lord Stonehouse wanted, she cried. The child was dead!

Miracle child! As she watched Eaton ride away she knew he would check. It was one of the things she had liked about him – he checked and double-checked, never leaving things to chance. Just as she did. He would check, and she knew what he would do.

Kate told the carter to take her to Matthew's hovel of a barn, although it was miles away. When she saw the child, the tinges of red hair beginning to show, she fell on her knees and wept for joy. She had no doubt, no doubt whatsoever that the Lord had brought him back from the dead. That was why, ever since, on that day in September, however difficult it was, and wherever he was, she left him a simnel cake, the cake of resurrection.

She told Matthew they must go, and go now, and that she would join them in their flight. She did not know where. Nor did she know how until she saw the plague cart. Few people would question, or even go near, a plague cart. When they were well away from the parish, they could paint over the red crosses and join the thin but steadily increasing stream of people escaping, like themselves, from some crime, or perceived crime, from the recurring threat of harvest failure, from shrinking wages and rising prices, from the loss of smallholdings, from enclosures or shrinking forest rights such as Lord Stonehouse was imposing, to the land of new opportunity: London.

31

Kate had forgotten I was there. She was hunched forward on the bench, her hands clasped, rocking slightly, and I swear that in her mind she was on the rutted road to safety, to London without, in the plague cart. She came to with a start, stared at me as if I was really risen, at that very moment, from the dead and fell on her knees.

'Forgive me! Forgive me!'

I pulled her up. I held her. I told her not to be stupid. There was nothing to forgive. I should go down on my knees to her. I duly did and she pulled me up, laughing. Then I wept. We wept together, great sobs shaking us as we held one another. The soldiers who had passed us earlier stopped again in astonishment. They had killed a pig to salt before leaving the next day and carried great haunches, still dripping blood, on their shoulders. I shouted to them to leave some unsalted for our feast tonight and one of them joked back – for your wedding feast?

'A reunion!' I cried. 'A reunion!'

The rain had cleared, but there was more on the way. The birds were silent. Eaton had taught me to listen to them in one of his jingles that sat oddly on his lips: when the birds come not out, there's more rain about. Soldiers were cleaning muskets and Will was striding about, ordering the packing of wagons that were already packed, the repair of a broken wheel which I thought would be done faster without his interference. Luke was sealing a dispatch, then a letter to Charity, which he handed to a waiting rider. There was a sense of purpose that had been missing for days. I felt it in myself. Purpose, excitement, and, rising steadily inside me, anger. I told Kate that all this time I had been trying to find my father, but I no longer cared. Who needed fathers when I had such mothers as Susannah and Kate? I kissed her again.

She pulled away, laughing. 'I am not your mother, Tom!'

'Then you are very like.'

'You will forget all this then, and go back to London?'

I fell silent. We went inside the great hall and I stared up at the landing. I took two things over all else from Kate's story. One was her steadfast love, the other my birth mother's burning hatred. I felt she had given me that hatred in my blood. Just as she believed Lord Stonehouse had killed her father, I believed – no, I knew – he and his sons had killed my mother. I could see them, the three of them, watching from above as Kate and Mrs Morland half-led, half-carried her down the great stairway while I was being born. I am sure she knew what I was seeing, as I answered her at last, for she kept looking at the stairs, then looking away, trembling.

'No. I am going to stay,' I said. 'I want to find out what happened. I want the truth.'

'You want revenge! You are becoming like her – I *knew* this would happen. This is the worst possible reason for wanting Highpoint.'

I could feel that blood, my mother's blood, rising to my cheeks as I struggled to keep my voice steady. 'Where is Matthew?'

'I won't tell you!'

'I'll find him.'

She began hurrying up the stairs. 'I wish I'd told you nothing!'

I followed her. 'The minister Eaton gave you the name of – who did secret marriages – he's at Shadwell?'

'He was dismissed. After the scandal.'

'Shadwell is where Mrs Morland's funeral is being held tomorrow?'

She whirled round. 'You cannot go there! Edward Stonehouse is taking the service! They will kill you!'

'Then tell me where Matthew is.'

She ran, disappearing just as she had done for most of my life. I saw her only later that evening, when the pork had been roasted on a spit and the soldiers were drunk on perry cider they had found. The hospital had become a servants' dining room again, with only Eaton left. Ben would not let me go in, pulling me back in the dark doorway.

'It is a miracle,' he whispered.

Eaton was propped up in a truckle bed. Candles were lit only at that end of the room, and Kate moved in and out of the light, dipping a cold compress into a bowl, then dabbing Eaton's face with it.

'She has been with him all afternoon and evening,' Ben whispered. 'From the moment she came he opened his eyes and – look, look!'

His scar had been weeping prodigiously, but when Kate brought the compress away it was clean. He shifted restlessly. Kate murmured something and his voice had some of its old strength.

'I see. You came because of Tom. Is that all?'

I was sure it was not – otherwise why had she not come before I told her how he had confessed his love and remorse to me? But when she said, 'All? You saved his life!' his old violent self seemed to return, and he went into a vehement, barely coherent ramble saying that was rich! He had only saved my life to bring me into great danger.

'He knows that.'

'He does not know that – he knows nothing! He must leave here! He must go now!' Alarmed he would relapse, she threatened to go unless he was quiet and he gave her a look like that of a trapped, partly tamed animal, a mixture of burning resentment and need. Several times he opened his mouth to speak, but what he had to say would have been difficult enough in full health, and he closed it under that quiet gaze, until his resentment faded under the need for those gentle movements, the soft rustle of her skirts along the floor and then, quite suddenly, he slept.

32

One of the strangest things about the war was that, although both the King and Parliament vowed they were fighting for God and the people, as soon as either side appeared, the people disappeared, taking their food and animals with them. So it was at Highpoint. When the soldiers were there, there was only Kate and Rose, looking after Mrs Morland. The morning Will's unit left, in some mysterious way the news of their departure had reached every corner of the valley, from Earl Staynton in the west to the Grey Horse in the east.

I went into the kitchen to find some food. A stout woman was scolding a kitchen maid, as if she was responsible for the dirt and grease left by the soldiers on the spit. They were taken aback to see me. I apologised for the mess, but the woman, whom I learned later was Mrs Adams, the cook, turned her back on me.

Other servants disappeared as I approached. At first I took it as an understandable resentment of the unit leaving the house in such a state. But it was more than that. They knew who I was. Edward Stonehouse would be taking Mrs Morland's funeral that morning. I heard someone ask if Richard would be there. I was a usurper.

When I smiled at Rose, who had at first given me such pretty curtseys, she gave me a frightened look and I saw she was being beckoned away by an old man dressed in rusty black. This, I guessed, was Mr Fawcett, the house steward. He had bulging, frog-like eyes which slid from side to side, checking Rose's dress, and those of other servants. All were in black, filing out towards two carts which would take them to the funeral. I heard Fawcett mutter to a barrel-chested man, whom I thought I had seen somewhere before: 'That whore's bastard.'

The blood burned in my cheeks and I took a step towards Fawcett, before stopping myself. Had I learnt from Eaton how to channel rage into such cold bitterness? Or had I inherited it from my mother?

I watched them board the carts. My anger at her treatment mounted as I watched the carts pull away and I went to the stables. I would finish what my mother had begun.

Patch wanted to gallop but I kept her on a tight rein as I followed the carts through a ford, then travelled upward to bleaker country. An uncomfortable silence fell over the carts. Once I caught Mrs Adams's black scarf as it blew off. I handed it to her with as much courtesy as I could muster. She took it without a glance or a word, and let it hang in the wind before wearing it, as if I had given it some contagion. The only person who would meet my eye was the barrel-chested, bearded man I was sure I had seen before somewhere, but could not think where.

Behind me, as we approached Shadwell, I could see a coach climbing the hill. I fell back from the carts and checked my pistol. The village was a huddle of cottages round the church, which was the only substantial building. Apart from a few smallholdings, people seemed to depend for their survival on sheep, which grazed right up to the graveyard. I did not dismount, but waited while the mourners filed into the church and the coach drew up.

First to emerge was Edward Stonehouse, dignified in his clerical robes, prayer book in hand, face solemnly prepared for the service. I stared down at him with interest. It was the closest I had been to him. He gazed up at me in astonishment, the heavy iron spectacles slipping down his nose. It was more than astonishment. His hands shook, almost dropping his prayer book, and his ruddy face lost colour, becoming pallid against his black robes, and he stopped abruptly. His wife, being helped out by the coachman, collided into the back of him.

'Do be careful, Edward. You are in such a dream this morning!'

Her voice was sharp and impatient. She looked as if she had just swallowed a whole bottle of vinegar; her eyes were screwed up and her lips so thin they almost vanished into her face. If Edward had been Margaret Pearce's lover he had had a bad bargain with his wife, I thought; except Luke had told me she had brought him a small fortune, which probably paid for the gleaming coach with the Stonehouse arms, and the coachman's livery.

'What is it? Who is it?' Her eyes were slits as they peered up at me. I returned her gaze with interest while my horse peacefully cropped the grass. She gripped Edward's arm. 'Impertinence! Tell the coachman –'

Whether she intended him to tell the coachman to take his whip to me I never knew, for Edward gripped her arm and almost pulled her through the lych gate. Clearly unused to this treatment, she protested loudly until my identity must have dawned on her for, as she reached the porch, she said, 'It's not *him*, is it?' and twisted round to stare at me. Meanwhile, a governess was ushering the children from the coach. There was one boy, about ten, resplendent in a black doublet who might have attracted Lord Stonehouse as a possible heir, but Phillip (again according to Luke) came from Edward's wife's first marriage. Her husband had been carried off in the same plague that had killed Edward's first wife and the grandson Lord Stonehouse doted on. The other children, all girls, could be my half-sisters. All stared back at me, as children will do, without inhibition, and I gave them as interested a stare back until Phillip demanded of the harassed governess: 'Who is that man?'

'A man on a horse,' she replied.

'I can see that,' he said, with withering scorn. 'Why is he staring at me?'

'Mama said he was impertinent,' the eldest girl whispered to him, simpering.

'Did she! Did she now!' He broke free from the governess's grip and strode up to my horse, which began to back restlessly until I quietened her and made her hold her ground. 'Here – you, sir! Clear off! Unless you want a good thrashing!'

Mrs Stonehouse reappeared at the porch. 'Phillip! Come here! You are at a funeral!'

Phillip looked as arrogant and hot-tempered as his step-uncle Richard, but – giving me a final 'This is a private family funeral, sir, and strangers are not welcome!' – reluctantly joined his sisters trooping into the church. So far I had gained an unexpected enjoyment from this, but now began to feel increasingly uneasy. There was no sign of Richard, or of an approaching coach. He might be in the church, but it was unlikely he would go in before the servants. I had never believed Will's story that Richard had gone to join the King, but was less concerned to question it while his soldiers were there. If Richard and Mrs Morland were as close as she said, I would have expected him to be at her funeral. I hesitated, gazing as if for inspiration at the only elaborate feature of that simple church: a doorway carved with man tempted by fruit from the Tree of Life. I wondered if my mother had gone through that porch to marry. And to whom.

I found a copse where I tethered my horse as best I could from prying eyes. As I returned, I glimpsed a man running from the back of the church towards the village. Edward's reed-like voice was magnified by the bare stone and echoed round me as I pushed open the church door: 'We brought nothing into this world . . .' He stopped as the old, swollen wood grated against the stone flags. Illuminated in the doorway, I felt like a player on a stage as every head swivelled. I had to endure the door's protesting groan again before the cold, musty dimness closed round me.

Heads jerked back as Edward continued, his eyes following me as I stumbled down the aisle, trying to find a place: 'And it is certain we can carry nothing out . . .'

There were places further along the benches, but people would not move, remaining in the aisle seats as still as the stone effigies, staring rigidly ahead, or with bowed heads and hands clasped in prayer. I tripped over a protruding flagstone and would have fallen if I had not grabbed the meaty shoulder of Mrs Adams. I muttered an apology, but she acted as if nothing had happened, apparently too deep in her devotions. Finally, someone did move, albeit grudgingly, leaving me the end of a bench on which I could precariously balance one buttock. It was Henry, the coachman. I nodded my thanks, but he too remained stolidly unaware of me.

Edward might have chosen the psalm deliberately for me. The candle flames in the sconce above his pulpit bent with his movements as he stared accusingly at me: 'Lord, take thy plague away from me!'

'Amen,' said Mrs Stonehouse, from her pew in the front, her children, then the whole congregation echoing her.

Edward gripped the pulpit, his voice carrying an avenging strength. 'Hear my prayer! . . . For I am a stranger with thee: a sojourner, as all my fathers were . . . spare me a little, before I go hence, and be no more seen.'

I shuddered, for although the words were addressed to the coffin below him, they seemed to be directed at me. I felt I had committed a blasphemy, like a thief in the night stealing memories which I had never shared. While the congregation prayed fervently for the soul of Mrs Morland on its final journey, I struggled to join in but the words stuck in my throat. I could feel her presence. She was reluctant to start on that journey while I was there. A malevolence clung round the coffin, as tangible as the damp, cloying scent of rosemary on its lid. Panic rose in me and I was on the verge of running from the church when I remembered I *did* have memories, Kate's memories, as real to me as if I held them myself. I could picture Mrs Morland snatching up my mother's dress as if drawing back a curtain, as I came out into the world.

I covered my face with my hands and prayed, not for Mrs Morland, but for my mother, who was buried in this place, probably quietly and secretly. I wept, standing clumsily, awkwardly as the coffin was lifted, and borne down the aisle, the children briefly scampering to pick up drifting rose petals until they were stopped by their mother.

Through my blurred vision I saw, beyond the swaying coffin, the list of incumbents, beginning with Hugh Bertrand in 1112. I wiped my eyes on my cuff. The incumbent from 1622 to 1625 was Mark Stevens. Then there was a gap until 1627, when Edward Stonehouse gained the benefice, together with Highpoint. Abruptly, I realised I was holding up the people on my bench. All brushed hurriedly past me, as if I had the plague Edward had obliquely suggested, except Henry, who dropped his hat. By the time he picked it up, most people had filed out of the church, following the coffin.

'Upper Vale,' Henry said. Henry's eyes met mine, and I realised he must be the coachman who had helped Kate build a fire for my mother after he had driven them to that remote farmhouse. 'Mark Stevens is at Upper Vale.'

'Thank you,' I said, but he had already gone.

The church had been left open, presumably for the recording of the death. On a small table in the vestry was a bound book ready for signing, a quill and a horn of ink. The book was open, the breeze tugging at the pages, which were weighted down by a seal. I jumped as there was a clattering sound in the church. A pewter bowl used in baptism had fallen from the font and was rolling on the flags. Through the doorway, I could glimpse the coffin being lowered into the grave.

The book contained the parish records of births, marriages and deaths going back to 1604, when the Church tried to tighten its grip on marriage. Before then people might be married (or believed they were) by agreement between parents, spousals before witnesses or even, with poor people in remote areas, a 'handfast' without the blessing of the Church.

I turned back the pages to 1625. They were stuck together. No wonder my hands trembled. Ever since this business began, I had struggled with the stain of illegitimacy. Only now, when it might be disproved, did I fully realise what a weight it had been on my soul, however much I tried to rationalise it away, or shrug it off with bravado. I was in such a haste I tore one page. I struggled to control myself. There was nothing in 1626, which I could understand, for there had been a gap between Mark Stevens leaving and Edward Stonehouse taking the benefice. But, to my acute disappointment, there was nothing in 1625 either. I fumbled wildly with the page, convinced a pair must be stuck together, but it remained firmly, stubbornly, one page. There had been no marriage, and I must remain a bastard forever. It had either never taken place, or been a fantasy in my mother's mind.

Then, as I returned the book to its previous page, I noticed something only someone as zealously trained as I had been by Mr Black would have done: a little flake of paper with a bound edge, caught in a globule of glue, like a fly in amber. I turned the book on its end, towards the light and squinted down the binding. Yes. There was no doubt about it. The page for 1625 had been removed, and the binding re-glued. I was so taken by my own cleverness at this discovery I was unaware someone had crept into the room until the pistol was snatched from my belt. I fell against the table, dropping the book, sending splashes of ink from the horn and the quill spinning to the floor.

The pistol was levelled straight at me by Edward's son Phillip, a triumphant expression on his face.

'Stand away, sir, or I shall fire!'

'Let me have that.'

'No, sir! Stay there or I will shoot you!' The pistol was not cocked, but he must have watched a gamekeeper or perhaps even have been taught to shoot, for he was fumbling to cock it. He backed away. The pistol with its long barrel was too heavy for him, wavering this way and that but, by dint of trial and error, he found the dog lock and at any moment would fire. I dived at him, grabbing at the pistol, jamming the cock with my fingers. He jerked backwards, hitting his head against the door jamb and falling stunned. In an instant he went from being a little man to a boy again, looking about to cry. As I moved to help him, he scrambled away from me and cried that if I shot him – and in church too – I would certainly go to hell. I assured him I had no intention of shooting him, although he would have done the same to me, and would that not have sent him to the same place?

'No, sir!' He got up, with a sullen glare, his courage flooding back to him. 'For I am good and noble, and you are bad and base. You are a *thief*, sir, and I shall tell my father and he shall have you *hung!*'

I squatted down so I was on the same level as him. 'I am no thief, Phillip. I am trying to catch one.'

He scowled at me unbelievingly. 'Who? What did he steal?'

'Me,' I said softly. 'Who I am.' For the first time he looked at me uncertainly, understanding my manner, if not what I said. I pointed to the parish book. 'Perhaps you could ask your father who tore out the page of marriages in 1625.'

He stared at me a moment longer, before abruptly running away. I shouted after him: 'What would you say if I was your step-brother?'

He stopped at the church door, shouting, 'I'd say you were a liar, sir!' before running out.

There was one more thing I had to do. I walked between the gravestones, some blank, others with skulls or winged angels. One after another the servants were picking up earth and scattering it on the coffin. The barrel-chested man picked up his handful of soil. Unlike the others he stared at me again directly, meeting my eyes, but my attention was drawn elsewhere.

Phillip was talking urgently to his mother, making his hand into a pistol. Perhaps he often told stories because, with incredulity on her face she tried to gesture him into silence, only giving her stunned attention when Edward's voice faltered and, in the most familiar passage of all, he put ashes and dust in the wrong order. This disjunction spread along the line of mourners: two, bending to scoop up soil, bumped into one another, one almost falling into the pile of earth, with hurriedly stifled laughter. The regular patter of stones on wood was broken. As I went past, I caught Mrs Stonehouse urging her husband to set the men on me for my insolent blasphemy.

'Be quiet!'

The two words rang round the graveyard. Her mouth dropped open with the astonishment of a woman who had never been spoken to like that in her life. Before she could respond, he continued, hoping Mrs Morland would find eternal life, speaking at such speed he spurred the mourners on so the rattle of stones on the lid became almost continuous.

By some instinct I moved to the north aspect, to a wild overgrown section near the sheep, which scattered as I approached, their bells a thin skeleton of sound. Here, most graves were buried in the undergrowth, few had stones, and fewer still were marked. Burrs clung to my breeches, and the fluffy white seeds of old man's beard eddied around me, drifting where the wind carried them as I searched among the stones.

'Margaret Pearce is there –'

Edward had appeared by my side. He pointed to a stone, jammed against the drystone wall, barely visible among brambles and weeds. I tore them aside, ignoring thorns and nettles. It had no name but at one time had been scratched and scrawled with some obscenity in redding, the dye with which farmers mark their sheep. I fell on my knees and scrabbled the weeds away with both hands.

'Tear away!' Edward said. 'The weeds will grow all the faster – that spot will support nothing else!'

I leapt up. 'I will put a fresh stone there!'

'You will not!'

'I have a right.'

'You have no rights here! Neither has she! She is lucky to be buried on consecrated ground. If it still is! She has soured it, cursed it – nothing will grow in this corner but weeds!'

His chest was rising and falling. He still had the prayer book in his hands, plucking fretfully at a tear in its spine. Everyone had moved from the grave to stare at us. The youngest child, a toddler, was walking towards us before Phillip grabbed him and, imitating his mother's scolds, thrust him at the governess.

'If you do not go, I will have you arrested!'

'For checking marriage records?'

Mrs Stonehouse was moving towards him with a determined expression on her face but he rounded on her so violently she stopped, holding her hat on in the wind, straining to hear.

'Why was a page torn out in 1625?'

He lost all colour and I thought he was going to faint. In spite of everything, in spite of the long journey I had taken to find the truth, my heart went out to him. I was a confused jumble of emotions: anger at his complicity in what had happened to my mother, joy that I might at last have found my father.

'Can we talk elsewhere? Later?'

'There is nothing to talk about!' he said violently.

His reaction was so extreme, his face so full of guilt, I could not stop the word coming to my lips. 'Father –'

For the barest split second he took it as a term of his calling, then jumped as if I had stabbed him. 'I am not your father!' His wife must have heard him, for she now came forward with a look that a cavalry charge could not have stopped.

'The marriage was declared illegal!' Edward said.

'By who? By Lord Stonehouse?' I said.

Suddenly we were all talking at once. The mourners edged forward, open-mouthed.

'What marriage?' Edward's wife said. 'What are you talking about? Who is this man? Is he the b—'

'Bastard? No, madam,' I said, taking off my hat. 'I no longer think you can call me that.'

She stared at Edward, who suddenly turned not on me, but on my mother's grave, over which the weeds and nettles already seemed to be creeping back. '*Origo mali!*' he said, spitting out the words. Then he swung round on me, losing control of himself completely. 'She was a cheat and a thief! She tricked me into agreeing to go away with her, claiming she had money. Money! The only money she had was the pendant she stole that afternoon. That was nothing to do with me – I had no part in it, nothing. I was horrified when she showed me it – horrified!' His voice was now full of bitterness. 'She fooled everyone – she certainly fooled me! You are base born, you are nothing to do with me, *nothing* – and *that* is the whole truth of it!'

33

He had every reason to lie. His wife was standing there. His children had stopped playing, gazing awe-struck at their normally mild-mannered father ranting with the venom of a radical preacher at me, stabbing a finger towards my mother's grave. They had on their faces the look only children have, when they have some terrible foreboding that a disaster is about to strike, but do not understand why or what is happening. The two youngest had run to their governess's arms, and she was whispering to them, comforting them.

Origo mali – the source of the evil. He was wrong to point to my mother's grave. The source of the evil was all around me. The land. The rich valley below me that led to Highpoint and beyond to what had once been the Pearces'. That was the source of the evil, the reason for the feud between the Stonehouses and the Pearces, which probably went back to Tudor times or even further, the true source long forgotten, buried generations back. And I was prolonging it. I could understand now why Kate kept urging me to leave. If I did find out the truth, would that be the end of it? No – it would lead only to more bitterness and conflict. I suddenly had a great longing to be with Will, Luke and Ben in a righteous conflict I could understand, and, if I survived, to return to Anne. I could feel her in my arms. I longed for her and London – the whole wretched stink of it!

But that urge lasted only as long as it took me to find my horse. If I rode away, it would not end. Ever since I had been born, the Stonehouses had tried to kill me. First the father. Then Richard. Now Edward, at the end of his tether, looked capable of doing so. My hands as I gripped the reins were blotched red and white with the nettles and scored with scratches from the brambles I had torn from my mother's grave. I knew her now. Whatever else I was, I was my mother's son. I would finish what she had begun, or end with her in that limbo of weeds, more suited to my nature as to hers than any comfortable, tended, consecrated spot. I could hear her voice, whispering in the wind: *I shall have one of them . . . The father is my lord . . . the estate is entailed to Richard . . . a complete boor! . . . Edward has a head on his shoulders, but is as weak as water . . .*

I had thought for a time I was Lord Stonehouse's son, but now it looked as if I was Edward's. He admitted he had been prepared to run away with Margaret Pearce, but when the money did not appear and she stole the pendant, that was too much for him. He would have been not much older than me. Young. Gullible. Easy to catch. And all the time Lord Stonehouse was, in his cautious, secretive way, harbouring a passion for her.

She laughed, Mrs Morland said: 'Marriage! That's what I want to talk to you about!' Laughter has different meanings, according to who hears it. Mrs Morland heard the mocking laughter of a whore. I heard laughter that was bitter, ironic. If only she had waited, she would have landed the biggest fish of all.

I turned into the lane that ran past the church. Edward was closing the door, talking to the verger who held the parish records. The children, chattering in the coach, became silent when I appeared. So did the mourners in the carts. Perhaps they expected me to follow them, as I had done on the way here, as a curlew follows a traveller over a moor. But I turned Patch the other way.

* * *

On our way to Highpoint, Eaton had pointed out the way to Upper Vale, where the coachman, Henry, had told me I would find Mark Stevens. It was less than an hour's ride from Shadwell, but was as different again as Shadwell from Highpoint.

It was strange, barren land I rode through, rock and heath from which even sheep would derive little sustenance. Strange, yet curiously familiar. It was like the marshland round Poplar; it was Stonehouse without – outside his jurisdiction.

The land improved as I descended from the heath to a straggle of small villages, of which Upper Vale was the first. And the first building, a little distance from the village, was a run-down church. The cottage next to it looked more prosperous, the thatch new and the chimney smoking. A clattering sound came from the yard at the back as I approached. Perhaps I had been stupid to trust Henry. He seemed genuine but, after all, he worked for Lord Stonehouse. I slipped from the saddle, eased out my pistol and crept round the back. A sudden movement made me cock my pistol. I found myself staring into the face of a sorry-looking nag who had just kicked over his pail of water. I righted the pail so he could take the last mouthful and tethered Patch next to him.

The back door was invitingly half-open. Still suspecting a trap, I thrust my boot at it. The draught blew a tang of woodsmoke at me. It did not take long to see the cottage was empty: it was one room, with a ladder to an upper-storey for sleeping. The fire was almost out, producing more smoke than warmth. It was neat and tidy, but there was no sign of a clergyman living here: no books, no papers, only a shelf of herbs.

As I approached the church, I realised it was not run-down, but pillaged. Brasses had been ripped from their matrices. Spikes of broken stained glass were strewn outside a window. Shards of it crunched under my boots as I walked up the aisle. The glass was mixed with splinters of wood from the altar rails, which had been hacked away, as Eaton and I had seen some Parliamentary troops doing on our journey to Highpoint, in an excess of religious zeal and alcohol. They took the rails for firewood, and as a substitute for burning Catholics.

A man was there, a cleric. I saw at first only the fluttering of his black surplice in the breeze from the broken windows, a gentle movement in the darkness of the chancel; I thought he had ascended the pulpit and was gazing towards the ceiling. Then I realised: he was hanging from the tie beam, the knot in the rope tilting his head upwards. I scrambled up to the pulpit, struggling to reach him. The more I tried, the more he spun away from me, like an erratic pendulum. His hand moved with the motion, as if it was trying to reach mine. At last, I managed to grab him and cut at the rope, but he pulled me away with him. For a nightmare moment I was swinging alongside him; the rope seemed alive, wriggling like a snake, about to wrap itself round my neck before it snapped under the double weight and we fell to the floor together.

I broke a nail clawing the rope away from the deepening purple groove in his neck. There was no heartbeat. He was cold, but there was no resistance when I moved his arms: he had been dead just over an hour, perhaps two. There was blood on my hands. No, not blood – dye. It looked like redding, the same dye that had marked my mother's grave. Gently I smoothed out the crumpled surplice. The letters were smeared and incomplete, but I could still make them out: PAPIST. Not far from his body was a scarf – the same orange colour I was wearing which identified the Parliamentary troops.

I was so deep in the horror of this I scarcely registered Patch's distant whinny and snort, until it was combined with his hooves on the flags and the grating creak of a gate. I ran towards the cottage. A man was riding the nag I had given water to and letting my horse out of the yard. If the gate had not stuck he would have succeeded. I dived forward, catching at the edge of his coat. I glimpsed a beard, a mouth bared with few teeth as he tried to bring his whip down on me but I pulled him off and we were on the ground together. I brought back my fist before I saw who it was.

'Matthew!'

He stared at me for such a long, long moment I began to think I was mistaken. I was too young to realise that the distance between forty and fifty, given the losing of teeth and a good deal of hair is much less than that between eight and seventeen. He stretched out a tentative hand, feeling my stubbly beard, touching my red hair, then gave me a very slow, crooked, almost toothless smile.

'Why, Tom!' he said. 'How are you?'

We had no time for a leisurely reunion – if we had stayed much longer, I would have been hanged myself.

Matthew pointed to an angry crowd gathering where the village began, a short distance away, armed with clubs and pitchforks. One man had a hammer, and was still wearing his blacksmith's soot-stained apron. Later in the war, villagers, maddened by the atrocities and plundering they suffered from both Cavaliers and Roundheads, formed themselves into large associations called Clubmen, to protect themselves. Incidents like this were the seeds of it.

'I thought you were one of the people who killed poor Mark,' Matthew said. 'So do they. Take off that orange scarf, for God's sake, otherwise they'll hang you! I'll pretend to be chasing you, otherwise I'll not be able to return.' He threw a punch at me which caught me in the face. I staggered backwards. 'Go on!'

There was a roar from the crowd. 'Get him, Matt!'

I scrambled on to my horse as the blacksmith came running towards me. He threw his hammer, which glanced off the wall as I galloped away. He ran beside me, grabbing at my saddle. Tight as I had the girths, he was immensely strong and I felt the saddle twisting round. The ground and his grinning face swayed towards me. I saw myself hanging from that beam. I wrenched at the reins. Patch reared. The blacksmith's momentum flung him forward, but still he clung on to the slipping saddle. I lashed out with my boot, the spur catching him in his face. He gave a single grunt and fell. I righted myself in the saddle. The crowd had stopped, silent now their leader was down, blood pouring from his face. I stopped, full of guilt and bewilderment. What was I doing, what were we all doing, fighting one another? They were like me, like the crowd who had fought and demonstrated for those words I had rescued from the mud. I would help him, talk to them! So I thought wildly, until the blacksmith stirred, the crowd began to mutter angrily and I kicked my heels into Patch and rode on.

I waited on the heath, by a stream, until Matthew joined me. He marvelled at my height, at my beard, while I could not believe he was so small and, well, so . . .

'Shrunk and wizened?' he said. 'It's good for business as a cunning man. The older I get, the more people believe me.'

I laughed, touching him, still not quite able to take in that he was here, that he would not disappear at any minute; in one moment I could look at him in awe, the next in disbelief. I hugged him with delight and wonder, for he was my past, all the stories he had told me . . . but then, as I felt his bony chest against me, my hands crept down to where, under his shirt, he kept the belt and the pouch.

I had dreamed of this moment ever since Eaton and I had travelled together. Just as it had been in front of the flickering dockyard fire he would take the pouch from his belt and the pendant from the pouch. I could feel nothing but skin and bone. I pointed back towards the village.

'Is it down there?'

He looked as directly at me as he had ever done in my life.

'I don't have it, Tom.'

'You're lying! Where is it?'

'I don't have it!'

'Tell me! Tell me!' I shook him. I was like a maniac. He pulled backwards, stumbled and almost fell in the stream, then yanked his shirt so violently from his britches the old, rotting fabric tore. His ribs stood out in the greying, puckering flesh.

'I don't have it, I tell you! I did what Kate told me to and got rid of it – and that's the truth!'

34

I sat on a stone by the stream, unable to move or think. In one part of the sky rain clouds were building up again, merging with the heath, but in the west the sky was white as milk. The horses were sucking contentedly in the stream. The constant heath wind rippled the hair tufted round Matthew's bald crown as he took some bread and cheese from his saddle bag.

'Did me no good and it would have done you no good, Tom,' he said softly.

I said nothing. I had carried the memory of him all these years and tried to tell myself I still loved him, but the truth was I did not. I loved the memory of him building ships and telling me stories of foreign lands, and making things happen by magic and bringing out the pendant, the falcon flashing and dipping and flying in the firelight as he told me my fortune. But I knew now he had never left England and the stories were from sailors in the docks; there was no magic but that of persuading people his herbs would work; and, he was now telling me, no pendant.

I noticed how bent his back was and that the bread he was preparing to eat was mouldy. He offered me some, admitting it did not look much, but fresh air and a dip of spring water was a very fine sauce.

'What is it, Tom?' he said gently. 'Art thou not pleased to see me?'

'Yes, yes, of course I am,' I said, against the curious sort of lump that seemed to be forming in my throat. Then: 'No! No! No! I am not!'

I seized the lump of mouldy bread and flung it into the stream. He stared in astonishment as it drifted away, bumping and eddying against a rock before being swept out of sight. He was even more astonished at the torrent of bitterness that poured out of me. So was I. I had no idea that it had been sealed up in the deepest caverns of my heart all these years. He had deserted me. He had deserted Susannah, leaving her to be murdered. Burned. Did he know that?

'Of course I know that!' He rounded on me with a sudden venom. 'Why do you think I got rid of it? Ever since I picked it up it's been a curse on me, and it would have been a curse on you. Do you think there's been a day when I haven't thought about Susannah? About you?'

That cut me, but like everything Matthew said it was true and not true. There was something he was holding back from me. He knew where I was in the City, I retorted, because he had remained in touch with Kate. Yet he had made no effort to contact me. Why should I be pleased to see him? To care about him?

He stood by the stream, fidgeting with the lump of cheese, putting a crumb of it in his mouth. When he gave no answer and I made a furious move towards him to demand he at least look at me, he jerked his cheese away as if afraid I would throw that in the water too. The movement both filled me with shame and irritated me beyond endurance.

'I have not been a good father,' he mumbled.

'You are not my father!' I shouted, so loudly the horses lifted their dripping mouths from the stream to stare at me.

'That too,' he said. 'That too.' He scratched his bald patch. All life's puzzlements seemed to be in that scratch, as he stared across the barren heath which, with its scrub and rock, always seemed to retain something of evening. In places it was almost one with the lowering sky, which looked heavy with more rain, in others brighter than noon with flickering patches of light. I thought for a moment he was whistling through his front tooth, but it was the wind, shredded by the thorns. Furtively, he eased another crumb of cheese into his mouth.

I could not look at him or keep still. I strode to my horse, feeling I never wanted to see him again. Patch shook herself, spraying me with water, but I scarcely felt it. I stopped, strode back to see Matthew sucking some morsel from a crevice in his tooth and turned to my horse again, plunging my hands in my pockets, as I always did when I did not know which way to turn. My fingers closed on the coin. I whirled back, overwhelmed by a great rush of guilt, staring at his bent figure, his cheeks hollowed, then ballooned out by his scouring tongue. After what he did, how could I have said he was not a good father?

'I'm sorry,' I wept, 'I'm sorry.'

I went over and hugged him properly. He jumped, dropping his cheese, afraid I had gone crazy and was about to throw him in the stream too, then saw the coin in my hand. 'Kate told me it was dangerous to get in touch with you. You were leading a different life. You *are* different.' He took the coin. 'Is that it? My Judas coin? Is that really it?' He turned it on the edge, saw the fleur de lys, weighed it in his hand and moved to give it back to me. He told me what I have related, that when he threw what he thought was a dead child into the cart there was a fiendish cry of an evil spirit pursuing him. The faster he went, the louder and more piercing it became, until he could stand it no longer. He stopped, intending to fling out the child. But the fearsome cry stopped as soon as he went round the cart.

'You looks at me. And I looks at you. And you looks as though you're about to cry up to the heavens again, so I puts you inside my jacket and, God help me, you goes to sleep! After taking you to Susannah, I show Mr Eaton a dead baby from the cart and –'

He flipped the coin in the air, caught it, looked at it rather regretfully, then flung it in the stream. I looked at him with the same astonishment that he had shown when I threw away the bread. I ran down the stream, saw it glinting in the water, but as I stretched out to get it, he put his hand on my arm.

'Leave it, Tom. It's finished now. It's no more good to you. Nor is the pendant.'

'You still have it.'

'No, Tom.'

'I need it to find out who my real father is. I don't want to keep it!'

'Is that true?'

'Yes!'

He gave a great sigh. He stared at the coin glinting in the eddying water. 'I put it back.'

'Back? Where?'

'Highpoint. So no one could accuse me of stealing it. I gave it to Kate. She put it in the jewellery drawer in Frances's bedroom.'

I gaped at him. 'In the – Anyone could find it. I could have found it.' He shook his head. 'It's a secret drawer. It's true!' he said when he saw my disbelieving expression, with the desperate vehemence of a habitual liar who cannot get anyone to believe him when he does tell the truth. 'Where do you think I learned carpentry? Before I got the plague cart I delivered wood to the cabinet maker. I watched him shape that secret drawer.'

I rounded sceptically on him again. 'Then how did my mother know where to look for –' I shivered. It was not just the evening cold that was coming with the advancing rain clouds that crept slowly over the heath, gradually staining the paler sky like spilled ink. I knew the answer to my question before I put it. 'You told my mother, didn't you?' I shook him. 'Didn't you?'

He sighed a very deep sigh and said he used to tell stories about the pendant which everyone had marvelled about when Frances

Stonehouse wore it in church. He boasted he knew where it was. That afternoon in September, Margaret Pearce came to him. She threatened to tell everyone neither his love philtres nor his whore's physic worked if he did not tell her about the drawer.

He sighed again and dropped his head in his hands, staring at the coin in the water. 'You know everything now. Satisfied?'

Satisfied? I dragged Matthew up from the stone and hugged him and danced him around until he nearly fell in the water.

'Come on! Let's go!'

'Where?'

'Highpoint. Before the light goes.' I pulled him to his horse and cupped my hands to give his old bones an easy lift.

'Wait.' He would not move an inch until I told him everything that had happened. When he learnt that the Parliamentary soldiers had left a day ago, he backed away.

'Then who killed Mark?'

'I don't know. But I'll bet it was Cavaliers, working for Richard Stonehouse.'

'Mark wasn't a papist.'

'They killed him to destroy the last evidence of the wedding. They wore orange scarves like mine to pretend to be Roundheads.'

Lightning lit up the heath. The horses lifted their heads and trod restlessly, waiting uneasily for the low mutter of thunder. The prospect of a downpour on open country made it easier to urge him on his horse. Halfway in the saddle he stopped.

'They've been waiting until you find me, then they can get us both and the pendant.'

'I've worked that out. We're both storytellers, Matthew.'

'There's a difference between telling a story and being in it. We're riding into a trap.'

'Not if we know it is one.' I could feel myself being pulled towards Highpoint, like a compass needle towards north. And I felt as cold and hard as the metal itself, as the ice that is supposed to cover the northern climes and the frost spirits who had ice for their hearts. 'We can avenge Mark's death. And my mother's.'

'Are you mad? We can't fight an army of Cavaliers.'

'No.' I swung on to my horse. 'But we can take the pendant.'

He clapped his hand to his head with such force I thought it would fly off. '*Steal it – again!*'

'Return it to Lord Stonehouse properly.'

Lightning scored the sky again, and this time the thunder was closer. A wind sprang up, rippling the heather. I urged my horse on to the track, but Matthew pulled his back.

'Tom, don't be a fool. It's not you riding the horse – it's the pendant.'

I hesitated, but only for a moment. 'You may be right. You're wiser than I am, Matthew. But one thing I have learned – you can't keep running away for ever.'

He looked as if I had cut him across the face with a whip – it hurt him more than anything else I had said or done. It was meant to.

35

I heard a shout and galloping hooves as I left the heath to descend to Shadwell. When Matthew caught me up he pointed to a path that led through the copse where I had tethered Patch during the funeral service. No one knew that country better than Matthew, not even Eaton. He had lived on his herbs and his wits for years, travelling on little-known paths between Upper Vale and Oxford. As the rain came down as though it was being poured from pitchers he led me through a wood which became part of the Great Forest. It was slow riding but a much shorter route and, when we reached the spreading impenetrable oaks, gave us some shelter both from the downpour and what might await us at Highpoint.

We reached the edge of the forest and stared down at the house. The rain had slackened to a steady drizzle, punctuated by large cold splashes dripping from the trees. The moon, when it appeared, threw long black shadows of the house. It was exactly the same moon as the night I was born, Matthew said. I scornfully told him he was imagining things, but so was I, seeing my mother being put in the coach, lurching wildly down that avenue black with rain.

We forded the river and Matthew led me through a copse where we left our horses and mounds of leaves deadened our approach. Candles were lit in the hall and we saw a maid lighting them in one of the lower rooms. There was no sign of anyone else, and no sound except the occasional distant clatter from the kitchens and the steady patter of rain. We worked our way round to the outermost wing, where I planned to climb up and break through a window, but first I tried a servants' door. It was open.

'I don't like this,' Matthew whispered.

'Listen.' I pointed towards the stables.

'I hear nothing.'

'Exactly. No horses.'

'They'd leave them out of earshot.'

I hesitated, but felt the pendant was so close it was pulling me inside. I slipped into the dark passage. There was a smell of stale cooking. After a moment he followed me. Light spilled from an open door and I ducked back as Mrs Adams appeared, throwing some slops into a bucket in the passage. I watched her disappear, shouting at someone: 'D'you call that clean? Scour it! Scour the soldiers away! Thank the good Lord He's delivered us from them!'

We climbed the back stairs, stopping in the shadows at the edge of the gallery, blinking at the light. Every candle in every sconce was lit. Once across it we would be in the maze of dark corridors that led to Frances's bedroom. I was about to dart across when there was a woman's cry. It came from a large reception room with double doors across the landing and was followed by a murmur of voices. I jumped back into the shadow of the stairs.

Eaton came out of the room. I could see Kate, but no one else. It *was* a miracle. I never thought to see him walking again and ran towards him. He did not look glad to see me, but then he never looked glad to see anyone. I embraced him and he started to say something but it was lost in the sudden tumult of doors opening and swords being drawn.

'You can release him from your fond embrace, Eaton,' Richard said.

He leaned against the wall, looking as if he was dressed for court, in a red doublet, over which he wore a short cloak with a jewelled clasp bearing the Stonehouse falcon, which seemed to flutter as he moved. Behind him were several men. At the door of the room from which Eaton had emerged was Captain Gardiner, very much as I first met him in the stink of Smithfield, except his new beaver hat was freshly brushed. He was leaning near the room from which Eaton had emerged, the flame of a candle reflected in the rapier in his hand.

'Where's the other one?' Richard said sharply. 'Idiots! The back stairs!'

As usual, Matthew had vanished. How he managed it, I did not know, but, I thought sourly, he had had plenty of practice at it. For once I felt glad. They would soon have got out of him where the pendant was. I forgot Matthew, my attention, all my bitter attention, turning on Eaton, who stared just as bitterly back at me. 'I trusted you,' I said. 'I thought you were my friend.'

'You trusted Eaton!' said Richard incredulously. 'You thought he was your friend!'

There was an avalanche of laughter and I realised that all the servants who had been in the congregation that morning had appeared, from doors, down in the hall, halfway up the stairway where the barrel-chested bearded man's face was split into a wide grin; the cook stood at the door to the back stairs, her vast frame shaking. Like the King, in his attempt to arrest Pym and the other five members in the House, Richard Stonehouse had an acute sense of theatre. Everything had to have style, be part of a performance, to impress upon the people where power lay.

'Eaton has no friends – have you, Eaton?' Richard said.

'None,' Eaton said savagely.

'Eaton is the best liar, the best cheat I have ever known, aren't you, Eaton?'

Eaton said nothing, but there was a murmur of anger among the servants, and the cook looked about to spit at him.

'I only found out how he had cheated my father for years when

I got the papers from that other crook Turville's chambers. That is why you brought the pretender here, isn't it, Eaton? Because I threatened to give proof of it to my father.' There was another burst of anger from the servants, but Richard silenced them with a gesture. 'But, to be fair, Eaton built up the estate. He is good at contracts, and we made a contract. Bring me him and you can keep your position. I shall need a good steward.'

He clapped Eaton on the back. Eaton staggered and I realised how ill he still was, the livid palpitation of his scar the only colour in his face. He gripped the balustrade behind him to steady himself, glancing at the reception room he had emerged from. Following his gaze I saw that Kate was being held by a soldier, who had a knife at her throat. My numbness went. I had been a fool, but not a complete fool.

Eaton *had* changed during the journey here – nay, long before that. The thought of Kate, the prospect of seeing her again, had fought with the bitter alienated part of his nature fearful of losing what he had built up over a lifetime. I could now see signs of that struggle during the journey – half-warnings, surly rejections – even welcoming death as preferable to a struggle he had become too exhausted to believe he could ever win or resolve. Then Kate had come to him. Richard no longer had a hold on him, so he had had to take her hostage. I could read this in Eaton's agonised look towards Kate, in the look he gave me.

Perhaps Richard picked this up too. His mocking tone went. I saw his father in him then, in the brooding, almost morose manner he put on like a robe. He said there had been a great crime, an attempt to impersonate the family name in which, unfortunately, his father had been almost deceived, before turning on me.

'Where is the pendant?'

'I don't know.'

'Answer my lord,' said Captain Gardiner.

I said nothing. Perhaps it was the signal from Richard, the

movement of his cloak that, in the shifting candlelight, made me think the falcon had struck with a whirr of wings, slashing my cheek with its beak. Gardiner's rapier was back at rest, the point still quivering before I felt the oozing of blood and its slow trickle down my cheek and neck.

'Where is the pendant?'

I stared back at him and bit my lip so I would not cry out when the second cut came, but Richard stopped Gardiner and said something to one of his soldiers, who took out his pistol, pointing it at Eaton.

'Take his pistol, Eaton,' Richard said. Eaton did not move. We were a pair then: me with my fresh cut, and Eaton with his old scar, which seemed to unnerve Richard even then. I remembered Eaton telling me that Lord Stonehouse would threaten his sons that, if they were disobedient, Eaton would come to them in the middle of the night. '*Take it!*' Richard snapped.

The sour, rancid smell of Eaton's sickness hung round me as he removed the pistol from my belt. I swallowed down bile.

'Is it loaded?'

'Yes, my lord,' Eaton replied.

Richard looked gratified at the form of address. He seemed to need Eaton's humiliation as much as he needed mine. 'Cock it.' The soldier still kept his pistol trained on Eaton as he did so. 'Eaton's a good shot, aren't you, Eaton? I know. The best. You taught me.'

'Thank you, my lord.'

'Stretch out your hand,' Richard said to me. When I did not move, he said, equably, almost pleasantly, 'Eaton can shoot you in the elbow or the shoulder, it's all the same to him, isn't it, Eaton?' Eaton nodded indifferently, and raised the pistol. 'But I deem it more appropriate, because of your seditious pamphlets against King and Church, to remove the offending hand which will, at least, leave you your arm.'

Slowly, very slowly, I lifted my arm and stretched out my hand, willing it not to tremble, but the cursed thing did so. 'Wait, Eaton – do not fire until I give you the signal.' He turned to me. 'I will spare your hand if you tell me where the pendant is.'

Torturers have much in common with those who break children. Like Gloomy George, Richard had an instinct for weak spots. I felt my whole life, everything of meaning I had ever done was in that hand; I had written the poem to Anne with it, inked the Grand Remonstrance with those fingers that would not stop shaking. I wanted to shut my eyes but would not give him that pleasure, although the servants were the worst of it: shuffling hurriedly out of the firing line, giggling, whispering, their craning faces like those of people round a pit betting and watching cocks or dogs tear at one another. Only Rose turned away, looking white and sick, but Richard, always with an eye for a pretty face, smiled and beckoned her to the front, as if he was doing her a favour. The soldier pointing his pistol lowered it for a better view, and the man holding the knife to Kate's throat craned forward.

Richard said he would give me until the count of five – since I was apprenticed I no doubt knew my numbers? There was a titter of laughter, then total silence as he began to count. When he reached three, counting slowly, leisurely, I could no longer stand it, and tried to speak, to blurt out where the pendant was. He stopped counting. Bile rose in my throat, but my mouth was so dry I could not swallow it and could not speak. He waited. And as he waited he smiled. That smile of triumph welled up in me all the stubbornness and hatred for people like him that years of beatings had bred in me and I would not speak. His smile went and he continued counting. At five I shut my eyes.

Eaton fired.

36

I was deafened by the explosion, spun round expecting the blow and the violent, searing pain in my right hand, which I knew would no longer be there. Yet in almost the same moment I was being pushed against the balustrade by Eaton. His lips were moving, but I could not hear a word for the ringing in my ears. Beyond Eaton, I could see the man who had been holding Kate, his one eye staring rigidly from his shattered face as he slowly slipped to the ground. Gardiner was on the floor, trying to retrieve his rapier from amongst the feet of the panic-stricken fleeing servants. Most inexplicable of all, my right hand was still there, bleeding but still there. I realised that Eaton had used the rapt attention of the audience to draw the man holding Kate into a vulnerable position, then had knocked Gardiner down with the discharged pistol.

I winced as the hearing rushed back to my ears. 'Jump!' Eaton yelled. Richard's determination to discredit me before the servants now told against him as they ran, screaming and pushing towards the stairway, blocking the efforts of his soldiers to reach me. I scrambled up on to the balustrade to jump down into the hall below, expecting Eaton to follow me. But he ran to Kate. A soldier aimed his pistol at Eaton's back. I jumped back down from the rail into the gallery, sending the soldier sprawling, his shot hitting a candle sconce, spraying shards of glass and molten wax down on Richard as he came at me with his sword. I ran to the room where Kate was, just before Eaton slammed the doors, shoving a table under the handles. Kate looked about to remonstrate with him but, realising it would be useless, helped me bring up more furniture to block the door.

'I told you to jump!' Eaton yelled at me.

'You've saved my life too many times for me not to repay the compliment.'

'I told you! Only fools are heroes. There's an ante room – a window – go.'

Lifting a chair, he almost lost his balance. I caught him. His face was parchment yellow, and I could hear the violent thudding of his heart, in tune with his palpitating scar, which seemed to be opening up his whole face. But his manner was as surly as ever, his voice almost a snarl. 'I didn't do it for *you*. Don't think it! I did it for the estate. Everything – even the thieving – was to keep the estate together, to stop them mortgaging it piece by piece. I realised too late you are the one to do that – go.'

He shoved me away so violently I fell near the body of the soldier who had been guarding Kate.

'Here – this way! Quick, Tom!' Kate opened the door to an ante room as there was a shot, the ball tearing a hole in the door and sending one of the handles flying. Eaton attempted to hold the makeshift barrier together with his failing weight but the table grated back inexorably and one of the doors jerked open, catapulting a soldier into the room. Eaton struck him with a chair.

I was scrambling up to run into the ante room when Gardiner lunged over the remains of the barrier. I saw the tip of his sword come through Eaton's back before Gardiner withdrew it. Kate was shouting at me but I made nothing of the words, for Eaton still stood there, only staggering a little. I suppose, from our journey together, I had grown to think him invulnerable. Perhaps everyone in some measure thought that, for there was a brief silence, a stillness. He was like a great tree which, after no matter how many blows, shows no inclination to fall. He was still holding the chair with which he had struck the soldier, and he made a movement to strike back at Gardiner. Then the chair dropped, and, slowly, he fell.

All I could see was Richard's triumphant face in the doorway. I seized the sword from the dead soldier and ran at him. I had none of Gardiner or Richard's fancy Italian swordsmanship. If the Trained Band taught anything, it was the old-fashioned cut and thrust. But I had foolishness, plenty of that, and blind rage at the sight of Eaton falling, a great deal of that, as well as a liberal dash of surprise and leapt on the table, bringing the sword down on him. For a moment he staggered, but I had been deceived by the billowing cloak as he ducked away, giving him no more than a glancing blow in the arm, before the cloak twisted my sword away and I was dragged from the table. If Richard wanted to demonstrate to the servants that I was the lowest of low life I gave him full measure then. I returned, as if there had been no interval of time between now and then, to how I had been when George first locked me in the cellar, screaming and kicking and biting and scratching until, I suppose, I was like the wild animal Eaton had been before the Stonehouses subdued him.

I believe – I was slipping in and out of consciousness – Richard intended to hold the trial the next day, but a mud-splashed messenger arrived, telling him he had to leave early in the morning. I was kicked and jeered at and told the King was going to have his own again: there was to be a great battle in Warwickshire and what a pity I would not be there to take part in it.

Richard told me I was to be charged with murder. He said something about mitigating circumstances if I gave him information about the pendant, but by this time I had reached a state of indifference about what was going to happen to me. As I was dragged away I held in my mind the picture of Kate cradling Eaton in her arms, of her bending to kiss him, of the blood suddenly spurting from his mouth, and of her kissing him anyway, blood and all, and holding him tight to her. While Richard was talking about what seemed to me unimportant, meaningless things, all I could see was this, and it struck me with great force how alike we were, in that Eaton had never known his father, and I was constantly searching for, yet never finding mine, and that the main difference, perhaps the only difference between us, was that I had found love early.

They brought a man into the room whom I did not at first recognise, until I realised he was the blacksmith from Upper Vale without his apron. He testified that I was one of four Parliamentary troopers who had desecrated the church and hanged Mark Stevens.

Nothing brings a man to his senses more acutely than lies, particularly when they are so cunningly interwoven they seem to be the truth, and the more you protest, the tighter the net closes round you. The only way out is to stop struggling and try to find the one knot that holds the whole mesh together.

The trial was designed to break me further so I would reveal where the pendant was. Richard even had Mr Fawcett, the house steward, taking notes like a judge's clerk. But when Edward entered, in his clerical robes and holding a prayer book, it took on a different tone. Richard told a soldier to prepare the horses. He would ride by night if the sky kept clear and would leave in half an hour. They really meant to hang me. It was evident in Richard's eyes. Evident in the way the troops held me when, at that moment of realisation, my legs suddenly buckled and would not support me.

Half an hour. There was a lantern clock behind the desk where Richard sat, which had just struck nine. It had a design of intertwined tulips on the face, and the hand was still, in the centre of one petal. I stared at it as if, absurdly, I could stop it.

A whispered argument between the two brothers gave me a shred of hope. Edward, at least, seemed to grasp the enormity of what they were doing. Much as he wanted to see me dead, he was afraid, nay terrified, of his father. 'What if the King doesn't win?' I heard him say.

Richard dismissed any possibility of that, but I could see he feared it, and his father's reaction. That was why he had to justify what he was about to do with this trumped-up charge. My only chance was to play upon that fear, to try and drive a wedge between the two brothers.

'Why would I kill Mark Stevens?' I said.

They looked at me, startled, as if at that point I was already a body to be disposed of, not a real person.

'Because he would not give you the information you wanted,' said Richard.

'But he did,' I lied. 'He told me he married Edward at Shadwell to my mother.'

All the agitation that had been present in Edward that morning rushed back in him. Before Richard could stop him, he cried: 'The marriage was illegal.'

'Then why did your father have the records removed?'

'Because I told my father the truth that night!'

'Shut up, Edward,' said Richard, but it was impossible to stop his brother. His glasses were askew, his face distorted. It was one of those faces where the shape of youth lives on well into middle age, and I could imagine him that night, facing his father, terrified.

'I told him you were not my child.'

'How did you know?'

'How did he know?' said Richard contemptuously. 'Because he never fucked her – he says.'

'It's true!' screamed Edward at his brother. 'I did not know she was pregnant when I married her!'

Richard was suddenly aware of the steward, his protruding eyes standing out even more than usual, scribbling as fast as he could. 'Strike that,' he snapped. 'Give me the book. Go! All of you go, except you –' He pointed to Gardiner. 'Wait! None of you heard that, is that understood?'

They bowed and left. Edward was gripping his prayer book, saying some Latin line of prayer, over and over again. To my surprise, Richard went to him and put his arm round him with a real gesture of affection. 'Eddie, don't let him get at you. That's just what he wants, can't you see?'

'Then who is my father?' I asked.

Richard pointed to his father's picture. 'You would think he is, after what he has done for you. You don't know, do you? You have no idea what you have done to this family.'

I stared back at him, astonished. 'I have done nothing to you, nothing.'

'Ever since you were born . . . reborn –' He rounded on his brother, who was still muttering the line of Latin prayer. 'For God's sake, Eddie, stop saying that. If God hasn't heard you by now, He never will.'

Edward stopped, but his lips continued moving soundlessly as Richard marched over to his father's desk. He pulled fruitlessly at a drawer, then gestured to Gardiner, who prised away the lock with his dagger. From the drawer Richard took a bundle of documents sealed with red wax, and another of letters which he threw on the desk. Then he drew out a bundle of childish drawings, pages of figures and lines of Latin repeated again and again. His hands shook as he tried to separate pages stuck together, until he finally found what he was looking for.

The single hand of the lantern clock made a small grating sound as it jerked forward. Richard glanced at it. I felt the last half-hour of life he had allotted to me was almost done, and in those circumstances the yellowing piece of paper Richard thrust in front of my eyes was the last thing I expected to see.

'Do you recognise that?'

I took it and stared at it in bewilderment. It was a crudely written Latin tag, repeated again and again: *omnes deteriores sum licentia.*

'It's Terence, isn't it?' I said. 'Odd from a former slave: "too much freedom debases us". But it should be sumus, not sum –'

He snatched it back. 'Oh, *you* would know that, wouldn't you.'

I ought to. I had written the same line tediously, again and again. I told him so.

'Perfectly!' he said. 'Perfectly written, perfectly declined –'

I told him that I had been as full of mistakes as anyone and beaten more than most, but he would have none of it. While Edward exclaimed in wonder at finding passages in Greek he had written, Richard said in a sarcasm brittle with rage that I was perfect, had a perfect hand, was a perfect scholar, and on top of that a perfect gentleman. I laughed at this idiotic picture of myself when I remembered the wild, uncouth apprentice who, at first, had to be forced into wearing boots. He caught me a stinging slap across my face.

I understood then. I had always thought, from the moment I discovered it was Richard who wanted to kill me, that it was because I threatened his inheritance. And, of course, it was that. But it was about more, much more. After my pitch burn, when Lord Stonehouse picked me up, he had returned to Highpoint and called Richard and Edward into this room. I could see the scene, as Richard bitterly, compulsively told it.

Lord Stonehouse wore what the two brothers called his hanging face. He told them he had seen a child with Stonehouse features and hair as red as fire. Moreover, the child was with that wretch Matthew Neave, who drove the plague cart that night in 1625. Lord Stonehouse went over again what his two sons had told him that September night ten years before – that Edward had been tricked into marriage, and that the child had been fathered by Margaret Pearce's cousin, John Lloyd. Richard again supported his brother, saying everyone knew Margaret Pearce had been infatuated with John Lloyd. Lord Stonehouse made them swear on the Bible that their accounts were true, as if they were in a court of law.

And that, they thought, was the end of it.

But it was not. It was as if what had been buried in the pit had crept out and attached itself to Richard like a leech. That was how he described it, although he did not at first connect the change in his father's attitude to me. Before his visit to the shipyard at Poplar, Lord Stonehouse had resigned himself to the fact that Richard had no ambitions beyond the estate and his own pleasure, principally the latter. After he found me, his old desire for his eldest son to establish a place at court and in the affairs of state was rekindled. He wanted him to read Latin again, resume dusty lessons in rhetoric he had long forgotten. He was *twenty-seven!* His father cut his allowance until he conformed. He told him the Stonehouse name and fortune was not built on the *contra guardia* and *ricavatione* of the rapier, but on the *ethos*, *pathos* and *logos* of persuasion and argument.

Belief, emotion and reason! Make them believe, make them feel and make them think. How often had I been beaten with the same three sticks! I had been taught by Dr Gill but the hidden hand behind the lessons was that of Lord Stonehouse. I had been whipped through exactly the same series of hoops as Richard.

One day Lord Stonehouse put Richard's Latin text next to the same text in another hand. Compared with Richard's misshapen letters, it was perfect.

'It is writ by a scrivener,' said Richard, with contempt. 'No gentleman would write like that. When I need a letter, I employ a scrivener.'

'A gentleman cannot be illiterate, sir,' snapped his father. 'Your hand is unreadable.' He tapped the other text. 'This is written by a boy of ten.'

Whether or not Lord Stonehouse intended Richard to know about me I cannot tell, but from that moment I became the leech sucking not just at his inheritance but, in his eyes, his whole manhood. He found out about the payments to Mr Black, which, in Lord Stonehouse's careful management of his affairs, exactly balanced the reduction in Richard's allowance (or so it appeared to his now fevered imagination). Then he saw my picture.

I understood more and more, but grew more and more bewildered. 'But if what you told him about John Lloyd is true,' I burst out, 'why should you be so concerned about him finding the pendant? Surely you *want* it found?'

'You know,' Richard said. 'You know why.'

'I do not know.'

'Tell him, Rich. Tell him.' Edward broke in. '*Because he wants to change it, of course!*'

'He knows that,' Richard said.

'I do not. I swear I do not.'

'Liar!' Richard lashed his hand across the deepening wound in my face. 'Where is it? Where is the pendant?'

Change it? Lord Stonehouse was devious enough, but what was important to him was the bloodline, surely. One of them was lying, probably both. There was something not right . . . something Kate had told me . . . In the dizziness, pain and confusion I could not think – but I *had* to think.

Richard stared at the portrait of his father 'He wants you,' he said, with savage bitterness. 'He wants you to inherit.'

'That's not true.'

'I saw you at Queen Street. Dressed for the part.'

'I deceived the footman at the door. Your father did not know I was there.'

'Liar! Did he send you up here for the pendant? Of course he did. Where is it? Tell me! Tell me!'

Now it was Edward who pulled his brother away, whispering to him. I heard the word 'cellar'. They must have seen Mr Black's reports of my childhood fears, the cellar, the rats. My flesh began to crawl at the thought of it. They were grinning and whispering like two ghoulish schoolboys discovering a new form of torture for their victim.

'Eddie' – Richard struck the desk in triumph – 'that is a stroke! That is genius! I always said you were the brains of the family.'

Edward beamed, and I could see he had no greater pleasure in life than praise from his elder brother. Richard ordered a soldier to go and get Bryson. I had no idea who Bryson was, and when he turned out to be the barrel-chested, bearded man who had shown an interest in me at Mrs Morland's funeral I was at first none the wiser. Then, like a sudden blow to the head, it struck me where I had seen him before. It was when I was leaving Oxford with Eaton, and he stopped at the plague pit to chat about how business was to the man depositing bodies from his cart. Bryson was the driver of the plague cart.

37

It took four soldiers to hold me down. Richard regained control of himself as I lost it. I took a blow to the head and, as I slipped in and out of consciousness, I was dimly aware of him issuing orders for his ride north to the King, telling Gardiner to take me with Bryson to the pit, confident – as well he might be – that when I smelt the lime, I would talk.

The bitter cold outside brought me round. They bound my hands and Gardiner and a soldier called Nat pushed me stumbling through the trees. Nat started back as out of the gloom a man appeared who seemed to have no face. The man moved into a patch of moonlight and became Bryson, masked so that only his eyes showed. He wore a long leather coat like my old Joseph coat, which bore the marks of his trade, staining it like an ancient map of the world.

'Just beyond the trees, Captain,' he said.

Gardiner stopped short. 'D'you have another mask?'

'No, I ain't. Sorry.' Bryson gestured reassuringly. 'You'll be all right. Not many customers this year. Habit wi' me, that's all. Just keep well back.'

Nat looked far from reassured as he pushed me forward. The horse harnessed to the plague cart looked up, then went on cropping the grass peacefully. Some of the miasma, that distinctive plague smell, hung round the cart, a sour reek of pus and sweat mixed with the milky-sweet odour of lime. The tail of the cart was down and, sprawled in the rotting straw, I could see two bodies. They were men, stripped naked. Deep shadows made it seem as if they had been dismembered. I glimpsed a putrefying face in which I could see the glint of bone, silvered by the moon, and a twisted, decomposing arm. Nat muttered a prayer and even Gardiner turned away.

Bryson shifted the bodies as if they were sacks of turnips, making room in the wet, dark-brown straw. 'Did I not tell you I had two customers in there already, Captain?'

Gardiner swallowed and found his usual swagger. 'Ah yes. I forgot. So you did. Well, come on,' he snapped at Nat. 'Don't just stand there – get on with it!'

Bryson lit a clay, lifting the mask to take a few puffs, saying it was a special mixture of Virginia and herbs, good against the plague, the pox and diverse other complaints.

Gardiner bent over me, speaking gently, conversationally. 'Now listen, Tom. You know the plague. The screaming fever.'

'Vomiting blood,' said Bryson.

'Black boils.'

Gardiner nodded towards the cart. 'That's just a taste of what's coming. You're going to talk eventually, so why not be sensible and talk now, mmm?'

I stared up at him. I knew that if they threw me into that charnel cart I was as good as dead. If they took me to the house I stood a chance. However slim, I would rather die quickly than slowly of the plague.

'That's it, that's it,' said Gardiner, as however much I tried to stop them, tears filmed my eyes. It was the kindness, the sudden normality, however spurious, that did it. That and total exhaustion. 'Tell us and you can have a hot perry and sugar.'

'With spices,' said Bryson, smacking his lips.

'With spices. Better a live bastard than a dead Stonehouse, eh?' Gardiner patted me reassuringly on the cheek. Perhaps it was the pat. Perhaps it was the wink he gave Bryson. Perhaps it was the memory of all those moments I had almost given in to George, then reacted with a rush of fury, as much at my own weakness as at him. Whatever it was, a mindless rage overcame me. I bit him. He roared with pain, lurching backwards as my teeth clamped round his finger, but I would not let go until he half-lifted me from the ground and my own weight dragged my teeth away, tearing his flesh. Gardiner sucked and stared at his mangled finger before giving me two vicious kicks. Bryson removed the clay from his mouth. He and the soldier looked at me in awe.

'Well, I will say this for him,' Bryson said: 'he's a game one.'

'On the cart! Throw him on the cart!' Gardiner screamed at them.

They hesitated. I suppose they had thought it would never come to this. Gardiner shoved the reluctant Nat forward: 'On the cart!' Bryson shrugged, pulled down his mask, and in one swift movement they hurled me on. I landed face-down in the dank, fetid straw, struggling to sit up, spitting and spitting the clammy, rotting spikes from my mouth. An eye, or the opalescent remains of it, shifted in its socket to stare at me. I opened my mouth to scream but then gagged as I saw the movement was a maggot. The corpse was crawling with them. I twisted away, vomiting, striking my head again and again at the side of the cart as if I could break my way through it, before collapsing in the straw.

'I'm going to the house for a mask,' Gardiner snarled.

I heard him sucking at his finger as he walked away, then the scrape of a flint as Bryson relit his clay. He told Nat to watch me while he went into the woods for a crap. I spat out straw and acid flecks of vomit, and managed painfully slowly to twist myself into a sitting position, struggling to avert my head from my travelling companions. The tail of the cart was down. Wildly I thought about rolling off it, but as if he read my intention, Nat drew his sword. An animal cry from the woods made both of us jump. Gardiner, now masked, rode up as Bryson emerged from the trees, buttoning his breeches and still puffing at his clay. He slammed the tail of the cart into place. Gardiner dismissed Nat and rode behind the cart as Bryson clicked his horse into motion.

It was that strange time when the moon has not quite died nor the sun been born. The barest glimmer of light picked out the shapes of trees, almost threadbare of leaves, through which I could see an inn that seemed familiar. The sign creaked in unison with the jolting cart wheels: it was the inn just outside Oxford where Eaton had stabled our horses, a short distance from the plague pit.

In that moment I knew I would talk. Plague or no plague. I wanted life, whether it was three days of agony, or an hour or one minute: every second was precious. I had not lived. I had written no real poetry, only a few wretched pamphlets; snatched a few kisses, but never made love. Everything was preparing for life except me. The first bird was making a ghostly, hesitant sound followed by another, then another. Gardiner was yawning and stretching himself. He was no fool. He knew that even the cart, with its crawling maggots, was life compared with the pit. He knew I would tell him, for at least I would live until he had checked whether I was telling him the truth.

The cart stopped. I sat up. Gardiner had checked his horse a little distance away, and was scratching at the morning's first flea. Bryson was stumbling sleepily through thick, white-streaked mud, shoving open the gate marked with faded red crosses. I began to shout to Gardiner, to tell him where the pendant was, but half-swallowed a prickly stalk of straw which stuck in my throat. I coughed and coughed but could not get it out or talk. Now I began to panic I would be too late. Bryson bent over me, a shadowy figure of whom I could see little but the eyes above his mask. I spat out the straw and spluttered: 'The pendant is –'

Bryson clamped his hand over my mouth.

Gardiner rode closer. 'What did he say?'

"'I'll see you in hell,'" Bryson said.

'Then let him see hell.' Gardiner jumped off his horse. I stared up at Bryson in bewilderment, starting to splutter into speech again but stopped as Bryson took a knife to the ropes binding my hands, fraying them partly through. To complete my astonishment Bryson thrust the knife into my belt as he dragged me from the cart. My scattered wits could only fleetingly bring up the explanation that it was a more exquisite form of torture; they were playing some kind of game with me to improve the sport, like the Romans arming gladiators against wild animals. My legs were already dead and I swayed and staggered in the mud until Bryson prodded me forward with a heavy stick used for propping open the gate. Gardiner drew his rapier and followed us, gripping his mask tight to his face.

I stumbled over muddy circular furrows ploughed by constantly turning carts. The mud sucked at my boots, reluctantly releasing them; it splashed up to my cheeks and seemed to streak the gradually lightening sky. The awful stench was less suffocating than the cart, but only because it was overlaid with the stealthy, sickeningly sweet smell of lime. The two men goading me on fell silent and I stopped and would go no further. The paintings of hell I had seen could not match that picture; they were a lie, a Mayday farce of festival devils and fairground monstrosities. Better to burn and scream in those mock fires than lie lifeless in that pit. Some attempt at covering the bodies with earth had been made, but the recent rains had formed a cold fetid lake covered with a thick, chalky scum, penetrated by the occasional bubble of gas in which could be seen the bones of a hand or the frozen stare of a child.

I backed away, blundering into Bryson, who held me, stolid and unconcerned as a street scavenger whose daily business is decay and rubbish. Gardiner flicked his rapier towards me, but the stench kept him at a distance, pressing his mask to his nose. 'I can see this is unlocking your tongue, Tom . . .'

I said nothing, pulling at the frayed ropes round my wrists, but they would not break.

'Where is it?' he snapped. 'Take him closer, Mr Bryson. It will sharpen his mind.'

Even Bryson seemed reluctant. 'You do it, Captain. Your rapier be longer than my stick.'

Gardiner swore and drove me forward. I yanked at the ropes fruitlessly, slipped and fell. He shoved me nearer the edge with his boot. 'Are you going to tell me? If you don't I swear I –'

Bryson lifted his stick above his head and brought it down on Gardiner. It would have knocked him insensible but for his beaver hat, which cushioned the blow and flew into the pit. My mind was as numbed as if it had been tied up like my legs, into which the feeling was flowing back in painful surges. I gazed up at Gardiner, who swayed in a daze above me for a moment then gave a roar and drove his rapier at Bryson. Bryson half-parried it with the stick, but Gardiner struck it out of his hand, then flicked the mask away from his face. It was Matthew.

It seemed to take for ever running through the mud, which sucked me back at every step. For ever seeing the sword drawn back before I jumped, sending Gardiner sprawling, his rapier flying through the air. He rolled free and went for his sword, kicking Matthew away. I wrenched at the ropes, searing my skin raw, but at last snapped them. I tore off his mask and got his arm in a lock, but he levered his legs up and flung me from him. He picked up his sword as I took the knife from my belt. Matthew was lying motionless.

Blood trickled from the tear in the jerkin over Gardiner's left arm. 'Pendant or no pendant,' he said, 'you are going where he should have put you in the first place –' He kicked at Matthew, who was coming round, groaning. 'And where he –' he gave Matthew another kick '– will keep you company.'

I did not know then the *contra cavatione*, nor the *ricavatione*, the various feints and deceptions which, by my instinctive reactions to the whirling, flickering blade, however I tried to avoid it, were driving me back closer and closer towards the edge of the pit. But I knew the *stoccata lunga*, the method of delivering the point by the shortest and fastest means to the heart – or, at least, engraved in my mind were the sequence of movements he had made when he killed Eaton. The glittering blade – there seemed several of them – darted at me from every angle, hypnotising me, but I knew I must not look at the blade but at his footwork. When his left foot went back and his right knee was moving to bend forward he would lunge. He had me where he wanted me, right on the edge. The smell was overpowering. His left foot went back. I threw the knife. It caught him in his chest, diverting but not stopping the lunge. He cannoned into me, then, carried by his own momentum, plunged into the pit. I slipped, teetering on the edge, struggling to keep my balance before Matthew grabbed me and pulled me back.

Gardiner's screams were choked by the chalk-coloured slime, threaded with blood, which frothed and bubbled as it drew him under, until all that was left, floating on the surface as the scum began to form again, was the beaver hat. I turned away, shaking, unable to stop, and Matthew held me as he had not held me since I was a little boy.

'I thought it was about time I stopped running,' he said.

38

Matthew wanted to dump the two bodies that had travelled with me into the pit, not just to get rid of them, but because three was a lucky number. I would not hear of it. Ghastly they might look, I said, but they had been my companions on what I thought was my last journey, and they deserved a better resting place.

'You are a strange one, Tom,' he said. 'You always were, and I do believe you always will be.'

But he allowed me my whim, and we found a spot under a willow, which Matthew said had a kinder spirit than the yews further downstream. I told him I was glad of that, for I might like to be buried there, if a church could not be found for me.

He paused on his spade. 'Why are you talking about your burial, Tom? I have every intention of going first.'

'Why?' My voice faltered. 'I was with them. And they died of the plague.'

'Ah.' He dug a little longer and looked at me searchingly. 'Are you a little hot?'

'Yes, yes. I am.'

He felt my forehead, my pulse, and then squeezed my groin. 'Is it tender here?'

I winced in pain. 'Yes, yes! How long do I have?'

'Oh, Tom, Tom . . . you will bury me yet.'

'Don't make game of me. Tell me the truth.'

He held me. 'You're much braver than I am. And taller. And a soldier.'

'That doesn't make me any less afraid.'

'No. But it should tell you what this is.' He turned the corpse with the opalescent eye over.

'A musket wound.'

'And this?' He pointed to a terrible wound which had half-severed the neck from the body.

'A sabre cut! They're soldiers – they died of their wounds.'

He grinned. 'Very bad year for the plague, this. They were trying to frighten you. Do you feel better? Fever gone down?'

Better? Miraculously all my symptoms had disappeared, and I told Matthew I wished his magic was as effective as his more rational explanations. I hope the poor soldiers will forgive me, but I danced round their grave feeling I could defeat the whole King's army. At least I was able to attend to them more reverently, searching the rotting jerkin of one, the breeches of the other for some form of identity, but there was none. So we put them in a grave with no marks and I said a short prayer for them and their mothers and sweethearts or wives who would never know whether they were alive or dead.

We eventually came to a fork in the road. Matthew pointed his whip and said that way was Highpoint and the other London, and recommended the latter. I shook my head and pointed to the former.

'You'll get no peace, Tom,' he said quietly.

'I told you: I want to give it back to its rightful owner,' I said hotly.

'Ah,' he said. 'Is that so?'

He said nothing more, but clicked at the horse, and turned the cart on to the Highpoint road.

The house was silent again. The servants were there, or at least I saw a face at a window, but they must have seen me alight from the cart, for they vanished again. The doors in the reception room where Eaton had built the barricade were leaning drunkenly from the hinges. The piled-up furniture had been cleared, and on the floor was a large dark stain. There was no sign of Kate. I reached Frances's bedroom well ahead of Matthew, lifted the lid of an oak chest, pulling out a drawer, flinging out necklaces and bodice ornaments as if they were playhouse baubles. The drawer looked perfectly normal. I shook it. There was no telltale rattle. I emptied the second drawer. Again there was nothing.

'You're lying,' I said to Matthew as he entered.

'Tom. When have I ever lied to you?'

'You may not lie, but you never tell the truth.'

'Patience, patience. Look at yourself. You're changing.'

I thought this was another of his jokes, but then looked in a mirror, started and glanced back, almost thinking Eaton, or the spirit of him, was standing behind me. The cut Gardiner had given me had opened up my cheek in a livid wound that turned me from a fresh-faced boy into a man. In the portrait I could see the boy who had run into the Guildhall that day, full of dreams that he would be a freeman and marry the master's daughter. The man staring back at me from the mirror had dreams, but they were tempered with the first shadows of caution and bitterness. Matthew appeared in the mirror.

'Do you still want me to open it?'

'Yes.'

He lifted up a drawer. 'Look. See the difference between the two thicknesses?'

I snatched it from him and would have battered it open but he stopped me and with irritating slowness showed me the carefully glued wooden plugs that concealed wooden screws. It seemed to take him an age to take out the plugs and screws and remove the false bottom. Cushioned in velvet was the Stonehouse pendant. It was as if the room was on fire. I started back as the falcon seemed to strike at me with its emerald beak. Its nest was a huge, polished ruby, surrounded by a miniature forest of enamelled flowers and insects, set in a framework of gold.

Matthew did not try and stop me now. Whatever power had drawn me to it now silenced him. He watched as I struggled to remember which jewels Lucy Hay had pressed, and in which order. There were two small emeralds, a deeper green than the rest – old mine green, she called it – on the edge of the miniature forest. I held one down, then pressed the other. I ducked as the falcon almost hit me in the eye. The ruby had sprung clear of its mount, exposing an oval space in which a portrait might be kept, or painted. Only there was no portrait.

I had accepted the legend that my father's picture would stare out at me so completely I sat stunned, unable to believe that there was nothing there, unable to see what was there.

'Look –' Matthew pointed to a small piece of folded paper, wedged at the bottom of the compartment.

I remembered what Kate told me my mother had said: *If anything happens to me, give it to the child. In the portrait compartment is my hold on the child's father.* Not a portrait, but her 'hold on him' – whatever that was.

Carefully I teased out the paper and unfolded it, expecting a name, but like the will o' the wisp, the truth constantly came close, then eluded me. There was no name, but some kind of cipher. My eyes blurred as I struggled to read the letters, for legends are so strong and simple but ultimately absurd. Where would my mother, in the chaos of that day and evening, have found a portrait of my father to put in the pendant she had stolen? What actually must have happened was far more poignant. The wavering letters were a faded brown and did not look as if they had been written in ink. She had got this scrap of paper from somewhere and, in the blood of my birth, had written, with her nail possibly, two words, the latter being so badly smudged I could read only the first letter:

BOWNDERY L—

I read them out to Matthew. He stared at the pendant, then at the floor, scraping his hand against his beard.

'What does it mean?'

For answer he took me to the copse where we had left our horses the previous night. They had broken free, but I called Patch and eventually found her with the other. We rode to what, just before I was born, was the boundary between the Pearce and Stonehouse estates. Now the fences had gone, it was all Stonehouse land, but Matthew knew exactly where the old boundary was. We tethered our horses by a stream, which he said was the water released by Eaton after Kate had freed him from the trap. Following the stream upwards, we came to a well-worn path crossing it. It was an unexpected sheltered spot, the sort of place in which children delight to hide. A group of trees grew over a jutting lip of rock, under which was a small cavern. The path ran just below it, downwards to Highpoint and upwards in the opposite direction to the ruins of what had once been a house.

'What's that?'

There had been a fall of rock in the cavern, and Matthew was clearing it. He looked round, then carried on clearing the rock before he answered. 'That was where your mother used to live.'

I walked a little way along the path towards it, until I could see from the line where the foundations were it must have been a substantial manor house. Stones had been taken from it for other buildings, leaving one roofless wing, overgrown with ivy. In a few years that too would be gone. I walked slowly back in the cutting wind which snatched at my hat and coat. This must be the path my mother had taken to Highpoint, or to this spot to meet her lover. Or lovers. *I shall have one of them, Kate. Who do you think it shall be?*

Matthew had cleared the stones, and crawled to a lower, shadowy part of the cave, feeling over the wall.

'Did she meet her lovers here?'

He scratched his head. 'I remember her meeting her cousin.'

'John Lloyd?'

'That's right.'

'When did he come back from Ireland?'

'He didn't. He was killed in the fighting there.' Matthew cut his finger, swore and sucked it. 'I used to leave her herbs here.'

'Love potions?'

'Something like that.'

Where I had swallowed everything he said as a child, I now recognised the shift in his tone, his evasive grin. 'Something like that to get rid of me?'

He continued to grope for a moment before saying: 'Didn't work very well, did it? . . . Ah!' He found the niche he was looking for, pulled away a stone, then scrabbled his fingers deeper in to tease something out. I snatched it from him. It was a small pot, stoppered crudely with a piece of flint. L. Letters! Inside the pot was a small bundle of them. When I read them, exactly where my mother had collected them, I recognised the hand immediately and everything that had happened to her that year – and to me, growing inside her – fell into place.

PART THREE

Edgehill

October 1642–April 1643

39

Once more Matthew and I came to a fork in the road. Again he pointed with his whip. That way was to Warwickshire, that to London. He pleaded with me to take the road south with him, but the pendant, which I now kept close to my skin just as Matthew had done, drew me north like a compass. We embraced each other tightly, silently; then, with a heavy heart, I watched him until he was out of sight, on the road he had taken in the plague cart seventeen years before.

I caught up with the Parliamentary baggage train south of Worcester. No one knew what they were doing, or where they were going – or if they did, they would not tell me. Passing a good-sized inn, I had an inspiration. Eaton had always headed for a town's main inn. The landlord had barred the door against soldiers, and when I kept hammering on it opened it only to point a pistol in my face. I said my name was Eaton, and I was on Lord Stonehouse's business. He lowered the pistol a little, stared at my scar, then poured me a small beer and gave me a message sealed with the familiar falcon.

Lord Stonehouse's letter was curt and to the point, demanding to hear from his steward who, as Eaton had said, had done his dirty work for him for so long.

'Any reply?' said the innkeeper.

'No reply,' I said.

I spent the night at the inn, setting off at dawn. It was October the twenty-third. Unusually for that autumn there was no rain that day, and the sun came up in a cloudless sky. Lord Stonehouse's letter had been sent from a manor house in Chadshunt, two hours' ride away. It told me that all the Stonehouses would be in Warwickshire that day. It touched me that both brothers, although they had taken the opposite side to their father, had written to him. Richard was with Prince Rupert's cavalry, and Edward was a chaplain with the King's infantry.

At Chadshunt I was told that Lord Stonehouse was at church in the nearby village of Kineton. The service was almost over. Instead of going in, I prayed outside for God to give me guidance in what I had discovered, and in what to say to Lord Stonehouse. I waited just inside the lych gate. While I was in prayers, the lane outside became as busy as St Paul's Churchyard, with as many people trying to go one way as the other, and a minister in his black robes trying to force his horse through. There were even hawkers selling protective amulets. One held up to me the tattered remains of a pocket Bible, which he claimed had stopped a musket ball and had special powers. For a shilling, it would save my life. I pulled him back so the minister's horse would get through, and found myself staring into the eyes of Edward Stonehouse. For a moment they were unfamiliar, the blinking desiccated eyes which normally lived behind glasses, surrounded by the whorl of wrinkles formed by constantly squeezing to see. The two armies were now less than two miles apart in places, and a man with good sight might suddenly find himself in the wrong one, let alone someone with blurred vision.

Edward peered down at me. What colour there was in his cheeks left them in an instant. He gave a gabble of terror, saying that the plague child had come from the pit for him and dug his spurs in his horse.

I sprang forward, shouting that I must talk to him and almost caught his reins. But I was hampered on the one side by the hawker, saying surely I wanted to save my life for a shilling, and on the other by two pairs of hands slapping down on my shoulders in a tight grip.

'I like the scar!' said Luke.

'That'll terrify the Cavaliers!' said Will.

They fell on me with delight, Will immediately claiming the half crown he had bet that I would be there for the fight, Luke disputing that there would be one.

'Essex will cut and run, like he's done before.'

By this time Edward had gone, and I discovered that, once again, I had missed Lord Stonehouse. Luke found out that Lord Stonehouse had left with Essex, and promised to show me where to find him. But when I walked Patch back to their camp there were orders to strike it.

There was a ditch for a privy, but it had become so choked and foul, men preferred to shit where they found themselves. Thousands of men spread over fields and hamlets were struggling to pack their knapsacks and check – or find – their weapons, for theft was rife. They were loaded like pack horses, with pot helmets and body armour – which many discarded in order to move more freely. Musketeers not only had to carry their cumbersome weapons but musket rests and bandoleers of gunpowder charges round their necks. These bounced and rattled in the wind as I saw a familiar shape, head and shoulders above everyone else, lifting his pike.

I could not say I hugged Big Jed, for I could not get my arms round his body, but he squeezed every breath from mine, half-lifting me from the ground.

'I have something for thee,' he said. 'A carrier reached us just after we left Highpoint.'

He took a letter from his knapsack. It looked as if it had travelled from place to place to reach the unit. It was covered with grease marks from a piece of cheese which almost obliterated my name, but my heart thumped painfully as I recognised the childish hand and broke what remained of the seal. I felt a rush of joy and guilt that Anne, who had painstakingly struggled to learn to write that summer, had got a letter through, where I, who wrote so easily, had not even tried. It was short.

I wood have wrote longer but it is Mye first Lettre & the Carrier is waiting to go to Warre. I Hope Youe doe Think of Mee as I of Youe and not of Your Countess.

My Countess? What on earth did she mean?

I Knowe your Poeme by heart noue & can reed it. I Praye for Thee Every Daye & God send you back to your lovinge Anne, Amen.

I read it, kissed it, folded it to put it in my jerkin, unfolded it, read it again to make sure the words were still there, doing this several times until I realised Luke was watching me, grinning. I stuffed the letter in my jerkin, whereupon Luke opened his to show me his letter from Charity.

'The war is turning women into writers,' he said.

The field, which had been crowded, was half-empty. I looked round for Patch, but she was nowhere in sight. Nobody had seen her go. She had become more than a horse to me; she had shared everything since leaving London; she *was* London. People looked at me indifferently as I ran around calling for her.

'She's probably been requisitioned,' said Will. 'I'll give you a chit.'

'I don't want a bloody chit,' I screamed at him. 'I want my horse.'

'You're foot. Not cavalry.'

'I've got to find Lord Stonehouse.'

'Here,' said Jed, putting a pike, almost three times as tall as myself, into my hand. 'I've just requisitioned it.'

*   *   *

Towards the end of that morning Edward Stonehouse finally found his way to the Royalist army on high ground overlooking some of the most fertile land in England, an escarpment known locally as Edgehill. Only then, at the sight of his King, did he become calmer. Scarlet standard flying, black armour glittering, Charles was riding through his troops with his officers and peers. He had always portrayed himself as a warrior prince, but Englishmen had not fought one another on English soil since the Wars of the Roses almost two centuries ago. Wars happened elsewhere – in Europe, Ireland or Scotland. In the century so far, all across the great stretch of these green fields had been peace, disturbed only by sporadic food riots. All of Henry VIII's peers had experienced war abroad; of the peers crowding close to listen to Charles, only one in five had done so. Like their King, most still felt they were performing in a masque. But as he went on, discarding many of his usual flourishes, his voice took on a new strength, an urgency of tone.

'I see by all your loyal faces . . . that just as no son can relinquish his father, no subject can relinquish his lawful king . . .'

Struggling to focus by squeezing his eyes tight, Edward picked out the familiar shape of his brother, sitting straight on his horse, head bowed.

'My regal authority being obtained from God, we have marched long in the hope the enemy will realise their error, but now we have come upon them. Matters are to be decided not by the word, but the sword, and we must try the doubtful hazard of war. May the justness of our cause make you courageous, and God make you victorious!'

The resounding cheers reached us on the meadows below. To Will's disgust, we arrived late and were in the reserves on the left flank, near abandoned farm buildings straddling the Kineton road. I caught a glimpse of the King's upraised sword and an arm of black armour. The sun came out and glinted on it, and a murmur rippled through the ranks as some soldiers took it as a sign against us.

A Puritan preacher responded by chanting: 'Let the saints be joyful in their glory . . .' Soldiers round him joined in: 'Let the high praises of God be in their mouths!'

The single roar of a cannon silenced both the cheers and the chanting.

It was two o'clock. The two armies were now less than a mile apart. Essex had decided it was impracticable to retreat, but was in no hurry to fight. It would be suicidal to attack uphill. His cannon might have dislodged them from their superior position, but the range was too great. Like those of the answering cannon, the balls merely dropped in the soft mud of the meadows. Essex could see several peers grouped round the King. It seemed as though some kind of argument was taking place. The disagreement was between the sixty-year-old Earl of Lindsey, in charge of the infantry, and Richard's hero, Prince Rupert, who wanted to command the infantry as well as the horse. As Richard, spellbound, watched Lindsey throw down his baton and say if he was not fit to be a general he would die as a colonel at the head of his regiment, he saw his brother. He knew only too well that agitated state and moved to be with him. He put an arm round Edward's shoulder, calming him as he heard about the devil pursuing him, and led him to the lip of the escarpment. His eyes were as strong as his brother's were weak. He could see our banner: a red cross lettered with FOR GOD AND PARLIAMENT. He glimpsed my red hair.

'Has he seen father?' Richard asked Edward.

'He was looking for him.'

Richard could see Essex's banner, a good half mile away on the other flank. He picked me out again, among the pikemen, laughed and said he could see not a drop of lime on me, unfortunately. I was just like the rest, one of the rabble. Edward thanked God for his elder brother supporting him, just as he had done on that dreadful night when he stood up for him before his father, saying the child could not possibly be Edward's since their relationship was only a few months old.

Fortified by Richard's support, Edward went as one of the chaplains to Sir Jacob Astley, who had taken over from Lindsey, joining now with especial fervour in his brief prayer: 'O Lord, thou knowest how busy I must be this day. If I forget thee, do not thou forget me.'

It was mid-afternoon, still clear, but what warmth there had been in the day was beginning to leave it. I was convinced we would not fight that day – there would only be more circling and manoeuvring, more psalms and speeches. Then we saw their cavalry delicately, carefully, almost sedately, picking their way down the steep escarpment. There was a fall of rocks and one horse almost fell. On more gently sloping ground the cavalry broke into a trot, then the trumpet sounded the charge.

Stupidly I watched, thrilled at the sight and sound, the colours of the pennants, the flash of their drawn sabres, as if I was staring at a performance in an arena. I was a boy again, watching the sights of London, the pageantry, the royal processions. Other faces gaped. We were all Londoners, wood turners, tailors, tanners, bakers and printers, carters and watermen. Some still wore the clothes of their trade. We had been rigorously trained, but in drill manoeuvres and weapon orders – there were forty-eight musket orders, and sixty-five for the pike. The only experience of fighting for most of us was as part of the London mob. Like me, most seemed hypnotised by the wonderful spectacle galloping across Kineton meadows towards us.

'Ground your bloody pike,' said Jed, who had much less imagination but far more sense.

Muskets were as little use in that first charge as the cannon. A horse was hit and I saw a man's head disappear, his horse riding on, one hand clutching at the reins, the other at his slipping sabre. Most muskets were fired too soon and there was no time to reload. Their riders came at an angle, smashing into the flank of the Parliamentary cavalry, sweeping through into the first lines of infantry, which duly fled. A man ran screaming towards us, blood spurting from a sabre cut in his neck. He fell, Jed half-stumbling on him before shoving him away.

'Hold your pikes!' yelled Will. 'If you run, you're dead!'

He stood, beating at and pleading with the fleeing soldiers to stay and fight, while Luke, who had broken all the rules in the reloading of muskets, tried to bring calm to the scattering musketeers with a kind of forced, dazed politeness.

'Match cord. Reload. Present.'

Whinnying horses, nostrils flaring, were as terrified as the men. One ran at the stand of pikes as if they were a fence at a hunt and came down, impaling himself, yellow guts spilling out on a meadow that was disappearing into churned-up mud. The bandoleer of gunpowder charges round the neck of one of Luke's musketeers caught alight, one charge setting off another. The man spun round like a screaming firework, beating at his burning clothes, falling into the back of our line as the thrashing, dying horse fell into the front. Slashing, hacking, the Cavaliers cut through and careered straight on. Only one checked his horse and wheeled. Even at that moment I thought it a superb piece of horsemanship. Richard was crouched low on the saddle, the slightest of smiles on his face, focusing his whole being on the point not the blade. I was transfixed by the sight, the blade inches from me, when there was a great roar, more animal than man. Jed brought up the butt of his pike, deflecting the blade. Richard slashed at him. Jed stumbled, dropping his pike. Screaming, I brought up my pike. Richard's horse reared, almost unseating him, before he was swept on by the hindmost of the charging horses.

Then, just as suddenly as they had appeared, they were gone, carrying a group of our stationary horses with them. If they had turned on our rear, it would all have been over. But they were no more disciplined than we were. The fleeing troops were to them like so many foxes, vermin who troubled their estates, but who also gave them the delight of the hunt. They rode down and killed stragglers for about two miles, until they reached the Parliamentary baggage trains at Kineton, and then they looted.

There was a strange, stupefied lull in which the yelling and the thunder of the horses were replaced by the cries of the wounded. I could not see Jed. I was stumbling about like a drunk, as were many others. At the sight of a blackened, bloody face lurching towards me, I brought up my pike only to discover it was Will. Wordlessly, he shoved me forward. I thought it was over, but we were lining up again. Unbelievably, their infantry were coming our way. Unlike the horses, which tore through us in a crashing wave, they were a slow-moving sea, inching inexorably forward. There were many more of them, and if they had been properly armed that, too, would have been the end of it. But many had only cudgels, picking up swords or muskets from the dead and wounded as they walked over them.

It was what the manuals called 'push of pike' in planned regular movements which bore no relationship to the chaos and carnage as each side gained a yard then lost it, stumbling over bodies, ducking, weaving, slipping over grass that had vanished in mud pooled with blood.

Luke was running low on match cord and went down the line with it, struggling to keep some kind of order, but that soon vanished. We were like ants which, when a nest is disturbed, scurry around performing tasks endlessly, repetitively, trampling over fallers to take their places. They were demons before us, with blackened, bloodied faces. My particular demon had an open mouth with broken teeth and a large wart at the side of his nose. When my pike went through him there was a bloodthirsty howl of satisfaction. It was a moment before I realised the howl came from my own throat.

Slowly, imperceptibly, the sun went down. Through the gloom I saw a group of Royalist cavalry on the Kineton road and thought, almost with indifference, that they would finish us. But they were surprised by a unit of Roundhead cavalry, led by a tousle-headed man who had lost his helmet, which charged ferociously to scatter them.

When it was almost too dark to see, both sides, as if by mutual consent, retreated a number of paces. They were like two wounded beasts, reluctant to give ground but too exhausted to fight or even to move one limb after another. There were a few scattered musket shots. One or two men stumbled away. Most did nothing but stand there, clutching their weapons, swaying in a daze, staring across at the fading, ghost-like shapes opposite.

Finally we dragged ourselves back to where we had started from. So did they, each side doggedly clinging to the tradition that to leave the field of battle would be an admission of defeat.

The moon rose. I scarcely noticed at first it was Ben bandaging a wound in my leg. I could not remember when it had happened, but it was throbbing painfully. Ben had been with the baggage train, but had managed to rescue his medical supplies before the Cavaliers looted it. I had not spoken since I got back, but now I found my voice.

'Jed is out there . . . He was wounded.'

'He got back. I've seen to him.' Ben went to Luke, who had a head wound. 'He may lose his arm. Get some water.'

Near the abandoned farm buildings was a small stream. I took a bucket and limped across to it. It was a clear night and there was already a nip of frost in the air which carried sharply the cries from the battlefield – men calling out for God or their mothers. There was nothing I could do, and I wished I could shut it out, for it was returning me to a painful humanity I did not want. Not yet. I wanted to remain in this numb, unfeeling state. Then my mind picked out from that dreadful chorus a sound of sanity – the snicker of a horse.

'Patch!' I cried.

I ran round the buildings as fast as my leg would allow me and found the stables. In the dim light I was sure it was Patch until I was a few paces away. Then I saw the horse was black, and several hands higher than mine. Still, it was a horse and, at that moment,

I felt closer to it than to any human being. I put down the bucket and clicked softly to the horse.

'Are you a horse stealer as well?'

Richard's relaxed, mocking tone sent a chill running through me. I spun round but before I could reach my knife the point of his sword was at my throat. His face was in darkness, the tattered folds of his cloak hanging over his sword arm.

'I have no quarrel with you, Father,' I said, as steadily as my voice would allow.

He smiled, moving into the weak shaft of moonlight that spilled through the door. 'You're an ingenious child. First you pretend to be Father's child, then Edward's, and now it's my turn. I told you: you are John Lloyd's child.'

'He came back from the grave to make love to her then. John Lloyd went to Ireland the previous summer and was killed there.'

'There is still no proof you are my child!'

'I have the letters you sent to my mother. From the first lines of undying love to "here is a crown for some whore's physic". I showed them to your father this morning.'

He was quite still. The point came down to my heart. I was aware all the time of his feet, his balance. If his balance shifted to his right foot, I had a split second before he killed me. The bucket had dropped on a bale of straw. I stretched my hand towards it but could only agonisingly brush it with my fingertips.

The blade lowered fractionally – then came back sharply. 'You're lying. My brother said you were looking for Father. You never found him, did you? I was watching. You would never have ended up with the pikemen if you'd found him.'

I began to move towards him; not away from the blade but into it. I stopped watching his feet and looked directly into his eyes. I tried to become that human being I was before the battlefield. It was one thing for him to get someone else to kill me, another for a father to kill his own son. I struggled to say as much.

'That's because you're part of the rabble. Nobles do it all the time,' he said with contempt. But he kept evading my gaze, then being drawn back to it with an awful fascination. I could almost see the thought slipping in and out of his eyes: *My child. My child . . .* I must not plead. I must not beg. That was what the rabble did. I must somehow stop being the plague child in his eyes. I must become the child he might have wanted. All the while, as I moved forward he was backing towards the wall of the stable. The point penetrated my jerkin, pricking my flesh, but he was too close to me to make a fatal thrust.

'I don't want the inheritance, Father. I just want –'

'Don't call me that!' he shouted.

'Tom –' Luke called.

Richard flung me across the stable to crash into the opposite wall. The sword blade leapt forward like the tongue of a snake. I fought with every instinct to keep my eyes open, staring into his.

The sword blade stopped at the last moment and steadied. 'Shout back.'

I swallowed, panting, and for a moment could get no word out.

He was swallowing too, breathing heavily. 'Shout back!'

I managed one word: 'Coming!'

From where he had thrown me, near the door, I could just see the edge of the encampment. Luke, his head now bandaged, walked across the light of the fire, glancing in the direction of the stables. Keep him talking, I urged myself, keep him talking . . . But my mind was jammed. All I could utter was an inane mumble.

'Did you love her?'

'Love her?' He gave an incredulous laugh. 'I saw what she was after right from the start.'

His father, his dear father, he said, and there was both a longing and a hatred in his voice, never gave him credit for anything. But he saw through Margaret Pearce when she was in deepest black at her father's funeral. Attracted to her? Of course he was attracted to her. Everybody was. But he knew women. He had had enough of them.

'Like Jane,' I could not help interjecting, remembering the story she had told me at Turville's.

'Jane?' he said.

He had forgotten her. I cursed myself for distracting him, but it made no difference. He went on compulsively, driven to talk about something he had never talked about to a living soul before. Fathers and sons, fathers and sons! Almost every word he said rang with pride for and hatred of his father. His father was the cleverest, shrewdest of men – but he was a total fool with women! His wife had twisted him round her little finger. When she died, he never stopped mourning her – until he saw Margaret Pearce in deepest black.

Oh, there was not a man at the funeral who did not feel for her, Richard said. Both up there – he struck his head – and down there – he slapped his groin. Oh, he wanted her! He wanted her all right!

Luke was saying something to Ben, their shadows dipping and swaying in the firelight. He left Ben and slowly, casually, looking as if he was enjoying the cold sharpness of the air after the heat of the fire, began to stroll towards the stables. I prayed he was wearing his sword.

The day after the funeral, Richard said, he was called into his father's study. When Lord Stonehouse had been through his misdoings, and he was on the point of leaving, his father said: Margaret Pearce – respect her grief. That was all. Respect her grief, with a penetrating look from those black eyes.

'I was – how old are you?'

'Seventeen.'

'I was nineteen! Nineteen! I believe he only ever knew my mother. I had had whores, servants, even a lady-in-waiting old enough to be my mother who showed me more of the deceits in women's hearts than my dear father ever dreamed existed. Respect her grief! In other words, keep away from her, she's mine. He was blind to what he was walking into, what she was doing. I knew what she was using her grief for! Seduction, the subtlest form of seduction.'

There was a grudging admiration in his voice now, and I suddenly saw that my mother and he were two of a kind. His eyes shone and the sword trembled. Perhaps, in his own way, he had been in love with her and, in her own way, she with him. Then his voice took on a sharp, bitter edge.

'I knew exactly what she was doing.'

'Plotting to take over the estate,' I said.

His sword dropped. 'How do you know?'

I thought of what Kate had told me, and shook my head. *Origo mali*, the source of the evil. The estate. Wildly, for the first time I had the barest glimmer of hope that we might reach out to one another, perhaps even one day understand one another. I took a tentative step towards him. The sword came up. Luke strolled towards the stables, but I noticed him only when he stopped. He must have seen the glint of Richard's sword in the doorway, for his hand went towards his belt.

'Why didn't you tell him?'

'Tell him? There was no point in telling him. I was nineteen. What did *I* know about grief, love? What did *I* know about *anything*?'

There was such a deep well of bitterness inside him that had been dammed up for so long he was shaking, the sword a trembling glint of silver. I moved a fraction closer. Perhaps some of my own rebelliousness came from him – and perhaps he read that thought, for the sword drifted lower. Another step and I could duck under the sword and seize his arm.

'The estate was entailed to me, but I knew women like that. If she could not unwrap the entail, she would persuade him to leave everything outside it – whole streets of London properties – to her.'

'Then why did she not just pursue him?'

'Oh, she did! Of course she did. But my dear father, so clever, but so naive with women, respected her grief too long. He is as tight with his feelings as a miser with his money and she thought she would get nowhere. So she turned to me. I played the innocent. I was easier. And young . . . and we both, for a time, were attracted to one another and – you are too young to know anything about love.'

'As your father said about you.'

He gave me an angry stare, the sword jerking up again. Then laughed shortly. His arm relaxed, the sword drifting downwards again. That was the moment. One step. Half a step and I could have taken him, twisted the sword out of his hand. I could have done it. I know it. But in that moment I was as compulsively drawn into the story as he was in the telling of it.

'What happened?'

'I got her pregnant. She thought I would marry her. I told her I knew what her game was and to get rid of it . . . I never, not in a million years, thought she would turn her eyes on my fool of a brother . . .'

He dropped his guard completely. I could have taken him then or perhaps even kept him talking. Perhaps, perhaps . . . I shall never know. There was a deep frost that night, beginning to sparkle on the blades of grass where the moon touched them. I heard Luke's boot crunching on it. Caught the glint of his sword.

'No, Luke, no!' I shouted.

He was halfway through his thrust. My shout both caused him to partly check his thrust and alerted my father. He was too late to parry the sword but twisted away so Luke caught him in the side. My father lunged forward at him with such force he could not withdraw the sword as Luke fell. I caught him as he struggled to pull out the sword. There was a look of surprise, of complete disbelief on his face, and then a shadow of his disarming smile.

'I thought I'd . . . got . . . away with it . . . old fr—'

Blood abruptly poured from his mouth. I screamed for Ben and held Luke to me as he struggled to speak again. 'Tell Charity I love her, I will see her in heav—'

Ben pulled me to one side and knelt by Luke. He could not get the jerkin open because of the sword, and slit it with a knife. He peeled away the bloodsoaked letter Charity had sent. He made a vain attempt to stop the blood, then shook his head.

I heard the horse and glimpsed my father riding away. Howling like an inmate of Bedlam, I went after him in a limping run, dragging the knife from my belt.

Some time later Ben found me on the battlefield, where, as the frost deepened, the dead and wounded still lay. I was repeatedly stabbing a man who was already dead. Near me was Richard's tattered cloak. The man I was stabbing was not Richard. My mind was blank. I could not tell Ben why I was stabbing the man. I had never seen him before, nor had Ben. Nor was it possible to say which side he had been on, for, like many of the corpses around him, he had been stripped naked by men who took rings, boots, belts – anything they could use or sell. As Ben led me back to the camp we could still hear them, moving about the field, like wolves in the night.

40

The Bedlam I went through was part of a greater Bedlam. Both sides claimed victory. Fleeing Parliamentary deserters reaching Oxford said the whole army was retreating and the King on his way to London. In London on 25 October, two days after the battle, someone who called himself 'A Gentleman of Quality' – it may have been Crop-Eared Jack – printed a smudged quarto claiming a great Parliamentary victory in which Prince Rupert had been captured.

What neither side expected was a stalemate. Each thought such a bitter conflict would resolve everything, one way or the other. The King did march on London. Rupert sacked Brentford, ten miles west of London, on 13 November. Londoners both panicked and were outraged. Fear of losing their property caused many Royalists to support Parliament. The following day, at Turnham Green, the Royalist army found itself facing an army of Londoners, enlarged to twenty-four thousand with Trained Bands from Hertfordshire, Essex and Surrey. A few shots were fired. The King had faced far superior numbers, but it was more than that which made him retreat to winter in Oxford. The memory of Edgehill hung like a miasma over everyone. Both the King and Essex had spent that frozen night on the battlefield. The King had stared at the sixty corpses which lay where his standard had stood before crouching over a camp fire, unable to sleep for the cries of the wounded. Nobody wished to fight again. But although half-hearted negotiations began, neither side was prepared to give an inch.

It was mid-December when a carter carrying the last of the season's frost-bitten fruit from an orchard in Chiswick took me into the City.

I went up Holborn and into Cloth Fair, the snow still falling but not settling. The City was silent. The air was strangely clear. The smell of Smithfield was a ghost of its former stench, for there was little meat coming in. I stood at the opening of Half Moon Court, an inexplicable panic seizing me, for I felt I had done something terrible, but knew not what. From the printing shop came a steady rhythmic clank. I knew and loved every sound, the groan of the platen – the press needed oil – the sigh as it met the paper. Before Edgehill I had longed to be here, picturing myself running across that courtyard into Anne's arms, seizing her and kissing her under the apple tree. Yet I stood there, reluctant to go on, the panic rising in me, staring through the drifting snow at the bare tree, at the window in the jutting gable, from which I had gazed with so many dreams.

There was the sound of raised voices inside and then Sarah came out to empty some slops, calling after her that it was more than her life was worth. She was followed by Anne. Whatever was happening to my mind, my heart was still there. It hopped, skipped, jumped, stopped, then started again at twice the rate when I saw her. Yet . . . why did I not jump towards her? Why did I just stand there gawping? – as Sarah used to put it when I was an apprentice who refused to wear boots. She was as beautiful as I remembered. No, no. More so. She wore an old blue dress, her hair was tangled and she wrapped a shawl of her mother's tightly round her shoulders as she engaged in the most mundane of exchanges with Sarah, but I loved and swallowed hungrily every word, every movement.

'Pleeeease, Sarah. One bucket.'

'Master said no more coal till nightfall.'

Anne wheedlingly stroked her cheek. 'Feel my hand. It's freezing.'

'Don't you know there's a blockade at Newcastle?'

'You'll be sorry when I freeze to death.' She went in, slamming the door behind her.

'Sorry? Good riddance!' Sarah muttered, dumping the slops and looking towards me.

That was why the air was so clear: few chimneys were smoking. I turned away. I was wearing a battered wide-brimmed hat I had picked up from God knows where and my breeches and jerkin were fit only to throw on the pile of slops. What was left of the sole of one of my boots kept company with the upper only by courtesy of a piece of string.

'Another bloody tinker, pretending to come back from the war,' Sarah grumbled as if to herself, but deliberately pitching it loud enough for me to hear.

I could not stay a moment longer. Could not face any of them. Least of all the girl I loved. I needed the safety, the anonymity of the road.

'Stop! Here, you –' She came after me, fumbling in the pocket of her apron, where she kept dry crusts for beggars. She held out a crust to me, then dropped both it and the pail. 'The good Lord be praised! It's Tom! Tom!' She hugged me, then she recoiled. 'Your face. What on earth have you done with yourself? You stink like the slop pile.' Then she hugged me again, eyes shining. 'It's Tom! Tom!'

The house seemed about to fall into the courtyard there was so much opening of doors and shouting. The printing machine stopped in mid-cycle. A window flew open and Mrs Black leaned out.

'Oh, my goodness! And I aren't dressed yet to receive him. Jane!'

Anne ran out, shawl flying from her shoulders. 'Tom . . . Tom . . . you've come back . . . you've –' She stopped and clapped a hand over her mouth, choking off a scream. 'I thought you were Eaton for a moment.'

'Eaton's dead.'

'Thank God.'

'God rest his soul,' I said, with the first burst of passion that had risen up in me for a long time.

'What's wrong, Tom?' she whispered. 'What's wrong?'

I still wanted to run, and yet I longed to hold her. How could that be? 'I don't know,' I said. 'I don't know.'

She pulled me to her and kissed me and then we were overwhelmed, Mr Black seizing me by the hand and drawing me inside, shouting at Sarah to put coal on the fire – did she not realise how cold it was? His voice still slurred a little, but was almost back to its old, deep pitch. He thought it was a great victory. Was it true that the King was suing for peace? He had something on the press now that depended on it. I fought for something to say as he sat me down on his chair by the fire, which Sarah was hastily raking out and building up.

'The press needs oil, sir,' I said.

He laughed and clapped me on the shoulder. 'D'you hear that? Once a printer, always a printer. Nehemiah!' he shouted, and an apprentice, as small and sullen and ink-blacked as I used to be, stared in from the shop. 'Stick to your calling and you may grow up to be like Tom.'

I could see from the expression on Nehemiah's face the last thing he wanted to be was a bedraggled creature like me.

'Go on! You heard him! Oil the press!' Mr Black bellowed, just as he used to shout at me. 'Anne! Stop staring at his scar – it's a badge of honour! Get wine!'

Mrs Black made her entrance, sweeping up to me with every intention to embrace me as I stood up but, stopped by my smell, growing in pungency from the heat of the fire, extended first her hand, then her fingertips. 'The charts said you would be here before Christmas. I kept telling Anne, but she would believe you were dead. She was weeping her heart out.'

'I was not, Mother,' said Anne furiously.

'I told her to do something useful, but all she would do was try to write to you.' Anne turned away, her eyes shining, as her mother wagged a chiding finger at me. 'Shame on you, Tom! And you a poet!' She would never use the word pamphleteer. 'Not one letter!'

Mr Black was already well into his second glass of wine, and wagged a finger in his turn at his wife. 'Come, come, Mrs Black. You don't carry your quill and ink with your musket into the field, do you, Tom, eh?'

He spoke man to man, as if he had experience, or at least a conception of 'the field', and I saw with a sense of dread that he would expect me to write something like the pamphlet *An Exact Account of the Most Dangerous and Bloody Fighte near Kineton* I had seen but been unable to bring myself to read. I was struggling again to find something to say when I saw Jane in the background. With a lurch of guilt I remembered that, somewhere in my knapsack, was the letter I had promised to give to Mrs Morland.

She greeted my shyly and asked if I had seen her mother. I blurted out abruptly: 'Your mother's dead.' My clumsiness silenced everyone and she asked if I had seen her. 'Yes. Yes. Yes, I did.' Each word felt like a piece of lead dropping from my mouth. 'I gave her your letter,' I lied. 'She forgave you and gave you her blessing.'

She closed her eyes and clasped her hands in a silent prayer, then opened her eyes and gave me the most wonderful smile. 'God bless you, Tom.'

I burst into tears.

There was a moment's awful silence, then everyone crowded around me talking at once, but I could hear nothing. Their faces were a blur through the tears which, feeling intense shame, I struggled to stop but could not. I tried to get away from them, stumbled over my knapsack and found myself looking into the shop, Nehemiah gawping at me. He was oiling the press and, distracted from his task, the oil dribbled over his boots. They were laced in true apprentice fashion, that is to say, scarce laced at all. For some reason this redoubled my tears.

'What have you done, Tom?' said Mr Black, with all his old sternness.

'I don't know, sir.' I did not, and that made me weep all the more, until I thought I would never stop. 'I don't know, I don't know!'

'He needs rest,' Jane said. 'He can have my bed. His old bed.' She coloured as Anne gave her a jealous look.

'He can have my bed,' she said.

'Anne!' cried Mrs Black, scandalised.

'I can sleep in your room,' she said.

Before they could argue, she led me upstairs like a child.

41

For I do not know how many days I fell asleep in her room, but awoke at Edgehill with the acrid smell of gunpowder in my nose or, sometimes, the curious, clean fresh smell of blood. Or I would sit up with a start, with the order to 'Palm your pike – charge your pike!' ringing in my ears and find I had gone through the movements in my sleep. Or I would hear Luke's relaxed, almost lazy voice: 'Try your match . . . guard your pan . . . present . . . fire.' They brought the doctor, who tried to bleed me, but I could not stand the sight of blood. They brought the minister, Mr Tooley, who tried to cast out my devils, quoting Luke to me where Jesus cast out a legion of devils into swine. But I argued, apparently – I do not remember this – that I did not understand why the poor swine had to suffer, throwing themselves from a cliff, and I preferred to keep my devils.

They all shook their heads at me except Anne, who after the minister had left said she saw no devils and refused to let anyone else into the room, bringing me food and drink, meeting with tight lips her mother berating her for behaving like a servant.

Gradually the devils, or visions or whatever they were, faded. One day I woke up and snatches of that battlefield had, as usual, come into my dreams, but that morning it was different. There had come back into my mind as much as I was ever likely to remember

of what had happened after I had run from Luke on to the battlefield after my father. Mr Black had told me that Edward Stonehouse
had been killed, blindly finding himself in the wrong part of the
battlefield. Richard Stonehouse had been posted in one of the
pamphlets as missing. His body had not been found. I felt I had to
see Lord Stonehouse as soon as possible. I got out of bed and almost
fell, clutching on to a chair. Anne came running in and told me to
get back into bed. I shook my head, but sat down heavily in the
chair.

'Are you back?' she whispered.

I nodded.

'Are you Tom?'

I nodded.

'Can you speak?'

I smiled. 'Yes.'

'It does funny things to your scar. Smile again.' I laughed. She
flung her arms round me and kissed me. 'I love you!'

'I love you.'

'As much as the Countess?'

'What *is* this Countess stuff?'

I felt automatically for her letter, which I had carried beneath my
shirt, and she produced it. 'I helped you undress. With Sarah . . . You
don't remember?' She blushed. 'Only the top part. My mother was
horrified.'

I read again *I Hope Youe doe Think of Mee as I of Youe and not
of Your Countess* – and was mortified when she told me what led
up to that sentence. When Eaton and I returned from Poplar to stay
at the Seven Stars, before going on to Highpoint, I had gone to
Bedford Square in search of Kate, at the same time as the Countess
had sent me a letter asking me to meet Mr Pym. The letter sat in
some state over the fire in Half Moon Court, its elegant hand and
impressive seal sending daggers of jealousy into Anne's heart. That
it was a love letter, she had no doubt. Every time she saw it she felt

an urge to throw it in the fire, but dare not. At last she could stand it no longer and went to Bedford Square.

I covered my face with my hands and got up, unable to listen or speak for a moment. It was so childish, so unwomanly, so undignified. It was more than that, although I did not see it then. I had taken a step into that world, perhaps more than a step, and it was my private world, for which she was quite unsuited and had no place. I was deeply in love with her, but deeply embarrassed at the thought of her turning up in Bedford Square. If ever the time came to resolve this problem, which now seemed more unlikely than ever, it was my part to do so, not hers. She waited as if she was aware of this, hands clasped, head bowed, until I sat down.

'A foul animal of a footman told me to go round the back,' she said.

'I know him,' I said faintly.

'Then she came out.'

I covered my face with my hands again, visualising Lucy Hay sending poor Anne packing, seeing her wandering away from Bedford Square humiliated, as I had done so many times in the past. But it was worse, much worse than that.

'She took me up to her with-with—'

'Withdrawing chamber.'

'And gave me a drink of cho-cho—'

'Chocolate.'

'She's *old*.'

'She is a very beautiful woman,' I said coldly.

'She wears beautiful paint. She gave me some. Look –'

I stared speechless as Anne, with great excitement, dabbed her cheek from a pot, producing a smear of red. Apparently the misunderstanding over the Countess's letter was soon dealt with. Anne never said as much, but I could not stand the thought that they must have been talking about me. I could not believe how intimate they had become in such a short space of time; so intimate, I found myself listening open-mouthed to things about Lucy Hay I never knew. Before I was born (Anne emphasised that) Lucy Hay was seriously ill and lost her first and only child, who was still-born. Then her husband died. It was such a terrible tragedy, Anne said, having apparently gone from hating Lucy Hay to adoring her in the space of a cup of chocolate. 'But it made her as a woman.'

'Did it? How so?'

Anne was literally wringing her hands, twisting her small fingers together, looking faintly ridiculous with a smear of cochineal on one cheek, like a half-made-up player on Bankside.

'Have you heard of Sir Thomas More?'

'Of course.'

'He said if female soil be more productive of weeds than fruit it should be cult-cult—'

'Cultivated?'

'Thank you. It should be culti-vated with learning.'

A little writing was one thing, but I did not much care for the sound of this, nor when she referred to a short period in the last century when women like Queen Elizabeth and Lady Jane Grey had become as familiar with the classics as men. But it was what she said next that really shocked me.

'Lucy,' she said, 'advised me to have no more than four children.'

I told her that was unnatural nonsense. The typical remark of a woman who could not perform her natural function. She replied that it gave women a better chance to help men, since women had cooler heads than men, who sometimes needed their judgement.

'Judgement? Oh, Anne, I love you, not your judgement. What judgement do you have? I don't know what she's playing at, but she's an intriguer, a meddler! You mustn't listen to her, do you hear me?'

She bit her lip rebelliously. 'Are you jealous I went to see her?'

'Jealous? What an odd thing to say. No. Of course I'm not jealous.'

She dropped her head and plucked at her dress in silence for a few moments, then sighed, and gave me a resigned, supplicating look. I normally gained fresh life and energy from the love and nonsense we talked together, as a bee sucks nectar from a flower, but I found this conversation confusing and exhausting. I went to the window. It was beginning to snow again. Sarah was feeding the robin, which she always claimed was the same one every year.

'She also said you were one of the most intelligent and capable men she had ever met.'

I whirled round, staring suspiciously at her, but her face was eager and earnest, with not a trace of a smile. I could not help reflecting that eagerness. 'Did she? Did she really?'

'Yes, and you are, you know you are, Monkey!' She dived across the room and flung herself at my feet, eyes sparkling. I seized her to kiss her, but she wriggled away from me. 'Wait! Wait! Stay there! Don't move! Don't look!'

She rushed to a scrap of mirror and there was an intriguing rustling and fumbling and peering into the mirror with her back towards me.

'Cheat! You're looking!'

I turned away, covering my face with my hands. This was a form of silliness I much preferred. In the endearing way in which women pick up a fashion one moment and discard it the next, she seemed already to have forgotten about learning Latin and Greek. There was an intense little silence in which I could hear her breathing and murmuring to herself. Then a rustle of skirts.

'You may look,' she said, commandingly.

She had turned herself into a woman of the court, her lips reddened, her cheeks flushed pink, her eyebrows blackened, emphasising the astonishing, imperious grey of her eyes. But it was not that that made me react as I did. She had unbuttoned the top of her dress, folding down the collar. On her breast was the pendant. It seemed to fill the whole room with a virulent light, the falcon's venomous eyes staring at me from its enamelled nest.

I leapt across the room at her. 'Take it off! Take that thing off!' I wrenched at the pendant. She screamed as the chain bit into her neck. The clasp broke and I threw the thing across the room. The bird seemed to flutter and hiss at me. 'You have been into my pack!' I shouted. 'Never do that again! Never touch that thing again!'

Her mother appeared at the door and Anne flung herself into her arms, sobbing. 'I thought he was going to kill me! I thought he was going to kill me!'

42

Lord Stonehouse was good at mourning. It was his natural habitat. My mother must have known this instinctively when she chose the clothes for her father's funeral. I thought as I went into Queen Street that morning she would have cherished this moment. I felt that I knew her then, that I was closer to her than to any living person, even Anne.

Richard Stonehouse was still posted as missing. The great town house was in mourning for Edward. Hangings were half-drawn and there was an air of sepulchral quiet in the black-and-white chequerboard hall, where the Greek busts and the footman looked at me askance. Sarah had mended an old jerkin, and stitched a new collar on a shirt she had beaten almost white under the pump. I carried my soldier's knapsack. They searched the pack for gunpowder, which I suppose in a way the contents were.

'Name?'

'Thomas Neave.'

'Business?'

'I have concluded a mission for Lord Stonehouse.'

Lord Stonehouse was in a meeting and continued his business as punctiliously as usual. When I was eventually shown into his study I stood waiting as I had stood before, some distance from the desk, while the single hand of the clock jerked on and Mr Cole shook sand on his signature, sealed the document, bowed and went out. Lord Stonehouse was wearing reading glasses I had not seen before. He put them in a case and beckoned me forward.

'You have it?'

It was as if he was referring to a run-of-the-mill dispatch from some informant in Oxford. Yet there was something comforting in his abstract, weary tone, in his remoteness, his coldness, which I was beginning to understand, above all in what he did not say. He did not, as might have been expected, refer to Edgehill, or 'our great victory' as some called it. He knew. He understood. There was, at least, that bond between us.

He became alive when I took the pendant from my pack, swooping on it like a falcon on its prey. It seemed to fill the whole of that dark sombre room with light, reflecting from the polished oak of his desk, glittering in his black eyes. He gave a great sigh, stroking the falcon as if he was smoothing out its feathers. The light only seemed to die down when he noticed that I had put two other things on his desk: a small pile of letters and Richard's tattered cloak.

Slowly he put down the pendant and picked up the cloak, putting his hand through the rent in it, staring at the dark brown stains at its edges, then at me, as malevolently as the falcon, which now seemed to slumber in the jewel.

I told him how Richard had confronted me, killed Luke and ridden away. How I had run after him, drawing my dagger, but could remember nothing else, until I returned to London. Gradually what had happened that night had been coming back to me, patchily, incompletely, in nightmare flashes.

Lord Stonehouse smoothed the torn cloak, his sceptical eyes never leaving me as I told him I lost Richard before I got to the meadows, which were no longer meadows, but a dark marsh of the dead and dying. I kept on running, kept on hearing his horse, or thought I heard it, but it was a will o' the wisp sound, leading me this way, then that, until I saw the escarpment looming above me as the clouds drifted from the moon. Not far away was a camp fire. Dipping in and out of the light of it was a familiar face: the hollowed eyes and the spade-like beard of the King. Other figures rose in the firelight, staring at me. I stumbled away, too exhausted to run, but nobody followed me. Perhaps they thought I was a spirit. Then I saw it. Richard's horse. Doing something unbelievable in that place. It was peacefully cropping grass. It sniffed indifferently at a man with half a mouth and twisted, sightless eyes before browsing for another patch. From the pommel of the saddle trailed Richard's cloak.

I took the cloak and went from body to body, some dead, some still crying out, their cries redoubling as I approached them. I looked, or turned over body after body until I came upon two men who were manhandling a corpse, one removing the dead man's jerkin, the other his boots. They snarled at me like wolves.

'This is our patch!'

'Find your own!'

But when they saw I was taking nothing, simply turning corpses over, they ignored me and fell to quarrelling over the boots. I came to one man, face buried in the grass, who had a jacket I thought was Richard's. He was still, moonlight shining on small crystals of hoar frost forming on his cheek in the intense cold. I turned him over. He was alive, the movement lifting him out of his frozen coma.

'Help me,' he whispered. 'Dear mother, help me.'

At first I had not seen anything wrong, but now I saw a terrible wound in his stomach, from which the guts spilled. I turned away, retching, but he had found a last strength, clutching at my arm, shrieking at me: 'Kill me, kill me, kill me!'

He would not let me go. I stabbed him until his arm fell away from me and the cries stopped. Even then I could not stop. I was still stabbing him when Ben found me.

My hands were covering my face. I brought them down slowly, fearing I was still in those meadows, but I was in the study with Lord Stonehouse whose expression was as cold as the frost that night. My shirt clung to my back with sweat, but I was shivering as if I was still on that freezing field.

'Did you find Richard?'

'I don't know, my lord.'

He stared at the cloak. 'Did you kill him?' he said softly.

'I don't know. Don't you understand? I don't even know whether I'm really remembering or whether it's part of the nightmares I have.'

He stood up, his voice rising abruptly. 'Did you kill my son?'

'I don't know,' I screamed back at him.

The door flew open and the servants who were always outside rushed in. Lord Stonehouse made a violent gesture for them to go and they almost fell over themselves in an effort to turn, bow, leave and close the door again, all at the same time. After the door was closed, all you could hear was our jerky breathing. Lord Stonehouse so rarely lost control he looked unfamiliar with it, touching his desk as if to make sure it was solid, then sitting and folding Richard's cloak into a meticulous square until his hands stopped shaking. He turned to the letters, and I told him how I found them.

Letters, papers were meat and drink to him, and he could extract the meat from the fat faster than any man I knew. He skimmed through the pages rapidly.

'I thought as much.'

There was not a word about me, that I was his grandson, nothing. 'You thought as much?'

'I am not a fool.' He leaned forward, his black eyes venomous and unpitying as the falcon his ancestors had chosen as a symbol. 'One last time: did you kill my son?'

Those eyes made me feel as if I was halfway to the gallows, and brought out in me, unexpectedly, not what he dreaded to hear, but what I did. 'I do not know. What I do know is that I killed my friend.'

There it was. I had said out loud what I had never admitted to myself before. It was there, unlike what had happened to Richard, but slippery memory had been assiduously burying it. Now I had said it. Admitted it. I felt, with a welling of grief, a profound relief. I could now do what I had avoided thinking about, let alone doing. I could go to Charity, give her his ring, and tell her how Luke died.

Lord Stonehouse swept his hand across his desk, dismissing what I had said as of no importance, irrelevant. Perhaps to him it was. I heard he had no friends. That gesture, reducing someone I loved to a triviality, goaded me into a fury. He moved his hand to the bell to summon the servants, but I no longer cared who he was, what he said, what he did to me. I jumped forward, bending over him, gripping the edges of the desk.

'He was my dearest friend. If I had not shouted to stop him, Luke would have killed your son. Instead, Richard killed him.'

The words choked in my throat. He kept his hand near the bell. His voice was cold with scepticism. 'Why did you shout to stop your dearest friend?'

'Why? Why? Because Richard is my father, as well as your son! Do you think, my lord, that having found him, my instinct was to kill him?'

'From what you say, he tried to kill you.'

'From what I say! Ask your servants at Highpoint. How much proof do you need? You brought us up to hate one another. First you try and make Richard into something he's not – then me.'

Lord Stonehouse stabbed angrily at the bell. The servants sprang in, hovering round me. I tensed, clenching my fists. I was not going to be dragged away as I was before. But Lord Stonehouse took a sip of the wine that was always on his desk, dabbed his lips, and told them to get his secretary.

As the door closed, I said: 'When it came to it, I don't think my father could do the job himself. Or perhaps,' I added bitterly, 'I'm naive, and that is what I like to think.'

Lord Stonehouse jumped as the coals settled and a flame lit up his lined face, which was the colour of old parchment. He stared at the bundle of letters written to my mother, part deceit, but part love, or perhaps again that is what I like to think. He read one page, then another. The secretary, Mr Cole, entered and stood in the required position, legs slightly straddled, files under his arm. On one of them, I noticed, was the heading *Mr Richard*.

Lord Stonehouse finished the letters, tapped them square with his fingertips, put them in the drawer, the first on the right-hand side which I now knew to be Richard's, and locked it.

'Mr Cole, I believe we have an agreement with Mr Neave?'

With a flourish the secretary drew out the document he had witnessed and I had signed – years ago, it felt, as an arrogant youth, full of certainty and ideals. That arrogance was even there in my signature, with the ridiculous squiggle underlining it, which I had been so proud of, but now made me wince.

'I believe it was one pendant for the freehold of . . .'

'Half Moon Court, my lord.' With another flourish, Mr Cole set a document, heavy with seals and legal language in front of me.

I signed for the receipt of it, my signature now being a very sparse one, with no squiggle. Lord Stonehouse gazed at it, and the other, but made no comment. It was a moment or two before I realised I was dismissed. At the door I turned.

'And . . . the marriage, my lord?'

'What? Oh. Old Black's daughter. Why should I stand in your way? Make you into what you are not? Mmm?'

Before he had finished the sentence, Lord Stonehouse was immersed in the file Mr Cole had placed in front of him, back in his familiar world of paper.

43

The file they were discussing was the one on Richard. Lord Stonehouse would not rest until he knew what had happened to his eldest son. No doubt he was already setting Mr Cole to work to find out whether I had killed him. Not a word about me being his grandson. Nothing. I was Mr Neave. His father was tight on his feelings, Richard had said. Tight? Feelings? All he cared about, after all this, was his eldest son, the entail, the estate! I worked myself up in this manner until I realised it must have been exactly the state of mind Richard was in when he first saw my portrait.

I told myself I was free. I had everything I had ever wanted, and tried to return to the mood of the previous, idyllic summer. But I was so morose when I returned to Half Moon Court that Mr Black called me into his office fearing the worst. Indifferently I put the freehold on his desk. At first he would not look at it, thinking it was another notice to quit. Then he saw the seal. Read the clauses, threw the document in the air with a whoop of joy, caught it, read the clauses again to make sure they had not fallen from the paper and got lost, and shouted for his wife. I was happy then. Grinning all over my face as he poured wine and went over brick after brick of the place saying, 'This is ours – thanks to Tom! And this! And this!' Suddenly I was not mad, talked about in whispers, but a saviour.

'Shouldn't you post the banns,' Anne whispered, 'in case you go away again?'

I kissed her and said I would go right away to see Mr Tooley, but while the wine gave me courage, went to see Charity instead. She was bewildered when I stumbled out that, but for me, Luke would be alive.

'But the sword was not in your hand.'

'No, no, but –'

I gave up. What she wanted to hear, again and again, was that he loved her, and would see her in heaven. All the guilt I had tortured myself with was dismissed, was nothing compared with that. She even asked me if I would be little Luke's godfather, and when I said I would gripped my hands and said: 'What exactly did he say? Tell me again.'

As well as giving Mr Black the freehold, Lord Stonehouse seemed to take in earnest my decision to be a printer and put government work our way. Parliament ruled by ordinance, and we printed ordinances on loans to put the navy to sea, ordinances to 'find' sailors (in other words, press them), ordinances on armaments, on manuals for armaments (making what was already complex incomprehensible), ordinances to trench, stop and to fortify the highways (such as they were), to build a great wall round the City, and ordinances to raise rates to pay for all this. Parliamentary rule was not the Eden foretold by the Grand Remonstrance I ran so eagerly through the streets with, and its demands for money started to make the King's previous excesses look frugal. And it was as dull as ditchwater. I grew sick of the sight of the word ordinance.

To relieve the tedium, Mr Black wanted me to go to Westminster as I used to, but I refused. Be a printer's runner again? I was a journeyman, near to being my own master! Nehemiah should go. So Nehemiah went, and came back, eyes shining, saying he had seen Mr Pym. As surly as my hands were black, I snarled at him to get on with the presswork. I had not heard a word from Mr Pym. Nor from the Countess. Not a word. I remembered the heady evening, before I left London with Eaton, when I met Mr Pym at Bedford

Square. But, of course, all they were interested in was my prospect of becoming a Stonehouse, which I had traded in for Half Moon Court.

I struggled to concentrate on composing the grubby text that Nehemiah had brought me, which was an Ordinance on the Rightfull Printing of Ordinances.

The only letter I received was from Kate. After leaving me on the road to Warwickshire, Matthew had returned to Highpoint. He and Kate had travelled back to London, as they had done many years before, in the only vehicle that could get through both warring sides unhindered – the plague cart. Poplar was thriving. A ship was being built for the navy and Matthew was – or called himself – a shipwright.

One bleak day tempers were at their shortest. The ice was half an inch thick in the pail in the yard where Sarah crunched and slipped over layers of dirty frozen snow to return from the bakers with only two small loaves of black rye bread. There were so many ordinances I was setting type while Nehemiah worked the press. I smelt beer on his breath and accused him of going to the Pot. He denied ever going there, which made matters worse, for I had seen him there once before and said nothing.

I lashed out at him with my composing stick, catching him on the forehead. The type I had set up flew in every direction, making me even more furious. I drew back the stick again. A trickle of blood was making its way down Nehemiah's forehead. I stopped as Nehemiah flung up his hands. I saw myself crouching there, biting my lips so I would not cry out when the next blow hit me.

I hurled the stick across the shop and went into the house. I saw Mr Black's startled face as he came out of the office, but went straight upstairs into my old bedroom in the garret. I wrapped a blanket round me, for it was bitter cold up there. The morning's frost patterns were still on the window. I pushed away Susannah's Bible, which I had not opened for a long time, sat on the window seat, breathed a hole in the patterns and stared out. My knees brushed against my pack and I had a sudden deep, profound longing to put it on my back and go, wherever my feet took me.

I heard a step on the landing, and thought that Mr Black had followed me. The door opened, but I continued staring out.

'I'm sorry,' I said.

There was a touch, the gentlest, most hesitant of touches on my shoulder. It was Anne. I knew what she had come for. Wearily I said: 'I'm sorry. I haven't seen Mr Tooley yet for the banns but –'

'I do not want you to see him.'

Irritably I thought – first Nehemiah, now Anne. She was already at the door, going. 'I promise you –'

'I do not want you to see him,' she flared.

'Come on, come on.' I stopped her and held her in my arms. She lifted her face, looking at me searchingly, with a wildness I had not seen in her before. It sent a thrill of desire through me and I bent to kiss her. At the last moment she turned her lips away. That only redoubled my excitement and I pulled her more tightly to me. She struggled, trying to speak, but I shut her lips with mine. We had twisted back inside the room and I had a brief glimpse of the apple tree and I remembered Eaton throwing the apple core away and saying, *Show her who's master! Give her the whip!* He was right. Stupid that we had lived together, so close for so long, and never done this. The more she struggled, the more her fists struck and her nails bit, the more inflamed I got, until I had her over the bed, about to fling her on it when she gave me the most infernal blow to the head.

No. Not her, the beam – that wretched beam! But it was as if she had wielded it as she pulled away and ran to the door. I staggered and sat down heavily on the bed, my head ringing. She took a step or two back towards me. I could not look at her. The force of the blow had caused me to bite my tongue, and my voice came out thick and dazed. 'I . . . I . . . will go now . . . to Mr T-T—'

'You don't understand, Tom. I don't want to marry you.'

I shook my head dizzily. 'Don't be silly.'

She clenched her fists with a sudden ferocity. 'I am not being silly! I do not want to marry you.'

I got up giddily, the room swaying until I was able to focus on her tight lips, her determined eyes. The top of her dress was torn and the curve of her breasts rose and fell quickly. She said something so low and mumbled that I could not follow it.

'What?'

'You – do – not – want – to – marry – me.'

The words came out in such great gulps, tears welling, my heart went out to her. At the same time I laughed, I was so astonished. 'Oh, Anne! What nonsense! I love you. I've always loved you, always wanted to marry you.'

She dashed the tears away from her eyes with a violent gesture of her hand. 'You may love me, but you don't want to marry me. You will never be happy with me.'

Beneath the anger she was shaking. I felt that her whole life, and mine, was falling to pieces and longed to hold her, to comfort her, but feared from her look another outburst. 'I will never be happy with anyone else,' I said quietly.

'You will never be happy with me,' she repeated, just as quietly. 'We are not suited.'

'Not suited? Of course we are suited. We have always been suited.'

As if every word was being torn out of her, she said: 'I've stopped you . . . being . . . having . . . a position.'

'Don't be stupid. This is what I want.'

'This? Is it?' She had stopped trembling and was quite calm now, staring round the garret at Sarah's bed, with the sacking she used for blankets, at mine, still unmade. Mr Black must have joined Nehemiah at the press, because it was now working at a regular rhythm, sending a little tremor through the house every time the platen came down on the paper, then jerked back for the next pass. She came closer, staring steadily into my eyes. 'Is it?'

She made me look at things I had been refusing to face, look inside myself in a way that was so painful I could not speak. I turned away from her and almost cracked my head on the beam again. I drove my fist viciously into it and grimaced, clutching my hand, feeling I had broken every bone in it. I sat in the window seat breathing so heavily the last of the ice patterns melted.

'Here.' She brought me a cloth. 'Your lip's bleeding.'

I wiped it and indicated her torn dress. 'I'm sorry.'

'It's nothing. I'll sew it. That's what women are for.' It was the only sign of bitterness she showed. 'What did Lord Stonehouse say?'

'He thinks I killed his son.'

She was very still. 'Did you?'

'I don't know.' I told her all I knew, all I remembered. She was silent until I told her what I had said to Lord Stonehouse, how what he had done had caused Richard and I, father and son, although he did not know it, to hate one another. I thought it was true, it hurt him and was meant to hurt him and I was glad I had said it, but she stared at me, appalled.

'You cannot talk to your betters like that.'

'Betters?' I snarled at her. 'How is he better than me?'

'He is a lord!'

'He is a lord,' I mocked. 'He is a cheat and a murderer.' I told her about the contract and she was, if anything, even more appalled.

'You fool!'

It was one thing for me to feel it, quite another for her to call me it. She backed away as I only just stopped myself from flying at her, as I did when she wore the pendant. Even then I felt it was the pendant that had somehow poisoned things between us. 'Yes. I am a fool. I could have got myself a position, I suppose. Is that what you mean? I did it for *you!* God knows why! You are right – we are not suited at all! I will go!'

She was so pale it seemed as if every drop of blood had been drained from her face. 'Yes,' she whispered. 'It's best you go. Go now. I wish you'd never come here.'

It was all the more terrible because she said it so quietly. She turned at the door and I thought she was going to say more, but if she was the words would not come. She went and I heard her say something to her mother, again quietly, evenly, as if nothing had happened, then her bedroom door closed. Half a dozen – no, a dozen times – I went to go downstairs to tap at her door but returned to stare down at the frozen apple tree. She knew me better than I knew myself. I had been bitten by the pendant, by the falcon, and wanted more than this – what, I did not know. She was right. I would have married her, stayed here, or somewhere like it, become restless, perhaps grown to hate her. Instead she had refused me – refused me! It made me love her more deeply than ever and resent her bitterly at the same time. She had given me my freedom, but there is nothing more terrible than freedom when you do not know what to do with it.

The press stopped, and the house seemed to steady itself, as it always did, like a ship coming to anchor. They would be spreading out the printed copies to dry now; Mr Black carefully, meticulously, inspecting every one, criticising one here, another there. I listened. Yes, there was his sharp voice, the sound of a blow aimed, but it produced only a snivel not a cry. He had not the strength now, as he had had with me. Ah, if I could only go back, start again, how I would welcome that blow. If I could go back, correct my mistakes – and my hopeless aspirations . . .

I picked up my pack. There were a few hours of daylight left. I put my clothes in my pack and checked my boots, with a sudden desire to leave without delay. There was only one thing left to pack, which was what I came with – Susannah's Bible. I picked it up to thrust it in, but seemed to hear her voice saying: 'Tom, whenever you need guidance, open the book.'

I had not opened it for many a month and God knows I needed guidance then. I fell on my knees before the window seat and opened the book at random, as she used to do, only making the choice of the New Testament, not the Old, for that meant to me the blood and vengeance of Edgehill. I shut my eyes and put my finger between the pages, as Susannah used to, and opened them to see that passage in

John where Jesus feeds the five thousand with five loaves and two fishes. I stared at it but I could not for the life of me understand what meaning it had for me. The only bread in the house was rye bread, and it was difficult to break that at all, let alone for five thousand.

I pored over it, and puzzled over it, but I had not Susannah's belief nor Matthew's guile to extract a meaning. Finally I closed it with a thwack, thrust it in my pack and went to the door. The house shook, but it was not the tremor of the press. It was a carriage approaching, and not a bone-rattling hackney carriage, but a carriage and pair. I could see the fine horses edging carefully into the narrow entrance. There flashed through me that only my lack of belief, my insistence in believing there must be a riddle when there was none, had prevented me from seeing the obvious. Susannah would have seen the meaning in the passage straight away. A miracle was about to happen! Now the sceptics may say that the real miracle was that, had I not pored and puzzled over that passage, the pack would have been on my back by now and I on the road, unreachable.

In that moment, I knew with absolute certainty that Lord Stonehouse, overcome by remorse at the hatred he had fed between father and son, had come to beg forgiveness. I saw him again as the kindly old man who had taken me in his arms when I had the pitch burn. Great treasure. It was exactly what Matthew had foretold in the pendant. Exactly the ending that a story or ballad should have. I ran down the twisting stairs into a house of turmoil, with Mrs Black colliding with me as she shrieked to Jane to get her best dress, and Mr Black and Nehemiah coming out of the shop, jaws dropping.

Only Sarah, wiping her hands on a cloth, seemed unmoved. 'He'll never get that thing through there,' she said.

I ran into the yard, slipped on the ice and fell, finding myself staring at the liveried legs of a footman, then into the disdainful eyes of Jenkins, my old enemy from Bedford Square, who was placing the steps for the Countess to descend.

44

They were overawed, but they loved her. I never knew anyone more capable of being charming and dismissive in the same breath. Lucy Hay complimented Mrs Black on the exquisite cloth of her shawl ('Who is your merchant?') and Mr Black on being London's Voice of Liberty (a phrase I could see him setting up there and then, with due acknowledgements) and begged for the opportunity to see me and Anne alone.

I feared she wanted to tell Anne she was standing in my way. So did Anne, I believe, for she refused to come down. Only dire threats from her mother and father brought her down eventually, very pale in the face, with her dress repaired. The last of the coals were heaped on the fire, wine pressed into our hands and we were left alone. The Countess kept her fur cloak on, for the coals Sarah tipped on the fire had practically extinguished it. She sipped at her wine, grimaced and, since I had swallowed mine at one gulp, poured the rest into my glass.

'You've heard the news about Richard Stonehouse?' she said in the tone of one who was quite sure we had not. I went very still, suddenly certain that his body had been found. Normally she was the most tantalising person in drawing the most from a piece of news that no one else knew, but she saw my expression and said: 'He's alive. Very much so.'

Relief was followed by a confusion of emotions. That, and what I had said to Lord Stonehouse, finished any hope of a position with him. He had not contacted me to tell me this, although Richard was my father and he must at least have had an inkling of the torment I had been through. A miracle. Lord Stonehouse overcome by remorse. What an idiotic fool I was! I should go back to my ballads and pamphlets – it was all I was fit for. I scarcely listened to what the Countess was saying. Richard had got back to Royalist lines. He was Sir Richard now, she told us. He was in France with the Queen's retinue, recruiting English soldiers from Continental armies. There was still enough daylight left for me to go. I stared at my pack, which I had dropped by the door. I finished the wine, unable to meet Anne's eyes, wishing the Countess would leave, but she rattled on, saying that Lord Stonehouse wanted to celebrate the news that his son was alive but deemed it inappropriate to hold a function for an important Royalist commander.

The fire had at last blazed up, and the Countess sighed with pleasure, dropping the fur cloak from her shoulders. The twin of the falcon pendant, which I had first seen in her carriage, was glittering between her breasts. 'Men,' she said to Anne, shaking her head, 'have no idea how to resolve such a conflict of interests.'

Anne stared at her mutely. I reddened for her, sure she had no idea what the Countess was talking about, and stared into the fire.

'Everything all right between you two?'

Anne sat bolt upright, screwing her hands together. I wanted to hold her, to protect her from this prying, inquisitive woman, who was like a bloodsucking flea, gaining her nourishment from the intimate secrets of other people's lives.

'I see. It seems I came at the right time.' I leaned forward to tell her not to interfere but she held up an imperious hand. 'I am having one of my occasions for Lord Stonehouse tonight – not on the face of it about Richard, but it will enable him to, er . . . discreetly celebrate. Warwick will be there. Bedford. Mr Pym, of course. All the right people. I want you to be there.'

I was looking into the fire and turned to stare at her. After all that had happened, she expected me to celebrate Richard's return to life. On the other hand, Mr Pym would be there and the great earls who employed him, Bedford and Warwick, who ran the navy.

'I don't know,' I said, looking away off-handedly into the fire. 'I don't know if I should go –'

'Oh, not *you*!' she said. 'That would be not be right at all.'

She was not looking at me, but at Anne. I stared at the Countess in amazement, Anne in abject terror.

'I need a lady in waiting. All the lively ones are in Paris with the Queen, or Oxford with the King. There is no reason why righteousness should not be attractive, but Puritan women are as dull as dumplings.' I tried to interrupt her again, but nothing could stop her. 'We live in an upside-down world where, as the ballad has it, war makes lords peasants and peasants lords. But for the moment I shall call you Lady Black. Men like a mystery. Come on, Anne. We have little time.'

She rose, gesturing Anne to follow her. Anne leapt up, but there her obedience ended. She backed away, twisting her hands together as if she would tear them off. 'I cannot. I cannot.'

'Nonsense. Of course you can.'

'I would not know what to say,' Anne cried in agony, 'what to do!'

I came between them, shielding her from the Countess. 'She's right. It's ridiculous. How can she have a conversation with Mr Pym? Or Lord Stonehouse?'

Before the Countess could answer, Anne rounded on me like a spitting cat. 'Do you think I have learned nothing from you, the way you endlessly go on about politics? Nothing from there?' She pointed to the print shop. 'Nothing about the war? Do you? Do you?' She turned away, tears springing into her eyes, gulping out the last words.

'Exactly,' the Countess said soothingly, comfortingly. 'You listen beautifully, Anne, and ask questions charmingly, which is all men ever expect of us – isn't that right, Tom?'

She smiled at me sweetly. I hated her. I hated her like poison. I could not understand why I had ever found her beautiful, ever been so fascinated by her. But even with all her scheming I did not think she would persuade Anne. She was panic-stricken at the prospect, too over-awed by what she called her betters. Sure enough, she dropped back in her chair and huddled before the fire again, shaking her head stubbornly.

'It's impossible. What could I wear? I've only this dress and one or two other rags.'

'Well,' the Countess said, 'you could wear this, for a start.'

Anne turned, staring, the tears in her eyes glittering like the diamonds in the pendant the Countess was removing from her neck.

All the humiliation I ever suffered from Anne when I first came to that house with no boots on my feet was as nothing to seeing her being helped into the coach by Jenkins. Her terror seemed to have vanished in excitement. There seemed to be a familiarity between her and Jenkins, who was back to giving me his old looks of disdain at my crumpled clothes, my blackened hands. Of course! Anne had not been once to the Countess, but several times. Lucy Hay had dropped me for a new favourite.

The whole household turned out to see them off, Mrs Black curtseying and Mr Black lifting his hat like a pair in a puppet show at Bartholomew Fair. Half the porters came out of Smithfield to help the coach back into Cloth Fair. Some of them thought the Countess was the Queen, the way she smiled and raised her hand. Anne waved to me, but I could not, would not, wave back. There was too much in that wave, in the look she gave me, that reminded me of the time when she had called me Monkey in disdain.

'Some of us go up, and some of us go down,' Sarah said. 'But what do we do now for coal?'

It was freezing, and far too late to leave now. After supper I took my pack upstairs and went to bed early, but could not sleep for thinking about Anne. Now, as I tossed and turned, my envy and burning resentment vanished in an agony of concern. I knew her so well. Her panic would come back. They would know who, or at least what she was. I could not stand the thought of Lord Stonehouse's black, penetrating eyes on her, what he would say. I sprang out of bed, and went out into the cold night.

There was no sound except the watchman's cry. Not a dog barked. Even in the inns, people seemed huddled over fires. I stopped, my breath hanging frozen in the air as the watchman passed me. He said something but I caught not a word. What was I doing, hurrying across London, on this bleakest night of winter, to care and comfort her, forsaking all others, as the marriage service puts it, if I did not love her beyond anything else? I felt as I had when we had our first kiss. No! When I longed for it. I whooped. Ran. Fell, picked myself up laughing, and in this manner reached Bedford Square.

I could not see her among the glittering array of people caught in the blaze of candlelight, or hidden in deep shadow. I saw Jenkins serving drinks, and the Countess in earnest conversation with Mr Pym, before passing to another group. Perhaps Anne was in the back where I used to be, ignominiously bundled into the kitchens. Or – it would be like her – had fled there.

I took a step to go round the side, where I had so often delivered letters, and saw her. Or, it would be more accurate to say, saw the pendant. For a moment I still did not recognise the woman wearing it. She came out of the shadows with Lord Stonehouse. She was Anne, yet not Anne. Her rosy lips and cheeks stood out in sharp relief from the rest of her pure white skin, set off by the pendant, which sparkled on the swell of her small breasts. She was nodding, tilting her chin earnestly, deferentially at Lord Stonehouse, drawing up the long, smooth line of her neck. At the same time, within the frame of beautifully, tightly curled ringlets of hair her large blue eyes shone brilliantly, coquettishly up at Lord Stonehouse, in a way I had never seen before. She reminded me of somebody, but try as I might, I could not call her to mind.

45

She did not return that night. Torn with jealousy, I slept little. Having stood there, still and frozen as an icicle, until the first carriages came, I awoke next morning with a thickening cold and a fever. I realised who, gazing up at that window, she had reminded me of. It was not someone I had ever known, but only imagined: my mother.

In my growing fever, the two merged together, until I felt I no longer knew who Anne was, just as I lost my own certainty when I saw my portrait at Highpoint. The pendant at Anne's breast became the pendant Matthew was picking up from the wet bushes and I thought I must leave, but in this slipping, fading vision I was holding her hand and we were leaving together.

'*Cream Ice!*' Mrs Black shrieked.

I lifted my head to hear the murmur of Anne's voice. I was covered in sweat and my nose was as swollen as a pig's bladder. From the weak sun filtering through the fresh ice patterns on the window it was past noon. Someone had piled extra blankets and coats on me. I heaved them off and immediately began to shiver. Mrs Black shrieked again.

'The earl of *who?*'

I slumped back on the bed and dragged the blanket over my head. A little later Anne came in, calling my name. When I did not move she began piling the coats and blankets over me again. Irritably I shoved them away, telling her in a thick, croaking voice I was too hot.

'Poor Tom. You sound dreadful.' I blinked at her. She had been in my dreams so much as she was at the window in Bedford Square that it was bewildering to see her in the thick old dressing gown of her mother's. She wore it over the dress I had torn, which she had repaired so neatly the stitches were scarcely visible.

'Here –' She put down a hot posset.

'Thank you.' I buried my head on the pillow.

'Don't you want to hear what happened?'

'I just want to sleep,' I mumbled, 'Lady Black.'

She touched my head. 'You're jealous.'

I sprang up shouting: 'I am not jealous! I just want to slee—' I broke into a fit of coughing. She put a pillow behind my back and I swallowed some of the posset. 'What did you say to Lord Stonehouse?'

'How do you know I talked to him?'

'Because I saw you.'

'Saw me? How?'

I blew my nose. 'Through the window. I thought you would be . . . terrified . . . out of your . . .'

'Oh, Tom, Tom!' She held me.

I sneezed. 'I thought . . . up there . . . you were so much above me.'

She pulled away. 'What do you think *I* have felt since this business began? That's why Lucy – the Countess – after I had gone that first time gave me lessons.'

'I see. I see.'

'I didn't talk to Lord Stonehouse. He talked to me. He likes that, because he can't hear very well. Didn't you realise that?'

I shook my head at how obtuse and self-centred I was not to have picked it up. It explained why he shouted and was so brusque and non-committal about some of the things I said. Lucy Hay used his deafness. She introduced Anne as Lady Black and only when Lord Stonehouse had been talking to her for some time – he said she reminded him of his wife when he first met her – did Lucy reveal who she was, saying he must have misheard, for she had introduced her as her lady-in-waiting, Anne Black.

'What did he do?'

'He cut me.'

That she had so soon adopted salon language, and the despair I read in her dropped head and shaking shoulders, made me think my fears she would be cruelly rejected had been realised. I put my arms indignantly, protectively round her – and then slowly withdrew them. She was not crying, but laughing. Her blue eyes, the pupils still enlarged with the belladonna Lucy had evidently dropped in them the previous evening, were sparkling wickedly.

'Bedford came over –'

'The Treasurer?'

'Is he?'

'Go on.'

She caught the urbane tone of the fifth earl I had often heard in the lobby to perfection. 'He said if the uneasy truce persisted and I happened to find myself in Hertfordshire . . . Then he was interrupted by Warwick who talked about some jewels, captured from the Spaniards by a privateer, *Resolution*, owned by him and Lord Stonehouse, which would just match my pendant . . .'

Resolution was the ship Matthew helped to build, the one I had run with the pitch to caulk. I stared at the scar on my leg from the pitch burn, after which Lord Stonehouse had picked me up.

'He just cut you? Lord Stonehouse?'

'Yes. But once he saw Bedford and Warwick talking to me . . . he seemed to, well . . . to see me differently.'

'Differently?'

'Perhaps he was jealous. I don't know.' There was a mischievous glint in her eyes I had never seen before. Now she mimicked Lord Stonehouse's rough, abrupt tone. '"You're Black's girl," he said. He was surprised I could read and was interested in estate management and –'

I gaped at her. 'You know nothing about estate management.'

'He does. I listened.' Her voice faltered. She clasped her hands and stared at me earnestly. 'Do you think I made a fool of myself?'

I stared at her suspiciously, but she continued to return my gaze modestly, meekly. I was no longer quite sure where I was with her. However rattle-brained Mrs Black might be, she always looked upon Mr Black as the master of the house and was obedient to him, which was as it should be, since a man's honour was so tightly bound up with his ability to rule his own household. I hated the thought of the hot eyes of those nobles on her, but was avid for the information she had gleaned from them.

'Did Lord Stonehouse say anything about me?'

She looked at the floor and shook her head unconvincingly.

'What did he say?' I said sharply.

'He said . . .' she trembled and bit her lip, then abruptly the words spurted out in a burst of laughter '. . . you talked too much.'

I continued to stare at her coldly until she choked off the laughter. 'Are you going to Hertfordshire in the spring?' I said. 'Or to look at Warwick's jewels?'

She burst out laughing again. 'Oh, Tom, Tom – you are a million times more to me than those rich old men.'

'Am I?' I said stupidly. 'You are a million times more to me than Lord Stonehouse.'

To hell with it. To hell with honour, Lord Stonehouse, the King – if this was the upside-down world, I wanted to be in it.

'You'll get my cold,' I said, as she kissed me.

'We'll share it,' she said.

*   *   *

I returned to the print shop. My mind was made up. I would like to be, to do, much more than ordinances, but if it had to be ordinances, so be it, so long as Anne and I were together.

I no sooner picked up my composing stick than I saw Nehemiah cringe. A stab of guilt went through me, and I told him, I swore it, that I would never hit him again. He sniffed and backed away uncertainly, sure I was only planning a more subtle form of torture. Mr Black heard me, and took me to one side and told me I would ruin the boy.

'It is how I see the world now, sir,' I said.

'Well, it is a most peculiar way to see it. I never liked beating you, Tom, but it formed your character, did it not?'

I said nothing and he went away sighing something about youth and change and the old solid ways being disrupted by the war, and the sooner it was over, the better.

It was a fine March day and ice in the yard was turning into slush when Nehemiah came running back from Westminster, full of excitement. He apologised for losing his hat – in the past he would never have dared tell me – but he had an important letter for me. Lord Stonehouse's falcon stared out at me from the seal. I had become resigned to expecting nothing from him, but at the sight of the seal all my old hopes and aspirations rushed back. My fingers shook as I broke the seal. I stared at the short, abrupt sentences, almost sick with disappointment.

It was not from Lord Stonehouse but his secretary, Mr Cole. It said there was a Parliamentary meeting in two days' time at Westminster and his lordship required me to take notes.

'It seems an honour to me,' said Anne, meekly.

'An honour? Taking notes like a common scrivener?'

'It is not what you hoped for, certainly.'

'Not what I hoped for? It is an insult!'

I crumpled up the letter and hurled it into the fire. It bounced out and she fished it from the grate, smoothing it out. She read slowly, but in a thoughtful way, her lips spelling out the difficult words. 'His manner is, perhaps, a little unfortunate.'

'A little —' Several times a week now she went to Lucy and she was picking up phrases, mannerisms. I wondered whether she had picked up anything else. 'Do you know anything about this?'

'No. No. Why should I?' She gave me a look I was beginning to recognise, tentative and submissive but calculating, a look that preceded her suggesting I did the exact opposite of what I was planning. 'Except . . . I think it might be about Edgehill.'

Edgehill was a running sore. Locals claimed the place was haunted. On New Year's Day on Kineton meadows, between three and four o'clock on a cold, misty afternoon, strange apparitions had been seen of musketeers and pikemen. The boom of cannons was heard and the shrieks and groans of dying men. Troops of horsemen charged one another, then vanished into the mist. The following day many people witnessed a full-scale battle, which began at midnight, the ghostly apparitions, many of them littered about the meadow, vanishing at sunrise.

So said the pamphlet *A great vvonder in Heaven: shewing the late Apparitions and prodigious noises of War and Battels, seen on Edge-Hill.* The King authenticated the events, sending six observers who witnessed the apparitions, identifying some of them, including Sir Edmund Verney, who had died holding the King's standard. They were taken by many as a sign of God's displeasure at the spilling of so much Christian blood. Nehemiah went to a large demonstration of apprentices in Covent Garden calling for peace, and there were riots in the City calling for an end to the war. The prosperous were now finding Parliamentary tax ordinances much worse than the Ship Money the King had imposed on them.

The King was gradually strengthening his position. He held the North, from Newcastle to York; Wales and the Midlands down to

Oxford, and Cornwall and Devon. Bristol, still in Parliamentary hands, was being encircled by Prince Rupert. Abroad, the Queen was successfully raising money for Charles.

In the face of this increasing threat from the King, Parliament was split. Denzil Holles, one of the five members whom the King tried to arrest for treason in the House, led a strong faction who wanted peace on almost any terms. Holles had fought long for Parliament, but had been sobered by Prince Rupert slaughtering a third of his regiment at Brentford, just before the stand-off at Turnham Green. He was prepared to barter civil control of Government for freedom of religion. Mr Pym argued this would be a disaster; if Parliament laid down its arms – the King's first demand before drawing up a treaty – they would lose all the ground gained, and he would be the first to walk to the scaffold.

It was against this gloomy background that I went into a large, draughty committee room near the Painted Chamber in Westminster. Lord Stonehouse greeted me tersely, told me he wanted my note by seven o'clock that evening at Queen Street, and pointed me towards the scrivener's table. It was a hastily cobbled together *ad hoc* committee of Lords and Commons members, whose real object was to raise yet more money, and whose loosely defined purpose was military requirements in the light of Edgehill – in other words, one of those meetings where the real work is done.

'Tom! You are one of us now!'

It was Mr Ink, splashed to his collar, embracing me. I felt a pang at being back almost where I had started, but we laughed at old times, when he had pressed into my hand the words that would change the world.

'I still believe words can light a fire in people's hearts, Tom,' he cried fervently.

Dear Mr Ink! I told him sadly words had become ordinances, but then I was tapped on the shoulder by Mr Pym. He fired questions at me about Edgehill, shaking his head as I told him I did not recognise in the accounts given by London pamphlets the battle I had been through.

'Why haven't you written your own?'

'Mr Black works for the Government.'

'Governments need to listen.' He tugged at his spade-like beard in that nervous, jerky way of his. 'Sit here,' he said abruptly, pointing to a chair next to him.

I told him I was a scrivener, but as he was close to the scrivener's desk he gestured impatiently that it made no difference, and by the time I made sure my quill was sharp the chairman's gavel went. It was as I feared. The chairman was fulsome in his praise of Lord Essex's great victory, although, he added, no victory was so great that lessons could not be learned from it.

In our corner the quills scratched dutifully, mine in tune with the rest. If I had been deaf, I could have written out what Lord Essex said in reply, it was such common currency. In a word, the lesson of Edgehill was money. He needed numbers to defeat the King. He reeled off numbers. Men, horses, cannon, weapons – if a large enough army was assembled, and the King was slowly starved of provisions, that would bring him to the negotiating table. Mr Pym shook his head at the mention of negotiation, but there were resigned nods of approval from Holles and his supporters. Most people round the table, including Lord Stonehouse, showed no reaction, one way or the other.

When Essex had finished, there was the sort of lengthy pause that follows an argument so weighed down with facts and figures it appears irrefutable. There was no argument that more money was needed. It always is. Quills scraped gradually to a stop. People coughed, shifted in their chairs, shuffled papers. Someone caught the chairman's eye.

'Mr Cromwell,' he said.

I had scarcely noticed the MP for Cambridge since I had heard him say in the lobby that if the Grand Remonstrance, which had begun the path to war, had not been passed he would have sailed for New England. In Parliament he had been a stolid, unexceptional supporter of Mr Pym. He was one of those Puritans who had found God after a youth of debauchery. I suspected that the sins he had committed were exaggerated both by himself and others, for he had that tortured look of a man who, glancing a mite too long at a woman's skirts, prays as vehemently to God to forgive him as if he had raped her. He surprised an acquaintance by giving him money he had won at dice years earlier. The man had forgotten all about it, but Cromwell insisted on him having it, saying it would be a great sin for him to keep it.

In action, often precipitate action, this self-torture lifted. Where other people dithered, he was not held back by self-questioning. He had done that with God, and God had given him the answers. Long before the King raised his standard, a group of Royalists rode to East Anglia 'to protect' the silver plate of the Cambridge colleges. Cromwell lined the Great North Road with musketeers. He marched on King's and other colleges, drums beating, flags flying, seizing plate worth twenty thousand pounds for Parliament.

None of this was evident in this rough, raw-boned man, forty or so, who had the reddened face of a countryman over his white collar, which Sarah would have said could have done with a good wash or two to beat the grey out of it. Nor did there seem any expectation of what he would say, beyond praising Essex. He was a supporter, having originally moved the motion for Essex to be made general. And indeed he praised him for his fortitude, for his steadfastness of command. That air of torpor began to steal round the room when people feel a consensus has been reached and the restless begin to think of food and drink.

Then Cromwell paused and ran his hand through his tousled hair. He pushed aside his notes, and gazed over the heads of the people in the room. It was a gaze of a man of the country he came from, for the Fens are said to be so flat that no one there believes the world is round.

'My lords, gentlemen, the Lord granted us that we did not suffer defeat at Edgehill,' he said. 'But can we describe it as victory? Are we being blasphemous in doing so? Would God have allowed us to be driven back to London? Rupert to carry out his bloody massacre at Brentford? To sue for a peace which would give us a penny or two of what we asked for and lose some of us our heads? My lords, I see in all this God's disapproval, but also His infinite wisdom, in giving us another chance – the opportunity to learn lessons.'

His language became rougher, his accent thicker. 'On my first going into engagement at Edgehill, I saw our men being beaten at every hand. We need new regiments. Money, numbers . . . I agree, my lord. Yes. But we need to spend the money on the right sort of men. Your troopers –' he looked round everyone at the table '– are mainly decayed old serving-men, tapsters and such like. Their troopers are gentlemen's sons and persons of quality. Do you think your base and mean fellows can ever defeat gentlemen with courage, honour and resolution?'

I did not care for the sound of that, for I thought of Jed, and hadn't I, too, been base and mean when I was not the other? But he qualified that by saying he would rather have a plain russet-coated captain that knew what he fought for, and loved what he knew, than one who was a gentleman and nothing else. I would have died for him then.

You were either Cromwell's man or Cromwell's bitter enemy, and from that moment, as his harsh urgent voice rang round that room, I was Cromwell's man. My hand flew over the paper as my feet had flown over the streets when I had carried the Grand Remonstrance. I was fired up by him as I had not been since those first heady months. No preacher ever inspired me like him. As he spoke, I believed the world was going to change, and change utterly. It was not that he spoke as others did, in large numbers and grand visions.

Quite the opposite. Vision he left to God, and he was His practical servant. He spoke about what he knew, his corner of England, for which his simple desire was to raise regiments.

It was the way in which he talked about them that nearly made me leap from my seat, for his description met all the weaknesses I had seen at Edgehill. Men would be carefully selected, God-fearing and disciplined. They would be trained from what had been learned in combat, not from military manuals. Above all, they would centre round the cavalry – not on slow cumbersome positioning, as if a battle were a formal duel obeying court rules, but on movement and surprise.

Cromwell's speech was such an attack. It was an ambush that took Essex by surprise. Denzil Holles, for whom attack was the last, not the first resort, looked furious. But he saw some of the lords nod in agreement, as did Mr Pym, and held his fire. Lord Stonehouse neither nodded nor shook his head, but stared round the table at other people's reactions. He was one of those men who, at this stage in a meeting, would rather give away money than give away his thoughts.

When Cromwell had done, Holles launched his own attack. His argument was simple, but savage. 'You were not at Edgehill, *Colonel* Cromwell,' he said, emphasising his rank in a belittling way.

'I arrived late, it is true,' Cromwell began. 'But –'

Several people began speaking at once. The chairman called for order but could not control them. I dropped my pen on the floor in my agitation and rose to pick it up. It was such a cheap, intemperate attack by Holles I opened my mouth to speak but caught what I took to be a warning glance from Lord Stonehouse. Mr Pym said something to me but in the noise I could not hear what he said. In my anxiety I was trampling my quill with my boot. I was remembering, in the evening gloom at Edgehill, watching a late Royalist cavalry charge being repulsed by Parliamentary cavalry led by a man who had lost his helmet.

'You were not there,' Holles was shouting.

I flung down my broken pen, trembling. 'I was there, sir,' I shouted. 'I saw Cromwell in the late afternoon, in a counter attack on the meadows.'

There was an abrupt silence. A ring of faces stared up at me, in the centre of which swam Lord Stonehouse's baleful black eyes. All I could think of was his one-line dismissal of me: he talks too much. It dried the words in my mouth. The sigh of the wind outside and the creaks in that draughty chamber were suddenly audible. I could not stop shaking. Who was I to talk in that august company? Base, mean – a scrivener! A man to write down opinions, not to have them – let alone express them. Then I saw Cromwell looking at me and I remembered his words – that he would rather have a man who knew what he fought for, and loved what he knew, than one who was a gentleman and nothing else. It was as if he had given me permission to find my own voice at last.

I told them what it was like to be a soldier in the line that day. How the line broke at the first charge of their horse. I told them that Colonel – and I looked at Holles as I stressed the rank with pride – that Colonel Cromwell was right. That cavalry must be the main weapon. But it must be disciplined cavalry. Their horse charged on to plunder the baggage train. If they had wheeled and attacked our rear, the day must have been lost.

It was youth, it was arrogance that drove me on, but mostly it was anger and bitterness at the senseless slaughter of untrained men, for again Cromwell was right. They had been trained to drill, not to fight. It took an apprentice seven years to become a cooper, printer, baker or goldsmith, but a soldier was expected to learn to fight in his spare time? Oh, I lost myself then. Every runaway horse has to come to a stop. I saw the ring of staring faces again as my voice slowed and faltered, saw Holles's red contemptuous face as my knees began to buckle and I remembered where I was and who I was – a scrivener, with a broken quill.

'And who, may I ask, are you, sir?' said Holles.

It was a question I had been asking myself all my life. 'Thomas,' I began miserably. 'Thomas –'

'Thomas Stonehouse,' said Lord Stonehouse, his harsh voice ringing round the room. 'He is Thomas Stonehouse, my grandson and heir.'

46

Did Lord Stonehouse make that astonishing announcement because he was proud of my performance? Because he wanted to make amends? Because he thought I was a worthy heir? Of course I believed that! What other motives could there be? There were small things that made me wonder – Anne fishing the letter out from the fire and persuading me to go the meeting, Mr Pym pulling me away from the scrivener's desk to sit with him at the committee table – but I brushed them aside.

I was walking on air when Lord Stonehouse – my grandfather, I should say – introduced me to Cromwell, who asked me where he might get in touch with me.

'Write to him at Queen Street, Oliver,' said Lord Stonehouse.

Cromwell bowed to him, then to me. Cromwell, bowing to me! Whatever lay behind Lord Stonehouse's decision, I left the House a very different person from the poor scrivener who went in. In the lobby I almost walked past Mr Ink. He was behind a pillar, looking at me in the way people do when they believe you are something. I put out my hand but he refused to take it, although mine was almost as black as his.

'Dear Mr Ink – come, I am no different.' You may judge that the first hint of patronage had crept into my voice.

'Oh, you are, sir. You talk different. You walk different.' Shyly he offered me two sheets of paper, as ink-splashed as the very first sheets of Mr Pym's words with which I had run through the streets. 'Your speech, sir.'

'Thank you. And God bless you, Mr Ink.' I laughed and hugged him, for he had taught me to believe in words and in hope for the future, and there is no better thing for a man to do.

It was only when I reached Queen Street just before seven that evening to take the proceedings of the meeting to Lord Stonehouse that doubt began to creep in. There was some catch. My footsteps faltered. But the servants bowed, Mr Cole offered me his congratulations and whisked me upstairs.

Only Lord Stonehouse – it is difficult to call a man Grandfather when he has once consigned you to the plague pit – was intimidatingly the same. I stood on the slightly worn patch of the oriental carpet – the patch Richard used to call the gallows spot – exactly as I had stood so many times before while Lord Stonehouse signed letters and gave them to Mr Cole to seal. When the secretary had gone he read the proceedings of the meeting, still without acknowledging my existence. My heart sank as he turned the pages. The catch must be Anne. He would never agree to my marrying her. And if he did not, I would walk away. He reached the end of Mr Ink's pages, removed his spectacles, coughed and cleared his throat.

'You spoke well.'

'Not too much, my lord?' I hazarded.

The lids lifted from his eyes, and he gave me his basilisk look. 'You failed at the peroration. Holles would have had you there.'

He opened the drawer which I now knew was mine, and paused for a moment before dropping in the speech. 'Did you see Cromwell at Edgehill?'

I was very far from the boy who had first come into this room, violent with dreams and words. I had learned not to move a muscle of my face in front of him. Holles was not alone in his attack on

Cromwell. His enemies were circulating a story that he had climbed a church bell tower, seen that Parliament was losing and fled.

'It was growing dark. I saw someone who was very like, my lord.'

Not a muscle in his face moved. 'Did you see Cromwell?'

'I am sure Cromwell would not lie, my lord.'

There was a slight tremor in his cheek, the vestige of a dry smile. He looked at the speech again, then dropped it in the drawer and locked it.

'Sit down.'

It was a novel experience for me in that room and I looked wildly about me. Silently he pointed to an elegant walnut chair, with a finely carved back in which the inevitable falcon glared at me malevolently as if he, at least, knew me as an impostor. Lord Stonehouse went to the window, his hands folded behind his back, and stared out over the dark street. A carriage rattled past, then it was so quiet I could hear the candles flicker. When he did speak, it was the last thing I expected him to say.

'Did your leg heal?'

I stared at his broad back in bewilderment. 'My leg?'

He swung round as if I had insulted him. 'Your leg!' he barked. 'Did it heal? From the pitch burn?'

'Yes, my lord. Well. There is a scar.'

'Show me.'

Embarrassed, I got up and unbuttoned my breeches, until my leg was as bare as it had been on the day the pitch fell on it. He stared at the reddened, puckered skin, touched it, then suddenly, clumsily embraced me. The embrace ended as quickly and abruptly as it had begun, and when he released me there was something as near to a twinkle as I ever saw in his dark, brooding eyes.

'How is Lady Black?'

* * *

'The marriage is to be in one of the chapels at St Paul's,' I said.

'St Paul's!' Mrs Black shrieked and fainted, Mr Black only just catching her in time. When Jane brought her round, with a vigorous application of salts and vinegar, the first words she murmured were: 'What on earth shall I wear?'

'Anyone would think it were her wedding,' said Sarah, the only one totally unmoved. She remained steadfast to her philosophy that people went up and people went down –

'– but it's best to stay where you are?' I grinned.

'More room in garret with your big feet out o' way,' she sniffed. 'Until you're back.'

She more than half believed it was one of my pamphlet stories. From time to time, so did I. While a house in Drury Lane from the Stonehouse estate was being prepared for us, I had nothing to do. Everything was taken care of by the steward, Banks, and by Jane. When Lord Stonehouse found out she was Mrs Morland's daughter, he insisted she must become housekeeper at Drury Lane. A positive side of his harsh, extreme paternalism was that he looked after his servants. When I offered her the post she could not speak, only nod and pink with pleasure. For her it was more than rehabilitation, it was a return to the estate where she had been brought up, and, for her, the estate was family.

Never in my whole life was I so idle. Mr Black would not allow me in the print shop. His formality with me was almost distressing. My hands grew whiter and whiter, and I itched to touch type once more. Anne was swept up by the Countess, who took charge of her clothes, her mother's clothes, their language, their manners, what was correct and what was not. Anne, too, became formal with me, calling me Thomas in a stupid stilted way, until I longed for her to call me Monkey again.

Neither Kate nor Matthew would attend the wedding. Kate wrote that Matthew was working night and day on a new ship, the *Endeavour*, but I believe the true reason was he was afraid of the long hand of Lord Stonehouse, and preferred to stay in the relatively lawless Poplar Without. He did, however, send me a wedding gift, which he said I might need after all. Wrapped up inside the letter was a tightly folded scrap of paper, torn from a shipwright's drawing. Inside that was a silver half-crown coin, the fluer de lys on the edge showing it had been minted in 1625. Sly as ever, unable to leave the coin in the stream at Upper Vale, he must have fished it out before galloping after me on our ride to Highpoint.

For herself, Kate wrote, her part was played now and she was at peace. But I know she was there, outside St Paul's, watching, vanishing like a will o' the wisp when I turned, for that wedding morning Jane, now ensconced at Drury Lane, had found a simnel cake on the doorstep.

Strutting in silver buttons and scarlet stockings I faltered at the sight of an imperious figure wearing a head-dress of gilt and flowers.

'Come on, Monkey,' Anne whispered, as the bride-cup was held aloft and the fiddlers began to play.

The wedding was marred for me only by Lord Stonehouse insisting that Anne wore the pendant. All the time we made our vows I felt the falcon's ruby eyes glowering at me as if I was an impostor.

'You should be grateful to it, Tom,' said Mr Pym at the wedding feast in Queen Street. 'The bird chose you.'

'The wretched bird chose me? What kind of a riddle is this?'

'In the sense that the bird is the great estate.'

'Stop it, John,' said Lucy. 'Let Tom enjoy his day.'

But we had drunk a good deal of wine, I had to crack the riddle, and they wanted to tell me. Like born conspirators, they moved me away from the throng in the reception room, into the shadows of the hall, near the statue of Minerva, behind which I had hidden the day when I had first coneyed myself into Queen Street. Mr Pym asked me why I thought Lord Stonehouse made his astonishing announcement at that meeting.

'Why? Because I made a brilliant speech,' I boasted. 'And in searching for the pendant I found myself and showed him I was the man to inherit.'

'All true,' said Mr Pym. 'All very true. It would not have happened without all that, certainly.'

'But . . .?'

He abruptly fell silent. Lord Stonehouse appeared at the entrance to the reception room. He had a glass in his hand, but still looked as if he had the affairs of state in his troubled face. Then he saw Anne talking to Warwick and a smile crossed his face as he went to join them.

'Power is a fragile thing,' Lucy said, suddenly sober.

'Stonehouse's loyalty to Parliament was being questioned. Rightly.'

'Rightly?' I said, staring across the hall at my grandfather, who, as Warwick slapped him on the back, was laughing, happier and more relaxed than I ever thought to see him.

'He helped Richard get to France.'

Not only that, I learned, he saw him off. Warwick controlled the sea and it was a hazardous passage. It was a ship in which Lord Stonehouse had a substantial share that took Richard. Warwick was informed of this by one of his commanders. It was also rumoured that Richard had been given funds by his father to pave his way in Paris.

'Best you know this,' Mr Pym said, lowering his voice still further. 'He keeps a foot in both camps. What really matters to him is the estate – the name. But he went too far in helping Richard, and in that meeting he was forced to make a decision about you – and declare his loyalty.'

Pym had engineered Cromwell's speech. And mine. And, if you like, my inheritance. I was glad my grandfather had helped Richard, at considerable risk, whom he had harmed in the past as much as me. Yet I thought of him touching the scar on my leg, and his clumsy embrace. In his own way he loved us both. But he was driven as he had always been driven by the falcon, the estate, and was hedging his bets. Suitably chastened, I drew from my pocket the lucky half crown Matthew had returned to me, spun it in the air and caught it. 'So in the end it all came down to this.'

Lucy laughed. 'Which way the coin falls.' She took it. 'Sixteen twenty-five. When Charles was crowned.'

'When I was born.' Something struck me. 'You mean – I may not inherit!'

'Of course you will!' Mr Pym beamed. Then his beam was modulated. 'So long as Parliament is in power.'

I pocketed the coin. I raised my glass and my voice rang round the hall. 'To Parliament!'

There was a sudden silence. Faces turned – then everyone raised their glasses. 'To Parliament!'

I suppose, from their smiles, Warwick, my grandfather and the rest saw in my flushed face and outburst a burning, youthful, naive enthusiasm for the cause, of the kind that had moved me that night when I ran down the street clutching in my hand the words of the Grand Remonstrance. And that, as Mr Pym would say, was true. Very true.

'What were you talking about so secretively?' said Anne in the carriage home.

'The falcon,' I said.

'Isn't she beautiful?' Anne said.

'Not as beautiful as you.' I kissed her, but could not kiss her properly until she had taken off the pendant, and locked it safely away, I hoped forever, and we drew the curtains round our marriage bed, and finally came together.

Historical Note

Tom and the Stonehouses are fiction, but that larger-than-life character, Lucy Hay, Countess of Carlisle is factually based. She was the mistress of the Earl of Strafford, the King's most powerful counsellor, who became a hate figure for Pym and the Parliamentary opposition. Reluctantly, out of political expediency and in an act he regretted for the rest of his life, King Charles signed his death warrant.

When Strafford was executed in May 1641, Lucy not only lost her lover, but her power base. Perhaps she loved power more than love. Perhaps it was a matter of survival; she was a woman on her own and felt the need to back both horses. At all events, while she kept the ear of the Queen she was revealing court secrets to John Pym in November 1641, when the Parliamentary opposition laid down its explosive demands to the King in the Grand Remonstrance.

Lucy was the sex symbol of her day, a scintillating figure at the Caroline court, but it was probably power, not sex, that brought her and Pym together, although gossip painted a more lurid picture. She was 'first charged in the fore-deck by Master Holles, in the Poop by Master Pym, while she clapped my Lord Holland under hatches,' wrote Henry Neville in 1647.

Pym and the other four members were all too aware of the threat the King would arrest them. The question was when. Most historians credit the warning given in a message from the French ambassador, but Diane Purkiss in the *English Civil War* makes a robust case for the warning coming from Lucy Hay (albeit in not quite the dramatic way described in this book). She argues that historians do not like the idea precisely because it sounds like something out of a novel. Yet she quotes several contemporary sources who believed it to be true: 'Thomas Burton . . . in his diary of Cromwell's Parliament, quotes Haselrig [one of the five members] as saying: "I shall never forget the kindness of that great lady, the Lady Carlisle, that gave timely notice."'

Although Tom passing Lucy's letter to Speaker Lenthall is my fiction, the dialogue he hears is from contemporary sources, and the Serjeant's suspicion that the letter contains a plague-sore dressing was all too credible. In what must have been one of the first biological assassination attempts, the previous month John Pym had received such a letter in the House, recorded in a pamphlet *A damnable Treason by a Contagious Plaster of a plague sore.*

This was the age of the pamphlet, and I am indebted to Joad Raymond's *Pamphlets and Pamphleteering in Early Modern Britain* for brilliantly bringing the age to life, just as the pamphlet brought politics not so much to life but into existence for the general public. It is difficult now, when government (theoretically) is accountable down to the very shopping lists of MPs, to imagine a time when it was accountable for nothing. The King either ruled by diktat or, when he ran out of money, called Parliament. Either way, it was a private affair. The public had nothing to do with it.

The Long Parliament which met in 1640 was different. The division between Parliament and the King was so great London was hungry for news. Scriveners like Mr Ink wrote proceedings of both Houses, published every Monday. The King was unaware at first that politics had suddenly gone public.

'Parliament was articulating a theory of responsible, representative government and public accountability,' Raymond writes, 'and this transcript of its proceedings was electric.'

It was the beginning of real news – but also the beginning of spin. MPs like Pym leaked transcripts or notes to promote or justify their actions. Since that heady month of November 1641, Britain has never been without newspapers. After war was declared in August 1642 the Royalists produced their own publications and an increasingly virulent, partisan press was born. In the following year, alarmed at having let the genie of freedom of speech out of the bottle, Parliament attempted to curb it, leading Milton to publish his famous pamphlet in defence of it, *Areopagitica*, having as its title epigram: 'This is true Liberty when free born men/Having to advise the public may speak free.'

So it is not specious when Tom thinks the words he is running with will change the world. Historians argue endlessly whether there was an English revolution, but no one can dispute that there was a revolution in public thought. Before the Civil War an average of 624 titles were published every year. In 1641 the number was 2042 and in 1642 this almost doubled to 4038 titles. The words opened up a new world not only for people like Tom, Will and Ben, but also for Anne.

The germs of feminism sprang up during the war, although were largely stifled after it. Like Susannah, women mainly found independence through radical religious sects, but there was the beginning of political consciousness. In February 1642, four hundred working women, independently from fathers and husbands and desperate from financial hardship, petitioned Parliament in what Lawrence Stone calls the first independent political action by women in English history. When the outraged Duke of Richmond cried, 'Away with these women, we were best have a Parliament of women,' the petitioners attacked him physically and broke his staff of office.

There is no written record of Cromwell being at Edgehill, but it is probable he was. In her biography, Antonia Fraser cites the Puritan MP Nathanial Fiennes who, in trying to check the Parliamentary rout, was joined by troops including those of Cromwell, and they rode together to Kineton. Denzil Holles, who later became a bitter enemy of Cromwell, made no mention of his absence in his report, written with other MPs, a week after the battle.

The meeting in Westminster at which Tom claims to have seen Cromwell is fictional, but Cromwell's speech is based on his actual words, spoken in different contexts. Like so many ideas thrown up in the Civil War, some of which would take root in the formation of the modern state, Cromwell's approach was the germ of what would become the New Model Army, Britain's first regular fighting force.

Acknowledgements

Thanks to my agent, Felicity Rubinstein for her energy and encouragement, my editor, Clare Smith for her unerring capacity to put her finger on passages where rewriting made so much difference and to Deborah Rosario for her research and feeling for the seventeenth century. I'm grateful to all the friends who read the book and gave me feedback, particularly Eileen Horne, Libby Symon and Peter Smith. And thanks most of all to my wife Cynthia, for her support and her ability to be both encouraging and critical at the same time.

'A boy's story is the best that is ever told.'

CHARLES DICKENS

CONSTRUCTION AND CREATION
∙∙

A Word from the Author

AN IDEA, LIKE A GHOST
∙∙

Things to Think About

BEHIND THE SCENES

CONSTRUCTION AND CREATION

'The whole difference between construction and creation is exactly this: that a thing constructed can only be loved after it is constructed; but a thing created is loved before it exists.' So said Charles Dickens on the creative process. And yet the precise nature of the writer's craft is a mysterious one. What is it that inspires authors to put pen to paper: curiosity, sympathy, passion, obsession? In his own words, Peter Ransley reveals what inspired him to write *Plague Child*...

The origins of *Plague Child* go back to the 1980s, when I spent chilly nights on the Wiltshire Downs during lambing season.

I was adapting a book for the BBC called *A Shepherd's Life*. Written in 1910 by W. H. Hudson, it was described as 'a poignant portrait of country-life' – but there was disquiet beneath the surface. Hudson writes: 'It is a pity that the history of the rising of the agricultural labourer, the most patient and submissive of men, has never been written...' The rising was in the 1830s when labourers, half-starved amidst rural plenty, their patience and submission at breaking point, smashed threshing machines and burned ricks. They had their own mythical figure, Captain Swing, who would come out of the fog of the burning ricks, right all wrongs and return common land to the villagers.

At Salisbury thirty-four men were sentenced to death, thirty-three transported and ten got fourteen years imprisonment.

For the BBC programme, I went to the village Hudson wrote about, near Salisbury and, amazingly, there were still handed-down memories of this terrible time in circulation. I interviewed a seventy-year-old shepherd, Tom, who told me many of the stories and this was substantiated by research I did. There were records of shepherds, blacksmiths, labourers – the records of protest; pamphlets, prison documents, Home Office papers of food riots, court evidence of informers' reports and intercepted letters: material largely ignored by conventional history.

It was years later, when I read Diane Purkiss's *The English Civil War: A People's History* that I had the idea for *Plague Child*. I named my hero Tom, after the shepherd. I wanted to make it not just a thriller about an illegitimate boy searching for who he is, but have him searching also for 'something that will change the world'. In 1642 it might have been the philosopher's stone. Or the Second Coming. In Tom's case, it is words.

In 1642, politics was the preserve of peers and gentlemen in parliament; ultimately of the king, who could dissolve it at will. There was no reporting of parliament, and it was people like Tom who helped to change that. That's why I made Tom a printer's runner, then a pamphleteer.

Pamphlets had as great an effect then as the Web today – arguably greater, for they took politics out of parliament and began to give people a voice. In 1639, 624 pamphlets, mostly religious, were printed. In 1642, when the king raised his standard at Nottingham, there were 4,038 titles printed that year, mostly political.

What happens to Tom in *Plague Child* and the following books takes him through key events – not as history, but as something that is happening, that he believes will change the world – and did.

'We owe our state of government to it,' writes Purkiss, of the Civil War, but most of us have little idea who fought whom, or why. In a cry from the heart she says: 'Nor do most of us care…yet it made us the country we are, the people we are.'

Everyone knows a king was executed, but few realise that, proportionally, more English people were killed in the Civil War than in the First or the Second World War. It was the beginning of the modern age. From its pamphlets newspapers were born. There were visionaries, spies, women preachers – the first seeds of feminism. The war changed not only this country but the world: it spawned the American Revolution, and influenced the French revolutionaries.

Plague Child is a thriller. But I hope also that it may convey, as it did to me, how we have been formed by what happened in that tumultuous period – and possibly even more by what didn't.

AN IDEA, LIKE A GHOST

'An idea, like a ghost, must be spoken to a little before it will explain itself.'

CHARLES DICKENS

From Socrates to the salons of pre-Revolutionary France, the great minds of every age have debated the merits of literary offerings alongside questions of politics, social order and morality. Whether you love a book or loathe it, one of the pleasures of reading is the discussion books regularly inspire. Below are a few suggestions for topics of discussion about *Plague Child*...

- ► Peter Ransley sets the tale predominantly in Oxford and London in the seventeenth century. How successfully do you think he captures this era? In what ways does he do this?

- ► *Plague Child* is a work of historical fiction. What other genres do you think this novel falls under and why?

- ► The English Civil War acts as the backdrop to *Plague Child*. In what ways to you think this political crisis affects each of the characters? In your view, do you think politics divides characters that would otherwise get on with one another?

- ► Tom is taken advantage of by many of the novel's characters, but he also shows signs of strength. How would you characterise Tom? Is he a natural leader or an underdog?

- ► Throughout the novel Tom states how he felt loved by Susannah and Mathew. In what ways do they show parental love?

▶ *Plague Child* contains far more male characters than female ones. What impact, if any, did this have on you as a reader? How successfully do you think the female characters are portrayed by the author?

▶ Tom's opinion of Eaton changes throughout the novel. What were your views on Eaton and at what point did they change, if at all?

▶ In chapter thirteen, Tom manages to secure the clothing of a gentleman for himself, and it isn't too long before attitudes towards him change. How important do you think appearance was in seventeenth-century England and in what ways does the author illustrate its relationship to social class?

▶ The title *Plague Child* refers to Tom. Do you think this is a powerful title? Who in the novel do you think perceives Tom as merely a 'plague child'?

The next book in the Tom Neave trilogy ...

CROMWELL'S
BLESSING

Out in April 2012

Read an extract here ...

I

I could not stop shivering. That February morning in 1647 was the coldest, bleakest morning of the whole winter, but it was going to be far colder, far bleaker for Trooper Scogman when I told him he was going to be hanged.

Most mornings I woke up and knew exactly who I was: Major Thomas Stonehouse, heir to the great estate of Highpoint near Oxford, if my grandfather, Lord Stonehouse, was to be believed. Now the Civil War was over, sometimes, in that first moment of waking, I woke up as Tom Neave, one-time bastard, usurper and scurrilous pamphleteer.

That morning was one of them.

I should have left it up to Sergeant Potter to tell Scogman, but he would have relished it: taunted Scogman, left him in suspense. At least I would tell him straight out.

My regiment was billeted at a farm near Dutton's End, Essex, part of an estate seized by Parliament from a Royalist who had fled the country. The pail outside was solid ice. The dog opened one eye before curling back into a tight ball. Straw, frosted over in the yard, snapped under my boots like icicles. A crow seemed scarcely able to lift its wings as it drifted over the soldiers' tents.

More soldiers in their red uniforms were snoring in the barns, where horses were also stabled. We were a cavalry unit, the justification for calling Cromwell's New Model Army both new and a model for the future. Whereas the foot soldiers were pressed men, who would desert as soon as you turned your back, the cavalry were volunteers. They were the sons of yeomen or tradesmen, who brought to war the discipline of their Guilds. They joined not just for the better pay – and the horse which would carry their packs – but because they were God-fearing and believed in Parliament.

Except for Scogman.

I approached the wooden shed which was the camp's makeshift prison. I half-hoped Scogman had escaped, but I could see the padlock, still intact, and the guard asleep, huddled in blankets.

Scogman on the loose would have been worse. The countryside would have been up in arms. Villagers resented us enough when we were fighting the war. Now it was over, and we were still here, they hated us.

Six months had passed since the Royalist defeat at the battle of Naseby. Yet the King was in the hands of the Scots. We were supposed to be on the same side – but the Scots would not leave England until they were paid and there were rumours they were doing a secret deal with the King. In spite of the stone in his bladder, his piles and his liver, Lord Stonehouse was in Newcastle, negotiating for the release of the King.

'We could not govern with him,' he wrote tersely to me. 'But we cannot govern without him.'

The guard, Kenwick, was a stationer's son from Holborn – I knew them all by their trades. I prodded him gently with my boot. 'Still there, is he?'

Kenwick shot up, turning with a look of terror towards the shed, as if expecting to see the padlock broken, the door yawning open. He saluted, found the key and made up for being asleep on duty by bringing the butt of his musket down on a bundle of straw rising and falling in the corner. The bundle groaned but scarcely moved. Kenwick brought the butt down more viciously. The bundle swore at him and began to part. Somehow, I thought resentfully, even in these unpromising conditions, Scogman managed to build up a fug of heat not found anywhere else on camp.

I waved Kenwick away as, with a rattle of chains, Scogman stumbled to his feet. His hair was the colour of the dirty straw he emerged from, the broken nose on his cherub-like face giving him a look of injured innocence. Trade: farrier, although sometimes I thought all he knew about horses was how to steal them.

'At ease, Scogman.'

He shuffled his leg irons. 'If you remove these, sir, I will be able to obey your order. Major Stonehouse. Sir.' He brought up his cuffed hands in a clumsy salute.

Kenwick bit back a smile. I stared at Scogman coldly.

He was about my age, twenty-two, but looked younger, thin as a rake, although he ate with a voracious appetite. Scoggy was the regiment's scrounger. He stole for the hell of it, for the challenge. In normal life he would have been hanged long ago. But when a regiment lived off the land he became an asset.

It only took one person to point out a plump hen, and not only would chicken be on the menu that night, but a pot in which to cook it would mysteriously appear. There were many who looked the other way in the regiment, except for strict Presbyterians like Sergeant Potter and Colonel Greaves, but in war the odds had been on Scoggy's side. In this uneasy peace his luck had run out. Scoggy had been caught stealing not just cheese, but a silver spoon. Not only that. He had stolen it from Sir Lewis Challoner, the local magistrate.

I chewed on an empty pipe, knocked it against my boot and cleared my throat. Scogman could read my reluctance and in his eyes was a look of hope. I cursed myself for coming. I should have sent Sergeant Potter. Scoggy would have known, however Potter taunted him, there was no hope. I struggled to find the words. In my mouth was the taste of the roast suckling pig Scoggy had somehow conjured up after Naseby. Even Cromwell had eaten it, praising the Lord for providing such fare to match a great victory. Cromwell believed in the virtue of his cavalry to the point of naivety, but when they sinned, he was merciless. I must follow my mentor's lead.

'You know the penalty for stealing silver, Scogman?'

'Yes, sir. Permission to speak, sir.'

'Go on,' I said wearily.

'Wife and children in London, sir. Starving.'

He knew I had a son. We had talked over many a camp fire about children we had never or rarely seen. 'You should have waited for your wages like everyone else.'

'We're three months behind, sir. There's talk we're never going to be paid what we're owed.'

It was true Parliament was dragging its feet over the money the troops were owed, and a host of other problems, like indemnity and injury benefits. Meanwhile soldiers scraped by on meagre savings, borrowed or stole.

'That's nonsense. Of course you'll be paid. Eventually. You should tighten your belt like everyone else.'

Scogman glanced down at his belt, taut over the narrow waist of his red uniform. Again Kenwick repressed a smile. I took the spoon from my pocket. My breath fogged it over. It looked a miserable object to be hanged for. 'Why the hell did you steal a silver spoon?'

He couldn't resist it. 'Because I never had one in my mouth, sir.'

Kenwick showed no sign of laughing, after looking at my expression.

'You will go before the magistrate.'

Even then he didn't believe me. 'I'd rather be tried by you, sir.'

'I'll bet you would. Sir Lewis may be lenient. Lock him up, Kenwick.'

I turned away, but not before I caught Scogman's cockiness, his bravado, shrivel like a pricked bladder. Outside, while the crows flapped lazily away, I tried to do what Cromwell did when he ordered a man's death. He prayed for his soul; it was not his order, he told himself, but God's will. Then he would unclasp his hands and go on to his next business. Rising over the thud of the door and the rattle of the padlock came Scogman's voice.

'Lenient? Sir Lewis Challoner, sir? He's a hanging magistrate! Major Stonehouse!'

I put my hands together but could not find the words to form a prayer.